Tokens

Book 2 of The

Tokens of Legacy

Harriet M J Wood

Copyright © 2020 Harriet M J Wood
All rights reserved

ISBN 9798611148204

This novel is a work of fiction. Names and characters are products of the author's imagination and any resemblance to actual persons, living or dead, is entirely coincidental.

*For Bill from small sister
Always in my heart*

Chapter 1

There was a bird somewhere nearby singing as if it were the dawn of a world re-born and only his voice could herald its glorious beginning.
The man stirred as the vibrant melody penetrated his consciousness, slowly rousing him from the unplumbed depths of sleep. He rolled onto his back, stretched luxuriously and took a deep breath of the cool fresh air, his senses noting a medley of sweet aromas, grasses and flowers. Opening his eyes he gradually became aware of his surroundings; a shady room with muted colours on the walls; a bed so comfortable that he couldn't recall a better one. There was a large window to the right of where he lay, soft fingers of light creeping from behind the delicate drapes, their folds moving slightly in the gentle breeze.

He lay still for a while, rejoicing in a feeling of well-being but wondering why he should be surprised to feel thus. Was there something he should remember? Whatever it may have been the thought was as elusive as a will o' the wisp so he gave up the attempt to pin it down.

Eventually he sat up on the edge of the bed, stretching his arms and wiping the sleep from his eyes. He stood and walked across to where a small table stood, a bowl of fruit and a small flagon of liquid placed upon it. He poured a little into a fine crystal goblet and sipped appreciatively. A further table provided a jug of clear water and large bowl which he made use of to wash before dressing in the soft clean robes draped across a chair.

'What is this place?' he murmured quietly. Slipping on his comfortable sandals he opened the door, unsure what to expect. It gave out onto a small garden surrounded by a very low wall into which was set a wrought-iron gate. Beyond the gate stretched a vast rolling green plain, dotted with wooded areas; in the far distance a range of mountains rose, purple blue in the early light. He walked along the narrow garden path and through the gate, trying to remember if he had ever seen such a view before. After a few paces he turned to look back. The garden was gone; nor was there any sign of where he had come from. Although he thought it odd, it didn't worry him in the least. Instead he simply started walking towards the far hills.

Much later on – time seemed a bit irrelevant here – the man sat down on a large stone beside a slow running stretch of water. He could see silvery fish almost motionless in the shaded areas of small pools where overhanging trees permitted only dappled sunlight to penetrate, their bodies moving only slightly with the current. There were dragonflies darting here and there, iridescent blues and greens with flashes of gold, their gossamer wings almost a blur. A little way up from where he sat a bird dipped in and out of the shallower water sending tiny droplets flying. It was just so peaceful, the man was thinking. But where am I? Does it matter? Perhaps it's easier to just enjoy what you have.

He moved on, his long stride carrying him across the grassy plains, rich with wild flowers and herbs, through shady woods, shafts of sunlight striking the rich leafy loam of the ground, birds flashing from branch to branch. Eventually, as the light was beginning to fade he came across a very small low cottage type building in an open clearing. No one in sight, and no sign of occupation. It seemed as though he was meant to simply make use of whatever was provided – his mind didn't question how or why, and that didn't bother him. It's a bit like a dream was a fleeting thought.

He passed a very comfortable night and proceeded again the next day.

This pattern continued for a number of days; the man neither wondered why nor concerned himself with other questions, merely accepting everything around him.

However, as he was crossing a wide stream one morning, he caught sight of the figure of a man some distance ahead, sitting down in the shade of a silvery birch tree. Approaching, he could make out that the man was probably quite elderly, his hair almost white, his weather-beaten face showing lines of age.

'Welcome stranger,' said the old man in a surprisingly strong voice. 'You've come quite a long way, have you not?'

'I suppose I have. Although I can't recall quite where I started from.'

'That's no surprise really,' was the response. 'We occasionally see folk like you. Once you get to E'shariya you will find what you need.'

'Folk like me?'

The old man nodded and smiled gently.

'Yes,' he said. 'out of place – the wrong time for you yet. It will come to you soon, and then the questions will start. A new learning perhaps.'

'I think perhaps that this is merely a dream and you are just a part of my imagination,' said the traveller then. 'Yes, that makes more sense.'

'Do you know who you are?' asked the old man.

'Of course I do. I am . . ' he paused, struggling. Frowning slightly he shook his head. 'No, I can't – quite – remember. It's there but I cannot grasp it.'

The old man rose and laid a hand on the traveller's shoulder.

'Do not fret, it will come. It has started.'

'What do you mean?'

But the old man turned and walked off, disappearing as he passed beyond another stand of birch trees.

What has started, and who am I? For several minutes the man stood motionless, his mind a jumble of chaotic thoughts as he tried to make sense of the weird situation he found himself in. And failed.

So, I am on my way to this place, E'shariya, wherever or whatever that is. Is it a name I should know maybe? I suppose the only way to find out is to keep going.

And so he walked on, the mountains no longer so distant; indeed, the ground was rising inexorably the further he went, but for the moment there were no more people to distract his thoughts.

At one point he paused, turning to look at the soft rolling plains he had now left behind. Unbidden, the vision of a beautiful city presented itself, walls of gleaming silvery white marble, elaborate turrets reaching into the sky. Without warning, it was engulfed in a swirling black cloud with such an aura of dark evil that it caused him to gasp. Just as suddenly the entire vision was gone, leaving him shocked and confused. What did it mean? He had the feeling that the city was somehow familiar, a memory from his life before he found himself in this dream; but was this from the past, or a forewarning of what was to come?

Was it possible to feel everything in a dream, to touch and know what was soft and hard, to recognise the taste of water or wine, to smell the air around you and to be aware of the ground changing underfoot? Above all, would you not know who you are? Oh yes, the questions have started, he nodded to himself.

Chapter 2

The once beautiful city of Elagos was slowly recovering its glory. In the short period of time following the defeat of the Red Lord's forces both the residents and those who had been a part of the victorious onslaught had worked tirelessly to restore some kind of normality; vast amounts of rubble and debris had been cleared; the ruins of the magnificent entrance gate had been removed; homes had been restored to their rightful owners and almost all signs of the aggressor's occupation eradicated.

Much had also been achieved by pressing the enemy survivors into service. On the orders of Sirad, Lord Commander of the Knights of Pelenin and heir to Sothan, the present King in Pelamir, those of the enemy left after the battle were given the opportunity to earn their freedom by committing to serve the city of Elagos and the people of Galdesh for a year and a day. They would be housed and cared for until that time and in exchange would be obliged to assist with the rebuilding works within the city itself and in various places in the surrounding countryside where homes had been vandalised or destroyed. If willing, they would be taught new skills that they could take back to their own lands, should they decide to return after their period of detention. To say that these men were surprised at the terms offered where they had been told to expect no mercy would be an under-statement. There were those who were sceptical but who were soon won over; others, who had willingly worked for the Red Lord and whose hatred for the Alliance was overwhelming soon paid the penalty. Sirad, well known for his fairness, was too aware of the horrendous sufferings of so many and was not prepared to risk that those tainted with the evil of the Red Lord should ever affect others in the future. The rules of war are harsh.

The night was quiet and still with no discernible breeze and little to yet hint of the approach of autumn. The moon was nearly full and bathed the sleeping building with its brilliance, casting clear sharp shadows across the walls and avenues. For the moment, at least, the city knew peace.

They had been very fortunate so far, thought the young man; losses in the taking of Elagos had not been too great and consequently the morale of all concerned was running high. The men were fired with enthusiasm, eager to take the campaign to the south, riding on the wave of this first success. But there was so much that was still undisclosed; so much that if revealed would certainly cause the best of them to draw back and question their understanding of their own destinies.

During the recent celebrations when the city had feted its rescuers promises had been made on both sides; nothing wrong with that – they were well-intentioned and quite genuine. The problem was that no-one actually appreciated just how complex and deadly the whole situation was. It was not merely a case of one army battling against another for control of a stretch of country. That was simply the visible symptom of a potentially fatal disease. This disease was an evil thing, the cause unknown, the nature as yet undefined, but surely far more insidious and deadly that had so far been supposed. They were all in the dark and in sore need of something better than a bright moon to help them see their way.

He walked along the terrace and down a flight of wide steps; crossing the silent courtyard he continued at a thoughtful pace along the wide avenues down through the levels towards the site of the main gates. There was no sign of life from the houses he passed, their shutters tight against the cool air. The slight sound of his booted footsteps echoed faintly between high walls and once or twice some small animal scrabbled across the occasional pile of loose gravel.

Finally reaching the lower level he turned to walk along the inner curtain wall. As he approached one of the small access towers two figures materialised from the shadows, saluting as the moonlight plainly revealed the features of the young Lord Commander of the Riders, the Prince Sirad. He stopped briefly to exchange a few words with the guards before moving on to where he could survey the place where the main gates had once stood but where now a huge breach, over a hundred foot wide, now lay open to the plain upon which many thousands of men had died violently such a short time ago. The monstrous chunks of stone that had been scattered as if by a giant hand in the cataclysmic explosion of force generated by the bonded minds of the two newly-awakened Ben-Neterù had been laboriously shifted; soon they would be re-fashioned to create a new entrance way for the city.

Sirad propped himself on one of the blocks and thought back to that extraordinary moment. He saw again the faces of the men from Ancor staring in total disbelief as their late king's daughter challenged them to stand firm – a vision conjured from nowhere it seemed, though she had been in their midst all along. His beloved Alinor, now his betrothed, had defied all the odds and ridden with him to this, their first victory. Against the powers that Verun – Altalla, the Red Lord, call him what you will – was able to summon against them, they had had only one option; the linking of their two minds in the inexplicable Bond had generated such a force that it had not only disrupted the coercive mental field generated by Verun, but it had totally destroyed the enormous city gates as well.

The man could not recall any detail of that experience – the possession of the Power was still new to him, and although Alinor had come into her own inheritance as one of the Ben-Neteru before him, she too was struggling to come to terms with it. He remembered, though, how drained they had both been after the expenditure of this tremendous wave of power and how he had come close to losing his life in the aftermath, too badly wounded and weak to fully defend himself during the running fights inside the city. His foster brother Ben had been in time to stem the loss of blood and had searched for his Lady to come and direct her healing skills.

Ben. There was another problem. Alinor had said that Ben knew some of the truth; did he realise then the source of their power? No, he surely cannot have yet faced up to the knowledge that both Alinor and Sirad were of the Ben-Neteru, for that sort of secret he could never have concealed from the man who had been his closest friend since childhood. The two of them would have to talk, probably soon; she had said, give it time and it will be all right. Sirad could only hope that she was not giving him false comfort. He knew how much it had scared him when he found out – how would Ben deal with the pain of finding out his foster brother was not the man he had grown up with?

The young prince rose, stretching his left arm and feeling the tightness as it pulled on the wound in his side, healed now but still inclined to ache occasionally. He ought to go back and get some sleep for there was so much that needed his attention each day; but on many nights sleep eluded him and he had taken to walking off his restlessness.

He sent out a tentative mental probe to see that Alinor was sleeping deeply, thoroughly exhausted from spending hours helping amongst those who were still recovering from their wounds. The halls of the ancient palace no longer sheltered the wounded; those whose injuries needed greater time to heal had moved to the hospital, a sprawling but harmonious building with large gardens providing relaxing areas for its recovering patients. Within the palace the refurbished council meeting areas witnessed much activity as the remaining members of the ruling Council sought to fill the gaps in their number and restore the governing structures. The Elders had welcomed the presence of the young Prince of Pelenin; a wisdom uncommon in such a young man, they said to each other, and a skill in diplomacy that many would envy. The Lady of Ancor too attended a number of meetings, but she remained quietly in the background, listening intently, the first to acknowledge her own inexperience in the art of government. Since that fateful day nearly eighteen months ago when her father, Teleston of Ancor, had been savagely murdered in an ambush that wiped out everyone in her travelling party, and from which she unexpectedly escaped, Alinor's life had been changed beyond recognition and belief.

From a protected life that had seen her spend much of her time away from her father's court she had found herself alone in a strange country en route to try and fulfil a task the meaning of which had been kept from her. A determination to avenge her father's death nurtured the latent strength of will and character that had impressed the noble young Lord of Pelenin, along with admiration for her excellent skills with a sword. Without Sirad's intervention and that of her beloved Lore-Master Amiros, she would have died after those who had sought her death above all nearly succeeded in poisoning her.

The purpose of the fated trip had been to seek out Remon the Seer in Elagos. A Mage and Mind-Master of legendary fame he had helped the young woman to a realisation of part of her destiny. The knowledge she had learned and the skills which she had been obliged to develop in the limited time she was able to spend with the ancient Seer had been an ordeal beyond description. Even now she barely grasped a small part of the whole. Remon had explained that there was still a wealth of information locked within her mind, far too much for her to be able to process or even accept so early in her advancement. She would need time to progress and adapt as her true nature asserted itself.

That was the one most devastating truth that the old Mind-Master had revealed to her. Legend had told of the times before the Scattering Wars when the semi-mythical ruler Rakep-thos had united the lands in a time of peace and prosperity for time untold. He and his kin were known as the Ben-Neteru – eternals – whose life spans were measured in centuries and whose powers belied understanding. Everyone knew that these were marvellous legends with barely a hint of reality. But Alinor now knew better.

Of course, Rakep-thos was long gone, but some of the Ben-Neteru still lived, inconspicuous and unrecognised by ordinary people. There were those who whilst not full-blooded Ben-Neteru still possessed many of the legendary powers and whose lives were much extended. Alinor had learned that her own mother, the Lady Meriona-en-resaan had been a true Ben-Neteru and whilst her father only carried part of the heritage it had been possible for the full nature of these legendary beings to be passed on to her when her mother chose to pass from this life. The implications were overwhelming. Alinor had still not fully come to terms with the discovery; to live beyond the normal span of years and see those around you age and die was a prospect that terrified her. The friends and acquaintances she had left in Ancor, the people she had met on her travels, not to mention a certain young Lord for whom she felt more than just a passing attraction; these people would be lost to her. Remon, the most powerful Ben-Neteru since Rakep-thos himself, had reassured her that she was not alone and that she had already met another who would be the most important one in her new life. At first she had thought that he referred to himself and when he too chose to pass felt that her life had become unbearable.

Shortly after her return to Pelamir from her time with Remon in Elagos the young Lord of Pelenin revealed that he too had been brought to the realisation that his own mother, the Lady Galena, had made the same sacrifice of her life to gift her son with the full nature and abilities of the Ben-Neteru. Now they could both begin to understand how their destinies were inter-twined, a fact that their respective parents had long known but had kept from their children. Their early learning had been guided by the Lore-Master Amiros, in whose being the heritage of the Ben-Neteru was very strong and he had been instrumental in saving Alinor when a virulent poison had been used against her. Alinor particularly had relied heavily on the Lore-Master's support, but he had fallen foul of Verun, the disgraced but exceedingly powerful former pupil of Remon who had somehow come into possession of the mythical gem Mnethar the power of which he had used on Amiros with devastating effect. Verun sought total domination over all the lands and it was his forces that had taken control of the former neutral city of Elagos where the vicious Mage had hoped to confront his own former teacher. Thwarted by Remon's passing, he took out his anger on Amiros; as a result the Lore-Master now lay trapped in a seemingly permanent coma, his mind closed to any attempts by either Alinor or Sirad to reach him.

The past months had taken their toll on the young woman and Sirad was anxious to do anything he could to try to ease her current situation. Several days ago the prince had arranged for staff to care for the Lady of Ancor; it was unthinkable that a sovereign lady should stay anywhere without at least a token retinue. Different for him, he had the other Riders, and besides, he was still only the heir, whereas Alinor, although not yet crowned, was now the rightful queen of the northern lands. As the present Ancor entourage in Elagos consisted only of the elite palace guards Sirad had consulted with a couple of the city nobles and enlisted their assistance. As expected, Alinor had at first objected but, with a little gentle persuasion on his part, she relented and agreed to taking on at least one lady-in-waiting and perhaps two to three other personal staff. She had been too long without female companionship and the prince was well aware that his lady was under great strain and in need of the company of her own sex.

The duly appointed lady-in-waiting was named Semira – a lovely raven-haired young woman; not very tall, she had a delightful face and shapely figure. From one of the oldest families in the city, she had been well educated and was possessed of a definite mind of her own to the despair of her parents. She was sensible of the duties and formalities of rank, but quite unaffected in her manner. Sirad had spoken with her and simply asked that she take good care of the Lady's needs. Semira had accepted the task of course, before asking the prince to tell her some of what had happened over the past year, for, as she rightly pointed out, there was better chance of their getting on well if she had some idea of what the young woman had been through.

Sirad had laughed, but then did give a very brief outline, warning her that the Lady of Ancor was not one to suffer fools. 'Nor am I,' was the comment he had received as the dark-haired beauty made her exit.

The prince's judgement was vindicated when Alinor took an instant liking to Semira. She found that it was actually very nice to settle back into the role of a woman again after so many months in the guise of the youth Elukar, and Alinor was slowly starting to allow herself to relax even while knowing this respite could not last that long. Semira brought in another young girl Mina as a second maidservant and took as her first task the provision of some suitable gowns for her mistress. It did not take very long to capture Alinor's interest when she produced quite a number of bolts of glorious fabrics in a dazzling array of colours, and she encouraged her to indulge herself in all those luxuries which had been markedly absent for so long. Semira was also thoughtful enough to come up with suitable designs for the Lord Commander as well – for as she said, he couldn't wear uniform all the time.

There was a smile on the prince's face as he walked back up to the palace, remembering quiet and special moments spent with the woman he loved. The look on her face when Fehlen and Gerin had made that momentous presentation of the insignia at the celebratory feast had been unforgettable, a combination of total surprise, awe and pleasure. Come to think of it, he had not yet tackled those two captains about the matter; no doubt Ben and Osan had also been involved in the unprecedented occasion. Captain-Commander for Life was a supreme honour, rarely awarded; true, Alinor's father Teleston had received it, but he had been Sothan's ally and life-long friend, but there were very, very few other men who had been likewise named. Of course, Sirad had no objection to Alinor becoming the first woman to be thus recognised, but it was the sole prerogative of the sovereign and he would not have dreamt of going against protocol. The Riders' strict tenets and rituals did not favour admission of outsiders, yet his senior captains had taken it upon themselves to admit Alinor, the Lady of Ancor. Discipline in the ranks, thought the Lord Commander, is getting very lapse; one is tempted to find some suitable way of reprimanding such a flagrant breach of etiquette.

Sirad attended the first meeting of the day barely an hour after dawn, once more down by the damaged city walls. Representatives from the craft guilds were there, anyone connected with the re-building and re-shaping of Elagos. At earlier discussion with the city elders, the prince had suggested that the architects be asked to submit designs and costing for the necessary work, both on the defensive walls and for those parts of the city where the occupying forces had vandalised the existing structures and defaced some of the major edifices.

In a remarkably short space of time these craftsmen had produced a series of very practical proposals, efficient and cost-effective but very much in keeping with the original aesthetically well-balanced style of the ancient city. For an hour or more the dozen people involved talked, measured, compromised and generally pulled all the plans to pieces, finally agreeing on their worth. The actual projects would involve many months in the execution and temporary measures would be necessary to make the city safe before winter against the now unlikely prospect of a further attack. Massive building work necessitated a massive workforce, and the Council members were grateful for the boost in numbers provided by the presence of the prisoners pressed into service.

Sirad left the meeting, acknowledging the thanks from some of the elders there for his continued support, knowing that it was time that both he and Alinor thought about heading back to their respective homes. The other Alliance contingents from Lefnan-Ilos, Mindros and Harfeld had already set off on their return journeys to bear the news of the relief of Elagos. Any thoughts that Sirad had originally had about the armies taking the fight on to Mekad and Hansor to challenge the power of Verun had to be put on hold. Apart from the fact that to attempt to take on the enemy during the worst part of the year would be unwise, he recognised that the level of Verun's abilities was far, far greater than they had anticipated; the damage that he had inflicted on his old teacher Amiros with the use of the fearful gem Mnethar gave pause for serious thought. There were many questions that needed to be addressed, not least that of where Verun had actually found the gem. Both he and Alinor knew very little beyond the legends about the precious stone, although they suspected that the old tales barely did justice to the reality. It was said that it would destroy any unworthy body who even approached it; so how had Verun, so twisted in his mind, ever managed to get hold of it, let alone use it against another Mage with the undoubted powers that Amiros possessed? However, it did seem that Verun had suffered some kind of backlash when Alinor and Sirad had bonded to use their ability to destroy the gates of Elagos and interfere with the mind control that Verun had been utilising on his armies protecting the city. As yet, they did not know the extent of this set-back for the evil aggressor and it would take a little while for them to be able to get information back from Verun's stronghold and the areas around Mekad to provide some ideas of what was happening there. But this, hopefully, would give them much needed time to learn more of the dangers they would be facing, and how, if at all, they could defeat Verun.

There were other matters nearer home that took immediate precedence. Alinor was the Lady of Ancor, the rightful ruler following her father's death, but as yet, the news of her survival would barely have had time to reach the city of Thorgiliad itself, or the ears of Vixlan, former Steward to the king, who had wasted no time in taking control of the country for his own advantage. Vixlan had been open to the manipulations of Verun who had insidiously encouraged the little man's greed; all of Teleston's loyal retainers and advisors had been removed, by one means or another, from the court. Leaders in the Elite Guard had been dispersed around the country, their privileges curtailed, any thoughts of opposition slyly discouraged by unvoiced threats. When Sirad had approached the Steward to request assistance with the relief of Elagos, as was required amongst members of the Alliance, he had been shabbily treated and fobbed off with an absurdly small number of troops to support the venture. The memory of his insulting behaviour still rankled Sirad and he was well aware of Alinor's anger at what had been happening in her beloved home.

But – it suddenly dawned on him – he had been so taken up with a multitude of matters that he hadn't really seen Alinor for a couple of days now, and they had barely mind-spoken at all. When they had she seemed distracted and too quiet, the energy that had been carrying her along completely drained away. How could he have allowed himself to neglect her so badly?

Sirad returned to the palace and straight away went up to Alinor's apartment. Semira met him in the corridor.

'I am glad you have come, my lord; I am worried about her. No,' she put her hand out to stop him rushing into her rooms immediately. 'she is still sleeping, but she had bad dreams again last night – I heard her cry out once, but when I went in she fell quiet and did not stir afterward.

'I couldn't come to you before as she was very guarded about my leaving her.'

'That's not like her,' Sirad frowned. 'What has been going on?'

'It's difficult to explain really,' Semira sighed. 'It's like something and nothing, if you know what I mean. I can't put my finger on any one thing, but it is as if she's building up to some sort of crisis. She isn't sleeping well, more often she's half asleep during the day and she can't seem to concentrate on anything very long. I'm sure she was near to tears after Commander Dhalen visited her the other day, but gods forbid that she would show this to anyone else.'

Sirad shook his head, much disturbed by the woman's words.

'Could it be something to do with her father again?' she asked.

'Perhaps,' said Sirad slowly. 'It's been such an awful year for her . . .'

His voice trailed off.

'What day is it?' he asked suddenly.

'The first day of Benath,' Semira replied.

'Then you are right. It is about her father. Teleston's coronation day was celebrated on the first of Benath and has always been a significant occasion for the people of Ancor – how could I have forgotten? The memory of that will in itself cause her great distress, let alone her having been through so much afterward.

Thank you, young lady, you have provided the answer.'

He smiled gently and added, 'I suggest that you take a few hours off now; her Ladyship won't be needing you for a little while.'

Semira dropped a curtsey, relieved that the worrying concern was now in good hands. She had been very much in awe of the prince when he first arrived in the city but had quickly seen the depth of his feeling for the young northern queen who was now her mistress. Alinor herself she very much admired, having learned much more of her story in the short time that she had spent in her service. Semira's education had instilled in her a healthy respect for the former Grand Master and it was obvious from little things that had been said that the Lady Alinor had a lot in common with the ancient seer.

The man walked slowly on down the corridor, letting his mind reach to Alinor's to confirm that her rest was still untroubled. Turning the corning he saw two Riders on a terrace to his left, one sitting down, his arm in a sling, the other leaning against the balustrade talking quietly. Sirad hesitated a second, then schooling his face to a somewhat severe expression he strode quickly over towards them.

'Senior Captains, my apartment, one hour.'

Without waiting for any reaction he turned and marched briskly away, leaving the two men staring after him in some surprise. What they did not see was the way his mouth turned up and his eyes danced at the prospect of discomforting his companions.

'What on …?' Fehlen looked at Osan who rubbed a hand over his wounded arm.

'Search me,' Osan replied. 'But he didn't look too pleased about something.'

'I'd better go and find the others, I suppose. They shouldn't be too far away. Perhaps Ben's got an idea of what he wants.'

'I doubt it,' Osan shook his head. 'From what I've seen recently they don't seem to be talking much to each other – and that is *not* a good sign.'

'I thought Ben had gone a bit quiet. But then, there has been so much to do, so maybe it's not that serious.'

'I'll join you there,' said Osan as Fehlen hurried away.

In his apartments, Sirad read over a pile of reports as he ate a fugal breakfast, breaking off every now and then to stare unseeing out of the windows at the attractive gardens beyond. Any day now the messengers sent to Pelamir carrying news of the battle for Elagos should be returning. From there the news would have been sent on to the other nations advising them of the victory and giving advance warning of the imminent return of their own troops. Several companies of Riders would probably have left the capital by now but would travel at the normal, fairly fast rate, to Elagos. To invoke their spell-cast swiftness was unnecessary at this point. Supplies were urgently needed but they would be very much slower in reaching Galdesh. Fresh horses would be brought with the Riders to replace the numbers lost in the fighting.

Sirad spared a thought then for the loss of his own big bay, speared in the last ambush. He'd ridden that particular animal for over ten years and was deeply saddened by the loss. The strange relationship between Riders and their horses was hard for an outsider to appreciate. The entire culture of the country of Pelenin revolved around their extraordinary fey animals, a continuing reminder of ancient magics. Now the prince would be obliged to find a new horse – but, he thought, only for a couple of summers. It would not be long before Lightstar's new colt would be grown – what was it Alinor had said about him? Taukhet she had named him, but he didn't really understand what it meant – something about a spirit and fire - and hadn't got round to asking her. Too much else had happened.

There was a loud knock on the door and he brought his thoughts back to the present. That should be his wayward captains, he thought, and called out:

'Enter.'

The five captains, closest companions of the heir to the throne, marched in, bowed and remained at attention until their leader should signal otherwise.

Sirad continued to read his reports for another minute or so whilst the disconcerted men wondered just what was wrong. It was so unlike Sirad to behave in such a way and they exchanged worried glances.

Without looking up Sirad ordered:

'Report.'

One by one they saluted and stated their names and rank; Benharad, Fehlen, Leykar, Osan and Gerin – all senior captains and long-standing friends of the prince, although from the expression on his face that was not apparent. As the prince's second-in-command Ben gave a status report on the troops and horses, following it with details of present patrol and duty orders.

Sirad put his papers to one side and looked at the five men, acknowledging to himself that he was fortunate indeed to have such fine warriors as his friends; his face however gave no indication of what he was thinking, his grey eyes remaining dark and piercing.

'Good,' he said, standing up and walking round to the front of his table. 'That appears to be satisfactory.'

There was just the slightest emphasis on the word 'appears'.

'However,' the prince leaned on the edge of the table and waited for the sound of the word to die away before speaking again.

'This is the most important campaign that we have ever been involved in. Our success will hang on the performance of the Riders despite the presence of all the other nations. For most of those other troops this is the first time that they have come into close working contact with us and I know you will agree with me that first impressions are supremely important. '

He waited for a response and the five dutifully replied, 'Yes sir.'

'The mores of the Riders of Pelenin go far back in time and are *sacrosanct*,' he stressed the word. 'Our rituals have been guarded jealously and our customs honoured for centuries. It is unheard of that any Rider should break with the tradition of our nation.'

The five men were feeling distinctly uncomfortable, each wracking his brain to fathom out what could have prompted such a lecture from their Commander.

'Warfare is a bloody business, gentlemen, as you well know. There are many things that may happen in the heat of battle that only time will vindicate. However . . .'

He paused again, silently enjoying the effect his words were having.

'When, in the cold light of day, tradition is flaunted . . . I put it to you, *Captains,* that something must be done.'

He looked at each man in turn, knowing their thoughts were in a turmoil, trying to identify firstly what awful breach had occurred, and secondly, who could have been responsible. All without success.

'It grieves me,' the prince continued soberly, 'that the responsible parties appear to have no sense of guilt whatsoever. On the contrary they continue to act in such a fashion as to indicate to me that they consider themselves to be above censure.'

He stopped – the silence was palpable.

Ben was staring at Sirad as if the prince was out of his senses. Just then Sirad looked at him and the hapless captain read the laughter in his foster-brother's eyes.

'My lord,' said Ben firmly, 'such conduct as you have outlined is indeed reprehensible and would warrant the maximum sentence possible in the event of it being proven. However . . .'

It was now Ben's turn to make the emphasis and pause for effect. His fellow officers were all looking at him, nonplussed.

'Without doubt such a break with tradition could have been interpreted as something approaching a cavalier disregard at the highest level, but I have no hesitation in contesting your opinion.'

There was an audible gasp from the other four captains who were convinced that Ben had just forfeited his rank permanently, despite his intimacy with the prince.

For a few seconds the two men were locked eye to eye, and then to their amazement the prince burst out laughing, as did Ben.

'The Insignia,' said Gerin, finally catching on. 'That's what this is all about!'

They joined in the laughter for a few moments, admitting that Sirad had really caught them out. It was Ben who recovered first.

'Yes, my lord, we admit that we have apparently trespassed against the old customs, but we also have no intention of apologising for it. The Lady Alinor had won the right to recognition by the Riders, and we know that you would not have made the decision alone. And besides,' his face took on a little boy's innocent expression, 'the king said it was all right.'

'How on earth . . .?' Sirad exclaimed, shaking his head in disbelief. 'Captain Benharad, I don't know quite how you managed this – you will have to explain yourself eventually.'

'I don't think there's anything you can do under the circumstances,' observed Gerin, sharing Ben's innocent demeanour.

'All right, I give in,' laughed Sirad. 'But to be serious, I would like to thank you, and the others, for what you have done. She knows what it means to us, and the gesture only served to underline what I would dearly have liked to make public.'

'She is one very special lady,' said Osan quietly. 'It was obvious even before we reached the city, but then – well, you know better than us.'

'Yes, I suppose I do,' the young man responded with a wry smile.

'There is work to do, captains. Get out of here.'

Chapter 3

It was getting on towards mid-day by now and Sirad's thoughts turned once more to his beloved Lady; his conversation with Semira earlier had left him feeling guilty and concerned. Leaving his paperwork aside, he made his way to her apartments, knocked on the door and went straight in, crossing the gleaming floor with its richly coloured rugs scattered here and there, to where Alinor was leaning against a pillar, watching a couple of birds hopping around on the balcony. She looked up at him and smiled a little sadly, her eyes worried and tired. He took her in his arms and just held her close, saying nothing, sensing her deep need for comfort. After several minutes he kissed the top of her golden head and whispered:

'We are one, remember? How about sharing it with me, whatever it is that's hurting you so much, instead of blocking me out?'

Alinor sighed and held him tighter.

'I don't quite know what to say,' she whispered. 'I'm just so tired, and everything is . . . I don't know.'

'Come and sit down for a while.'

He led her over to a big couch and they sat down, her head resting on his shoulder, his arm remaining protectively around her. She had lost weight, he thought; she seemed so fragile. And she had taken pains to make sure that their exceptional mind link did not reveal the true depth of her unbearable thoughts and feelings. Gently he stroked her soft golden hair, remembering how she had first appeared that day in the forests of Harfeld – she'd cut it shorter then in keeping with her disguise; he'd been fooled for certain.

'Let it out, Alinor, don't bottle up all the feelings. It's no surprise that you are suffering a reaction to everything that's happened; it's been a long time coming, well overdue.'

He paused.

'I realise that it's your father's coronation anniversary.'

She nodded, eyes closed in remembered pain, unable to prevent the unforced tears glistening.

'The past eighteen months have been more than hard on you.'

Again she nodded.

'I miss him,' her voice was so quiet. 'So many things I want to tell him, so much I should have said but never did, and now it's too late.'

'He knows it all, I am sure, and understands.'

'Maybe, but I can't help but think about it just the same. And all this,' she looked up briefly, tears falling down her pale cheeks.

'Ben-Neteru, the power, Remon and Verun, and poor Amiros. What's it all about, Sirad? I'm so tired. I don't think I want to go on.'

The man enveloped her in his arms, the despair in her voice cutting him like a knife.

'I don't blame you for feeling this way, my love. There are times when it's almost beyond me too. But it will pass, these feelings you have now. You know it and I know it. Just try to let it all go – cry as much as you need to, let it all wash away with your tears.'

She did cry, quietly desolate, her salty tears cleansing her soul of the grief she still harboured for her father, her murdered countrymen and friends, the brave men who had helped to win the city but who did not live to celebrate that victory. And tears too for her beloved Lore-Master Amiros, somehow trapped in a living death because of Verun's spite.

The young prince said nothing at all until the tears were all spent. He fetched her some cold water to wash her face and a goblet of the healing *essuvar* to soothe away the strain.

For a while the then told her about everything that had been going on in the city, all the plans and discussions for rebuilding, the reports from the scouting patrols and news from Pelamir. Gradually the haunted look in her eyes faded and she started asking a few questions, her interest in the re-birth of the city re-kindled. Talking over, they just sat quietly, Alinor feeling secure enfolded in the man's strong arms, every now and then his fingers gently stroking her hair. Eventually she drifted off to sleep, totally exhausted; she didn't stir as he carried her into the bedroom and laid her so very gently on the bed, covering her with a fine blanket before slipping silently away.

His mind kept returning to one particularly distressing problem that faced the young couple, a problem that seemed insurmountable – that of the state of Amiros. The old man, as they still thought of him even though they had no idea really how old he was, seemed to be beyond their reach in the depths of his dark state. Early on they had taken him to Remon's house, hoping that the strange crystal globe housed there could bring him back; to no avail it seemed. It had eased away the all-pervading blackness that had first threatened his being but he showed no signs of awakening, and whilst his physical body appeared to be maintaining a stable condition, despite the lack of real food and drink, nothing anyone did made any impression.

Unknown to Alinor, Sirad had been having strange dreams again in which the crystal played a prominent part. Normally they would not hide anything from each other, and with minds so closely attuned it took only a thought to link themselves. But on occasion, they had both had cause to dissemble, usually to protect the other from worry or distress; there were enough things on Alinor's mind that it had not been difficult to keep her in the dark. He was aware that the strange crystal was a tool that Remon had used to assist Alinor in the development of her abilities; she had explained as best she could what had happened, but it was difficult to describe what was in essence indescribable.

When Alinor had returned to Pelamir after her time with Remon, she had used some of her new-found knowledge to assist Sirad, recently come to the awareness of his own heritage. She had warned him that it would not be possible for him to undergo the same sort of ordeal that Remon had inflicted on her without the assistance that the strange globe had provided and the protection of the Seer's abode. But there were many questions to which Sirad wanted, and needed, answers; Alinor was in no condition to help him, and he was pretty certain that she didn't have the knowledge anyway, so it was that he decided to go alone to the seer's house. Maybe, just maybe, he may find some of those answers there.

Knowing that the young woman would now sleep for a while, and not wanting to have to see anyone else just yet, he made for the nearest exit from the palace, making sure that none of his own people saw him. With long strides he crossed the squares, courtyards and avenues and reached the seer's house. The mysterious entrance doors were ornately carved but bore nothing that would indicate a means of opening them. Remembering the words that Alinor had used, he spoke them quietly and gently touched the warm wood; the huge doors opened to him just as they had for Alinor and quietly closed again behind him. Crossing the vast marbled hallway he ascended the magnificent stairway that curved up so elegantly to the first floor. He paused momentarily at the top to admire the intricate design with the soft roseate light streaming through the beautiful window that caused the warm stone to glow and highlighting the crystal patterning of wall and floor. Once again he became aware of the same sensation of welcome that seemed to flow from the very stones of the building. He crossed the wide corridor and entered what Alinor had called Remon's library. He was expecting to see the same untidy jumble that had so amused Alinor when she first met the Grand Master, but though the room was packed with books, manuscripts, charts, boxes, strange devices and suchlike, it now appeared quite ordered. He stood in the middle of the room taking in the details, wondering where to start now that he was here.

Too much, he thought. Where on earth would anyone begin?

There was one source of power and information that he could go to, and that was the crystal. It had been a key element in Alinor's learning, so perhaps he could start with that. He returned to the long corridor and entered the strange windowless room where the crystal globe rested on top of its tripod. As he entered, his feet cushioned by the rich blue carpet, the jewel seemed to send out a reassuring and welcoming glow; subsiding onto the soft cushions, the young man became aware of waves of energy washing over him. For several minutes he simply sat, relaxing under the influence of the jewel. But gradually he became aware that the gentle waves were turning into probes of increasing sharpness that assaulted his senses, testing his abilities to defend and protect. Alinor had mentioned this happening to her when Remon used the crystal in her training. Strong as he had been before, this onslaught was far greater than he had imagined; it forced the young man to adapt and strengthen his mind – not an easy task by any means – and before long he fell back, sweating and exhausted by the battering, his grey eyes closed and dark hair damp from his exertions. The fierce light that had been emanating from the globe dimmed to a gentle bluish shimmer, somehow restoring Sirad, as least bodily, though his mind was still a maelstrom of thoughts. Now I have some idea of what Alinor meant, he thought, when she described her stay in this house. If this is the sort of thing that Verun himself has gone through, and possibly is able to inflict on others, then we are still woefully unready to face him.

He had no idea of how long the strange jewel had held him, only that he badly needed a drink. Leaving the room he almost expected to find that evening had come, but the sun was still streaming through the windows. He returned to the so-called library and was not really surprised to see that there was a small chased gold wine flagon and delicate glass goblet on the small table by the fire. He knew they had not been there before. He went over and picked up the flagon; a delicate scent drifted from it. Hesitantly he poured some of the golden wine into the goblet.

Confident that nothing in the seer's house was likely to hurt him, he raised the goblet in a silent toast to the spirit of the departed seer and took a sip of the fragrant liquid; its coolness was infinitely refreshing and he drained the cup.

His attention fell on the long table at the far end of the room upon which several pieces of parchment had been laid out. He walked over and picked one of them up, running his eyes over the precisely elegant script.

As he took in the first words his eyes widened, and a knot formed in his stomach.

cd?bcqd cqdσ dcd cdmaqσ
cabbbm?acacq
bbιddτb τp cqdσ

Welcome, my son

I regret that we were never able to meet in person during my former lifetime for your mother told such tales of her beloved child, always understanding that you would come here one day. No matter. I have watched your progress with interest as I have also watched Alinor-Merion, and I find little fault.

You are here because you have questions that she cannot answer for you and you are worried for her safety. That is commendable but a waste of time. You know that you are her main protection, after the Tokens of Power, but that which must happen will surely do so.

Tokens of Legacy

The circumstances surrounding the awakening of your powers has been far from ideal. In Alinor's case it has caused some difficulties and she will need all the help that you can give her. You were always destined for each other, so do not be afraid to take her for your own. Your strength and love is her greatest support, and she in turn will fulfil your life.

You will find many of the answers to your questions here in this house – it is yours, for both of you to use. Within these walls you are protected and everything is directed to your well-being. You will discover in time that although the Ben-Neteru carry a heavy burden, their power can be used to bring great happiness and harmony. Do not grieve unnecessarily for those around you.

I believe that I may have underestimated my former student Verun and it is right that you should treat him with respect. He was always very capable and a quick learner; but he became greedy for power and enjoyed exercising that power over his less able colleagues. In that respect it is no surprise that he now seeks to obtain the Tokens of Power, but whether he works alone or under the influence of something more baleful I cannot yet say.

I am deeply saddened that the one you know as Miros has been put into such danger that it is uncertain whether he can be saved and I regret that it was not in my power to prevent this tragedy.

It may be that you will soon be needing the assistance of others of the Brotherhood in your quest. The healer Eldren may be found on the island of Mitos. Both you and Alinor will benefit from his knowledge.

I can tell you now that you were right to suppose that Verun did not escape totally unaffected. He will need to recover and you should make use of this time to further your own development. Alinor's sense of duty will not permit her to pursue the challenge that Verun poses just yet and so she will return to Ancor – at least for a while.

In due course you will come to understand better the destiny that the pair of you face; it is not my part to explain further at this time. Only know that the danger is very great, and the possibility of failure cannot be totally ruled out. However I, and others, have placed great trust in you and do not believe that this trust is misplaced.

Seek that which is yours by right, Sirad son of Sothan and Galena. Unite that which was lost and do not fear the future.

ᖆᘚᑯᘔ ᑯᶄᑯ ᴄᴄ|ᑫᶃᑯᖘ

    The young man read the paper twice, unable, or perhaps unwilling, to take in the extraordinary nature of the message. Perhaps he should not have been so surprised given that the Grand Master was who he was, but still it shook him to the core. How had Remon known he would come here today, and how had he written of things that had only occurred after his passing? He didn't understand the references to the Tokens of Power, though he felt he should. There was just something at the very back of his mind that seemed vaguely familiar, but try as he would it eluded him.

He helped himself to another goblet of wine and looked around the room again. So far he had only been in this room and the one where the crystal resided. Curiosity got the better of him and he went out to explore some of the other rooms in this strange house. He found the real library several doors away and gasped in astonishment at the piles of books stretching away before him. The Great Library in Pelamir was supremely impressive, but this defied description. There were spiral staircases going up to goodness knows where – from the outside there was no sign that this building was big enough to accommodate such an enormous room. He closed the door on the sight, too confused to even think about it.

He walked on and turned down to the left to a different wing. Here the colours of the stonework were bright, giving an airy feeling. A brilliant shaft of light fell through a high latticed window onto the pale blue marbling of the floor, picking out a design worked in gold and rose gems. He stopped short, staring at the intricate pattern. It was strangely familiar; he picked out the flying horse from the arms of Pelenin, and the crown and six stars. But worked in amongst that were the Swords of Bran from Ancor's coat of arms too, with a second crown and the tear-shaped gem he thought was probably Qanoor.

There was something a little eerie about it that made Sirad reluctant to go on. He didn't want to see any more without Alinor being with him. He got the impression that this whole area of the house just seemed to be quietly waiting for them; there was nothing menacing about it, just really weird.

He decided he'd had enough and retraced his steps, coming out into the afternoon sun. He took a long route back to the palace, re-thinking the unexpected message from Remon. There had been a suggestion, he thought, that perhaps the Lore-Master could be helped which was encouraging, and he wanted to talk to Alinor and tell her as soon as he could. But there had been other things in that letter that he would not share with her – they were personal to him and would stay that way for the time being.

Chapter 4

Semira went back to quietly put away some materials she had been working on in Alinor's apartments hoping to re-awaken some interest in her young mistress. She had been meaning to take various items to her mother for several days but had been unable to leave Alinor for long enough to go down into the city to where her parents had their home. The suggestion by Sirad that she could take a few hours off meant that she could catch up on some of her own personal chores. Filling a large basket with all the things that she had promised her mother she would find – a pile of trimmings and material pieces, some jars of ointment and herbal preparations, a small brooch as a gift and some fresh picked late flowers – she started out along one of the narrower paths behind the palace buildings, humming quietly to herself. The basket was awkward and quite heavy; on another occasion she would have had one of her parents' servants take it for her, but today she could not be bothered with looking for someone to help and decided to go alone.

It was the first time she had actually walked alone in the city since the early days of the occupation by the Red Lord's troops. The remembrance of their arrival caused her to shiver; although it had now been many months ago certain memories where still painfully fresh. During the first few weeks of their arrival the soldiers had behaved with characteristic brutality, setting upon and beating up unprotected civilians in the streets. Inflamed by heavy drinking they also sought to indulge their physical cravings with almost any female they could find. Although the excesses were eventually curtailed by the commanding officers it had not been until after many in the city had been made to suffer. Semira and one of her maids had been approached by five men one afternoon as they were returning from one of the many markets within the city. Unable to make their escape they were surrounded and taunted; their cries for help had gone unanswered and the men savagely raped them both, leaving them bruised and bleeding to find their way home. The horrific ordeal had left Semira ill for weeks, and even when she had recovered physically she refused to leave her home again until the city had finally been liberated. Her appointment as a companion to the Lady Alinor had been her parents' way of helping their daughter to return to something like a normal life. The plan had worked and she was now able to accept the presence of men, and more importantly soldiers, around her without panicking.

But now, out on the quiet street, she couldn't stop the feeling of unease starting to form. She took several deep breaths, telling herself that she had nothing to be afraid of, summoning her stubborn will to firmly quash the weakness that made her tremble. She re-settled the basket on her arm and walked on as briskly as she could.

Turning a corner she came face to face with two young men completely blocking her way. She made as if to pass them, but one shot out an arm and took hold of her basket, effectively pushing her against a wall. They were neither of them intending any harm, merely high-spirited and taking the opportunity to flirt with such an attractive girl.

'Please don't rush off, lovely lady!' said the first. 'There's surely no hurry on a day like this.'

'That basket is much too big for you to carry – we'll come along and help,' said the second.

'I don't need any help,' stammered Semira, 'please just let me go.'

'We mean you no harm, don't be worried.'

But Semira was worried, more than that she was terrified of a repeat of her previous ordeal and was unable to stifle her panic.

'Please,' she almost screamed, tugging to try and get the basket free.

The two found her reaction rather extreme and very amusing and merely stood their ground as she struggled to break away.

'What's going on?' demanded a voice, and a third man came into view, striding rapidly up from the turning further on down the lane.

The two jumped, quickly moving away from Semira who by this time was fighting back tears.

'It's nothing,' said the first, 'we were just having a chat with the maidservant here and she seemed to get upset. We haven't laid a finger on her.' It was the truth, but no consolation to the girl.

'Then your presence is obviously not welcome. Get on your way.'

They went quickly with just a brief backward glance and expression of indifference.

The man turned to where Semira stood, breathing rapidly but managing to regain control of herself.

'Are you all right?' he asked.

'Yes, thank you.'

He looked her up and down and she immediately thought how arrogant he was, those dark eyes and that hawk-like expression, judging her just like some bird of prey looking for its next meal, although she did sense somehow that she was in no danger from him.

'Rather well dressed for a maidservant, aren't you?' he said. 'Where have you come from?'

His tone angered her, banishing her former terrors completely.

'I am no maidservant,' she said caustically, 'and I am not obliged to answer such rudeness.'

'My apologies,' the man hinted at a bow.

'Perhaps my lady has lost her maid that she finds it necessary to carry her own basket?'

'You are insufferable. Just who do you think you are?'

'Ah, I am remiss. I forget our friends did not take the time for introductions. Rekar – formerly of Sistor, presently of Elagos – at your service, my lady.'

He did bow, properly, this time.

'Yes, I've heard of you,' responded Semira. 'The Lady Alinor has mentioned your name several times. I am her companion. My name is Semira.'

Rekar's eyes clouded for a moment, then he shrugged.

'Don't expect me to apologise,' he said. 'If you wander around the streets like that it's no surprise that you get mistaken for a servant.'

She scowled at him, but the gesture was wasted.

'I suppose I should escort you to wherever it is you are going.'

'Thank you, but that will be quite unnecessary. I would not like to keep you from important business.'

'Oh, nothing very important. I don't suppose a few minutes will do any harm.'

'Please, don't put yourself out on my behalf.'

'I won't,' said Rekar carelessly and took the basket from her. 'Which way?'

She looked at him, uncertain quite how to interpret his expression. She inclined her head and started off down the lane, he walking beside her but carefully not too close. They said nothing at all until she reached her home.

'Thank you,' she said, taking the basket. 'You didn't need to have come, you know.'

'Quite all right,' he said, nodded, turned on his heel and walked away.

'Of all the . . .' muttered Semira, feeling quite offended by his casual attitude. This man was supposed to be the local hero; no manners though, she thought, and went inside.

Alinor came to the dining hall that evening; she still looked pale, but most of the tenseness seemed to have left her and she even laughed when Semira made some comment, bringing a smile to Sirad's lips seeing his lady in better spirits. Dhalen, the senior commander of Ancor's elite guards and old friend of the new young queen, had obviously been waiting for her to put in an appearance and got up as soon as she entered, hurrying over to escort her to her place. He spoke to her in undertones and she nodded, that far-away look momentarily on her face again; but then it was gone and she smiled and made some reply to her faithful commander and continued over to where Sirad was waiting for her. He kissed her hand, mentally asking if she was all right. She smiled assuring him that she did indeed feel very much better following his earlier visit. The talk during the meal was varied and stimulating and the prince was relieved by Alinor's easiness; she seemed almost back to her usual self, though he knew she would still need time to recover fully.

Later in the evening as they strolled through the quiet halls of the palace, he told her about his visit to the Seer's house and that he had found the extraordinary letter from the departed Mind-Master in which he had left word about the possibility of Eldren being able to help in their quest – he rather hoped that as a healer Eldren would also be able to help Amiros. Alinor's surprise at Sirad's going there alone was lost in her enthusiasm to track down this previously unknown member of the Brotherhood and to see about getting the Lore-Master to him.

'Where is this island, Mitos?' I've never heard of it,' Alinor exclaimed.

'I think,' replied Sirad, 'I'm not certain mind you, that it's right out off the south-west coast of Lefnan-ilos. I'll have to speak to Fra'ilen about it – he'll know if anyone does. There's a whole string of islands out there stretching into the western sea. He'll be the best person to get us there.'

'But Fra'ilen's gone south already – we'll have to go and see him. We can leave early tomorrow, it won't take long.'

'Hold on a moment,' Sirad was quite firm. 'You are not going anywhere tomorrow, early or not. Whatever Fra'ilen can tell us, we have much to do before we can just rush off to some unknown island. I trust that you haven't forgotten that I need Fra'ilen and his men - we're still fighting a war for goodness' sake, and I may need him to help us find out what the enemy are now up to. We have no idea yet what has happened to Verun and what the current situation is in Mekad. Saving Elagos was only the first small step in what I fear may be a long and difficult journey for us; even Remon would not commit himself to saying that we would succeed.'

Alinor sighed deeply.

'I'm sorry; it's just that I have been so worried about Amiros. I know that his pain seems to have lessened, but he is still lost to us and I was so hoping that we could find some way to bring him back.'

Sirad wanted to reassure his beloved lady, well aware of the abiding love and respect she had for her old teacher. He too was dismayed by what had happened to the old man, and missed being able to talk matters over with him. True, Remon had offered a glimmer of hope, but there were no certainties.

'We don't really know what happened, do we? I mean when we were outside the gates and that vile black cloud was dispersed. Do you think that we should attempt to overlook Verun, find out what he is doing if we can?'

Sirad pursed his lips and shook his head.

'I'm not sure about that,' he said, 'it could be very risky, perhaps even more than it would have been before. We don't know how powerful he is, and we have no way of protecting ourselves. We could make a serious if not fatal error if we open ourselves to his attention.'

'But we *do* have protection,' Alinor was quick to interrupt. 'The house, Remon's house. Remember what he said, that we are safe from everything when we are within the house. If we are there we are free to use our power and Verun should not be able to retaliate.'

'Yes, but do we run the risk of showing him how much we have learned? No doubt we did surprise him at the gates, but surely the less we reveal of ourselves, the more time we may have to learn about our powers and what it is we are supposed to be seeking.'

Alinor looked at the young man and suddenly noticed how tired he was. She had been so wrapped up in her own problems that she had not given sufficient attention to his own well-being. The realisation gave her some anguish. She reached out and laid her hand on his cheek.

'I am sorry, my heart; I have been wanting to rush everything. You are right that we have to take time to think carefully about all this and where we go from here. My impatience is still my greatest fault.'

Sirad took her hand and gently kissed her palm; in a moment he had caught her to him, kissing her fiercely, holding her so tightly that she nearly cried out. She could feel his overwhelming emotions – they matched her own, and she rejoiced in that. She knew that they both wanted more and wished that they could . . . She stopped herself. Now was not yet the time and she knew it would be easy to allow herself to lead him on; but if she did they would be ignoring the conventions that had always ruled their lives and which still bound them.

With an effort Sirad pulled away from her.

'Oh my lady,' he whispered, 'how I love you.'

'And I you,' she replied.

'I think I had better go.'

She nodded reluctantly.

He kissed her fingertips, not daring to hold her close again, and then left quickly.

The Lady of Ancor was out in the city, exploring the craftsmith's area, pleased to see how well everyone was recovering, gradually returning to their previous, happy – and industrious – existence. The city was home to so many talented artisans, jewellers, potters, sculptors and glassmakers, it was a never-ending joy to wander the streets and marvel at the work offered for sale or glimpsed in the workshops . Alinor enjoyed spending time there, a brief escape from the officialdom of governmental re-organisation; and an escape also from the atmosphere of respectful awe with which she was treated, particularly within the palace. Her extraordinary ability as an Imager made it possible for her to assume a totally different appearance – a thought was all it took. So it was that the elegant, golden-haired Lady of Ancor might become a non-descript, brown-haired, middle-aged worker, going about his way, unremarked by the citizens of the city, occasionally stopping to chat about how things were improving and what hopes there were for the future. On another occasion she would be an old lady carrying some shopping back to her family, exchanging gossip with the women doing their laundry.

It was good to get away and distract her mind from the problems that she would soon have to face in returning to Thorgiliad and dealing with her traitorous Steward. She hadn't spoken much to Sirad about it; he had enough to worry about, she knew, and whilst they shared so much, she too preferred to keep some matters to herself, hard though it was.

She was just admiring some beautiful crystal glasses when Sirad's thoughts gently interrupted.

Yes, beautiful workmanship, aren't they? She nearly laughed out loud, but stopped herself just in time.

I always knew you had good taste! she thought back at him. But where are you now – I take it the meeting has finished?

Yes, and it went well. I feel confident now that things are really getting back to normal; the Council of Elders is back up to strength and they are looking to implement some quite far-sighted changes to take them forward. I think my task here is done.

Mm,' Alinor responded. 'I know it's nearly time. It's just . . .

Amiros. I know. But, while he still lives there is hope that he may return to us.

I'll come back now, she said, and perhaps we should take Amiros up to the house for one last time. I'm sure that his spending some time near the crystal globe is bound to help.

You may be right, he responded. We'll go now, but then we must really arrange to leave Elagos as soon as is practical. I need to talk with my father in person to tell him what is going on, and I know that you must return to Thorgiliad. You are their queen after all, and even with all that may lie ahead of us as far as challenging Verun is concerned, I know that you also have a need to address the wrongs that have been perpetrated since your father's death. He paused a moment. Sorry, got to go. Ben's chasing me for something. I'll see you shortly.

Alinor could see through Sirad's eyes that his foster brother Ben was indeed approaching rapidly. The two men started conferring about arrangements for their return to Pelamir; a large but subdued contingent of Riders had left Elagos a few weeks earlier, conveying the remains of their fallen comrades back with them to their families in Pelamir. Alinor withdrew her mind from the exchange, sparing a thought for the losses of her own countrymen. When she had consulted with her father's old friend Dhalen, senior commander of the King's personal bodyguard, he had told her that all his men had voted to bury their dead on the plain outside Elagos rather than make the very long journey back to Thorgiliad. In due course suitable memorials would be raised to commemorate the fallen of those countries involved in the conflict. Alinor was aware that their decision had been influenced also by the uncertainty of their reception whilst Vixlan was still holding the reins of power in Ancor. How he would react to Alinor's miraculous survival would be interesting, to say the least.

In the days following the re-taking of Elagos, the new young ruler of Ancor had spent many hours in discussion with the wise veteran, who had been overwhelmed by the totally unexpected and startling reappearance of his King's daughter. He had blamed himself for Teleston's demise, for despite all his efforts the King had refused him permission to accompany the fateful party that was to take Alinor to Elagos. But now he realised that in fact it had been for the best; the young woman now thrust prematurely onto the throne of Ancor would need all the help she could get from those who had remained steadfastly loyal to the late King. Although she would of course have the protection of the Riders of Pelenin under the very capable leadership of the young lord Sirad, her betrothed – what an extraordinary announcement that had been. Dhalen knew that the traitorous Vixlan had surrounded himself with a coterie of efficient guards, and established a network of officials throughout the country who had pledged their allegiance to him. Alinor's situation would be precarious and matters would need very careful handling if they were not to deteriorate into open aggression.

As yet, Alinor had not confided any specific strategy to remove the Steward; he didn't know if she even had formulated one at this stage. She had stressed the importance of obtaining far more information about exactly what control Vixlan had before making any firm decisions. She did not intend to initiate a bloodbath, which is exactly what could happen very easily if the situation wasn't handled very carefully. As far as Dhalen was concerned, her return to Thorgiliad should provide the catalyst to give heart back to her people and enable them to support her in whatever she eventually decided to do. Not without some trepidation he looked forward to their return to his home city and the restoration of fair government.

Chapter 5

Alinor gently laid her fingers on the brow of the sleeping man. He seemed peaceful enough, but her thoughts could not reach wherever it was his mind had travelled. Time and again both she and Sirad had sought some kind of response but without success. There was no change.

The three were alone in the Seer's house for a last visit before they would leave Elagos and make the journey back. Sirad would return to Pelenin, but he and Alinor would part as she went on to Thorgiliad. Sirad would not go with her immediately, but would follow later when she felt the timing was right. In the meantime they decided to take this opportunity to explore some of the vast collection of books that the Mind-Master had left in his study.

Leaving Amiros with the protective glow of the strange globe encompassing him, Alinor
and Sirad returned to where she had first encountered the Seer. The room remained much as she remembered, but, as Sirad had also thought, rather less of a muddle. There were shelves groaning under the weight of books, parchments and boxes of all shapes and sizes, any number of strange instruments on tables and shelves at whose purpose Alinor could not even hazard a guess. There were peculiar models of goodness knows what; diagrams spread out on yet another table, and a large chart covered with strange runes hung on one of the walls, partly obscuring a deep recess filled with shelves laden with bottles, jars and other containers, some leaning at drunken angles against each other. It was a true Magician's workroom and she smiled to herself remembering how she had asked the old man if he really could find what he wanted at the time. Once again, she was struck by the fact that she had never encountered another person in the house, despite her staying there for several days; food and drink had simply appeared, dishes had been removed, clothes had been laid out for her.

'This place is simply spellbound in the true sense of the word,' was Sirad's opinion. 'Somehow or other the power of Remon has created a place that is totally protected from the outside world and which almost has a life of its own. It's really odd.'

'You can say that again,' replied the young woman, running a hand through her hair, light from the ever-present fireplace catching the glints of gold in it.

For several minutes the pair simply explored, gazing at the strange constructions or gently reaching out to touch the soft leather spines of ancient books. There was a latent power in everything around them, they could feel the faintest hint of energy vibrating in the air.

'Do you think that Verun knows about this place?' Alinor asked Sirad.

'He'll know that the house exists, but whether he knows just what it contains is anyone's guess. But, I suspect that no one really grasps the extent of it. I know I don't, and something within me tells me that it is way beyond our present understanding.'

'I agree, and I think, though cannot remember clearly, that Remon may have hinted about things. Oh, but so much happened I still don't know the half of it.'

'I'm sure you're right in that.'

Sirad walked back to the big table where there was an open book, not particularly large, obviously ancient but whose fine, closely packed script was still clearly legible. The language was unfamiliar to him and he called Alinor over to see.

'This wasn't here when I came before,' he said, puzzled. 'What is it?'

She looked carefully, turning a few pages, feeling a trembling in her fingers.

'I'm not absolutely sure. But there is something about it that makes me think it is important – almost as if it were put here for us to find.'

'Do you recognise the language?' Sirad knew that Alinor had learned how she might use her own precious gem, Qanoor, The Firestone, to enhance her abilities and somehow enable her to understand ancient scripts in long-forgotten languages.

'This is a new one to me,' she responded, 'but I'm pretty sure that with a little assistance I should be able to make sense of it.'

They drew up a couple of chairs and sat at the table, the book between them. She drew out the silver chain around her neck and took the ancient teardrop gem in her hand. Like the mysterious globe it too radiated a pale light; it strengthened as her fingers closed around it. She closed her eyes and allowed the strange magic to penetrate her senses. After a few moments she looked over at Sirad, his grey eyes watching her intently, inwardly marvelling at this enchanting women and the astonishing powers that she possessed.

'I'll need to do a bit more work on this,' she said. 'I can read it, yes, but as yet don't quite understand all the words. I think,' she hesitated, 'I think it's something to do with The Firestone and with Mnethar. It's about talismans and tokens of power. See here,' she pointed to a few lines, 'it talks about Shenbran – my sword – and the other missing Sword of Bran.'

She linked her mind more closely with Sirad as they so often did; he felt what was now becoming a familiar jolt of power but it felt different from before and to his surprise he too began to make sense of the writings. In this strange house, she was able to share more of her abilities with him, her soul-mate, and as a hereditary Guardian of The Firestone enable Sirad to extend his not inconsiderable abilities further.

Sirad let out a breath in surprise.

'Oh boy, I was not expecting this!' he murmured, as he eagerly scanned the archaic text.

For an hour or more they were almost mesmerised by the ancient words; barely remembered childhood stories took form and meaning, bedtime tales no longer. Now they became fact, a truth that had been all but forgotten, hidden away for generations until such time as the rightful heirs should embark on their quest.

'Here,' Sirad pointed to a section. 'This mention of the Tokens of Power is what Remon talked about in his letter. I didn't really understand what he was getting at; I know it's to do with the Swords of Bran, but there are obviously a number of Tokens. I haven't found anything yet to say what they all are.'

'I couldn't find anything in the Library in Pelamir about them, though there was a lot of fascinating stuff.'

Alinor turned a page. 'Here, look –' she indicated a few words, 'this is about the missing Sword – Tauenbran – I never heard it called that before.'

'Nor I, but there is something about the name . . .' Sirad frowned, unable to bring whatever memory there was to mind. 'Qanoor is mentioned of course, but we need to find out much more about Mnethar. Until you were able to reach into Amiros' mind that awful night we found him I thought that Mnethar was simply an elaboration on the old myths – I never believed it could be real and that it could inflict such damage.'

'But it is, and it did,' Alinor said forcefully, getting up abruptly as the distressing memory of that terrible night brought tears to her eyes. 'We only felt a pale reflection of the pain that Amiros suffered at Verun's hands and that was enough.'

Sirad reached for Alinor's hand.

'We will save him,' he murmured to her. 'We must believe that.'

'I'm trying, I really am. But it's so hard to see him, day after day, alive but not truly alive.'

'We are together for a reason, my love. We don't have all the information that we need yet, and it may take us a while before we come to understand the extent of our quest, but we will find out. Remon believed that we could succeed, so we must also believe.'

Alinor rubbed her fingers over her eyes, wiping away the feeling of helplessness that threatened to overwhelm her given half a chance. She looked at him thoughtfully, this handsome man that she loved with all her being, knowing that he could share her life in the centuries to come, and knowing too that she had so much more to learn about both his and her own skills. The first time that their minds had come together, totally unexpectedly, on that day in the gardens of Pelamir they had experienced an overwhelming explosion of emotion and a momentary insight into how their unity extended and enhanced their individual abilities. In a fleeting instance they had both glimpsed some of the awesome heritage of the Ben-Neteru and each perceived something of the other's extraordinary nature. Since that day, even though their minds were always so closely attuned, and they had used their powerful bond to destroy Verun's protections at the gates of Elagos, the pair had not ventured to unite emotionally so completely.

Sirad felt her presence so strongly; she had become a part of him, so integral to his being that if anything were to happen to her he would be utterly destroyed. He longed to keep and protect her, determined that no harm should befall her, but he knew also that they would both face indescribable dangers from which there was no other protection except their own abilities. Ben-Neteru they were, but as Remon had pointed out to Alinor, they were still human, and their bodies could – and would – suffer when wounded, still feel hunger and thirst. Even though they shared a unity beyond the understanding of mere mortals, she would always remain her own person, beautiful, vibrant, the very essence of what it was to be a woman with the extraordinary strength that only a woman had. He looked into her blue-grey eyes, the unseen depths beckoning; he reached toward her and she came to him in an embrace so full of meaning. Their kiss was both gentle and all-encompassing, the air around them vibrating with an energy that would have been obvious had they not been where they were. They stood there holding each other for what could have been an eternity, neither wishing to move away, but finally, they broke apart knowing that it was time to leave. They would take the Lore-Master back to the hospital for the night, but in the morning they had made arrangements for him to start the long trek back to Pelamir where the Healers there could continue to care for him.

In the cool air of another fine morning the party bearing the unconscious body of Amiros, beloved Lore-Master and Mage, left Elagos on the slow trip back to Pelamir. He would once again be cared for by the taciturn dwarf Czaten, a former slave to Verun in his fortress at Mekad, who had been tasked with ensuring that Amiros, or what was left of him, should be safely returned to his friends in the north. Whilst the little man bore a burning hatred for Verun, for some reason he was absolutely devoted to Amiros and only grudgingly ever left his bedside. He had learned all that was necessary from the old healers in Elagos to keep his patient comfortable and for once became fairly vociferous about not requiring any other assistance on the journey.

Alinor had mixed feelings as she watched the company growing smaller in the distance. She was concerned for their safety, although the presence of a number of armed guards greatly reduced any risk. She still grieved at the loss of her mentor and friend, unwilling to build up too much hope in his recovery whilst also desperately looking towards bringing him back to them. There was a great deal of anger simmering within her that Verun had been able to wield such unholy powers as to bring the mage to his present state. Common sense told her that she would not help herself – or anyone else – by giving in to such emotions; there were other matters that needed, even demanded, her full attention.

It was time for her and Sirad to leave Elagos themselves; from there each would return to their own cities, Alinor travelling directly back to Thorgiliad, Sirad accompanying her only as far as the borders of Pelenin. He would have liked to be with her as she entered the city to take up her royal inheritance, but they had both agreed that any show of force may well have an adverse effect on her dealings with the Steward Vixlan. Above all, she wanted to keep the man in the dark as far as possible with regard to her true nature; hopefully, any stories that had emanated from the dreadful fighting at Elagos could be downplayed as simple exaggeration. Although she wished to return home as a queen, the rightful Lady of Ancor, she did not want that return to be loaded with pomp and ostentation. There would be plenty of time for that at her coronation, and that, she was determined, could not take place until Vixlan had been dealt with, and his corrupt setup totally wiped out. Besides which she also wanted to ensure that there should be some suitable commemoration for her father. She still needed to be able to publicly acknowledge and grieve for her father; when Sirad had briefly visited Thorgiliad to raise support for the relief of Elagos she had accompanied him, but she had gone disguised, appearing only to be one of his travelling companions. Under cover of night, when the palace was quiet, Alinor had spent some hours in the Hall of Kings at the marbled tomb of Teleston in quiet communion with his memory. Oh, how she missed him; his strength and majesty, his kindliness, his amused chiding of his somewhat stubborn and strong-willed daughter, his gentle comfort after her mother had died. No-one had ever expected that she would be forced into this position, having to accede to the throne and take up the reins of government so soon. Yes, it would happen eventually, but she felt abysmally ill-prepared, despite reassurances from her beloved Sirad. At least he had already spent a number of years acting for Sothan and, she had to admit, being a man had given him far more freedom. Whilst she more or less understood and had to accept the reasoning behind keeping her from the very public life at court, she could also regret that she had missed so much. Not much point in self-reproach, she told herself. Destiny makes its own rules; I must deal with the tasks allotted to me as best I can – I just wish I knew a little more about what lies ahead. She smiled to herself; 'The power will be yours when you need it.' So had said Amiros what seemed like an eternity ago. At least, she had *some* idea of what the powers she shared with Sirad were, although it was hard work schooling herself to control them, let alone feel comfortable with them.

    The Lady of Ancor would return home to Thorgiliad and her people; she had the immediate support of nearly five thousand battle-hardened men – not a huge number, but enough to start with until she could re-instate her father's elite guard. During their time in Elagos she had endeavoured to come to know as many of them as she could, with the steadfast assistance of Dhalen, and together they had identified those who had proved themselves as very capable leaders of their individual units. Some had received battlefield promotions, well-earned under savage conditions. Afterward, a number had been raised even further up the ranks; these men would be essential in restoring the balance of power and would be critical in the development of the superior fighting skills that Alinor knew would be required in the not too distant future. She would also need to place her own people in court, advisers, ministers, general staff – as yet she had no idea how many had remained faithful to her father. Although part of the challenge ahead could only be met by the powers possessed by Alinor and Sirad there would still be ugly and savage fighting amongst those controlled by their opponent. A disturbing thought crossed her mind, enforced by what Remon had written in his letter to Sirad; a chilling premonition that perhaps Verun was not alone. It was not a thought that she could bear to contemplate. Please, she told herself, one thing at a time. I cannot do more than I am doing right now and right now I must get ready to leave here.

The combined horsemen of Ancor and Pelenin were an impressive sight as they made their way from the plain surrounding Elagos up into the hill country. Morale was high amongst all the men; the Riders of Pelenin were content that all their hard training had proved effective against the might of the enemy, whilst the Elite Guard of Ancor were still celebrating the return of their Lady.

Sirad and Alinor had planned a couple of minor detours on the way back through Galdesh. The main body of men would proceed by the usual route via the Eastern High Road to southern Sarrent. With a handful of Riders and Guards the pair split away up the road to Dukonweld Hall, the large fortified holding that had become a base for the outlaws under Rekar, seized from the Red Lord's outlying forces with some help from Alinor. The intention was to let Rekar know that they were now on their way back to their respective countries, and just to have a quick catch-up to see how things were progressing amongst his people. The young outlaw had gathered a large following amongst the locals persecuted by Verun in his guise as Altalla and had been instrumental in enabling Alinor to reach Remon in Elagos. When the two had first met, Alinor had been travelling with Amiros, disguised as his assistant Luke. She had eventually been accepted by the arrogant young man, albeit a little grudgingly, and her help in freeing Rekar's teenage protégé Leni from the clutches of the enemy commander in Dukonweld had ensured a permanent welcome from all the other outlaws. When her true identity had finally been revealed it had proved to be an uncomfortable transition in their relationship, but once Rekar realised that neither Alinor nor Sirad had any intention of imposing any kind of authority over himself or his former outlaw band and indeed they in fact treated him as a valued comrade and friend the tensions were eased.

It was late afternoon when they rode through the gates of Dukonweld into the bustling activity of the first courtyard. A number of men came forward to greet them and accompany the party through to the main courtyard and the entrance to the Hall. Quite a lot had changed since Alinor and Sirad had left after the final planning meeting before the battle; for a start there were a number of women and children helping with the day to day running of the household. Months ago when the forces of the Red Lord first appeared in Galdesh to impose their dominance over the populace, there had been bloodshed when farmers opposed them. Rekar's father Radegan had tried to take a stand but paid the ultimate penalty; their lovely home, Sistor, had been vandalised and Rekar had become outlawed. The men who had joined him had sent their own families as far away as they could for safety but now, these families were returning to take up their rightful homes again and trying to recover their livelihoods. It would be a long hard struggle for them as so much had been destroyed by the occupying soldiers; they had been obliged to leave with only the minimum that they could travel with leaving all their animals behind. Rekar and his men had managed to create a safe camp up in the hills where they could house their horses and a number of stock animals too. Soon the traders would be returning and markets would resume in the war-torn villages and towns, but without being able to pay for goods, people were going to find it very hard, something the young Lord of Pelenin was very aware of. When they had entered Elagos and had chance to take stock of everything that the enemy had been controlling, Sirad had been pleased to find that all the monies collected in the area by fair means and foul were still stored in the strong rooms of the palace, perhaps because Altalla believed that under his control the city was now impregnable. A reserve of gold and silver coins which should have gone as payment to the enemy soldiers was still intact, swelling the amount. In consultation with Elders of the Council a plan was swiftly agreed to use much of this money to assist the local people who had lost their homes and livelihoods. Rekar had been tasked with recruiting some of his best men to help set up a suitable means of distributing monies amongst the families and also to ensure that essential goods could once again be brought into the region.

Leaving their horses in the care of the stablemen, Sirad and Alinor started towards the great entrance door to the Hall to be met by Hassa, Rekar's Master at Arms and closest colleague amongst the outlaws.

'You are most welcome, my Lord, my Lady,' he gave a slight bow, reaching out to grasp Sirad's hand in a firm grip. He smiled at Alinor, turning fully towards her, the recent scar down across his missing eye and cheek very noticeable.

'It is good to see you again, young Luke, if I may still call you that!'

Alinor laughed and nodded.

'Of course you may,' she responded, 'I do value our friendship, old man!'

At this jibe Hassa let out a guffaw and stood aside to usher them into the building.

'You've missed him by a couple of days, I'm afraid,' he said. 'He's gone back to Sistor to see about rebuilding his former home. Although I'm not sure that he really wants to go back to live there; mixed feelings I think.'

'He's been through a lot, I agree,' said Alinor.

'There's a weight of responsibility on his shoulders now,' Sirad swirled the wine in his goblet as the three sat at ease on one side of the huge dining hall.

'That's quite true,' responded Hassa, ' and he'll be staying here for a while I think. But he has said that he feels it would be right for me to take charge of Dukonweld so that we can train men here for the future. The fighting is not yet over, and even though I know Elagos will remain a neutral city; as long as the threat from the Red Lord remains the need for a good fighting force will also remain.'

Sirad nodded.

'He is certainly correct in that. We have dealt Altalla a wounding blow, but not a fatal one by any means. If you are able to continue the good work that I know you did,' Sirad glanced at Alinor who nodded in confirmation, 'it will be of great value.'

'I owe some thanks to a certain young northern lad who spent some time with us a few months back,' Hassa's deep voice was quiet. 'Even an old dog like me can occasionally learn a new trick or two.'

The tough old veteran stood and called over a young boy.

'Now, Barit, please take our esteemed guests to their quarters so that they can freshen up before dinner.'

For a moment Barit was overcome by shyness, suddenly thrust into the company of royalty; he glanced at Hassa who nodded.

'They don't bite, lad, go on.'

The boy had been considered too young to join the outlaws in their fight against the enemy, but he had now come to Dukonweld and heard all the stories – some of which were rather more fairy-tale than fact – about the strange northerner who had joined Rekar's men but who had turned out to be a real fairy-tale princess. And here she was with the Prince of Pelenin himself. Talk about a boy's dream come true! Just wait until he told his friends about this.

Once in her room Alinor pulled off her boots and over jacket; the water was warm and she thankfully washed the dust and dirt from her face and hands. She looked out of the small window onto the busy scene in the courtyard below, remembering what it had been like when Rekar's outlaw band had defeated Grosj and the Red Boar soldiers to take control of the Hall.

Psychologically it had been a huge boost to the men after so many months; now that Elagos had been liberated they were all in good heart and even more determined to finish the battle against the enemy that had destroyed so much of their lives. Sirad was right, though; it wasn't just a case of blindly taking the offensive and heading down to Mekad. Verun was a serious threat to them all, not least to herself and Sirad. It was important that she get back to Thorgiliad and deal with Vixlan; but how, she had no idea as yet. The Steward had obviously fallen under Verun's influence somehow, but she very much doubted that it had been a personal matter. Verun had spread his insidious thoughts far and wide, making use of those who were naturally greedy and who were prepared to do whatever was needed for their own advantage. Had Vixlan been involved with the attack on her father? Almost certainly he had provided the information about their supposedly secret journey to take her to Elagos. How else would the attack have come about?

A soft knock on the door alerted her to Sirad's arrival.

'Hassa has done a good job here,' he said, putting his arms around her and gently dropping a kiss on the top of her head.

'Rekar was right to put him in charge of the Hall; it makes a good base for them. Things will be changing soon; the people of Galdesh have always tended to keep themselves to themselves, with Elagos being the only real centre of attention. Perhaps it is time for them to open up a bit more – the outside world has really shattered their peace and nothing will be quite the same again.'

'I think that applies to all of us,' observed Alinor.

'I am concerned,' she continued, 'that there are such large gaps in our knowledge. I just get the feeling that there's more to it than just Verun's overwhelming greed for power, frightening though that is. I cannot see how we are ever to overcome him.'

Sirad shook his head.

'Nor me,' he responded, 'at least not yet I don't. But there has to be a way. We certainly have some time available to us – Remon confirmed that. Verun suffered in the attempt to block us; he'll have to work out a new approach, but how long that will take we have no idea. He still has control, I assume, over a huge number of troops in the south, but whether they will attempt further offensives before the year is out we don't know. I rather doubt it as they are not so naïve as to ignore the disadvantage of winter fighting, so that gives us a decent period to prepare our own forces and make plans.'

'Mmm, you're probably right,' allowed Alinor, 'which relieves me a bit. Now that we have put a little time between that awful fighting and getting back home, the urge I had to just charge off to take the fight directly to Verun has got a bit more perspective to it. I know it wouldn't have worked not just because of what our troops have suffered but because we still don't know exactly what we are getting into. You know far more than I do of the breaches that have developed in the Alliance – to be honest I'm not sure exactly what happened. But I think you would be in a good position now to help heal those breaches.'

Sirad nodded, breaking away from the young woman.

'Perhaps we've all become a bit complacent,' he said, running his hand over the closely woven blanket on the bed.

'My father sent me on quite a lot of trips to various places over the years,' he continued. 'I was received quite well,

I thought at the time, but when I came back and reported my visits, my father was fairly muted about it all. I believe he saw what I had missed; he was able to see a much larger picture than I was. I should have realised . . .'

'It's not your fault,' Alinor interrupted. 'You shouldn't blame yourself; your father is a very knowledgeable man and I suspect that even you do not have any real idea about all his experiences.'

The young prince nodded with a wry expression.

'You are probably right,' he said. 'But it's hard to accept one's own shortcomings. We've both had to face some startling truths in the last few months, and I'll admit to you that I have not really come to terms with them.'

'You and me both,' were Alinor's thoughts. 'But enough of that for now. What do you want to do now we're here? Do we go to Sistor to see Rekar – is there any point?'

'Probably not. We'll find out what's happening from Hassa I think, and then we should rejoin the return party home.'

Dinner in the Hall that evening was a fairly noisy affair. The food was plentiful – though not extravagant – and the two visitors were warmly welcomed by everyone. There was a steady stream of outlaws who wanted to speak to their former comrade Luke in particular; her easy manner let them forget she was a queen and they were eager to thank both her and Sirad for giving them back their homes. Alinor looked for her young friend Leni, but was told that he had gone with Rekar; they were not expected back for several days yet.

The two young royals spent several hours with Hassa the next morning discussing how matters were progressing and what plans they had. The veteran Master-at-Arms was in good spirits and confident that his men would be more than willing and able to act again when Sirad should call on them for support.

They left Dukonweld and rejoined the main party later that evening and the return march resumed the next day; the good weather continued enabling them to progress fairly rapidly on the long route home. Alinor was tempted to make further detours to catch up with those who had helped her and Amiros on their journey and who had worked hard to facilitate the movement of all their troops en route to Elagos, but the need to return to her home over-rode those ideas.

Travelling with the main party was one other person for whom the journey was something of an adventure. Semira had robustly rejected a tentative suggestion by Alinor that she may wish to remain in Elagos.

'You are my Lady now,' she had said, 'and where you go, so should I.'

Alinor had laughed.

'That may not be quite so simple as that,' she pointed out. 'I'm not sure that you quite understand what you are letting yourself in for.'

'Then perhaps my Lady would like to explain!' was the spirited response.

So it was that the Lady of Ancor developed a closeness with her companion that she had not known before with any other female of her acquaintance. They exchanged their stories, although Alinor did not reveal the full truth of her and Sirad's inheritance as Ben-Neteru or of their as yet ill-defined destiny; she shared enough to help the dark young beauty appreciate the implications of serving the young queen of Ancor. Whilst Semira had no great experience of riding, she took to it as if born to a life in the saddle and became a firm favourite with all of the Ancor guard, not to mention many of the Riders too. Her presence was a great support for Alinor and she proved to have a very able mind, quickly coming to an understanding of some of the many problems that faced her young mistress; this trip enabled her to finally put behind her the dreadful attack she had suffered and Alinor's strength and tenacity made a telling impression on her. The initial trepidation she had felt on leaving her home and family in Elagos for a strange country was soon replaced with a keen anticipation of making a new life; every day now would be a challenge to be relished and she rejoiced in a new-found enthusiasm for the future.

Chapter 6

There was a lark singing somewhere high above the grassy plain; the morning was filled with the promise of another bright warm day, the air redolent with the delicate scents of meadow grasses and herbs crushed beneath their feet.

The young couple stood looking out towards the distant mountains of the north, their minds linked as they made their farewells, their love for each other binding them ever closer. It was time to part; Sirad to return to Pelamir, and Alinor to finally return home as the new ruler of Ancor. He could be sure of his welcome but his beloved could not. He so much wanted to continue the journey with her, to be by her side as she entered Thorgiliad and her palace. But no, it could not be. This was something that she had to do alone, though the gods knew that he would be with her all the way in thought; he had the ability to see through her eyes just what happened, hear what was said, feel how she reacted to it all, but he knew that he would use it sparingly. He would not spy on her nor would he dream of influencing anything she did; she had the mastery of her heart and soul and he knew that whatever she decided to do would be the right thing, no matter how difficult or painful the experience. In time he would be able to go to Thorgiliad, for her coronation if not before; that was something to look forward to. They both still had much work to do on extracting information from the book that Remon had left for them. Alinor kept it with her for now, but with their strange mental bond they could choose to study it together. Priorities first though. For Alinor it was ensuring that she could take the throne safe from the machinations of Vixlan; for Sirad it was sharing their experiences in relieving Elagos with his father and hopefully learning a little more from whatever news his messengers and spies could bring back from their travels. Alinor's task would be far harder, he knew, but he also knew her strengths now and believed that the trust that the old Mind-Master had placed in them both was justified.

The lark disappeared and the two looked up to see the dark outline of a hawk circling slowly around, carried by the warm air current rising from the gently rolling plain. It was joined by a second bird and Alinor was suddenly reminded of that morning so long ago on a hillside in Mindros when she had been overtaken by the grief of her father's loss. Perhaps it was symbolic; she had found her pre-ordained partner in Sirad, though what their final destiny would be was still shrouded in mystery.

It was fairly late in the evening. Alinor was taking a few quiet moments while there was no-one else around to groom her beloved Elkana, the silvery mane flowing like a moonlit waterfall. In an undertone she shared some thoughts about the people she had seen that day, the mare's ears flicking back and forth, listening to her mistress. When she paused, Elkana nudged her gently, blowing softly in encouragement.

'I'm convinced you understand every word,' whispered Alinor.

The mare blew into her hand and delicately grabbed her thumb with soft lips, bringing a smile to the young woman. The big liquid brown eyes looked right at – or into – Alinor's misty blue ones. A wonderfully reassuring wave of comfort flowed over her, with a feeling of togetherness, love, trust, something that she didn't have words for.

'You do!' she said in awed surprise. 'You really do, don't you?'

Elkana tossed her head and Alinor could sense the mare's thoughts along the lines of 'it's taken you long enough to recognise it.'

Alinor let out a breath.

'Oh wow,' she murmured. 'This is something else.'

She ran her hand down the glistening neck and shoulder, then gently stroked the velvety nose.

'I always knew there was something special about you – that first day in the forest of Mindros. You came straight to me as if you knew.'

The mare's eyes blinked slowly.

'Yes, we were destined, weren't we? So, we've managed the first battle, but it may not be the last. We'd best take care of each other.'

The mare rested her head on Alinor's shoulder; theirs was more than just a horse and rider relationship, theirs was a deep bond of friendship.

'Thank you,' the young woman whispered as she gave the mare a final pat and returned to the campfire and dinner.

Alinor did not share this latest knowledge with Sirad as they mind-spoke that night. He and the Riders had already reached Pelamir the day before with a rejoicing slightly muted by the loss of some of their company. The Mindoran party bearing the still unconscious Amiros would be arriving the following day; their trip had been slow but uneventful. There was no change in the Lore-Master's condition, which could be taken as good news, but both Sirad and Alinor remained worried and puzzled the longer it continued.

What if he never wakes up again? Alinor asked tentatively. How long can he stay like that, it's not natural; that evil Verun has spell-cast him and he's trapped somehow.

I don't know, came Sirad's response. We don't know enough about what happened, and we certainly don't understand exactly what power is lodged in Mnethar that it can bring something like this about. I won't have had chance to continue reading that book yet?

Hardly. I really don't want others knowing that I have it.

Yes, I understand. You know I've seen some of what's been going on?

I was aware of you, even though I didn't exactly respond, I'm sorry.

No, not at all.' The young man's concern and love wrapped around her. It's going to be hard, I know, and I wish I could do something to help.

Just being there, and feeling your love, is enough for now, Alinor knew he too could feel her emotions matching his.

Your father is well? she asked.

Yes, thank you. He wanted a blow by blow account of what happened, so it did take some time in the telling. I think he was really relieved that we came through with less loss of life than might have been expected, knowing who was behind this.

He knew? queried Alinor.

Oh yes, it seems that my father actually knows a lot more than I gave him credit for. Maybe because of his friendship with your father and because of Amiros. Although how on earth he knows of Verun I don't understand. Still we did have a good heart to heart a couple of months back – that's when I found out about the Ben-Neteru and us – I don't think he told me everything. It may be that he himself doesn't understand it all, I couldn't say.

It would seem that everything is rather more complex than it first appears. The more we learn, the less we find we really know!

You are right in that, my love. Where it will lead us I have no idea, but for the moment we have to face what is immediately before us.

For a little while the two continued to share their thoughts, supporting each other and deriving comfort emotionally despite the distance between them. It would have to be enough for now, even though Alinor was longing to feel Sirad's arms around her, whilst he positively ached to hold her, to feel her warmth close to him. At least we have this, she thought, as she drifted off to sleep.

Some days seemed to just drag, thought Alinor. It wasn't possible to make great speed when travelling with such a large contingent of troops no matter how hard you willed it to be. She was getting restless having to have so many people around her; they were her own troops, and she was proud of them, but they were, she thought, a bit too zealous in wanting to protect their newly-returned Lady. Whatever she did there always seemed to be someone there, watching over her, waiting on her every word in case she wanted anything. I do want something, she thought, I want space to be me, on my own! She was reluctant to use her skill as an Imager - the fewer people who knew about it the better and thus the chance of it reaching the ears of those who still wished her harm would be minimised. But she was aware that there were unfriendly eyes following their progress up the Great North Road toward Ancor. Dhalen had maintained regular patrols all along their route and to some distance in all directions, but although they had found some evidence of unwelcome spies they had been unable to track them down. Verun's influence had spread wide in the time since Alinor's father had been cut down; there were tales of continuing banditry as roving bands of southerners still threatened the population, not merely those who posed an easy target away from towns and villages. Shades of Drak and his bunch was Alinor's first thought; on that occasion she had been hurt, but there had been a feeling of satisfaction in eliminating such a violent gang of thugs. The thought of similar groups possibly operating near or even in her own country was not a welcome one; who knows, they may enjoy a certain amount of protection from her conniving Steward. I am beginning to doubt everything these days, thought the young woman; it seems that finding those whom I can trust is no easy matter. But if I don't keep up my guard my whole future, and the futures of those I do care for, will be at risk. I didn't choose this – it was chosen for me and I will not betray their trust and belief in me.

A rare opportunity presented itself as the troops of Ancor prepared to set out one morning; it was a little dull, but the night's rain had stopped and the day would probably brighten within a few hours. As Semira was packing away a few belongings Alinor grabbed her favourite lightweight cloak and slung her precious sword Shenbran on her back out of sight.

'Say nothing to my guards,' she cautioned, 'but you can tell Dhalen that I am quite safe. I just need a little time to myself. On no account is he to attempt to come after me, and that is an absolute order. I shall rejoin everyone well before the light fails.'

She was gone before Semira had chance to say a word, not that anything she said would have made any difference.

Alinor slipped unnoticed over to the horse lines and quickly tacked up Elkana. Obviously pleased to see her mistress and keen to get going the mare nonetheless remained very calm so as not to invite notice. Within moments Alinor was heading away from the bustle; if she used a little of her skill to avoid detection she felt it was warranted and would not alert any watcher.

Once free of the camp she let Elkana stretch her legs; the extraordinary speed of the horses of Pelenin was not a myth, and even though Alinor had no need to spell-cast the mare – that ancient ritual used by the Riders of Pelenin in times of real need – the miles simply flew by. Alinor rejoiced in the feel of the wind blowing her hair like a golden banner as they galloped across expanses of grass and through open woodland. Elkana too was enjoying the opportunity to let off steam – travelling with ordinary horses was pretty boring. In the space of a couple of hours the pair had already gone way beyond where the troop caravan would have stopped for another night. Not following the road meant that they could shortcut the route anyway. Ancor was not that far away and for a moment she was tempted to continue. Not yet, she muttered, not yet. She dismounted by a small stream and left Elkana to crop the lush grass and get a drink.

Where are you, Verun? She wouldn't attempt to search out the dark magician even though she so wanted to find out what he may be doing, where he was hiding. Instead she sought awareness of anything untoward nearer to hand. She still needed to work on developing her mind further; she knew that there was much more that she would be able to do in time, but control was key if she was not to advertise her abilities. And so she let her mind roam, identifying where people were living and working, sensing whether it was a normal sort of working day, or whether they were worried or fearful. The worries mostly surrounded whether the weather would permit them to get jobs completed, or had they laid down sufficient feedstuffs to see them through the winter, would a child be all right after that silly fall when they were lucky not to break a leg. But just on the edge of her awareness Alinor could sense something a bit darker; carefully following the tenuous impression, she came to the conclusion that it came from two or three people, men almost certainly as there was that certain unmistakable male aggression in it. Curious, she called Elkana to her and remounted, heading towards the source of the uncomfortable emanation.

When she sensed that she was near the group, she left Elkana with a whispered 'Stay here,' and quietly made her way towards where three men were sat, passing around a flask of liquor of some kind whilst they rested their horses. There was some cover, not a lot, but Alinor knew that if she wished not to be visible they would be unable to see her as she blended with the shadow of an large oak tree.

'It's a waste of time,' said one of the three, 'they're being far too canny to let anyone sneak up on them.'

'Didn't reckon they'd feel the need to be so guarded,' said another. 'But I suppose they're thinking that they don't want the Lady to get lost again.'

'I wonder where she got to?' put in the first one. 'No one seems to know much about it.'

'Wherever she's been, it's the fact that she's come back that's got old Rat-face worried. He was absolutely fuming, I heard, but he is really panicked, though that doesn't show much.' The third man remembered when the news had reached Vixlan and had rather enjoyed the Steward's acute discomfort.

'I hear that he's got a lot of stuff hidden away in that hunting lodge of his way out east of the city. He won't want anyone knowing too much about it,' the first said.

'I've been there a few times,' replied the third man, obviously the real source of information in the group and a bit closer to the man who wielded power in the country – until the Lady returned that is.

'He's been very careful not to let too many know just what he's managed to gather; probably just as well now she's coming back, though I'm sure he never imagined it could happen. If she finds out – well, it's not going to bode well for him.'

'What about us?' asked the second man. 'I don't suppose we'll get much more useful work to do when she's back, and don't forget that Dhalen and his crew will be there. They are real trouble for us.'

'You're right there, Mak,' said the first, 'I'm thinking that she'll bring back all the old elite guard again – just when Rat-face had managed to get rid of them!'

Mak nodded, glumly contemplating the inevitable loss of income and even worse, the possibility of punishment being meted out for Vixlan's supporters.

'We'll just have to watch our backs, won't we.' The third man got up and stretched. 'Well, I think that any hope of interfering with them lot before they reach Thorgiliad is a non-starter. Picking off any of the patrols would be daft – they'd just send a bigger party out to catch us. Pity, but still. We'll just have to do what old Rat-face wanted and let him know numbers and status of these 'triumphant' returners. He'll need to put on some kind of decent welcome if he's got any sense.'

'Yeah, I suppose you're right. We might as well head on back. You never know, there's nothing to stop us having a bit of fun on the way.' The first man grinned at his companions. Alinor was pretty sure that the 'fun' for them would mean something very different for whoever they came across, but for the moment, there was really nothing she could do to prevent them harassing or harming some of her people. She could only trust that their route would not provide the distractions for which they were hoping.

She returned to where her mare was patiently waiting to be greeted with a gentle buffet.

'I know, I know,' she told her, 'I really would have preferred to remove the three of them, but that could have been counter-productive. I know them now, and once we get home I may be able to use them in some way – not sure yet. Anyway, we'd best be getting back before Dhalen feels the need to disobey my instructions!'

She vaulted lightly into the saddle and the two sped away back to rejoin her countrymen.

Dhalen had been on high alert as the royal party crossed the border into Ancor, though his weather-beaten face gave no indication of it. He had always felt a little uncomfortable with Vixlan, even though the king seemed to trust him and indeed, the man had worked hard and on the whole, he had to admit, had been a good Steward during the king's lifetime. However, there had been just something, he couldn't put his finger on it, that made him unsure of the man's reliability. Maybe it was the well-hidden vanities and the occasional arrogance that showed in unguarded moments; but now since Teleston was gone there had been nothing to stop the man who had soon been revealed in his true colours – far worse than the veteran soldier ever expected.

That day before the gates of Elagos when Alinor essentially returned from the dead as far as the loyal men of Ancor were concerned, Dhalen started to hope again. He and many of his loyal guards had spent weeks searching for their Lady to no avail; no demand for ransom had ever been received and thus the country could only presume her to be lost forever. Because of that they had been helpless to oppose the Steward's inexorable seizure of power in the country. Good friends who opposed Vixlan too strongly disappeared without trace; nearly all of the king's personal guard were in effect banished from the capital, given so-called 'important' duties spread far and wide in the country to prevent them from taking any action against the Steward. Of course, they had ways of keeping in touch, but they had despaired of being able to find a way to remove the man who had become a dictator in all but name.

Whilst recuperating from his serious leg injury in Elagos, there had been ample time for him to re-acquaint himself with his new queen. It was as if she had left Ancor a child but returned a warrior; she was so different, the veteran mused. She had such a presence and the strange skills that she now demonstrated – well, that was something else. He could remember her mother in those wonderful earlier days; Teleston at the height of his power, regal, wise, a ruler respected by all and beside him the lovely Lady Meriona-en-resaan, breathtakingly beautiful with an unmistakable air of magic about her, a true mythical goddess in human form. Oh, those were such wonderful days, and then, when Alinor was born, the happiness of the royal couple brought joy to everyone. Dhalen did not fully understand what had happened to change things, but he did remember that the king had been troubled by some news that the old Magician, Amiros, had brought him on one occasion. Everything seemed to be all right for a long time afterwards, but then, like a bolt from the blue, the lovely Lady Meriona died; Teleston had been bereft of course – their love had been so strong, but to Dhalen it seemed that somehow that her passing had not actually been unexpected by the king. From then on, Dhalen had quietly overseen the protection of the young princess; for her safety, or other undisclosed reasons, Teleston had been keen to keep her away from the Thorgiliad court; thus it was she spent most of her time in Coranien-dulat, a lovely city in a beautiful part of the country near the northern mountains.

He thought back on the times when the golden-haired child had followed him around, watching the training sessions with the elite guards, quick to understand exactly what each of the exercises they undertook was designed to accomplish. Dhalen himself would regularly travel to Coranien-dulat to oversee the guards who were stationed there. As the years progressed Alinor would join them in their training and he took enormous - though unspoken – pride in her undoubted skill with a sword. She had been tenacious and stubborn, refusing to give up until she had mastered each manoeuvre. It was obvious that in the time she had been lost to them, she had not neglected her training; even in the heat of the battle for Elagos he had seen the devastating effects of the young woman's sword and could only shake his head in amazement that his young protégé had become a true warrior queen to be honoured and respected by all.

Dhalen had been a trusted friend of the king and still mourned his passing; he too had ached to avenge Teleston's murder, but with Vixlan's actions effectively banishing most of the senior officers from the capital and dispersing the guard all around the country had made it virtually impossible for any of them to undertake a comprehensive search for the perpetrators. When Sirad had visited the court to request assistance in the offensive against the enemy in Elagos Vixlan had little choice but to show some kind of support for the Alliance. It was obvious that he hoped that by sending members of the elite guard to the battle front he could be able to rid himself of potential troublemakers. The overwhelming success of their onslaught had now put paid to that, and to crown it all, they were returning to Thorgiliad and bringing their lost Queen with them. She would not be safe though; Vixlan had surrounded himself with other self-serving individuals who would also not be happy to see Alinor restored. From his talks with her, he knew that she was well aware of the situation and had no desire to start a bloodbath of revenge. They were in for a tricky time. It's a shame that the young Lord of Pelenin didn't travel with them; he had enormous respect for Sothan's son and it warmed his heart to see the young couple together. He knew about the unspoken agreement to unite the houses of Thormeyern and Lanes-gilad and was quietly content that it would now definitely come about. But then, this was Alinor's problem and he knew her well enough to know that she would face it on her terms and without outside assistance. Thinking of that, Dhalen found himself actually looking forward to the demise of the Steward – it couldn't be too soon for his liking.

It would still be a week or more before they would reach Thorgiliad; the news of their arrival spread like wildfire and it seemed that the entire population of Ancor were making their way to greet the party along their route. From the smallest village to the largest towns, folk were turning out to offer what hospitality they could; when messengers had arrived following the relief of Elagos people had been stunned, barely able to believe that their beloved king's daughter was still alive. Now she was here, come back to them. They had hopes, yes, that Vixlan's stranglehold would be broken; that the exorbitant demands made upon them to satisfy the Steward's avaricious nature would stop; that excessive curbs on their freedoms would be wiped out; that their homes would again be safe havens of peace and happiness.

Alinor took time to respond to as many as possible along the way, thanking them for their welcome and reassuring them of her intentions to restore the harmony that had once been the traditional hallmark of the country. Dhalen could see that the plight of the less fortunate affected Alinor deeply, her anger at what had been happening since Teleston's murder fuelling her determination for justice. Occasionally she would mention a particular grievance to Dhalen and ask that he keep a record of such matters in order to make sure that they received the attention they deserved. It would not be an easy task, thought the old soldier, that she now set herself; so much damage had been done, lives affected or lost; the pain of the past months could not be dismissed with just a wave of the old Magician's wand. That was another sore point. Whatever had happened to the old mage had inflicted soul-wrenching grief upon the young woman for which there seemed no balm. Occasionally Dhalen found himself riding alongside his Lady's young companion Semira who he found to be both efficient and astute. It was obvious that in the short time she had been in her service she had formed a close bond with the young woman and was totally devoted to her well-being. Dhalen could not prevent Alinor from giving of herself to her subjects, but he could be satisfied that Semira would be there to help ease the young woman at the end of each day, ensuring that she did get a good meal and some rest – both being matters that Alinor would have paid little attention to if allowed.

Dhalen was anxious that they should reach Thorgiliad as soon as possible; the day after they had crossed into Ancor they had been met by a small party of soldiers sent from the capital. Ostensibly to greet their returning Lady, it was pretty obvious to Dhalen that Vixlan was keen to ascertain the status of the troops so that he could make some preparation for their arrival. He knew nothing of the day that Alinor had overheard the conversations with the three spies sent out earlier specifically for that task but was quite capable of reading the situation. That this would likely mean his taking precautions against Alinor finding out too much about his devious machinations went without saying. Dhalen recognised a couple of the soldiers, young men who, he was quietly pleased to see, were uncomfortable with their duties and careful with how they acted in front of the officer commanding them. He could only manage to grab a few private minutes with one of them; that was all it took to confirm what he had already been thinking. The Steward was unobtrusively panicking; urgent preparations were being made at the palace to receive Alinor and make it seem as if nothing had changed. It would be to little avail for Alinor had seen what she needed to when she accompanied Sirad to ask for military support; for that Dhalen allowed himself a smile. Vixlan was in for quite a surprise.

The sun was as high as it would reach, casting strong shadows as trees gave way to a rolling landscape. The richness of summer was gradually giving way to the colours of autumn, gold, red and bronze as if an artist's palette had emptied its warm tones onto the land.

'Ride with me this morning,' Alinor had said to Semira earlier. 'There's only a few miles before we shall catch our first sight of my home.'

The journey from Elagos had seen the two women's friendship develop apace, Alinor found she could be herself when with Semira, who, whilst acutely aware of her mistress' exalted status, treated her like a 'normal' person. The dark-haired beauty was not above disagreeing when she perceived something to be wrong – not in public of course - and would chide Alinor for neglecting herself if she thought it necessary. They were comfortable sharing their feelings on many subjects and would often laugh together.

Signalling to Dhalen that she did not want an escort, Alinor and Semira cantered on some way in front of the troop caravan.

'The view of Thorgiliad from up here is quite breath-taking,' said Alinor, 'I thought you might appreciate it.'

They reined in their horses as they reached the crest of a small hill. The turreted palace stood out above the bustling city which spread out over the undulating ground some miles away. The sun warmed the stone so that it took on a slightly golden hue. You could just make out an expanse of garden to one side of the palace and even though the city was quite large, it did not seem overcrowded, but rather it seemed comfortably organised; from this distance you could not tell how spacious it was, but it gave the impression of being a welcoming place.

'It's lovely,' Semira nodded her appreciation, 'so different from Elagos.'

'I hope you won't be too homesick.' Alinor looked carefully at Semira, wondering how her companion must feel.

'Of course I'll miss home, but it certainly won't be all the time and it couldn't possibly change my mind about coming with you. Besides, I expect you will not be spending all your time here . . .'

Alinor looked across in surprise, and then burst out laughing.

'I suppose you think that I won't be able to travel anywhere without my maid?'

'Something along those lines, yes,' came the reply, totalling ignoring what may have been a slightly censorious question.

'My lady – Alinor – I hope that I am right in thinking that I am not merely a servant. No,' she carried on quickly as Alinor was about to protest, 'don't say anything, just hear me out, I wish no disrespect. My life in Elagos was perfectly happy, but it lacked some purpose. I couldn't really say that there was anything really wrong, and I honestly didn't know what it was that was missing. But there was something missing for me and all I could do was hope that somehow, somewhere, the answer would turn up. But then they came,' her lovely face momentarily reflected the remembered pain, 'and everything turned dark. I wasn't sure that I would ever get over what happened, and in a way I nurtured the darkness inside. Then the day came when the Lord Commander spoke with me about needing someone to care for his Lady and my world changed. When I met you I realised that this was the something that I had been waiting for. I was awestruck at first,' Alinor was shaking her head at this, 'but I could recognise the pain you were carrying and I stopped feeling quite so sorry for myself.'

Alinor reached over to lay her hand gently on Semira's arm.

'Oh, Semira, I hardly know what to say,' she said quietly. 'You had every reason to feel sorry for yourself, and no-one would ever blame you for that. But yes, you are right. I do carry pain within, but I am learning to use that pain and not let it overwhelm me. I have the greatest gift of love from a man for whom I would lay down my life, but I also have your wonderful friendship,' she smiled and nodded. 'We've not known each other very long, but I am not wrong in my judgement of you. You are a very beautiful and clever woman and I am sure there is a lot more to you than that!'

There were tears brimming in Semira's eyes and she blinked rapidly, taking a deep breath before replying.

'I am honoured by your trust, my Lady – my friend. Although you have not spoken to me about it I know that much lies ahead of you, and I guess that it is way beyond my understanding, but I hope that you will, as much as possible, allow me to be with you on your journey.'

'You don't know what you are asking, Semira.' Alinor was darkly serious, instinctively wanting to protect her. 'I cannot possibly explain how dangerous life may become, but then, I think I know what to expect from you. Why, you are nearly as stubborn as I am,' Alinor finished with a laugh.

'That I am.'

'Well, that settles things. No point in arguing is there?'

'None at all, my lady.'

'In that case I suggest that you carry on with those surreptitious training exercises you've been doing and master the art of how to use a knife to good effect.'

Alinor wheeled her horse around, smiling at the surprised expression on the other woman's face.

'The others will catch up soon. It's time for me to go home.'

Chapter 7

The traveller wondered if he would ever reach this place that the old man had mentioned. He seemed to just be going on forever – not that he was at all uncomfortable, for the weather was balmy, the countryside very pleasant, the terrain changing just enough to remain interesting. Once or twice he thought that there was something familiar just up ahead, but it proved not to be so. Despite spending quite some time trying to remember his own name everything remained stubbornly blank; little flashes every now and then hinted at a memory but he couldn't grasp them.

If it is a dream, then at least it is not a nightmare, he decided, but - am I going to wake up at some stage? Does it matter?

Some time passed, difficult to say just how long, but finally the man crested a small hill and looked down onto a beautiful valley. There was a very large and rather magnificent house there, set amongst extensive gardens – impossible to say how big, they seemed to go on for miles. A gently winding track led down from where he stood to where large gates stood open to welcome travellers. From his distant viewpoint, the man could just make out people strolling along pathways among the lush flowers; the light of the sun made the stonework of the buildings scattered about the property glow with a pale gold warmth.

What an interesting place – quite unexpected, he thought. Without further hesitation he set off down the track, his long stride quickly covering the mile or more to reach the ornate gilded gates. There were no guards of any kind, no barriers to his entry; the impression was one of freedom to simply walk in. So he did.

Within moments he could see someone approaching; it was a fairly young-looking man dressed in a simple pale grey robe, a narrow silvery chain belt about his waist and an intricately tooled decorative disc hanging around his neck. He smiled in greeting.

'Welcome stranger,' his voice was mellow, 'I believe you have travelled far to come to us. Well, the journey is over and you may take your rest here – we have so much to offer. Please, come with me.'

'Thank you.'

It felt quite natural to walk with the young man on towards the main house, listening as he pointed out where pathways led off to left and right, to gardens obviously designed with themes of tranquillity, art or music; buildings housing beautiful collections of sculpture or metalwork, paintings or other forms of art. Any questions the new arrival may have had were forgotten; they were unimportant now as he experienced a wonderful feeling of peace.

The young man led the way in through a wide columned portico to a pleasantly cool courtyard where elegant fountains whispered musically as their crystal waters flowed into huge basins where delicately coloured lilies floated. From there they continued to a vast hall, the marbled floor patterned with sunlight pouring through high lattices; here and there hung sparkling crystals reaching down from the intricately carved ceiling above. There were several people sat around on carved stone benches, some were reading, or in quiet conversation. They looked up but then returned to what they had been doing.

'I expect you are hungry by now,' the young man said, 'I will show you to your rooms so that you may refresh yourself and some food will be brought to you. Please feel free to make yourself comfortable today; tomorrow I will take you to meet His Eminence.'

'You are very kind,' the traveller responded, 'I confess that I would appreciate something to eat; I hadn't realised it until you mentioned it now.'

'That's often the way. Here we are – these are your rooms now; you should find everything you need, but if not, you have but to ask.'

He was gone before the man thought to enquire exactly whom he should ask, but it didn't matter. He walked into what was quite a large airy room well-appointed with high quality items, dining table, chairs, desk, shelves containing a number of books, and harmoniously decorated with a number of classically beautiful items. An archway led through to an equally stylish sleeping chamber; walking past the tall windows he ran his fingers over the soft drapes suspended there, enjoying the silky feel of the delicate fabric. There were muted colours in the coverings of the bed which he knew instinctively would be very comfortable.

He rinsed away the dust of his travels in the large bowl of water placed for that purpose upon a side table and returned to the main room just as two women were laying out an appetising selection of food on the large table. They greeted him and bade him eat and enjoy before quietly slipping out the door before he had chance to reply. Looking at the spread before him he thought that by some chance they had managed to choose a great many of his favourite dishes and for the next half hour he took great pleasure in tasting all of them until he finally felt replete. He considered going for a walk, but the afternoon was now drawing on and he was beginning to get tired; returning to his sleeping chamber he decided to rest for a while. Stripping off his now tired looking travelling robes he slid into the supremely comfortable bed and within seconds drifted into a deep dreamless sleep.

It was obviously morning when he eventually awoke, somewhat surprised that he seemed to have slept for so many hours but well refreshed and relaxed. He sat up and looked around at his new found abode and saw another archway off the chamber that he had not noticed the day before. Curious he walked through and found himself in a marbled bathing room; water showered out from the mouth of a fantastical carved fish whilst several steps led down into a sunken heated pool. Soft towels had been placed on a long bench along one wall and he could hear the sound of gentle wind bells drifting in from the gardens outside. He stood under the shower for a few minutes, enjoying the sensation of the water flowing over his head and down his lean body. He made use of some soap thoughtfully placed in a dish carved into the wall to cleanse away any residual travel grime before stepping down into the warmth of the pool. Sheer bliss, he thought, this is truly wonderful. He found he could sit on a narrow submerged ledge, the water reaching up to his neck, and stayed there for quite some time.

Eventually he got up and dried himself, returning to the sleeping chamber where he found a set of new garments in which he dressed. Unsurprisingly there was food laid out on the table in the main room again and he broke his fast. He had just finished when a soft knock at the door heralded the arrival of the same young man who had met him yesterday.

'I trust you have found everything to your satisfaction?' he asked.

'Indeed yes,' the man replied, 'very comfortable. You seem to have thought of everything.'

'His Eminence takes great care to ensure the comfort of those who visit us. And now, I have come to take you to him. Please, follow me.'

The young man led the way along a number of corridors and through several large open areas where one or two people were walking; he did not speak to any of them but pointed out a few items that he thought his companion would find interesting. They came at last to a doorway upon which the young man knocked. A voice within bade them enter.

It was not a very large room, but it was well appointed and comfortable. The owner of the voice appeared to be quite an elderly man, simply dressed, sat in an easy chair beside a low table upon which had been placed a flagon and two goblets. He rose as the two entered.

'Thank you, you may leave us,' he said and the young guide nodded and left, closing the door quietly behind him.

'You have come quite a journey to find us,' he addressed his visitor, 'but now that you have finally reached your destination I am sure you will be very happy here.'

'Thank you for your generous hospitality,' the traveller responded, 'I feel most fortunate to have received such a welcome.'

'Not at all, it is the least we can do.' The old man indicated the table, 'Please share a little wine with me.'

He poured some pale coloured liquid into each of the goblets and handed one to the traveller. It was light and slightly sweet, a taste of fruit and honey but very delicate, redolent of lazy summer days, soft on the palate but altogether quite delicious – the sort of drink you could have at any time, and surely would leave you wanting more.

The old man, His Eminence seemed a fanciful title for him, indicated that they should sit.

'Do you know me?' asked the traveller, 'I'm afraid I seem to have forgotten my name, it's a bit strange.' He looked puzzled.

'Not at all,' was the reply, 'it's a more common state than you realise. The past is behind you now and is of no import. As for your name, why, that too is of little import; after all, what is a name? It has little bearing on who you really are. If you wish to refer to yourself I think that Elos is probably as good a name as any and is what I and my people will call you. As for this place, I do hope that you will come to consider it your home. We have so much here that you will enjoy; everything is designed to bring you peace and harmony. You will lack nothing, for anything you would wish for will be provided.'

The newly named Elos sipped his wine and felt reassured by the gentle voice. He was indeed fortunate to have found such a paradise, it was just like a fantastic dream, to be given everything you could want.

A dream? Was there really such a paradise within the reach of an ordinary man such as himself?

For a moment he looked into the eyes of the old man; there was a flash of something akin to recognition in the surprisingly piercing dark look – but then it was gone and the feeling of peace returned.

'I will let you go now to explore our beautiful grounds. It will be such a lovely day again, it is a shame to waste time inside.'

'Yes, of course, you are right,' agreed Elos. 'Once again thank you.'

'Oh no, I would thank you, Elos. I am so very pleased that you have come.'

It had been a strange meeting, but Elos thought nothing of that. Instead, he made his way out through an elegant courtyard, where soft green leaves whispered in a gentle breeze and blooms of every shade wafted their sweet fragrances to envelop him. Tiny birds in glowing colours flashed in and out of the trees and bees and insects hummed amongst the flowers. He walked on along paths which meandered through beautifully laid out gardens with ever changing vistas. Plants of every conceivable size and shape grew profusely; here and there seats had been placed and he stopped several times to simply sit and take in the atmosphere at once invigorating and yet tranquil.

The day wore on and as evening drew in he found his way back to his rooms. After another enjoyable dinner he looked at a couple of the books he found on the shelves before retiring to sleep soundly.

Days passed in calm serenity. The weather was always balmy – the odd gentle shower, mostly at night, ensured that the gardens were kept fresh and flourishing. Further out from the gardens the land gave way to meadows, bright with wildflower and herb, crossed with crystal streams feeding secluded pools and Elos walked for many hours, totally content.

On some days he spent time exploring some of the rooms in the vast mansion. There were a number of libraries, he discovered, and easily lost hours looking through the volumes contained therein. It seemed that books on every conceivable subject were housed there, enough to last a lifetime. On one afternoon Elos took down a small book that had been tucked away and almost lost amongst some hefty tomes on garden design. It contained some advice and suggestions for the care of certain healing plants and herbs and the preparation of various tisanes, infusions and ointments. One specific recipe struck a chord in his dormant memories – it was for *essuvar*.

I know this, he thought, I am sure I know this; but where from? For a few moments he sat, frowning in concentration until his head started to ache, followed by quite sharp stabbing pains. Returning the book to the shelf, he made his way back towards his rooms, but stopped to sit in the cool shade of a courtyard where the air itself took on a misty greenness. Trailing his fingers in the clear waters of a secluded pond he breathed deeply, allowing his mind to empty completely from any thoughts of the book he had been studying only a few minutes before. As he did so, the pain ceased and the headache disappeared. The pleasant smell of the foliage around him soothed him, restoring a sense of total well-being. The book was forgotten as he relaxed and gave in to the wave of tranquillity that now surrounded him, driving all other thoughts from his mind.

And so he continued to spend day after day contentedly walking, reading and studying the various sculptures and artworks that were carefully placed to please the eye both inside the various buildings and outside in the gardens.

He met a few people in his wanderings, but did not enter into much conversation with them. He didn't feel the need to talk particularly, and so made little effort.

One morning as he strolled into a new area of the gardens, he came across a small rustic style hut, more like a small barn. The double doors were open to the kind early light and he could see a middle-aged man sat at a writing table, papers strewn across it, pens and inks ready to hand. He was engrossed in completing a design accompanying a passage of closely written words, and did not look up as Elos approached. Moving quietly to one side so as not to block the man's light, Elos looked to see what was holding the man's attention. The writing was in an unfamiliar language was his first thought, or was it? But it was the design that intrigued him most. It was very complex and it took a moment to try and pick out any particular feature. He could see a couple of star shapes but then saw what was obviously a sword, almost hidden amongst the complex lines and curves that flowed around it.

'It will be good to get this finished,' said the writer, 'but it's going to take me a little more time yet.'

'You have an excellent eye for the work,' offered Elos, 'it is such an intricate piece of work. Is it a part of something else?'

'Oh yes, indeed it is. I am glad you see that.' The man looked hard at Elos. 'I have tried to ensure that the essential message has its place within the design.'

Elos looked again at the paper. Some aspect of the design looked familiar there, surely. Have I forgotten something, he thought, something important?

As he paused beside the table a shadow fell across the work. The young guide appeared in the doorway.

'Perhaps we should leave our artist in peace,' he said, his tone kindly but the message obvious. 'His Eminence has asked me to enquire how you are getting on, if everything is to your liking.'

'I cannot fault anything,' replied Elos, 'this is truly a place of beauty – one could easily lose oneself here in such glorious surroundings.'

If that was somewhat ironic, it did not strike Elos so at the time. The young man nodded his approval.

'His Eminence will be pleased to hear that,' he said, leading them both away from where the artist continued with his work. 'Our gardens are a great source of pride to us, but I believe that you are also enjoying our selection of written works also.'

'Yes certainly. I have always been a reader and have a great interest in many subjects. Books are not only a source of interest but also give great joy.'

'So true,' agreed his companion. 'However, on such a day as this it occurred to me that you may like to visit some unusual rock carvings that are further down in the valley. If you take this path here,' he indicated a track off to the right, 'and simply follow it down it will bring you to the lake of dreams, as we call it, and if you walk around to the left you will find the carvings set back in a small glen. They are quite curious.'

'How interesting,' said Elos, 'I should like to see them. Thank you for letting me know.'

With a slight nod, the young guide strode off on the left-hand pathway and disappeared from sight. Elos set off down the track indicated and eventually came to the lake. It stretched for some distance, reflecting the blue of the sky and providing a wonderful colour contrast to the pair of swans gliding silently near to the bank. He stood and watched them for a while, admiring their serenity; he remembered that swans mate for life, and if one is lost the other will remain solitary, devoted to its lost partner. Some creatures are happy to spend their time alone, he thought, whilst others find their strength in togetherness.

He walked off to the left as his guide had told him and soon found the little clearing amongst a stand of delicate silver birch trees, their heart-shaped leaves trembling in the breeze. In the middle of this space a huge lump of granite type rock erupted from the springy grass. Approaching it Elos could make out a series of stylised figures cut into the weathered faces of the stone. He thought he could make out a number of people, not obvious whether male or female, carrying what seemed to be offerings to another larger and more dominant figure. Further round a series of star shapes led on to where two figures, possibly a couple, walked hand in hand amongst a flower strewn meadow.

I am not sure if that is right, Elos thought, I may be being a bit fanciful. But it is easy to let one's imagination take over and perhaps see what is not there. Imagination is a very powerful part of one's mind, I suppose. One could easily just conjure up a picture of say, a dragonfly, iridescent in blue and green, and there it would be.

He stretched his hand out, and there it was, the dragonfly, just as he had thought, the jewel-like colours flashing in the sunlight.

He started, totally taken by surprise, and the illusion vanished.

'What on earth,' he spoke out loud, 'how could that be? All I did was think of it.'

He started to form the thought again, but, just as had happened when he had come across the recipe for *essuvar*, his head began to ache.

Must be too much sun, he thought and closed his eyes for a few minutes. The pain subsided.

Perhaps it is time to return to the house, he decided, and left the strange stone with its odd carvings looking oddly like a giant creature lying sleeping amongst the gently whispering trees. The headache did not return.

Chapter 8

So, I am finally home, Alinor told Sirad as she stood looking out of her window over the palace environs and towards the city. Lights still glowed in windows, but there were fewer now as the hour grew late.

I'm not sure how to feel about today, she continued, I suppose a mixture of relief tinged with sadness, but with a quite a lot of anger and a kind of fear all muddled in together.

It can't be easy, came Sirad's response, and when you are so tired – and I know you are, so don't deny it – things tend to be a bit worse.

Yes, Alinor sighed mentally. It was good, though, to see so many people with genuine welcome on their faces waiting on the way up to the palace. I was aware that Vixlan's men were trying to put a bit of a dampener on it, still wanting to maintain some kind of control, but I did manage to see that the city folk were actually getting their own back, out of sight of the parade! I just hope they won't suffer for it after as it's going to take a little while before Dhalen and the men can get back in control. I shall have to start straight in early tomorrow, not take a week or two to settle in as that weasel Vixlan so kindly encouraged me to do. Does he really think I would allow him time to cover up his misdeeds and steal more from me?

Sirad smiled to himself at Alinor's angry indignation. You wouldn't want to get in her way now, was his private thought; she will not be taking prisoners in this battle.

I suppose he was all sweetness and light? he asked Alinor.

Absolutely, she replied scornfully. Honestly, anyone would think he was a hero, the way he has tirelessly worked so hard for the continued wellbeing of the country following the awful demise of the king, with scarcely a thought for himself. Well, he's got another think coming. I'm going to put paid to his machinations right now.

Just be careful, my love. I am with you all the way on getting justice for your people, but never forget that Verun was probably behind a lot of this, even if Vixlan himself was not aware. You need to find out how all this came about, if you can; you may have more enemies at home than you appreciate and whilst I know how very capable you are, there is always a possibility of either of us making an error somewhere along the line. We have to be so careful.

I know, Alinor nodded – Sirad was right. She could so easily become distracted in her desire to put right the damage the twisted Steward had done and somehow prove to her father's shade that he could be proud of his wayward daughter.

I know, I know; you are right to warn me, she acknowledged. There is a lot to be done and of course I want to get things back to how they should be as soon as possible. I need to establish a council of people I can trust who will help govern Ancor in my absence for we both have a destiny to fulfil, tasks which must be undertaken; we have no idea how much time we will have before we will have to face Verun's spite again.

Talking of which, interrupted Sirad, I shall likely be making a trip down south and on towards Mekad before too much longer. Not sure how close I will get but certainly not so near as to risk falling into enemy hands, he added quickly as Alinor was about to object. I'll take Ben with me, I don't want to take the others – it would draw too much attention to us.

Alinor knew he referred to his closest captains of the Riders, Fehlen, Gerin and Osan. They had been with him the first day they met, fending off the unwelcome attentions of a southern-led ambush party. Normally there would be no question of the five running into any trouble they couldn't handle, but since Verun had come into their lives, nothing could be considered hazard free any longer.

Don't worry too much, Alinor. We will both be constantly on our guard; but I do need to spy out the lay of the land a bit more and find out as much as possible what is happening now. I have no intention of letting Verun find me.

That may be easier said than done, Alinor cautioned. It is so difficult knowing just how much we can do without him becoming aware of our presence or activities. But, you are right, we have to get as much information as we can. She paused. How is Amiros? Is there any change at all?

He is much the same, responded Sirad. I can sense no great feelings of distress or pain in him, but his mind is still closed to me. I don't know what I can do, or if there is anything that could be done.

The two young people's minds focused on their beloved Lore-Master; Oh Amiros, where are you? Alinor sent out her penetrating thought, trying to break through whatever barrier had been created between them. Surely, the energy that the two could direct at him would somehow reach him?

They could sense nothing, but still clung to the hopes that they would eventually find a way to bring him back to them. Neither was prepared to accept that he could be lost forever.

Alinor wiped a hand over eyes, yawned and sighed.

Get some sleep, my darling, you have a big challenge ahead tomorrow, Sirad urged. And take care!

And you too, my love. I miss being with you, even though we stay so close in mind, it's not the same.

I know, but I guess it won't be too long before we shall be together again. Remember, I love you.

And I you, with all my heart.

'A bit like old times,' said Ben to Sirad as they rode southwards, several days out from Pelenin.

'I wish it was,' the young Lord Commander replied. 'Believe me, I wish it was. But, things will never be quite the same again as you are well aware. Part of me enjoys the action and I almost look forward to taking the fight to the enemy, but then I feel guilty because men will lose their lives because I am leading them into such a perilous undertaking.'

'Don't take it like that; you know that any of us, all of us, would gladly ride with you whatever the odds. We were born to be Riders, we took the oath and we will give our lives without hesitation because that is who we are.'

'Yes, I know. But it doesn't necessarily make me feel any better.'

'How is she getting on? I know that in some way you talk with her.'

Sirad looked at his foster brother, wondering just how much he did know about their true natures.

'I think she's got her hands full dealing with that wretched Steward of hers. But, she'll find some way of bringing him to justice – although personally I'd like to strangle him and be done with it!'

'With you there!' laughed Ben but continued seriously , 'though I missed the last trip you took to Thorgiliad, I've heard all about it and he doesn't come out of it well.' He was quiet for a couple of minutes.

'She's lucky to have Dhalen to support her – he's a good man. I have a lot of respect for him.'

'He is, you're right about that. I can be reasonably confident of her safety with him close by her. And once the elite guards can be reformed matters will be a bit better.'

'Are you expecting that we'll meet up with any of the opposition soon?' Ben asked.

'Once over the border, I think things may start to get interesting,' replied his companion. You know as well as I that we want to try not to get noticed if we can help it. We really need to find out what kind of hold Verun has established down in Zarrakhen and the Sendure. Fra'ilen couldn't tell us much; in fact as he said, the communications between Lefnan-ilos and Zarrakhen were pretty much zero, although somehow Verun has managed not to invite too much curiosity about what he's been doing.

'We'll have to leave our horses here in Pelenin and change for others a little less obvious. We'd really stick out riding our own beauties, but it will slow us down a bit. I'd like to push on and reach the border this afternoon.'

'Good idea,' nodded Ben.

With the slightest of movements both men urged their horses forward, the animals keen to stretch their legs a bit more, covering the miles effortlessly as they sped on towards the border of Pelenin.

They changed mounts at a big traveller's inn about an hour's ride from where Pelenin gave way to Lefnan-ilos. It would not be the first time that Riders from Pelamir had opted to leave their precious horses behind, so no questions were asked. The owner of the establishment was away and the man left in charge was not familiar with the Lord Commander of the Riders, and failed to recognise the two men who appeared to be merchants of some kind. Sirad and Ben had dispensed with their customary uniforms and would easily pass unnoticed on their travels; however, look a little deeper and you may notice that for all their apparent simplicity, the two men were keenly alert to their surroundings, easy in the saddle, well-muscled and fit. There were still several hours of daylight left and having been able to get a couple of good southern horses they chose to continue their journey.

The next few days were uneventful; they would chat with people along the way, casual questions eliciting little new information. There had been a few incidents, the pair were told, where unfriendly groups of men would make their presences felt, not averse to answering any objections with violence, but ultimately not staying anywhere very long. They tended to be from the eastern part of the Sendure, was the opinion of locals who on the whole were not too worried about them at the moment.

'That may change,' observed Sirad to Ben. 'Maybe Verun isn't pushing too much this way yet. If only Amiros had been able to let us know a bit more. Czaten told me some of what was going on, but I could have done with the Lore-Master's take on matters.'

'Will he recover?' Ben asked. 'I didn't see that much of him since we were kids together, but I always thought him a kind sort, odd of course being a magician and all that, but I really liked him. He was always good to me even though I wasn't your real family.'

'You are my brother, Ben,' Sirad rebuked his companion, 'so don't ever think like that.'

That afternoon they had just stopped and dismounted to let their horses drink from a small stream bubbling out between some tumbled stones when they heard the sound of hoofbeats approaching rapidly.

A couple of minutes later four men appeared and approached the pair, drawing to a halt and obviously assessing whether they might be fair game.

'Where are you going?' asked one of them, presumably the leader of the little group. 'You traders or what?'

Ben glanced at Sirad and answered for them.

'Yes, we're merchants; just hoping to get some new business down here.'

'And what exactly is your business?'

One of the group edged his horse to one side, looking to see what takings might be on offer.

'Well,' continued Ben calmly, 'we deal in grain mostly, and beer too occasionally, though we'd like to expand that side.'

'Really?' said the man, hard eyes watching them intently. 'You don't seem to have much with you to show for it.'

'Not on this trip, no. We'll be meeting up with some existing customers whom we hope will give us some introductions to potential new buyers.'

Sirad took the opportunity to quietly move a little closer to their horses who seemed to be getting a bit restless. He had seen how the group were armed and instinctively recognised the characteristic arrogance that almost certainly presaged their intention to take whatever they could find of value from these two petty merchants.

'We should get on our way now,' Sirad said, 'the horses have had their break.'

Ben understood exactly what Sirad meant.

'Yes, I think you're right,' he replied and then addressed the dark man. 'More miles to go today I think, hopefully before it comes on to rain.'

He turned towards where Sirad waited.

'Not so quickly,' snarled the man, 'I think you could afford to be a little generous to fellow travellers.'

Two of the group dismounted and made as if to approach Sirad and Ben.

'I don't agree,' said Sirad, his sword drawn in the blink of an eye.

Without hesitation the would-be robbers drew their weapons and lunged at the Riders; simultaneous sword thrusts from Sirad and Ben eliminated the threat, the two men barely able to register surprise before they fell to the ground. Furious, the leader tried to ride them down, followed by his remaining companion. Avoiding the slashing blade, Sirad managed to grab the man's leg and pull him from his mount, dispatching him before he could regain control. Ben took a moment or two longer to finish off his opponent.

'Amateurs,' scorned Ben.

'Yes, a nuisance, but not much more than that. They're not really part of anything to do with Verun.'

'Do we move them?' asked Ben.

'I'd rather not. There's a town not too far ahead, we can say that we came across them and think that there were two groups who fell out with each other.'

That is what they did; Sirad sought out the town leader and told him of the bodies and thanks to a little mental coercion on the part of the Rider the man believed him completely. Sirad described their horror at such violence and told the man that he and his colleague would stay the night at the local inn as they were too shocked to want to continue.

That evening they learned that highway robbery had increased markedly over the past few months. People tended to travel in much larger groups than previously in order to discourage any attacks. The locals reckoned that Sirad and Ben had been very fortunate indeed not to have been caught up in the action.

It did rain that night, but had eased off by morning when the two set off again. However, but mid-day the skies had again turned leaden with the promise of serious downpours before the day was out.

'We could do with finding some shelter,' said Ben, 'I don't fancy our chances in this tonight!'

'Nor I. Perhaps they'll be something further up there,' Sirad gestured towards where the ground rose steeply; a rocky outcrop could be seen through the trees leading them to hope for possible caves where they could get the horses in under cover. They left the main track they'd been following and climbed up the hill. As they got nearer they could see where the rocks had thrust their way up from the ground, great fissures showing here and there, just the sort of features that frequently produced decent sized caves.

It took them about an hour skirting the base of the outcrop before they found a suitable spot. It wasn't obvious until you were almost on it, a large dark opening which led back and opened out into quite a wide cave, dry and sheltered from the wind which was getting up. They led the grateful horses inside and fed them from the supply of grain which they carried in the event of such an occurrence. Water was freely available, the now torrential rain outside filtering through the rock and pouring down the wall into a bowl shaped depression worn out over the years before flowing out in a narrow stream to continue its path down towards the valley below.

Later that evening the pair shared a drink as their small fire crackled and flamed, the sweet-smelling wood pleasant in the cool air. There was obviously some slight draught feeding through from the back of the cave which ensured that the smoke was carried away.

Curious, Sirad took a lit branch from the fire and went back to have a look at how far the cave extended. What he had assumed to be a blank wall was in fact broken; once he got close to it he could see that there was a gap leading behind a huge slab of rock. He expected a narrow fissure, but instead could make out quite a wide opening disappearing into blackness.

'Look at this, Ben,' called Sirad, 'it goes way back here.'

Ben came, bearing his own lit branch.

'It's wide enough for two people to walk abreast,' he said, surprised, 'I wonder where it leads.'

'Do you want to look?'

'Why not?'

Together they started down the passage; here and there the light of their torches reflected off glistening quartz crystals lacing through the rock. After about five minutes, Sirad stopped.

'Do you see this?' he reached out his right hand and ran it down the rockface.

'It looks like it's been worked,' said Ben. 'And on this side too. What does it mean?'

'I don't know, but I'd like to find out.'

They continued further, the passage jinking left and right but not narrowing at all.

'Here,' called Ben, 'there are carvings here.'

Sirad looked carefully.

'Runes,' he said, 'definitely runes, and quite clear too.' He frowned, lifting his torch to show more of the ancient writing.

'Can you read them?' asked Ben. 'I know you know more than you let on,' he continued as Sirad looked at him in the flickering light, 'and since you met Alinor you've changed a lot.'

Sirad would have said something but Ben continued.

'Oh come on, don't you think it's time you told me what's going on. You've said I'm your brother, so allow me that.'

'It's not as easy as that,' Sirad started, 'I'm not sure –'

'Of course it's not easy, I know that. Maybe there are some things I won't understand, but I think I deserve the truth.'

Sirad closed his eyes and took a deep breath; Ben was right, he did deserve the truth. But the truth would bring pain with it and to hurt his brother was the last thing he wanted.

'All right then, I suppose I'll have to tell you something to stop you going on at me,' he said, trying to lighten the tension. 'But please wait until later, once we've found out where this leads.'

'I'll agree to that, but you'll not put me off again.'

'Stubborn,' muttered Sirad under his breath.

'Yes, well, I can read some of the writing but it's a bit like a riddle. Something along the lines of "Where light strikes the water the jewel fits the rock; mend what is lost to open the path." And it goes on like that, I can't really make sense of it.'

He moved along the rockface, his fingers running over the indentations.

'Light and fire, the source is hidden, gold and fire, - something - above, - something - below,' Sirad translated key words as best he could, but their meanings eluded him. The two walked on a bit further to where the passage made a sharp turn right; the rock in front was covered in strange symbols. Part way down were more runes and this time the message was clear to the young lord: the two, male and female, who carried fire and light would enter where the doom would protect its treasure for they had been chosen.

'What does it say?" Ben stared at the extraordinary collection of signs.

'I think it says we don't go any further,' responded Sirad. 'I'm pretty sure it is a warning of some kind and I'm not prepared to risk anything happening – no-one knows we are here. I've never encountered anything like this before; it's beyond me.'

'If you don't like it, then I'll take your word for it. Let's get back to the cave.'

The two men retraced their steps, Ben feeling a bit spooked by the strangeness of it, and Sirad wondering exactly what he and Alinor would find beyond that point, for it was obvious to him that the runes meant for the two of them, and only the two of them, should progress further into the mysterious darkness.

Returning to the cave they added more wood to the fire, checked the horses and settled down again. Ben offered Sirad a drink saying, 'Time to talk, I think.'

'Mmm,' Sirad started. 'Where to begin?'

'With your lovely Lady, I would suggest,' said Ben. 'When she first met us she was a bit of a mystery; understandable that she didn't want to reveal who she was after her father was killed. But then when you were away and she was recovering, I guessed who she was, but I did promise not to say anything to anyone else – that was what she wanted, so fine with me. But Amiros paid her a lot of attention, and then she disappeared into the Library for days on end. I don't know what she was looking for, but I think she found something because she changed, just a little bit, not obviously but she was different somehow.

'When she came back from Elagos, she was really different, and then so were you. No,' he put a hand on Sirad's arm, 'not in a bad way, but perhaps a bit distant, like you didn't want me to ask too much.'

'I'm sorry, Ben, if it seemed that way. I couldn't have answered you anyway just then.'

'That's OK, I do understand. But,' he paused, 'when we came back home now I got to thinking about what had happened and so I went to the Library myself.'

Sirad looked at his foster brother and realised that Ben had probably found out quite a lot more that he had realised.

'I don't know whether to believe any of the things I found there,' Ben continued, 'so perhaps you could tell me.'

'Oh brother, this is not going to be easy – I know, I said that before and I mean it. A lot of what you may have found in the Library is real. We know that all myths and legends have some kind of basis in real life if you look deep enough; that premise is true here. You know that both Alinor and I trace our lineage way back to Rakep-thos; that is fact. Rakep-thos today is thought of only in terms of legend, a superhuman being, but

I assure you that everything written about him was actually true. The Ben-Neteru were very real and their heritage has been passed down through the generations.

'Alinor went to Elagos to find Remon Mind-Master because he was one of the remaining Ben-Neteru.'

Ben let out a whistle. 'He was?'

'Yes he was, which was why his passing was such a blow. His knowledge was extraordinary and his power almost beyond understanding.'

'Why was it so important that Alinor had to see him?' asked Ben.

Sirad looked up at the roof of the cave and took a deep breath. Apart from the quiet crackling of the fire the cave was silent, as if waiting for what the man would say.

'Because she too is Ben-Neteru.'

Ben closed his eyes and dropped his head. He now knew for certain what he had only guessed at before.

'And so are you,' he whispered, startled to feel unwanted tears prickling his eyes.

'Yes.'

Ben got up and walked a few steps away to give himself a chance to regain a hold on his emotions. Sirad stayed still, knowing the turmoil that his brother felt. He had to consciously shut out the sound of Ben's thoughts which his concern had allowed to be clearly heard.

After some minutes Ben came and sat down again.

'I, um, had guessed,' he finally said, 'but to come out and say it makes it real. I don't know what to say.'

'Not sure that I do either,' responded Sirad. 'I haven't really got used to the idea myself.'

'What about us?'

'Oh Ben, nothing has changed between us, not really. We are, and will always be, brothers. I dread the thought of losing you – that's if Verun hasn't killed me off first.'

'It's frightening for me,' said Ben in a subdued voice, 'but I can see that the thought of possibly living for years beyond count must be pretty awful too.'

Sirad was grateful that Ben could look beyond his own hurt to recognise the burden that he himself would carry.

'There's more to it though, isn't there? You and she have powers, don't you? And then there's Verun who is obviously a force to be reckoned with and who also has power.'

'Yes, Verun was one of Remon's disciples, along with Amiros. But Verun was rejected for some reason and disappeared for such a long time that they never thought to see him again. I know that Verun had to be quite powerful or he would never have been a disciple, but it seems that he has found one of the jewels of power and has some control over it. That was what he used on Amiros to such awful effect. We don't yet know if the damage can be undone – that's one of the reasons for coming down this way. Apparently another one of the disciples lives on some island out from Lefnan-ilos and he might be able to help us.

Neither Alinor nor I yet understand the extent of our powers or how best to use them, but we know that together we managed somehow to fight off the influence of Verun at Elagos.'

'It was quite impressive, whatever it was that you did,' said Ben. 'I don't know that any of us really appreciated what was going on – it know I started to feel like we were never going win, I just wanted to give up.'

'Yes, that was Verun trying to influence all of us. It was an indication of the sort of power that he can bring to bear. Now you start to see why Remon was called Mind-Master.'

'And is that the sort of power that you and she can have?' Ben was daunted by the thought.

'Yes, but there is more to it than that.'

Ben shook his head.

'I'm lost for words, it is so, so – I don't know.'

They were both quiet for a while. Sirad put a small piece of wood on the fire.

'You can talk to her, can't you, when she's not here with us?'

'Yes, I can. I can hear what she is thinking, as she can with me – and Amiros. If I choose to I can also tell what other people are thinking, though Alinor is much better at that than I am.'

'You know what I am thinking?' Ben was horrified.

'Only if I deliberately chose to, Ben, but I have never and will never intrude on your mind unless you were to specifically ask it of me. If you were in danger, for instance, I believe that if you really wanted me to know, I would somehow get that message.'

The other man shook his head.

'That is really uncomfortable, Sirad. I don't know how to take that.'

'I confess it scared me at first – I don't want to know what others think, especially my friends. It offends me deeply. But, and you will appreciate this, if I were able to know what my enemy thinks, I could protect myself and others.'

'Yes, I suppose so,' Ben was hesitant. It was a lot to take in. This was his brother, his closest friend; he knew he could trust Sirad with his life, and gladly protect him with his own, were it necessary. But now, he had thought that he knew the man sat here beside him, but yet he had become someone quite different, strange, dangerous even. How to accept that?

'I know this is hard for you – it doesn't take magic skills to understand how much of a shock this must be. I need you, Ben.' Sirad's voice was heavy with emotion. 'I need you to be with me as my friend – that will never change, no matter what happens to Alinor and I.'

Ben nodded, unable to trust his voice. Part of him longed to turn back the clock, go back to the way life had been; he and Sirad had done so much together. He had worked hard and earned his captain's commission in the Riders without Sirad's help. He enjoyed the respect of those under him and was totally committed to serving his country. That wouldn't change, and maybe now, in the face of Verun's threat to their freedoms he too would face a new challenge. These powers that Sirad and Alinor possessed did not make them invincible, Ben knew, and he knew too that no matter how different they became, his loyalty remained absolute; he would try to protect and help both of them wherever possible.

Finally Ben spoke.

'Everything has changed, but some things cannot. We may not be blood, but we are brothers, I know. You are who you are, even though you did not always know it. You are coming into your powers and that is hard for me to accept as it is almost impossible to comprehend, but that should not change what we are to each other. I don't want to lose what we have, Sirad.'

'Nothing can take that from us.' It was Sirad's voice that broke now. He had dreaded this time coming, when Ben would learn the truth, and his heart was aching for this man beside him. But no-one, not Verun, not anyone, would take away the bond of friendship that they had.

'Perhaps we should sleep on it,' suggested Sirad. 'At least from now on we can talk a little more openly between ourselves.'

'Yes. A good idea, although I'm not sure how I can sleep after this. I think I'm going to have a lot of questions, but right now my brain just doesn't want to hear any more.'

Sirad nodded and checked the fire was safe for the night; the heavy cloaks which they had been wearing to keep the rain off had dried in the warm air and they laid them on the floor. The two men stood a moment looking at each other before they came together in a brief hug.

'Sleep well, brother,' whispered Sirad.

The following morning saw the two friends set off under clearing skies; it was fairly wet underfoot, but the rain seemed to have moved on for the time and Sirad was anxious to continue his search for information. They were heading south for the coast where he hoped to find out a little more about the location of this island Mitos where Remon had said that Eldren lived. He was toying with the idea of maybe finding a boat to take him there; he knew Alinor wanted to go, but if he went now, it would save a lot of time. He didn't even know for sure if Eldren could do anything to help Amiros. He raised the subject with Ben some days later.

'If the opportunity is there, I think you should go,' said Ben. 'I could stay behind and see what I can learn while you are away, so that we make the most of this trip.'

'Yes, that's a possibility. But I don't want you to get too close to Mekad or run the risk of being caught.'

'I think you can trust me to use a bit of common sense,' Ben mocked. 'Seriously though, I do know this is no laughing matter and I have no desire to see inside any of Verun's strongholds. I know that Amiros is important to you and Alinor and presumably to this whole venture – remember you haven't finished telling me just what it is yet – so go to this Eldren if you can.'

'OK, we'll see what the situation is when we reach the coast. I don't want to waste too much time searching out Fra'ilen; ideally I'd like to consult with him but he could be anywhere.'

'Most likely out at sea, playing at being a pirate!'

'Don't joke about it, Ben; he always was a pirate, even though he's supposed to be reformed.'

'I don't want to get involved,' Ben was shaking his head, 'he'll start pushing for me to sail with him again and I barely managed to escape last time!'

'You'd enjoy it really,' Sirad aimed a punch at Ben's arm, 'but then, you've not sailed before have you? Can't remember what you were doing when I came down this way, oh, that was a few years back now.'

'Seem to recall being sent off on a lengthy patrol and training exercise up north instead.'

'You'll get your chance again, I promise,' laughed Sirad. 'I've got a feeling that we shall definitely be broadening our horizons in the not too distant future. But now, let's give these well-meaning excuses for horses some proper exercise.'

Chapter 9

There simply weren't enough hours in the day for Alinor as she started to make herself familiar with everything and everyone around the palace and surrounding city. There seemed to be endless delegations of people needing to speak to her; some only to welcome her home and offer condolences on the loss of her father, others keen to get a look at the newly-returned Lady of Ancor. There were many wanting to air their grievances, hoping that she would redress the wrongs that been inflicted by Vixlan's heavy hand; they spoke warily, uncertain that the greedy Steward would not find a way of punishing them somehow. Alinor felt sympathy and anger in equal measure; she wanted to ease her people's lives, but she wasn't going to be a victim of her charitable nature. She knew she had to be careful that in showing undue care in any one situation she could open the door to a horde of other petitioners, some of whom may simply be out for anything they could get. She disciplined her wrath where Vixlan was concerned, maintaining a controlled demeanour whenever in his presence. She could hardly just banish him from the palace instantly no matter how appealing the thought was. First she needed to take time to find out exactly what the situation was, what laws were being implemented, and even more importantly, who was in the pay of the man. Only then could she start to build up a trusted core of officials who would be able to help govern her country and restore the harmony that had existed under her father's rule.

Semira had her work cut out for her. It didn't take that long to identify suitable staff for Alinor's personal care but she couldn't stop there. Curiosity fuelled her instinctive urge to organise and so from there she moved out to the next level and investigated what was happening in the huge palace kitchens. On the whole, the important members, cooks, had remained the same. A couple had left when Vixlan decided they weren't worth their salary, but the best of them who had been in service even since before Alinor was born still ruled their little kingdom and were overjoyed that she had returned. There were tales aplenty of days gone by, and Semira's knowledge grew apace as they insisted on sharing reminiscences. They were the people who were only too happy to identify some of the lazier staff who had joined under the Steward's tenure.

'I can't be having them, the lazy, good-for-nothing layabouts,' old Maesie was in her element as she told the Lady's personal maid her woes. 'They hang round here, nicking my food, helping themselves to beer and good wine and telling me they're on special jobs for the Grand Chancellor, or some other such name as he decides to call himself.'

'Are there many of them?' asked Semira.

'Far too many for my liking, I can tell you. After his majesty was lost, may the gods keep him, that nasty snake of a man saw where his opportunities lay and grabbed everything with both hands. Mind you, he didn't want to be left with no-one to prepare his food proper!'

The cook looked about just in case one of the aforesaid layabouts was lingering within earshot.

'I'm that glad she's back, really I am. But while *he's* still around it pays to be a bit careful like. There's good folk who talked out of turn and all of a sudden they were gone. You watch yourself, young lady; I wouldn't trust him an inch, I wouldn't.'

Maesie had risen through the kitchen ranks when Alinor's father was alive, becoming the unchallenged head of the kitchen household before Alinor's mother died. Plump, as all good cooks should be, she was as down to earth as they come, taking no nonsense from the other staff, who without fail respected both her cooking and her management. Her stern glance would ensure that even the labourers took no liberties in her domain, but her twinkling eyes betrayed a healthy sense of humour that meant the kitchens were on the whole a very merry place, despite the heavy workload.

'My Lady is determined to restore the household to what it was when the king was alive,' Semira assured the cook, 'but it will take time. She's not getting as much sleep as she should, and I really have to keep reminding her that she should eat!'

'I've got just the thing,' Maesie tapped Semira on the arm, 'you wait there a moment.'

She bustled off to one of the pantries and came back with a plate of small fruit tartlets.

'She used to love these,' she told her with a smile, 'she'd come down here and sneak them from the table – not that I minded, she was such a lovely child.'

'They look absolutely wonderful,' exclaimed Semira, 'can I try one?'

'Of course, my love, you help yourself. But I reckon these will cheer her Ladyship up!'

'Mmm,' was all Semira could manage in reply, her mouth full of glorious fruit and feather-light pastry. A satisfied swallow, then, 'If you're not careful, Maesie, it'll be me sneaking them,' she laughed.

'Don't you worry, I know just what to tempt your young mistress with; oh it'll be such a pleasure to have her back and be like it used to be – or very nearly.'

Semira gave the old lady a quick kiss on the cheek.

'She is lucky to have you, Maesie!'

'Oh go on with you,' the cook waved a hand at her, 'get out of my kitchen.' But she was smiling and perhaps had a little tear in her eye.

The self-styled Chancellor was twenty minutes into another of his presentations to Alinor, attempting to baffle her with minute details about trading agreements and how well he was controlling the situation. *I'm no expert on this sort of thing,* she was thinking, *but I don't need to read his mind to tell when he's talking absolute rubbish.* She had deliberately avoided using her probing mind up until now, taking time to reassure herself that there was no possibility of Verun's involvement and his being alerted to her use of power. Her efforts over the past few weeks had not indicated any kind of contact with the renegade magician; it would appear that Vixlan's innate greed had not required any great encouragement, and once set on the road Verun had simply left him alone to build his own little empire. The ambitious Steward was exactly the sort of tool that Verun wanted and he would allow him more or less free rein for as long as it suited him.

As her weaselly Steward droned on and on, Alinor listened to what his thoughts were telling her. The initial panic he had felt when he realised the Lady had survived and was returning to her kingdom had almost gone away; from everything she had said and done he had got the impression that she was totally unaware of how successful he had been in syphoning off vast sums of money from the coffers, not to mention goods of all descriptions from within the palace. His fawning efforts in showing her just what an excellent servant to his country he was seemed to be paying off. What he could never realise was that Alinor knew far more about him and the situation now and his days were surely numbered.

He's getting confident again, she thought. It's time I started to rattle the cage a bit.

'Thank you, Vixlan,' she interrupted the Steward in full flow, 'I do appreciate your very full reports. However,' she paused and looked hard at the man, 'I have given matters serious consideration and feel that the time is right to make some changes. You have been working very hard during my absence and perhaps it would be sensible to relieve you of some of your burden.'

His face was a picture; although he managed to regain control over his expression, she had seen the dismay and apprehension at the thought that he could lose his lucrative source of income. He was so glad that when he heard she had survived he had taken pains to get his hands on as much as possible and secrete it where she would not be able to find it. Alas for him, his thoughts were as clear as day to the young woman; what she had overheard from the three men on her journey to the capital was confirmed. Now she would investigate the clandestine property that Vixlan had thought so safe; no rush, she would take her time to fully identify the extent of his greed.

Alinor addressed a young man quietly sat further down the big table upon which piles of documents had been placed to bolster Vixlan's presentation.

'I understand you have been employed in this department for a number of years now, Temar?'

'Well, yes I have, your Ladyship,' the young man was surprised to be the object of her attention, blushing slightly under her scrutiny.

'I have heard good reports of your work and I understand that you have a good grasp of the mechanics of these agreements.'

'I have studied them in great detail, my Lady, and have attended many of the meetings where terms have been discussed.'

'So I gather. I would like you to take over the current workload from my hardworking Steward with immediate effect. I am sure that he will give you every assistance to ensure a smooth changeover, won't you Vixlan?'

Her pointed question had the uncomfortable Steward nodding.

'Of course, my Lady, I will help Temar as best I can, but it may take a little while – these are complex matters.' Vixlan was frantically trying to play for time to enable him to manipulate matters and cover up the discrepancies.

'I am sure that Temar is well up to the challenge,' Alinor stated, looking at the surprised young man.

'I, I - I am sure I shall be,' he responded eagerly, overcoming his initial shock. 'Thank you my Lady for your confidence.'

The Steward didn't know where to look. His mind was a riot of thoughts and Alinor smiled to herself; that would show the little weasel who was in charge here. She couldn't help feeling a bit smug. This was *her* country, and she was taking control.

'I would like to discuss some financial arrangements for our military forces; I suggest that we meet, say the day after tomorrow?'

Vixlan drew in a breath, she was moving rather too quickly for his liking.

'That doesn't give me much time, your Ladyship,' he whined.

'I'm sure you will manage it, Vixlan, you seem to have everything else well in hand,' she purred. 'I will arrange for the senior officers to be present as well. I would like everyone involved to attend. Yes?'

'Of course, of course; I'll get right on to it.'

Vixlan hastily started gathering up bits of paperwork, some of which promptly scattered on the floor in his distraction. Temar couldn't hide a quick smile at the way his former boss had been so firmly put in his place. As he looked up again, he caught a glance from the Lady, who just nodded very slightly at him as if recognising that he had worked hard to get where he was, putting up with Vixlan's arrogance in the hope that one day the man would be caught out and get the punishment he deserved.

A couple of hours later Alinor was talking with Dhalen down in the barracks area. He had heard about what happened at the earlier meeting and was pleased that Alinor was starting to make her presence felt.

'He'll do a good job, Temar. I've known him since a lad; he's a good head on his shoulders and was always very quick to learn.'

'Yes, I've had nothing but good reports of him, so it's high time he moved up the ladder. We need good young minds with common sense to deal with these matters. I have my eye on a few other good candidates to take over in various departments. Vixlan won't know what's hit him!'

'You've no idea how glad it makes me to have you here to deal with that vermin!' Dhalen grinned at her. 'Just say the word and I will be happy to take permanent care of him.'

'Not yet, Dhalen, not yet!' Alinor laughed. 'There's a bit to do before we get to that point. Unfortunately,' she added somewhat ruefully.

'I suppose so,' the doughty warrior was mildly regretful. 'This next meeting should be interesting too.'

'Yes, I wanted to check up with you now to see how you are getting on with the restructuring of the guard. Have you managed to get everyone back that you wanted?'

'Just about. We did lose a few in the early days, after your father died. I know, but cannot prove, that Vixlan had them removed – permanently - because they didn't like what he was doing. There's a few who I know are thinking of leaving, unhappy to be effectively demoted to serving outside of the palace.'

'Are they all back here now, in Thorgiliad? I would like to be able to speak with them before they make their minds up finally. I need them to stay.'

'For you, my Lady, they will gladly stay, I am sure of that. But they will really be heartened if you address them directly.'

'Tomorrow then, old friend. Arrange it and I shall speak to them in the morning. Let's see the Elite Guard back as it was, for my father's sake if nothing else.'

'As you wish; but be assured, they will do it for you regardless.'

'There you are, Semira!' Alinor greeted her companion back in her chambers. She had wanted a few minutes to freshen up, have a drink and a couple of those mouth-watering tartlets that Semira now brought up regularly from the kitchen.

'You wanted me for something?' the young woman replied, a little surprised.

'I need some fresh air,' declared Alinor, 'so I think we'll take a ride out. I want to just go out and see my old nanny; she's gone to live with her daughter-in-law to help with her children as her son was just one of those who fell foul of my wretched Steward.'

'I'll just slip something more suitable on, if you don't mind,' said Semira, and quickly went off to her own rooms to change from the very attractive gown she had been wearing.

It wasn't possible for the Lady of Ancor to ride out without some kind of escort, so it was a small party, Alinor and Semira with four other Elite guards, who cantered out from the city towards the little farm where Nanny Freda now lived. It was only some ten or twelve miles, but enough for Alinor to feel refreshed by being free from the palace protocol for a few hours.

They found the old lady busy cooking some sweetmeats for the children, a boy of seven and a little girl of five, pale golden brown haired, excitedly laughing and trying to steal some of the mixture from the bowls on the big kitchen table. Hearing the arrival of visitors, the children came rushing out to see who it was, calling to their grandmother to come and see.

Hurriedly wiping her hands on her apron she appeared at the door and exclaimed in surprise.

'Little Alinor! Oh, I mean, Your Ladyship, what on earth brings you here? I never expected to see you come here.'

'Nanny Freda, it's so good to see you,' Alinor vaulted down lightly from Elkana's saddle. 'It's been too long – are you well? No need to answer, I see that you are.' She reached out and pulled the old lady into a warm hug.

'Well, well, you have grown up all of a sudden,' Freda declared, eyeing her old charge closely. 'A proper queen in the making, I always said, and here you are, visiting an old woman.'

'A very special old woman, and not that old!' Alinor corrected. 'I heard that you were out here – I am sorry to learn about your son. It must have been hard, for all of you.'

'It was, it was, especially for Lianna here, with two small children to care for. She works really hard to run the farm, to make enough to keep body and soul together and give the children a decent life.'

'I don't remember Lianna, I'm sorry to say, I'm not sure I ever met her. But I do remember Callen, we'd play together sometimes when I was at the palace.'

'Run and find your mother,' Freda told the children, 'she has important visitors.'

The two hurtled off around to the back of the house and towards the outbuilding, shouting, 'Mum, Mum, come quick!'

'Please, come inside,' Freda gestured. 'Have a drink of my lemonade; you used to like it when you were small.'

'Indeed I did, I can remember it clearly,' Alinor exclaimed. She told the guards to stay outside with the horses, then indicated where Semira was standing quietly, not wishing to intrude.

'This is my companion Semira, Nanny.'

Freda nodded in approval.

'Both of you, come in, come in. It's not much, but it's comfortable.'

They had just sat down on the bench by the fireplace when the children erupted into the room, dragging their poor mother with them.

'Lianna, this is my Alinor, come back to see me.'

Lianna's eyes were wide with surprise. She dropped into a deep curtsey.

'Your Ladyship, we are greatly honoured,' she managed to say.

'Not at all. I have come to visit a very old family friend,' said Alinor, 'and to see how you are faring.'

Lianna didn't know quite how to respond. She was a pretty girl, with long soft brown hair tied back, wearing a scarf over her head. Her face reflected the hours she spent working outside in all weathers and her hands bore the marks of hard physical labour. She could do with carrying a bit more weight, thought Alinor, she's as thin as a rake.

They talked for a while about all sorts of things, Alinor wanting know all about their lives now. Unbidden a memory stirred of another young farming couple, Orian and Meri, who had suffered at the hands of outlaws. She hoped that they were doing well – they would have had their first child by now. Lianna couldn't afford to pay for a man to labour on the farm, relying only on what she could manage for herself.

'Are you getting your annuity from the palace?' Alinor asked Freda.

The old lady looked surprised.

'No,' she responded, 'no-one ever said anything about that. I had hoped there might be a little something when I left, but it never happened.'

'Well, that's going to change,' said Alinor briskly. 'You gave my family years of service, and you are entitled to help now.'

She had a little money with her and placed it on the table in front of an amazed Freda.

'When I get back I will sort this out. You will receive an amount every month, and I will ensure that you also get what you are owed since leaving.'

'Oh my girl, you don't know what this means to us,' Freda brushed away a tear.

'I think I do, and I am only sorry that you have had to suffer so long.'

Lianna hugged the children to her, her face full of love.

'Thank you, my Lady, thank you from the bottom of my heart.'

'I don't want thanks, Lianna, Freda. You have a chance now to make a better life for your family.'

The visiting party stayed only a few minutes longer before Alinor declared they needed to be getting back.

'I will come and see you again, don't worry,' she called out as they mounted up and prepared to leave. 'But if you need anything, let me know.'

'You take care of yourself, little Alinor,' called Freda as the party headed off.

'Don't worry about me, Nanny, I shall be all right.'

'What a lovely family,' said Semira, 'and what a shame she lost her husband. It must be so hard for her.'

'Yes, and it shouldn't have been,' replied Alinor. 'We always used to look after our old retainers, and that rat Vixlan has betrayed the trust they put in us. That's just one more thing he will end up regretting.'

Despite her deep annoyance at how Freda had been treated, Alinor felt pleased at having come out to see her. It made a pleasant change to get out without a whole retinue to accompany her and the two women conversed happily as they rode on in the afternoon sun. At one point the track skirted an expanse of forest, the deepening shadows discouraging anyone from following the paths into its depths. For a short distance there were huge trees on either side of their way, their branches stretching across to shut out much of the light.

'I used to enjoy climbing trees such as these magnificent specimens,' Alinor remarked to Semira, 'much to Nanny's dismay. She tried to impress on me that it was not a ladylike occupation!'

'Without success I assume?'

'Invariably,' laughed Alinor.

Without warning, Elkana baulked and jumped sideways.

Danger – was the clear thought in her horse's mind, realised Alinor, her eyes searching all around.

Above us – Alinor saw how Elkana was looking up into the dark leaves of a sturdy branch a little way in front.

The others had reacted somewhat slower than the sensitive mare and were unsure what to do. There was the faintest rustling sound followed by an enormous black shape hurtling out of the shadows to land merely a foot or two in front of Alinor.

Elkana backed rapidly as Alinor drew her sword, ready to leap down and defend herself and her horse from this apparition.

'Stay back,' she shouted at the others, her weapon blazing with unnatural fire.

The creature's dark orange eyes seemed to glow as it seemed to consider whether to take down this puny human. It was a huge cat, its rich coat black and mottled grey, its head quite large and its fangs intimidating; it simply radiated power. For a long moment it hesitated and stared at Alinor as if to say, I can kill you with ease if I so choose. With a great roar, the creature turned away, disappearing in seconds into the darkness of the forest.

'No, don't go after it,' Alinor called to the guards who were showing signs of doing just that. 'You'll never catch it, and it might just decide to attack you.'

'What on earth was it?' Semira had been quite frightened by the unexpected ambush but recovered herself quickly.

'I'm not really sure,' Alinor was thinking rapidly. 'It seemed to be like one of those big cats that are found way south – I've never seen a real one before, only drawings from travellers – but it was a lot bigger than I expected. They don't live in this part of the world at all, so I can't understand what it was doing here.'

'We've not heard of any big cats around,' said one of the guards, 'and I would have thought that people would soon be shouting if they saw something like that.'

'It could kill a cow or horse easily,' said another, clearly alarmed at the prospect.

'Once we get back make sure you get the word out for people to take great care, and to let us know if they see it,' Alinor instructed. Her mind was trying to interpret the aura of menace that the cat had radiated; it wasn't totally natural, she knew that. Was this Verun's doing? Was he trying to find a way to get at her? The cat had paid no attention at all to the others in her party, its sole focus had been her and she knew this would not be the last time that they would cross paths.

She laid a comforting hand on her horse's neck. Thank you Elkana, she thought at the mare, you probably saved my life. The horse tossed her head as if to say, what else would I do, and the group quickly moved on out from the trees and continued back to Thorgiliad.

By the time Alinor and her party had returned and she had put the wheels in motion for Freda to receive her monies it was getting late. She had intended to look in the library for some information about the big cat, but it went out of her mind as she dealt with a number of other queries waiting for her. She had that meeting about the Elite Guard due in the morning which she was actually looking forward to. Dhalen had been busy restoring order to Thorgiliad's troops and Alinor was feeling far more confident about security now that she had really started to erode Vixlan's stranglehold. She wanted to run a few ideas past her trusted commander with regard to other placements in the governmental scheme and knew there were few better judges of character and ability than the veteran warrior. This was a time when she missed being able to talk with Amiros; he had been a valuable mentor for so long it was not easy to take on this enormous challenge of rulership without his continued guidance. She could almost hear his voice telling her to stop waffling and get on with it as she was more than capable of succeeding her father. I just hope you are right, old friend, she sighed.

It had been another busy, not to say eventful day, but she slept deeply untroubled by any dreams and awoke feeling fresh and ready for whatever this day would bring. Semira made sure she ate a good breakfast, knowing how likely it would be that her mistress wouldn't remember to stop for a mid-day meal. Her own plans were to continue with her assessment of the palace staff so that the ideas she had already started to form could be finalised and discussed with Alinor. In the past few days she had been approached several times by those who were now seeking to join the palace staff and serve the new queen. That boded well, she thought, at least it means that we have some willing candidates; a couple were very promising and she intended that they should work closely with the most experienced – and more importantly reliable – of the staff with the idea of succeeding them in due course. This place needs new blood, Semira had decided, to inject a bit more enthusiasm and commitment, and I'm going to do my best to make sure that happens.

Dressed in her comfortable hunting clothes rather than a stylish gown – Alinor didn't mind being the elegant Lady but when she wanted to work she found the flowing skirts a bit of a hindrance – Alinor made her way down to the huge training courtyard beside the Guards' barracks. She could hear the clanging of the metal-workers and farriers in their workshops down the street to the south; there was a constant requirement for armour to be repaired and new equipment to be provided. According to Dhalen the standards had dropped alarmingly under the Steward's rule; this was partly because Vixlan didn't want the troops to be too effective and certainly didn't want to spend any more money that he had to, but also because the craftsmen had quietly agreed amongst themselves that they would not produce their best work for the upstart. Consequently, the fires now burned long and hot as the masters put their hearts into their skilled undertakings.

There was plenty of activity in the courtyard as Alinor slipped through the small door leading out from one of the large storage buildings. Dhalen wasn't in sight, but there were a number of officers directing messages here and there to their subordinates. Busy, but not disorganised, thought Alinor, just as it should be.

She crossed over to where the Commander had his office and walked in through the open door. Dhalen had just finished giving instructions to his acting second-in-command and stood to attention as her shadow filled the doorway.

'My Lady.' He saluted, as did the other man.

'Good morning Commander,' said Alinor, for the sake of formality. 'And Captain Herran, is it not?'

'Yes, my Lady.' The man was still a little in awe of this woman who had appeared out of nowhere at the Battle of Elagos and fought side by side with her troops to such devastating effect. Yes, he had exchanged a few words during the return journey, and seen her a number of times here at the palace, but as yet wasn't quite used to her company, unsure exactly how to behave with his sovereign.

'Well, gentlemen, we've got a lot to talk about, but I would like to talk to the men first, if that is convenient.'

'Of course,' said Dhalen and sent the Captain out to call order.

'How's he shaping up?' Alinor asked.

'A good man,' replied Dhalen. 'I've had my eye on him for quite a while, but since we lost Neril he's really stepped up. He's an excellent swordsman, a good all-rounder, and has a way with the other men.'

'Good enough to take over from you – in due course that is,' Alinor added quickly as Dhalen's face registered momentary shock.

'In time, yes. He needs a year or three at least.'

'Oh, don't worry old man, I'm not going to make you retire,' Alinor laughed at his discomfort. 'The Guard need you for a while yet, as do I, but you do also need someone whom you can rely on in your absence.'

'He fills that bill well, my Lady, and will be an outstanding Commander in time.'

'I doubt he would ever truly fill your shoes, old friend, but it's good that you think so highly of him. So, before we get down to talking, let's get out there so I can speak to them all.'

Alinor noticed that Dhalen still had a slight limp as they left the office – legacy of the serious wound received in the battle – and confronted the ranks of Elite Guard, the sovereign's personal troops, the embodiment of the highest quality of fighting men. They stood stiffly to attention, their boots polished, armour glinting in the sun, each man proud of the uniform he wore.

'At ease, gentlemen,' Alinor instructed, her voice pitched to reach all the ranks arrayed before her. 'I have called you here today for several reasons. The Elite Guard have always been the sovereign's own personal men. Your history has been one of outstanding service and loyalty and remains so to this day. I am aware that since the king died there has been a deal of uncertainty. That is over now. The Guard are back where they belong and under my authority. It is inevitable that over time there will be some changes, but I assure you that your existence and your role is not under any threat. My father was proud of his Guard, as am I. The murder of my father has not yet been avenged, but I swear before you all that I shall not allow the man who perpetrated that crime to go free. Somehow, somewhere, his day of reckoning will come and I reserve as my legitimate right the final execution of justice.'

There was a wave of murmured approval at her words.

'You will know by now that we, and other countries within the Alliance, are facing a threat of the highest magnitude, a threat such as has not been seen since the Battle of Zimlat. Be aware, I do not talk lightly. I know this from personal experience. Many of you were at Elagos and have seen just a small manifestation of the evil that is seeking to overthrow our peace. I do not yet know for certain if this evil can be destroyed, but I give you my oath that I and Prince Sirad of Pelenin, my betrothed, will be at the forefront of the fight against it. I, our country, and our friends across the land need all the support we can muster. I need my Elite Guard, all of you, to stand by your own oaths of loyalty to the crown, to defend and protect our precious homeland, and to fight of the right of freedom for all.'

To a man the Guards raised their fists and shouted, 'For Ancor, for the crown!'

Alinor let the noise die down before continuing.

'Thank you. My thanks to all of you. I knew my trust would not be misplaced. But now, we have work to do. It is essential that the Guard be fully restored to strength – I mourn with you those we lost at Elagos – but we have no time to waste. You have the reputation of being the best of fighting men, well, we are going to make sure that remains so and even the best may become better still. I have complete confidence in Senior Commander, Dhalen, and I am pleased to confirm Senior Captain Herran's appointment as Second-in-Command with the rank of Commander. There are promotions in line for a number of officers of which you will be advised shortly. All shortfalls in recent pay will be corrected.'

Alinor sensed a corporate sigh of relief at that last news – just another thing for which Vixlan had been responsible. If he had hoped to demoralise her Guards, he had failed miserably.

'Once again, I thank you for your loyalty. We have a great challenge before us, but I know that I can rely on your support. That is all.'

She turned to say a word to Dhalen, but was deafened by round of cheers from the assembled ranks. To a man they had been impressed by her sincerity and bolstered by her undoubted confidence in their support. The pride of the Elite Guard had been restored and they would follow her wherever she would lead them.

She followed Dhalen back into his office, to be joined a moment later by the newly promoted Commander Herran having dismissed the ranks.

'May I take this opportunity to express my sincere thanks, my Lady,' he started.

'No need, Commander. You have earned the rank and I will expect great things from you in the future. And, whilst we are in private, please do not stand on ceremony!'

Herran felt it would take a while to get used to Alinor's easy manner; he was over the moon at his unexpected promotion and couldn't hide the grin which lit up his boyish good looks. Above average height, he made an imposing figure, the light bringing up the glints in his dark hair, muscular build and almost perfect features completing the image of a picture-book warrior.

'Get used to it,' Dhalen advised, 'you'll find it brings a lot more work and responsibility to your life.'

'I know, sir, and I look forward to it. If I can be half as good as you, then I know I shall be all right!'

'Ok, cut the flattery, Herran,' growled Dhalen, not at all displeased. 'We have a meeting to attend tomorrow,' he looked at Alinor who nodded, 'and I believe that we need to decide who else should be there.'

'I want to ensure that we have good representation on our military defence side,' said Alinor. She went over to make sure that the door to the office was firmly shut.

'I may be the sovereign now, but I want to put in place a reliable and realistic system of government. I am not my father, and I do not have all his years of experience. I rely heavily on the advice and support of good councillors in whose hands I can safely leave the day to day running of this country. The challenge we face will mean that there will be periods when I shall be absent, possibly for long periods of time.'

Dhalen opened his mouth to make some kind of objection but was silenced by a gesture from Alinor.

'No Dhalen, my absences will be necessary I assure you and it will likely not be possible for you or any of the Guard to accompany me. The matter will not be open for discussion.'

The veteran warrior snorted quietly and shook his head, knowing there was nothing he could do.

'It is essential that such a situation that we have experienced with Vixlan can never happen again. No one person will be able to control matters either here at the palace or across the country.'

The two men nodded their agreement.

'I will be discussing personnel with Herran later today,' said Dhalen, sitting at his desk to take the weight off his lame leg. 'We'll come up with some suitable candidates and prepare them for tomorrow's meeting.'

'I know I can leave matters in your capable hands. Commanders,' Alinor nodded at them both, turned and left them to start planning.

Chapter 10

The breeze was fresh and the waters slightly choppy as the boat forged on two days out from the shelter of the village harbour. Sirad leaned against the timbers near the bow and gazed out towards the horizon, hazy grey-blue in the distance. Seabirds occasionally passed overhead, gliding effortlessly over the miles of water; there had been dolphins accompanying the vessel for several hours earlier that day and Sirad had been totally absorbed watching their acrobatics as they leapt above the waves and cavorted beside and in front of the bows as if in play. He had heard about these wonderful creatures, but this was the first time he had ever seen them and was amazed to find that the stories he had heard appeared to be quite true. He looked up at the lateen sails, tautly filled with wind and watched as members of the crew moved easily around the craft as she pitched occasionally, sure-footed and confident in their chosen element, carrying out their many tasks efficiently and quickly.

It may take them three or four days to reach Mitos, so Garel'en had told Sirad, depending on wind and weather, but they shouldn't have a difficult trip. The little caravel-type craft was very manoeuvrable, necessary because they needed to get close into the shore of the island to be able to moor safely. Garel'en had been to Mitos on several occasions bringing supplies for the small number of residents there, trading for the smoked fish that the islanders specialised in and which was very popular back on the mainland.

Sirad and Ben had reached the coast some four days earlier; enquiries about how Sirad could get to Mitos had led to meeting up with Garel'en, a former compatriot of Fra'ilen. The Riders had been sampling the brew at a small hostelry on the edge of the harbour when the tall figure of the captain had approached them, taking a seat at their table.

'I take it you are not here in an official capacity, my Lord,' the seaman asked, his voice gravelly and low.

If Ben was surprised that they had been recognised, it did not show. Sirad looked closely at the leathery features of the man, his skin tanned dark from the wind and sun, his deep-set eyes seeing everything around him.

'We have met before, I think,' he said, 'but I regret that I do not recall either your name or where it was.'

'No matter,' responded the captain, 'it was a while ago and the meeting was brief enough. But I remember what my former captain Fra'ilen had to say about you – and yes,' he smiled, 'it was quite complimentary, for him that is.'

Sirad laughed, imagining what the big man had said. Ben echoed the laughter, recalling that Sirad himself had once described Fra'ilen as a 'dipsomaniac pirate'.

'I understand you are looking to get to Mitos,' Garel'en continued. 'I reckon I can help you there. I have a good little boat that I use whenever I have to go there; conditions are reasonable at the moment, though this time of year the weather can be pretty changeable. Not the easiest place to get into, but I know the waters so there shouldn't be a problem.'

'Thank you, captain - ?'

'Garel'en's the name, my lord.'

'Thank you Garel'en, your assistance is much appreciated. But please, as you said, my visit is not official and I would appreciate it if you would ignore my rank for the duration.'

'Fine by me,' responded the seaman. 'You're wanting to find Eldren, I gather?'

'I am,' Sirad nodded. 'Do you know him yourself?'

'Not really. I've seen him a couple of times, but he lives a pretty isolated sort of life as far as I know, but having said that, he does get a number of visitors over the course of the year. May I ask why you are looking for him in particular?'

Sirad hesitated for a moment.

'Let's just say he may be able to assist a friend of mine who is unable to come himself, so I have come in his stead.'

'Then it must be fairly serious,' the captain rubbed his chin with a calloused finger, 'to bring you here for one of the

Brotherhood. Yes, I am aware of who Eldren is, though not many of them round here are. As I said, he keeps himself to himself, but he is well thought of as a healer and takes care of those who live on the island.'

'I would be glad of your help, and for your silence too.'

The captain shrugged.

'No need to speak further of it,' he said. 'I take it you want to leave as soon as possible? It's a four or five day trip, all being well.'

Sirad nodded.

'We can go on tomorrow morning's tide. Come down to the harbour – you'll see my boat, Seahawk, near the largest warehouse. Don't be late.'

This last was said with a grin as the captain rose from the table.

'I won't,' confirmed Sirad as he too rose and shook the captain's hand.

'A bit of luck, that,' commented Ben as the pair now walked along the front looking for all the world as if they were merchants discussing their business.

'Yes, I was afraid it would take a bit longer to find a passage.'

'Well, that'll give me nearly a couple of weeks to pursue enquiries in the direction of Mekad.'

'Just be very careful, Ben – oh I know you are more than capable, but you've seen some of what Verun can do, and there's no shortage of bandit robbers roaming about. You'll be vulnerable on your own.'

'Trust me, my brother, I won't be doing anything stupid. I'm too fond of my skin to take unnecessary risks!'

By the fourth day the weather had turned overcast, the wind was fretful, gusting fiercely every now and then causing the sails to snap and billow, keeping the crew busy. Garel'en could be heard occasionally cursing as the boat pitched and yawed in the uncertain waters.

'I did warn you the weather could be fickle,' he growled at Sirad, 'but we could do without it turning any worse.'

'Can we run before it?' asked Sirad.

'Maybe, but it's not certain which way it's going at the moment. It'll be a rough night I think.'

He wasn't wrong, and Sirad found sleeping difficult as the wind starting whining through the rigging and the waves played with the little craft. But she was well built and well crewed and sailed gamely on through the worst of it.

By morning it had eased a bit, though the skies were leaden and rain blew in at intervals.

'With a bit of luck we'll still be able to get into shelter by tomorrow night,' the captain answered Sirad's queries. 'Not the easiest approach as the water is none too deep with a lot of rocks just below the surface. But we've done it enough times before, it shouldn't be too bad.'

I certainly hope you're right, was Sirad's thought. His sailing experience was limited and he had nothing but admiration for the men who took to the seas in all conditions, braving such a challenging and frequently dangerous environment.

Sure enough it took all their skill to bring the boat into the comparative calm of the narrow bay as night was falling the next day. Sails were rigged quickly and everything secured before all aboard could breathe a sigh of relief at their safe arrival.

'Will your business here be done in a couple of days?' asked Garel'en. 'I'd like to think we could get away again three days' hence.'

'I hope so,' responded Sirad, 'and I'm hoping too that Eldren will agree to come back with me.'

The captain looked a bit surprised at that but said nothing.

'I'll go ashore first thing,' continued Sirad, 'I don't want to waste what time I have available.'

After a somewhat calmer night, Sirad was rowed ashore by a couple of the crew in the early light. Already there were fishermen out tending their nets and fishing gear and Sirad approached the nearest to enquire about Eldren's whereabouts. He would have several hours of walking, it seemed, to reach where this somewhat reclusive member of the Brotherhood lived. Keen to pursue his objective Sirad set out immediately upon the track leading up from the waterside. It was a steep climb up to the top of the cliffs and he paused momentarily to get his breath back, taking in the view of the small town nestling way below him by the water's edge. The wind up here on the tops was brisk and he pushed on following the track inland to more sheltered ground. It was reasonably easy going as the track avoided the higher rocky parts; there were more trees away from the coast and some good grazing for the cattle, sheep and goats. He passed the time of day with the quiet folk he met en route, confirming that he was still on the right path to find Eldren.

I just hope that he will be able to help Amiros, Sirad was thinking. I'm sure Remon wouldn't have mentioned him unless there was a good chance. It will also be interesting to hear what this man has to say about Amiros and the Brotherhood, we know so little of the background.

Sirad stopped for a quick drink from the water bubbling over the rocks of a narrow stream. As he rested a moment he became aware of Alinor's thoughts faintly reaching out to him. He didn't really want to tell her about this venture to find Eldren just yet or get her hopes up, she had more than enough to deal with in Thorgiliad. One of the benefits of his previous visit to the Mind-master's house had been an increased ability to control their mind-sharing so that Alinor would not be aware of his surroundings – he didn't like to keep things from her, but felt it best in the circumstances that he did not completely disclose what he was up to.

How's it going? he asked her. More to the point, how are you feeling?

It's not easy, she responded, but I never thought it would be. I think I am making progress at last but – and he could feel her anger – I am absolutely fuming about what Vixlan has been doing. He has caused so much hurt and damage in my kingdom.

Sirad was actually pleased to hear her talk of 'her' kingdom. She seemed to have moved on now from thinking in terms of it being her father's kingdom and was taking the responsibility on board. It was a huge burden to carry, he knew that, but he knew too that she would learn quickly. She was strong, determined and brave; she would make a good queen for Ancor, he knew that, and however much he wished he could have been with her, it was right that she faced that challenge alone.

His time will come, Sirad reassured her, I know you'll see to that.

Indeed I will. But Sirad, you seem sort of far away. What are you doing?

Pretty busy, I told you we were doing a bit of exploring down south. Nothing too bad as yet, but we have to keep on our toes. Ben's just gone to look at something for me and I want to catch him up. I miss you, my darling and I worry about you.

I miss you too, of course, but I worry about you as well. Is there are news about Verun yet?

No, not yet, but I will let you know. I'm sorry, there are people coming and I have to go – Sirad was doing an excellent job of bluffing and for once Alinor was none the wiser.

Take care my love; the warmth of her thoughts filled Sirad with an almost painful longing.

I will, he responded, and you take care also.

Their connection broken, Sirad allowed himself a moment or two filled with images of his beautiful lady. But time was of the essence, and he strode on towards where he had been told he would find Eldren.

An hour later he crested a small hill; not far on was a small, low cottage that set comfortably into the surrounding countryside. There were a couple of small barn-type constructions off to one side and several areas of carefully tended garden surrounding three sides of the property. A flowering vine clambered up the cottage walls filling much of the spaces between the open door and windows; the gardens were crammed with every shade of green, with splashes of colour here and there. Every now and then he could see a little bit of smoke issuing from the chimney which leaned very slightly to one side at one end of the roof.

Relieved to know that at least someone was at home, Sirad crossed the small meadow and walked up the pathway between what were obviously herb gardens, judging from the mixture of aromas emanating from the lush growth.

As he approached the door a deep voice called out,

'Come in young man, come in.'

Reminding himself that this was the home of one of the Brotherhood, and thus anything was likely, Sirad ducked slightly to avoid the low lintel and entered the cottage. His first impression was of gleaming rows of bottles and jars filled with goodness knows what, glinting in the light from the long fireplace, above which a selection of cauldrons were suspended, bubbling or steaming gently giving forth an extraordinary concoction of smells. Bunches of leaves hung drying from every beam and the main part of the room was taken up with an enormous table laden with all the paraphernalia of the accomplished herbalist.

'You'll excuse me that I keep on working for the moment, I need to finish this mixture now – it's nearly ready.'

The rich voice came not from some big tall body as Sirad's mind had expected but from a short, plump little cherub of a man, his happy round face beaming a welcome for his unannounced visitor.

'Er, not at all,' was the young lord's response, slightly bemused by the unexpected situation.

Eldren busied himself mixing various crushed leaves taken from a row of bowls on the table and adding them to the bubbling cauldron over the fire. Using a long-handled ladle he stirred the aromatic brew, quietly muttering to himself as he concentrated on his art. After a few minutes he removed the cauldron and set it to one side.

Wiping his hands the russet coloured apron stretched across his front the little man turned to face his visitor for the first time.

'You look like your father,' he said, 'how is he these days?'

'He's . . . to be honest, he is not as well as he might be.'

Slightly nonplussed as he was by Eldren's directness, Sirad found it easy to respond to the unlikely magician. He had not thought that Eldren might know his father, but then, no reason that he should not; after all, he and Amiros were comrades. When he thought about it, what did he himself know of the past? There were many people his father knew, long before he'd been born, and despite their closeness, he was aware that there was still much his father had not told him, so maybe Amiros was not the only member of the Brotherhood who had either visited Pelamir, or had met with Sothan at some other place.

'Do you know what is wrong?' Eldren sounded genuinely concerned.

'Age has something to do with it, but is not the main problem. I believe he is suffering from some kind of illness, but our Healers have so far been unable to do more than alleviate the pain.'

'But that is not why you have come today, is it? Although I do not doubt that you would come if you had thought that I may help your father, he is not the reason now. I am aware of Remon's passing,' the little man's face registered a deep grief for his former teacher. 'We all knew that it would come in due course, but it was still a source of great sadness for us. There has never been such a mind as his since the time of Rakep-thos. But now he is gone.'

He shook his head and sat down on a stool by the fire, indicating to Sirad that he should take a chair opposite.

After a pause he looked up at Sirad, the deep-set eyes looking right into him, so Sirad felt.

'Could it be that it is to do with my fellow brother Amiros? We used to be quite close at one time but have not met for quite a number of years now. No-one amongst us has been able to locate him, which is very puzzling. Doreus, one of the brothers, says that a story has reached him that the body of Amiros had been brought back from Elagos to Pelamir, but we would know if he were dead, so how can that be true?'

'It is and it isn't,' Sirad started to explain as the little herbalist registered confusion. 'I don't know if you are aware that Verun has returned?'

'I heard rumours.'

'Well, they are true, but the only thing that interests Verun is power. It was because of his presence that Remon passed so soon, before Verun had chance to take him, and believe me Verun has serious power now. He has in his possession the stone Mnethar.'

Eldren drew in a sharp breath.

'That cannot be,' he exclaimed, clearly upset. 'Mnethar was hidden and then lost. How on earth could Verun have found it, let alone taken it for himself. The danger, the risk, was enormous!'

'Well, he did and has. What's more he has used it against Amiros with devastating effect. He then made sure that Amiros, or what's left of him, was returned to us.'

Eldren bowed his head, overtaken by emotion, his thoughts a positive turmoil as his own knowledge fuelled understanding of what power the awful stone possessed.

Sirad remained silent whilst the magician mastered himself and was ready to continue.

'Tell me what happened, as much as you know, from the beginning,' he prompted.

The young man started with the death of Teleston and Alinor's quest to reach Remon; how she had parted company with Amiros who had gone in search of information about Verun's whereabouts and plans; how days before they were aiming to relieve the city of Elagos Amiros' tortured body had been brought to their camp by the dwarf Czaten; how he, Sirad, and Alinor had done their best to heal the bodily wounds but were unable to reach his ravaged mind. Eldren listened intently as he told how they had carried him to Remon's house hoping that the crystal there would somehow bring their beloved Lore-Master back, to no avail.

Eldren frowned, chewed his lip and shook his head a couple of times.

'You say that his physical body is mending?'

Sirad nodded.

'But he is not conscious at all?'

Sirad nodded again.

'It's really strange though,' the young man said, 'because although he shows no signs of being awake, it is possible to get him to take liquids without choking. Even without proper food, there is no sign of his body fading, it's just that his mind is nowhere we can reach.'

Eldren got up and paced the limited space round the table. Once or twice he looked hard at Sirad, who became aware of some kind of power within the little man; nothing overt, but just tingling at the edge of his own mind.

'It has come,' he said finally. 'You and she have come into your inheritance. How else would Amiros have survived? But even your minds have been unable to reach where Amiros has gone.'

He nodded, ran a hand through his hair, obviously once dark but now liberally streaked with silver.

'What do you mean, where he has gone?' Sirad was puzzled.

'Not easy to explain, young man,' said the magician. 'There is an existence between life and death, so we are taught, where a soul may travel if caught before it's expected time. It would seem that the destructive power of Mnethar has been used by Verun to banish Amiros to this existence.'

'But can we get him back?' Sirad was almost afraid to ask lest the answer was negative.

'That I do not know for certain,' was the response. 'It is said that unless the soul wishes to return to this life, it may remain trapped there for ever, or until the body finally dies.'

'But that is – ' Sirad couldn't find the right words to express his horror.

'I know, I know. It is terrible to contemplate. As I see it, someone, somehow, has to attempt to reach him to try and persuade him to return. And even then, after what he has been through, there is no guarantee that he will wish to.'

The fire crackled and sparked as a log shifted.

The two men were silent for several long minutes.

'Are there others in the Brotherhood who may be able to help us?' Sirad asked quietly.

'I doubt it,' Eldren was thoughtful. 'You should know that we have been scattered for many years since our time studying with the great seer. Remon told us that it would not be his task to bring on any more disciples; that would be for the one who succeeded him as the next Mind-Master. There was plenty of time, so we all thought, and simply got on with our own lives, developing the skills that best suited us. There was never much need for any discussion about who would take on Remon's mantle. But now, with Amiros in such dire straits, the situation has become critical. We will have to at least try to bring him back.'

'Can we not approach whoever was closest to Remon?' asked Sirad anxiously.

'Ah, I see I was not clear. It was Amiros who was always closest. We all understood that in time, once Alinor and yourself came into your inheritances, Amiros would be released from the obligations that had bound him and would finally come into his own.'

'You mean that Amiros would become the Mind-Master, as Remon had been?' Sirad's voice was unsteady.

'Not quite the same, as Amiros is not a full Ben-Neteru as Remon was, or like you and Alinor. Yes, I have detected it in you – I also knew your mothers and what was likely to happen. I know they gave their lives in order to endow you with your powers.'

The young man didn't know what to think, how to feel. This was all just so strange, and Eldren's prognosis wasn't exactly encouraging.

'I believe that I shall have to see if I can find Mirantha. She may be able to help us, but I don't know quite where she's got to recently. Her last correspondence was a bit vague.'

Eldren bustled about, apparently searching for some kind of missive.

'Who is Mirantha?'

'One of you,' replied the magician. 'She's full Ben-Neteru. I learned much of my healing skills from her many years back – a very clever woman. Not much more than a girl still I should say – she's quite young in Ben-Neteru years. Oh,' he caught the expression on Sirad's face, 'you weren't expecting to find others were you? Well, you're not completely alone you know!'

'No, actually, I wasn't really, though I hoped there might be some others. I know it worried Alinor a lot when she first found out about herself – it frightened her.' He didn't mention his own discomfort as well.

'No surprise, that. It is a heavy burden to bear, especially when it has come as such an unexpected development – for both of you.'

Eldren stopped his searching and instead poured out a cup of dark liquid from a large bottle up on a high shelf to the left of the fireplace.

'I have neglected simple courtesy, young man. Here,' he handed the cup to Sirad, 'drink this; it will help restore you in mind and body.'

It smelled like autumn fruits and tasted just as good, with just a hint of something else that Sirad couldn't identify. He could feel a calmness flowing into him after the revelations of their conversation.

'A bit like the effect of *kalantas*,' he said. 'That's always been good as a restorative.'

'Just so,' nodded Eldren. 'I always did like that recipe.'

'You didn't . . ?'

'No, no, it was around before my time; I just used it as the basis for developing similar potions.'

It was getting late now and Eldren set about making a meal for them both, an appetising stew using meat supplied by one of his patients with assorted vegetables grown in his own garden.

The pair talked on as darkness fell.

'Get some sleep now,' said Eldren finally. 'I'll need to set things straight here before I can leave, and we ought to be away by mid-day if we are to reach the town at a sensible hour.'

He showed Sirad to a comfortable bunk. After all this, thought Sirad, I'll be lucky to get any sleep at all tonight. He was fast asleep within two minutes and never stirred until well after dawn.

There was no sign of his host when Sirad awoke feeling refreshed after his deep relaxed sleep. For a few minutes he simply sat on the edge of the bed, thinking over their conversation of the previous day. He had learned more about the esoteric nature of the Brotherhood and how Verun had been an unsettling member of their number before Remon had been obliged to dismiss him. At one time there had been ten other students studying with the Mind-Master, their skills diverse, but Eldren would not elaborate as to exactly what they were. It seemed that Amiros was the most senior amongst them and had been particularly close to the ancient seer. As far as the other Brothers were concerned, it was a foregone conclusion that Amiros would be the one to succeed to their leadership and they were a little surprised when he disappeared before the end of their allotted time with Remon. Over the years that followed, Amiros would appear unexpectedly and meet up with some of them, but never stopped in one place very long. Eldren recalled that he would occasionally mention spending time in Ancor and Pelenin, which he seemed to enjoy, but that he had travelled to other places of which Eldren had never even heard. This had Sirad wondering about his old tutor; Amiros was obviously a talented mage, a highly respected Lore-Master, but neither Alinor nor he had ever thought him to be much more than that. Glimpses of a greater knowledge and power in recent months had come as a surprise, but taking into consideration what Eldren had now told him Amiros was indeed a far greater force to be reckoned with. He could appreciate why the little herbalist had been galvanised into action at the thought that Amiros had possibly been lost to them.

A cheerful humming heralded the return of Eldren.

'You slept well, I trust,' he said, not waiting for a response. 'Help yourself to some food there,' he pointed to a table and cupboard, 'small beer is in the cask by the door.'

He bustled about clearing jars from the table and stacking them tidily on the many shelves before straining out the contents of two of the cauldrons into various containers, labelling them neatly. He emptied the liquor from the third cauldron into a huge flagon and placed it carefully in one corner. He disappeared into a small store-room and returned with two packs, one quite large, into which he started to put an assortment of potions.

'I'll leave these in town for my patients to collect while I'm gone,' he told Sirad. 'It should be enough to tide them over for a while.'

In the smaller of the packs he put some spare clothes, two or three small books and other miscellaneous items for the journey. He spent several minutes going round all the shelves checking for anything else he thought he may need and added a couple more objects.

'Once we get over to the mainland I should be able to meet up with Mirantha and we'll make our own way to Pelenin. I'm just waiting for Hadmar to arrive to get a message to her; shouldn't be long now.'

Sirad cleared away the breakfast items and tidied away the blankets from his bed, pleased that Eldren had already decided to return with him without being asked. He had just finished when Eldren looked up, listening for something.

'Ah, that should be Hadmar,' and he hurried outside.

Sirad followed, curious to see who it was that would convey a message to the mysterious Mirantha, who certainly did not reside on the island.

The two men stood outside in the morning sunshine, Sirad watching the track but Eldren looking up at the sky. Sirad followed the man's gaze and spied a dark shape heading towards them. As it neared he could make out a huge bird, a bit like an eagle only with finer, curving wings and not such a heavy body. A piercing whistle announced its arrival as it dropped rapidly to land on a wooden post close to where they stood.

It was a beautiful creature, the colour of its feathers ranging from brown-black to russet red, with wingtips of cream and gold and bars on its tail. The eyes were huge round orbs, gold with dark green pupils; the bird surveyed them both, not recognising the magician's companion but returning to focus on Eldren.

'Thank you for coming so quickly,' the little man said, 'I am in need of your help. Please, take this message,' he pulled a small capsule from one of his pockets and attached it to the bird's scaly leg. 'Deliver it to Mirantha as soon as you can – it is important.'

The bird looked down at the capsule and then back at Eldren, blinked once, and then spread its enormous wings and took to the air, climbing rapidly until it disappeared from sight heading northwards.

'What a magnificent creature,' exclaimed Sirad, 'I've never seen one like it.'

'They are rare indeed,' Eldren's deep voice answered the curiosity of his companion. 'Not many left now; they keep themselves to themselves, avoiding the predations of men. They have long served the Brotherhood as messengers for those of us who have less skill at long distance mind communications.'

So it's not just us, thought Sirad, who have the ability to communicate in thought, but if I understand correctly now it is only some of the Brotherhood who can do it.

'Well now, it's just a case of finally damping down the fire before we go,' Eldren turned to Sirad who indicated that he would do that job. They took up their packs and with a final glance round set off to return to the town. Once there, Eldren left his medicaments with the elderly landlord at the tiny tavern on the harbourside with instructions to pass the word around that he would be away for some time, he didn't know how long, but they could collect their supply from the tavern instead.

The two purchased some bread and ale and went outside to sit on the harbour wall. About half an hour later two of Garel'en's crew strolled up to join them.

'We were in town by chance, so we can take you back to the boat with us,' they said. 'The Captain will be pleased; he doesn't want to risk the weather changing and stopping us from getting away.'

'Quite right,' said Eldren, 'we could have an interesting return trip.'

The two crewmen hadn't met the little herbalist before and had been apprehensive at the thought of carrying a real magician on their boat. The sight of this chubby little man and his round friendly face put them more at their ease, though his comment made them think that he knew more than most land-lubbers about the vagaries of the sea.

'There's a good moon tonight,' Garel'en greeted his passengers, 'and the tide will be right for us to leave very early. My bones tell me there's bad weather heading this way so we need to make as much speed as possible on our return.'

Their packs stowed safely away, the two joined some of the crew in getting a few hours rest before sails were hoist and they slipped out from the shelter of the bay into a freshening wind. A few clouds scudded across the night sky, but as Garel'en had said, the moon was bright and gave them enough to see their way safely past the rocks on the high water.

True enough, over the next day the winds increased and the waves repeatedly carried the little boat up only to crash it down into the troughs in between, but she was a sturdy craft with an experienced crew and though it was distinctly uncomfortable, they still made good progress running before the worst of the weather. Sirad had not experienced rough sailing like this before, and whilst not actually sea-sick, was really looking forward to getting back to solid ground and drying out. The relentless spray weighed him down, and he felt pretty useless as the crew fought to keep the sails under control, not daring to put on too much lest they risk being overwhelmed.

The following day got worse and the captain was swearing about the distance they were being blown off course; nothing he could do about it without risking life and limb, they simply had to take what the weather gave them and hold firm.

It was somewhere around mid-day, though with no sun visible it was hard to be sure, and Sirad saw Eldren up at the bows, legs braced for balance and concentrating on holding fast to the rail. His eyes were closed and Sirad could sense an aura around him as the magician was drawing on some kind of power and directing it at the ominous clouds above them. Sirad focussed his mind on the little man and attempted to support him in a similar way to that he used with Alinor. He didn't know whether he was helping or not, but he did recognise that the storm was not entirely natural which was why Eldren was fighting it.

After what seemed an eternity Sirad felt Eldren draw back; though still very rough, the wind was not gusting so strongly and it was a little easier to keep upright on the heaving deck. Eldren made his way back to where Sirad was holding tightly to one of the stays.

'Thank you for your support, young man. I've not had to work that hard for a long time.'

'It wasn't natural, was it?'

'No, it wasn't. There is something out there that is not keen on whatever you are up to, and your presence was enough to stir it up.'

'Verun?'

'Maybe, but it wasn't that clear. It could be him or something else entirely, set like a trap.'

'Are we safe now?' Sirad was concerned that his presence had put others in danger.

'For now, certainly,' Eldren nodded. 'Yes, it will take us a little longer to get back because of the miles lost, but we should make safe harbour this time.'

'Thank you, Eldren, for myself and for the sake of this good crew. It is not their battle, though I unwittingly have put them in danger.'

'Nothing you can do about that, young man. You and that young lady are a very big threat to Verun and you would be wise to expect other traps along the way. But now, I could do with a drink and a rest.'

The two made their way down into the shelter of the little cabin below decks. Gradually over the next twenty-four hours the weather eased, to everyone's relief, and with a will the crew cleaned up and resumed their usual duties, bringing the craft safely back to her home port three days later.

Chapter 11

After another pleasant morning meandering in the delightful gardens Elos the traveller made his way back into the shade of the colonnaded corridors of the house. He had no particular activities in mind so simply wandered slowly along, admiring the statuary and designs inlaid along floor and walls as he had done on many days before. Every now and then other corridors led off to right or left; some he followed, others he just ignored as the fancy took him. This place seems endless, he thought, and still I see things I have not seen before today.

There were rooms opening off these corridors, their doors sometimes open, sometimes closed. A narrow door caught his eye for some reason; maybe it was the richness of the red woodwork, or the tiny gilded designs like musical notes that seemed to flow down its length. Curious, he grasped the handle and opened it; inside it was dim, curtains drawn against the bright sunshine in order to protect the beautiful array of musical instruments within. His attention fell immediately upon a small harp lying on a deep blue silken cushion; it was the kind of instrument a travelling bard would carry and he couldn't help but stretch his fingers out to touch it gently.

It seemed a familiar item, but from where in his past he couldn't immediately say. An urge prompted him to take it up from where it lay and to run his slender fingertips across the strings. The wonderful glissando filled the air around him; without hesitation he sat and balanced the exquisite instrument on his lap and started to play. Each note he drew from the strings filled his soul with an involuntary longing, but what for? The delicate harmonies surrounded him, lifting him up and somehow away from where his physical body remained. There was brightness everywhere, wonderful warmth and lights of every hue. He thought he could hear voices, very distant, he couldn't make out what they were saying or perhaps singing. As he strained to try and hear more, there came one voice clearer than all the rest: Where are you?

He was certain that it was meant for him. Someone was asking him a question, but he had no answer he could give. He didn't know where he was, if it was real, if it was something in the music he played. Then it was gone, the voices, the light; he was back in the dim room with the little harp.

It is not like my harp, he thought. But I don't have a harp, he corrected himself. He frowned, desperately seeking a memory that was at the bare edges of his mind. I did have a harp, he decided as a faint picture appeared in his thoughts; it was a lovely instrument and so very old. I remember telling that boy to be careful with it. What boy? Was it even a boy?

Surprised and confused, Elos stood and replaced the harp on its cushion.

Where am I? And what is this place? He knew that something had changed deep inside himself. It is not right, he thought, this place, this house, the gardens and all the perfection. It is unnatural, not at all right, I should not be here. But where am I supposed to be, well, that is another matter completely. I don't know. Surely I am the master of my own life? I seem to have forgotten how to be myself, whoever that may be, or even what I really am.

He looked around the room, taking in the classical artistry of it. He drove his mind to try and grasp at what he now believed his essential self to be. As he stood there, he thought that his vision was playing tricks as the room seemed to flicker; the paintings on the walls blurred and disappeared, leaving a broken stone façade in their place. But then it was all as it was before; a delusion perhaps, but which part of it was real?

The hint of a pain over his eyes interrupted his musings; why does this happen when I am close to thinking about who I am, he wondered. This is not too much sun or too much reading; there is something or someone who would rather I just stayed here and accepted this too perfect existence. He could stop the pain now, he found; it took effort but it could be done. If I can do that, what else can I do?

The voice he had heard echoed in his mind: Where are you?

I don't know, he answered it, but I do know this is not the right place for me. I need to leave and go wherever this strange fate leads me.

Leaving the room he retraced his steps back to where he once again recognised where he was in the house. Without returning to his rooms, he made his way outside and up the road towards where he knew the entrance gates had been. Although he had only passed that way the once, he was confident that he could find them again. After about twenty minutes of walking he caught sight of them in the distance and increased his pace slightly, anxious now to escape his illusory prison. As he got nearer he could see the young man who had been his guide on arrival waiting to intercept him.

'A lovely day, Elos,' he greeted the traveller, 'are you going far?'

His question may have been innocuous, but his voice held a hint of compunction, silently urging the traveller to forget his purpose.

'I would thank you for your hospitality,' replied Elos, 'but it is time for me to move on.'

'I am sure that His Eminence would be most upset if you left without saying good-bye.'

'Perhaps he would, but you will have to tell him yourself,' said Elos, his voice stronger than before, the unthinking compliance totally absent.

'But I really do think . . .'

Elos cut him off.

'No, I don't think you do at all,' he shook his head. 'I think you should leave me now.'

Elos turned on his heel and walked a few steps further. There was a strange sound behind him and he looked over his shoulder. There was no sign of the guide at all.

He strode rapidly on. The gates loomed large, and firmly shut. Undaunted Elos reached out and pushed against them. For a moment they resisted his touch, but in a heartbeat they simply disintegrated in a shower of light. The gateposts were gone, but so was everything else. Where once had been the enormous house and gardens there were simply rolling acres of grass and trees. Only the track remained, leading up and over the hill, quietly inviting the traveller to resume his search.

Elos, or whoever he was, felt that a weight had been lifted from his mind. I still don't know who or where I am, he thought, but I believe those questions will be answered. The old man I met said I should go to E'shariya, wherever that is, so that is what I shall do.

He lost count of the days he continued on his quest to try and reach E'shariya. It didn't matter, he was taken up with exploring his mind and finding out what he could do. He remembered the little dragonfly that he had conjured that day he had found the carvings on the rocks. If I did it once, I should be able to do it again, he reasoned. So he considered how his mind could be directed and visualised the fragile insect. No sooner than the thought had been framed the glittering dragonfly appeared in front of him, darting to and fro. Then a second and a third. He wondered about a fourth, but his control failed him and they all disappeared. Undaunted, he repeated the exercise several times then, and over the days that followed, creating various creatures and objects as he explored his skill.

Little flashes of memory started to stir giving him tantalising glimpses of what he knew had been another life. Faces, voices, places that were both strange and familiar, all filtered into his head. Whilst some of the memories were pleasant, he sensed there had been pain too, and he could not prevent himself from wishing to avoid those. Maybe it wasn't worth remembering too much, he thought, and spent a while considering whether to stop bothering trying to recall anything at all. But his mind would not leave it be and each day brought some reminder of what had been.

He awoke one morning to cloudy skies for the first time, and the temperature had dropped from the pleasant norm he had been experiencing. Until now, his journey had been enjoyable even outside of the strange paradise he had been caught up in, but things were changing. This dream he was living in was taking on another aspect, a little less comfortable, a little less friendly perhaps.

More real. It struck him suddenly; it was more like something that felt familiar, something from before? But before what? Have I been here before, or is this some kind of reflection? I don't understand.

All that day he continued with what now seemed to be an interminable journey. He slept fitfully that night in the shelter of a huge rock outcrop; no longer were there the mysterious lodgings that had miraculously appeared – and disappeared – to provide for his needs. I have done this before, he thought, many times in many places. As momentary pictures flashed into his mind, he could feel the cold and dampness, a weariness in his very bones. Then it was gone again.

Another day, and another after that. Will I ever reach my goal, he wondered; the journey was beginning to tire him as he climbed high into the hills only to drop steeply back down into wooded valleys. The forest trees showered him with raindrops, the cold seeping into his clothes. When he could go no further he sought out what shelter he could find, collecting some branches which he could push into the ground and create some protection from the gentle but cold breeze.

As if out of long habit he gathered wood to make a fire but then for a moment was perplexed by what he had done – how did he propose to light it? As you usually do, some voice inside his head prompted. And so he did, raising his hand and directing a flame into the heart of the sticks in front of him. The light from the flames suddenly flared and he put his hand up to shield his eyes from the pain that seared them. It only lasted a moment, but he felt frightened and it was several minutes before his heart stopped its frantic pounding in his chest and his breathing returned to its usual pattern. The memory was almost tangible now; burning light and excruciating pain followed by a darkness unlike any other. There had been a stone, a gem that radiated power and light, coruscating flashes that carried pain and destruction, the source of his banishment from the life he had known.

Mnethar, he breathed. The Stone of Power. It had been found and, against all the laws that bound mage and man alike, it had been used against him.

He dropped his head, breathing deeply as he faced the truth of his situation. Although there was much he could still not recall, he knew without doubt what had taken place that fateful day when he had faced Verun and been sentenced to an eternal punishment.

For a long time he could think of nothing more, almost drowning in waves of pain and despair, unable to cry out and barely able to breathe. Gradually the worst of it started to diminish; oddly enough he thought he heard faint music, as if from the strings of a harp.

'I am Amiros', he said aloud. 'I know who and what I am. You have not destroyed me, even though you have taken the life I knew.'

Taken by surprise by the extraordinary revelations he was totally exhausted by the trauma he had experienced. His whole body felt weak; collapsing onto the leaf strewn ground he fell into a deep sleep.

Far away, in another world, a young woman stood at a window in the palace of Thorgiliad and prayed for the soul of her beloved Lore-Master.

Chapter 12

It was a relief to be back on dry land Sirad decided.

'I don't think I'll be volunteering to join your crew in any great hurry,' he told Geral'en as they stood on the quayside with the sturdy Seahawk gently rising and falling beside them.

The Captain laughed.

'It wasn't so bad after all,' he said, 'didn't lose any sails, no timbers damaged. I've had a lot worse in my time.'

'I'm sure you have, but I think I prefer solid ground beneath my feet.'

Eldren rummaged around in his pack and came up with a small jar of ointment.

'Take this, captain. I noticed that one of your crew, Warek, had cut himself on the ropes quite deeply. It will heal faster if he uses this.'

Garel'en looked at it for a moment before taking it from the little man.

'Thank you, healer, that is good of you.'

'Not at all. I am grateful to you for bringing me here.'

The captain shrugged.

'Least I can do,' he said reaching to shake hands with both Sirad and Eldren. 'I wish you good fortune in your travels.'

He turned, strode quickly up the gangplank and disappeared into the depths of his boat.

'I know you are keen to get away,' Sirad addressed his companion, 'but at least stay tonight, have a good sleep and a decent meal before you set out. You didn't say exactly where you were going to meet Mirantha?'

'No, and no offence young lord, but I will not tell you even now. The less said the better in the circumstances. However, be assured that we will both get to Pelamir as soon as we can, for all our sakes.'

Sirad let out a deep sigh.

'I just hope that somehow you will be able to help reach Amiros and bring him back, wherever he is.'

'So do I, Sirad, so do I. But there are no certainties; my knowledge of this situation is very scant which is why I have asked Mirantha for help. But I don't know whether even she has the skill. When the time comes, we will need both you and the Lady of Ancor to assist if we are to stand any chance at all.'

The little magician's rich voice betrayed a wealth of feeling; Amiros was a brother, after all, and the bonds between all the Brotherhood lay deep. Sirad understood that in some way Amiros would be crucial to their quest, which as yet he himself did not fully comprehend.

The two men walked up the cobbled road to the inn where Sirad and Ben had parted almost a fortnight earlier. His companion had not yet returned, advised the landlord, but rather thought that he was expected soon.

No sooner had Eldren and Sirad sat down to eat a few hours later than a travel-stained Ben sauntered in through the door.

'Starting without me?' he asked, coming straight over to their table. 'I'm starving.'

Sirad jumped up and embraced his brother.

'You forgot to tell me what time you were coming,' he chided him, signalling urgently to the landlord to bring more food and drink.

'Oh, maybe I did at that. In that case, you're forgiven.'

Ben noticed the little herbalist smiling at their obvious delight in being together safely again, and glanced at Sirad for an introduction.

'Ben, come and meet Eldren. He insisted on coming back with me immediately. It's a long story,' he said quickly before Ben could ask, 'I'll tell you later. In the meantime let's eat.'

Ben was happy to take the advice; he'd been in the saddle all day, stopping only briefly to allow his horse to rest. He had intended to be back before now but various things had held him up. It was a relief to see Sirad safe for he had heard stories of a bad storm several days ago and had been worried in case his brother had been caught up in it.

Having eaten their fill mugs were re-filled and they chatted quietly; nothing specific, and certainly nothing relating to Sirad's visit to Mitos. All three were aware that these were uncertain times and it was all too easy for talk to be overheard and passed on to less friendly ears.

Their room at the inn was down the end of the corridor and big enough for the three of them; after a suitable time spent in the taproom they went up the uneven stairs, the creaking boards making an ideal alarm should unexpected visitors approach. Sirad bolted the door and settled himself in a black oak chair to one side of the fireplace with Eldren on the other. Ben threw his pack down with his cloak and poured out a large bowl of water to wash away the day's grime before he joined them both.

'You first,' directed Sirad.

'Well,' Ben pushed his damp hair back from his eyes. 'I've been a fair way into The Sendure and picked up a bit of gossip here and there, but not a great deal of concrete information. However, piecing it all together it would appear that Verun left Mekad very shortly after his army failed to hold Elagos. Where he went is a matter for conjecture; he simply packed up a load of stuff and set sail. He only took two ships, and neither has returned.'

'What about the forces in Mekad?' asked Sirad.

'Still there. Merchants are still sending goods up from the coast to supply the garrisons just like before, but no reinforcements have arrived; before Elagos there were soldiers coming in regularly from somewhere, but that seems to have stopped.'

'Where has he gone?'

'No idea. But no one is expecting him back in a hurry is the impression I got. The most senior officers in Mekad were thrown by the sudden departure of their leader, but soon got back into the swing of it, ensuring that they made the most of being in charge. I think they're still wary of him making a reappearance, but they're all cast in the same mould and are out for all they can get whilst seeming to be obedient servants of the Red Lord.'

'Reminds me of someone else,' murmured Sirad, his thoughts picturing Vixlan.

'The area is still very much under their control, but any further expansion has slowed down completely.'

'With luck, if Verun has gone off to lick his wounds, so to speak, and doesn't come back in a hurry, the lot left behind will concentrate more on fighting amongst themselves – it's a pretty likely scenario.'

Ben nodded.

'You could well be right. You did say before that you hadn't detected Verun's influence since Elagos.'

'That is so. Neither Alinor nor I could feel anything, but then, we didn't want to push our luck too much.'

Eldren had been silent listening to the two men but now spoke.

'From what you told me the other evening I would suspect that Verun has indeed suffered a damaging backlash, both from your crushing his mind-hold at Elagos and from using the stone.' He carefully avoided using the name of the gem; its very mention made him distinctly uncomfortable.

'Mirantha and I will investigate as best we can and I will advise you if we manage to trace our renegade Brother.'

Ben looked a bit lost at this and glanced at Sirad for some explanation.

'All right,' said the young lord, 'I will try and fill you in on some of what I have learned.'

For the next hour Sirad and Eldren laid out the bones of what they had discussed and what their plans should be from here.

The next morning Eldren left early, Sirad having arranged for a horse to speed his journey.

'I'm not much of a one for riding,' the little man said, 'but in this case it will serve to save a little time.'

'We'll see you in Pelamir, then,' said Sirad as they said their farewells outside the tavern. 'Safe travelling, friend.'

'And you too, young man. I won't say don't take any risks, you will do what you have to!'

Sirad laughed, slapped the sturdy horse on its rump and watched as the herbalist rode off.

'Well Ben, we'd best be getting on,' he turned to the other Rider.

The two planned to make a slight detour on their return route, heading slightly northeast before veering back to the borders of Pelenin. Sirad still wanted to get an idea for himself how much Verun's influence had spread. Ben's trip had been more to the south of The Sendure, this detour should fill in any gaps in their information.

It was a cool day, but not wet, and they covered a goodly distance without any problem. They met several groups of merchants along the way and heard what little news they had, still maintaining their own assumed identity as traders looking to expand. The general advice was to take care and not think about heading toward Mekad, all the merchants agreed it was an unfriendly area and not worth the inevitable trouble it would bring to any trying to enter it without the required permissions.

The next few day's riding brought similar comments from other travellers. Hansor was still many miles away and, as far as the two Riders were aware, was very much under enemy control. Even though Sirad would have liked to get nearer, now was not the time. He had gleaned useful information now from one merchant who had been there only three weeks ago. A sizeable garrison of the Red Lord's soldiers were in occupation and he had heard that they had plans to establish other strongholds further northwards towards the Sarrent. However, it did seem that some of the plans were on hold, and very few outposts had been completed.

'At least there is some good news,' said Sirad to Ben as they sat down, munching on some bread and cheese whilst their horses had a rest.

'I'll feel better when we can have a go at them,' responded Ben, 'I don't like the idea of giving them too much time to build numbers or improve their defences.'

'I tend to agree with you, but we won't be in a position for a major offensive against them for some time yet. It may be a long project when all is said and done. We won't be able to just charge down and attack Mekad; we will have to work steadily down across quite a long front to secure the whole area.'

'We'll have to work from Galdesh southwards too,' observed Ben, 'so that's going to be a huge job.'

'Yes, the more I think about it the more daunting a task it becomes. Even if all the Alliance are with us I'm not so convinced that an all-out attempt to remove them is going to be the right way forward.'

Ben looked hard at Sirad.

'Well, just think about it, Ben. A full campaign is almost certain to take years rather than months. It will involve the commitment of thousands of men with the inevitable impact back home that such a deployment would have. Despite all out efforts we don't know exactly how many we are up against, or possibly more important than that, quite how wide Verun's reach has become. We know that there are pockets of insurgents across the whole of the south and that they have been reaching ever further north into our territories. You only need to think about how Teleston was removed.'

'True,' said Ben thoughtfully. 'It would be easy just to say, let's go and annihilate them all, but I do know that it isn't as straightforward as that. From what you have said about Verun, I for one am feeling a lot more cautious.'

Sirad nodded.

'But you and Alinor have other things on your minds, don't you?'

It was Sirad's turn to look hard at Ben.

'Can't hide it from you, can I?'

'You're bound to want to go up against Verun himself; even though you haven't told me everything – no, don't look at me like that, of course you haven't. I told you before that I'm not sure I would understand it all anyway, but I'm working on it. After that talk with Eldren the other night, I'm beginning to see how some of the stuff I read about in the Library falls into place.'

Sirad stayed silent, washing down his snack with a draught of light wine. True, he hadn't told Ben everything, but that was because he hadn't got it straight in his own mind yet.

What were his priorities? Was it fighting the Red Lord's troops and liberating those who were currently being oppressed by them? What about Amiros? Well, until Eldren and Mirantha were on the scene he couldn't see what could be done. Maybe there really was nothing they could do, but he didn't want to even entertain that thought. The realisation that the Lore-Master should have succeeded Remon put a different slant on matters. It almost certainly meant that he could be crucial to his and Alinor's success in defeating the renegade magician.

'You are right, my brother, it was never easy to hide the way I'm thinking from you and with all that has happened you are bound to start linking things up. But,' Sirad let out a breath and shook his head, 'I still don't know enough to be able to make any useful decisions yet. So many loose ends, you could say. Too many hints and cryptic suggestions, indications that are so confusing that I cannot even start to see clearly.'

'Perhaps you are trying too hard,' offered Ben. 'Perhaps you need to back off a little and give things chance to fall into perspective. Worrying at all these things is making it difficult to get them into focus. You are worried about Amiros – no surprise there in view of what Eldren has told us. You cannot help but worry about Alinor and I feel for you. But that is one very capable lady who I have no doubt will sort out the problems that Vixlan has created. You've not told me much about how she is getting on?'

'Sorry, no I haven't. It would appear that that nasty little rat has really made a mess of things – Alinor was really upset about how he has just used people to enhance his own position, and how her people have been neglected and impoverished by his greed.'

'Doesn't sound too good,' growled Ben. 'But is she getting somewhere now?'

'Oh yes, she really has started to wield the metaphorical big stick!' laughed Sirad. 'I understand that she's got the military sorted out and installed a new head in the trade department. From what I gather, Vixlan was totally outmanoeuvred.'

'That would have been interesting to watch,' said Ben. 'But what's she actually going to do about Vixlan himself.'

'A work in progress, I think you could say. The man has accumulated a lot of wealth which he believes is safe from her – he may find that to be rather far from the truth. She's determined to relieve him of his ill-gotten gains before he manages to spirit them away from Ancor altogether.'

'I don't doubt she will succeed there.'

Ben paused.

'Are you going to Thorgiliad soon?'

'Mmm, not sure. Much as I would like to go right now I think I need to go back to Pelamir first. I hope that Eldren and Mirantha will get there soon and we can find out what they think about Amiros' prospects. After that, well maybe.'

The pair were silent for a little while. Then Ben ventured to ask, 'Any ideas about what she wants to do about her coronation? After what her people have been through it would surely help them to have a proper celebration.'

'Yes, I would agree there. She hasn't said much about it yet; not sure if she wanted to rid the place of Vixlan first, but maybe too long a delay is not what people need. Here, let's get on now. I think it's high time we went home again.'

The two men removed any signs of their presence, re-mounted and started heading back towards the Pelenin border, eventually reaching the inn where they had left their own horses on the outward trip. It was a relief to swap the sturdy southern mounts for their own sleek thoroughbreds and both felt their spirits rise as the nearer to their beloved city they rode.

There was no message from Eldren when Sirad enquired of the gate guards; he hadn't really expected anything. He wasn't going to worry unduly as he had no idea of where the herbalist was intending to meet up with Mirantha, and Eldren hadn't put a timescale on their likely arrival, although Sirad did hope it would not be too long a wait. The thought of meeting another of the Ben-Neteru was quite intriguing; perhaps she could explain a little more about their own nature and even about what was expected from Sirad and Alinor.

Sirad took himself back to the Library when he had time and searched again for anything there that might shed light on his current situation. He found only a passing reference to the otherworld state to which Amiros had been banished, but nothing he could find offered any kind of hope. I need those books that Remon has, he thought. If anyone knows it would have been him.

He shared some of his thoughts with his father. Sothan considered the news of his meeting with Eldren with interest. It had been many years since he had had the pleasure of the herbalist magician's company and was pleased to know that he was well and was in fact due to arrive in Pelamir soon. The time for keeping secrets from his son was over.

'You have done very well, my son, to find Eldren. I had almost forgotten his existence – very remiss of me. As for Mirantha, well, that really is something. I had come to think that any others of the Ben-Neteru had long left our shores. I believe I only saw her the once, when your mother and I were wed – what a wonderful day that was!'

There were tears in his eyes at the memory of his beautiful wife; the years could not fade the pictures in his mind nor the love in his heart. Grief at her passing was tempered by the warmth of his enduring love for her, seeing her in his son as he grew to manhood, a son any father would be proud of.

'Do you think that she and Eldren may be able to help Amiros?'

'I really don't know,' Sothan answered his son. 'Their knowledge and skill is way beyond anything we mere mortals can understand – oh yes, my boy, I am only too aware that you will soon outstrip us all . .'

Sirad started to speak, but fell silent again as his father continued.

'I know that you are still finding this hard, this burden that you feel weighs so heavily upon you. But I am well aware that you have found riches beyond compare with Alinor. If she loves you only half as much as the love I shared with your mother then you have nothing to fear. But whatever evil threatens the two of you will be strong.'

He laid his hand on his son's arm.

'You will face this, not alone, but with the support and love of an exceptional woman. I do not know what the future holds for us all, but I do have confidence in you. Perhaps it is time for history to reveal what really happened so long ago, and for ancient wrongs to be addressed.'

Sirad frowned.

'Do you have any idea what it is that she and I must do?'

'I am sorry, no, I do not. There was Power back then, and magical Tokens which . .'

'Remon talked of them,' Sirad interrupted. 'I didn't understand, still don't for that matter.'

'Did he not tell Alinor of them?' asked Sothan.

'No, it wasn't Alinor. I – ' the man hesitated, 'well I found a letter from Remon, addressed to me, in which he talked of Verun seeking to obtain the Tokens of Power, but he didn't explain any more than that.'

The old king nodded thoughtfully. Obviously there were things that Sirad wasn't going to tell him about the letter; it was curious that the Mind-Master had known to write to Sirad, but on second thoughts, perhaps it wasn't. After all, they were Ben-Neteru, and as such it was unlikely that anything could be kept from their knowledge, even though Sirad would need more time yet before his inheritance would be fully realised. For a moment Sothan felt overwhelmed with sympathy for his son and the load he now carried; he remembered his anguish when he had first found out what Galena would be bound to do in giving her life so that Sirad could come into his power. He couldn't argue with destiny, but it had still hurt deeply. It had been a pain that he could share with his closest friend Teleston, who had also faced the same situation. Another sadness, that Teleston had been so cruelly taken robbing him of the one person who had truly appreciated the enduring pain of their fate.

Putting aside his emotion, Sothan sought to reassure his son.

'Whatever is meant will come to pass, I am sure of it. You must do what you can, search for the knowledge and remain true to your nature. You have strength and power and your heart is honourable. Together with Alinor you will prevail.'

Sirad looked at his father, a man whom he had always regarded as the best role model any son could have, understanding but firm, fair and reliable, and above all a father who loved him.

'Thank you, father. Thank you for everything you have always done for me. I will not let you down.'

Their eyes locked, sharing unspoken feelings.

'Get on, lad, I'm sure there are matters that need your attention! I know I have work to do.'

'You're probably right, as usual,' laughed Sirad, rising and bowing to his father before striding out from the king's private quarters to resume his normal round of tasks within the Palace.

Chapter 13

Another morning, another meeting. Making progress though, Alinor reassured herself. Vixlan is really rattled now, she thought a little smugly. His power is slowly being whittled away, nothing too obvious to make him think I know what he is really up to.

She had taken great pains to impress upon the horrid man how she valued his efforts and how she only had his wellbeing at heart. It stuck in her throat much of the time, but the end would justify the means. She was confident that over the space the past few weeks she had put the right people in place to help govern her beloved country; people who cared as much as she did and who were willing to work hard for the good of all; people who above all would be loyal to the crown. There were some with many years' service and not a few many years younger who would grow up with the new era that her accession would bring about. That was a point too. Hints were being dropped about her coronation; when would be a suitable date – what about the mid-winter festival or was that leaving it too long? Surely it about time she introduced a bit of pomp and ceremony to show the other nations that the succession had been assured in Ancor; not to mention that no-one would object to having a good excuse to celebrate.

Alinor gazed out of her window; this was her city, her country. She would restore its glory as her father would have wished and she could sense his spirit there with her and knew that he was now content. On her instructions there had been a three-day period of remembrance throughout the country; after such a long period she had felt that it would be better spent in thanksgiving for Teleston's life rather than a grief-laden requiem. The people had suffered enough grief - it was time to move on with a new life, a new reign.

She nodded her satisfaction and turned to find Semira had just arrived to see if she needed anything else before she had to head down to the meeting room.

'No, I'm fine, thank you. But what are you up to this morning? How are things going with the household staff – I'm sorry I've rather left you to it and I never actually asked you to take on such a mammoth task.'

'Please don't worry about that,' laughed Semira, 'it was all my doing and I am quite enjoying the challenge. I admit that I got really worked up at first when I saw just what was going on here and it sort of got my inner organiser sufficiently offended that I had to do something about it! I do hope that I haven't overstepped the mark. I realise that I am supposed to be your personal handmaid, but on the grounds that you are, shall we say, rather independent and extremely capable of looking after yourself, you don't need or want me fussing around you unnecessarily. Hence I do have time on my hands to get to grips with making sure that your household runs properly. I suppose I get that from my mother who was always very strict about our home – in a nice way that is, she wasn't an ogre or anything, she didn't need to be.'

Alinor laughed.

'Believe me, I am extremely grateful to you Semira. You are right that I do loathe being fussed over, and the past year or so has rather reinforced that tendency. I know I can rely on you to instil some proper order – goodness knows the place needed taking in hand since so many of the original experienced staff left or were encouraged to leave. The running of the household is an extra task that I really don't need on my plate just now.'

'You don't need to concern yourself about it or me, my Lady. Matters are progressing very well, despite a bit of opposition in some quarters.'

'Oh?'

'Not too much of a problem, but there are just a few staff who are in Vixlan's camp and who were hoping to climb up the ladder higher than their skills or experience would warrant.'

'You're a foreigner here,' said Alinor thoughtfully, 'and it's no surprise that making any changes could be a bit of an uphill battle. It's hard for long-serving members of the house to accept that an outsider should suddenly be telling them what to do, especially when they are supposed only to be a "handmaid" to the Lady.'

Semira couldn't hide a smile at Alinor's tone.

'I believe there is one way to ease your path,' continued Alinor. 'From today you are officially the Mistress of the Queen's household.'

Semira's face was a picture, Alinor thought. The sudden promotion was a surprise, but she deserves it for the dedication she has shown since she came into my service.

'However,' Alinor looked sternly at the dark-haired young woman, 'this does *not* mean that you may slack in your attention to my welfare. I will still require your presence whenever summoned – and that includes being my companion when I travel. At some point you will need to identify someone else to eventually fill your post.'

Semira took a deep breath and curtseyed to her sovereign.

'Thank you, my Lady. I – er – hadn't expected such an honour,' she grinned then and added, 'and thank you for including the bit about travelling.'

'I hadn't forgotten our conversation that morning before we reached Thorgiliad. We are friends, and whilst the protocols may constrain our behaviour to some extent, when we are together we can at least be ourselves, if only for a little while.'

Alinor hugged her companion saying, 'Who knows what our future holds? But whatever happens we will look out for each other.'

'I cannot thank you enough, Alinor. I never thought to find such a friend as you.'

'Well, just your luck that there aren't too many like me!'

They laughed together at such an understatement, but it was time to get to work – for both of them.

Alinor wandered slowly through the marketplace, listening to the random gossip of the stallholders and their customers. The mood seemed much lighter than it had been in the early days of her return, and generally everyone appeared optimistic that their lives would return to the way they had been before their beloved king had been killed. Trading goods were arriving much as before, and she had heard that a shipment of elegant glass had been received from Elagos only the day prior. It was good that the way from Elagos was now open again, she thought as she studied a collection of pots and woodcarvings, tastefully displayed against some intricately patterned cloth. The smell of fresh bread from across the street made her mouth water and she made her way over to see what pastries there may be – not that she was hungry, but as a child she had always been tempted by the goods on offer and the scent brought back memories of hours spent exploring. In her current guise of a young man who could be either student or artist she purchased a custard pastry that melted in her mouth just as she recalled they used to. Moving on to a small square, she sat down near the fountain and observed the comings and goings; women describing their latest purchases with their friends, or how their children were getting on; men boasting about how lucrative their dealings had been, or arguing the toss with a rival.

All so normal, thought Alinor; they have no idea of the evil out there and I know I haven't seen the worst of it yet. Still, at least back here I can be reasonably happy that with the help I have received from so many good people we are getting much nearer to the restructuring of government that was urgently required. Her meeting earlier in the day had been productive, with the usual caveat that Vixlan was still not happy with the way his power was being eroded. Unaware of Alinor's mind-reading abilities he had been fuming about how she apparently took control with such ease and was blocking every move he wanted to make. His thoughts had been most unpleasant, if not downright treasonous she considered, but she still held off from making any accusations. There was one part of her that simply wanted him dead as the easiest way of getting him out of the picture, but she knew that it wasn't as easy as that. The last thing she wished her people to see was a vengeful queen who would cold-bloodedly eliminate any opponent. It just wasn't her, especially not here in her home. The battle at Elagos had been a totally different matter, kill or be killed; and as for Verun, well, there was hatred in her heart for what he was, no doubt of that. But that confrontation was in the future, and there was too much to do before it would come about.

I'm nearly ready to bring about that rat's downfall, she decided, remembering Vixlan's thoughts about the safety of his hidden hoard. Perhaps I could make a series of little trips out and about the countryside which will inevitably bring me to where he has his hideaway. I wonder what sort of excuse he could possibly come up with? Whatever it is it won't be enough to save his skin. I just want to be rid of him so my people will know their hardship is truly over.

She wandered further down through the city, crossing spacious tree-lined squares, past larger mansions with carefully tended gardens, imposing buildings home to wealthier merchants and noble families; there was a small park with fountains and streams, little copses of trees giving shade in the summer for families to sit out with their children. She was lost in thoughts of days past when a dog suddenly shot out from the shadows, tail between it legs, obviously scared by something. She started walking towards the cover but some instinct halted her steps; she froze, her mind seeking the source of her discomfort. There, just ahead of her, baleful eyes almost glowing with an almost palpable aura of savagery, was the big cat, waiting for her to come just that bit nearer. Before she could reach for her small dagger – no sword today – loud childish voices could be heard as a group of youngsters came running full pelt along the pathway. Shouting and laughing they distracted the cat who shook it head, growling quietly before slipping further back into the shadows and disappearing.

Alinor waited and watched for a minute or two, but the animal had gone. How on earth could such a big creature have got into the city and not be noticed by anyone? Cats, she thought, clever animals; they seemed to be able to survive anywhere and remain hidden from human eyes if they so wanted. This one wants me; it'll come again, that's for sure, and it could turn up anywhere.

Returning to the palace and her usual appearance, she went along to the library and asked the book-keeper if he would find her something about the big cats. After a short wait he came back with a hefty tome containing information about a plethora of foreign creatures. She leafed through it quickly, trying not to get side-tracked by some of the extraordinary pictures filling its pages, and eventually found the part she was seeking. The cat stalking her was a *bahlam*, the most fearful member of the cat family, a native of countries far to the south across the great western sea. The power of its jaws was legendary and it was known to hunt by day or night, on land or in shallow waters. It was quick, efficient and feared by the people who shared it territories.

Why is it here, mused Alinor, and pursuing me? This must be another ploy by Verun, although I am sure that he is not actually controlling it as such; whatever that magician does he corrupts men and creatures alike and sends them on their way to cause distress and harm. But this creature seems to be only interested in me; thanks to those children it was scared off, and the first time in the woods it wasn't keen on taking on so many people. If Verun has this creature going after me, what about Sirad? He may be in danger too.

In a split second her mind reached out to her beloved prince, finding him alone as he was making his way down to the Riders' workshops.

Are you alright? was his first reaction to her urgent thoughts.

Yes, I'm fine, don't worry. But something has happened and you need to know about it.

Go on, he stopped walking and leaned against a windowsill.

I didn't mention it before as I wasn't sure what to make of it but, when I visited my old nanny the other week there was a strange encounter on the way back. There was this huge cat, a *bahlam* I now know it to be, lying in wait above the track in the woods. Elkana spooked, warning me, and the cat jumped down in front of us, right where I would have been only moments later. It just looked at me as if to say, I'll get you next time, and then ran off into the woods.

Why didn't you tell me? For a moment Sirad was almost angry that he hadn't been there to protect her, but he knew that he could trust her and that Alinor was more than capable of looking after herself; he had to allow that she would hardly come to him with every little happening.

To be honest, I didn't think it was very serious. Unusual to find such a creature so far north in Ancor, but with so much going on I gave it little thought. Until today.

All right, I understand that, Sirad acknowledged. But now what?

I was down in the city, just taking a bit of time away to unwind a bit, when I was going through one of the parks. A scared dog came out from under the trees so I went to see what it was that had upset it.

She could sense Sirad raising his eyes at that.

Anyway, something made me hesitate and that was when I saw it again, almost hidden in the shadows, waiting for me. If it hadn't been for the bunch of kids that came charging past at that point I believe it would have attacked. As it was their presence seemed to discourage it and it disappeared again.

You say it's a *bahlam*? But there are none in this part of the world.

Exactly. I went and looked it up for a bit more detail. It's quite a fearsome beast, Sirad, and rarely fails if it attacks.

But you think it is just after you?

Yes, I do. I think that it's something to do with Verun. Somehow or other he's influenced this creature – it's no illusion, it's the real thing – and it is hunting me. No one else has reported seeing it, and as far as I know there hasn't been anything about people losing livestock or anything. It's really strange.

Please be careful, my love. I don't like the thought of Verun sending his creatures after you.

Neither do I. And of course I am being careful. But, consider this Sirad. If he has one diabolical cat after me, there may be something after you too.

Mmm. You could be right. I haven't come across anything yet, but that doesn't mean there isn't something out there waiting for the right opportunity. Your warning is timely, my love. We must both be on our guard even though Verun himself seems to be out of the picture at the moment.

Alinor shared her thoughts on how things were progressing and Sirad was pleased to find her confidence fully restored after what had been a slightly hesitant start when she first returned home.

On his part he was still awaiting the arrival of Eldren and Mirantha; Amiros' condition hadn't changed, though he had been restless several times but without showing any signs of returning consciousness.

I am sorry, Sirad tried to comfort Alinor. There is nothing else we can do at the moment. I know you are worried about him, but we must just hope and pray that between us all we will find a way. So, he tried changing the subject, what are your plans next?

The pair mind-spoke for a while, practical matters giving way to more private sharing. Eventually Sirad had to break off as company approached seeking a directive from him about palace matters. With a final loving thought they each went back to their tasks.

'I must confess,' said Semira as they made their way along a pretty green valley, 'that it is nice to get away from the palace for a while.'

Alinor nodded and stroked her mare's gleaming neck.

'I know what you mean. There has been so much to do since my return, but at last things are beginning to take the shape I would like. And I know that you,' she smiled at Semira, 'have been working wonders on the household.'

Her companion blushed at the unexpected praise.

'Don't think I don't get to hear about what is going on, or can see the improvements over the past weeks,' chided Alinor. 'My mind is not totally on what is happening with my government!'

'No,' responded Semira, 'I should know by now not to underestimate my Lady's grasp of what is happening.'

There were about thirty in the party that had left Thorgiliad a couple of days prior in the early morning of what had become a beautiful late autumn day. The previous week Alinor had announced her intention to make a series of tours about the country; the reason was twofold. Firstly so that she could familiarise herself better with the lay of the land and secondly, so that her people would be able to get to know her better. The intention was to spend four or five nights away, staying either in one of the large towns or at the homes of landed families who were eager to welcome their new sovereign, and perhaps, though none would be so vulgar as to say it out loud, raise themselves a little higher in the nobility stakes. Alinor was easily aware of all those hidden agendas, but did not find any fault with those who sought her company. Most of the families had been long-standing friends of the crown, some very close friends of her father; it was a pleasure to spend time hearing their stories of him, somehow bringing him closer to her. They in turn were impressed by her easy manner, a refusal to be weighed down by too much pomp, and her genuine interest in everyone and everything about her.

Semira too was enjoying the travel, learning about the country that was now her home. She watched over Alinor, admiring the way she was developing good relationships with her people, happy to listen to the humblest amongst them just as she did to the noblest. She learned the best ways to tactfully ensure that the Lady of Ancor did not get overtired by the continual calls on her time, for which that lady was very grateful. Alinor had not expected her trip to be quite so exhausting, but she was still enjoying every moment of it. Whilst her original thoughts had been to pave the way to

Vixlan's downfall, this trip, and the ones that would follow had been a really useful idea.

'We'll be reaching Foxenbale in an hour or so,' said Alinor, 'and after that go on to Nellchat. Berman's house is another ten miles or so further and will our furthest point on this particular visit. He is another very old friend of my father; I can recall seeing him a couple of times at court, but I believe his health is not so good anymore.'

'The countryside here is so different from around Elagos,' said Semira. 'I'd not done any real travelling until you came, but I really am enjoying this.'

Alinor was quietly pleased to see the real appreciation on her companion's face. She thought back to how she had had reservations at first when Sirad insisted that she needed to have a female handmaid/companion, but then Semira had so quickly demonstrated not only her talent for organisation but also her genuine care for her new mistress that Alinor had taken to her immediately and had found her to be a much needed friend.

'That is just as well as we're going to be racking quite a lot of miles in the next few weeks,' Alinor informed her. 'I think it is good for you to get acquainted with the folk of Ancor. But, I must ask, are you missing your home?'

Semira thought for a moment before replying.

'I would be lying if I said I didn't, but that is only natural when I had never been anywhere much before. Oh yes, I would love to see my mother and father, but I'm sure that you are bound to go there again in the not so distant future and you promised not to leave me behind, so I am more than happy to wait for that day. I am happy to be here and am enjoying making a new life for myself.'

Alinor smiled at her.

'I am glad to hear you speak that way. And of course, when the time comes to return to Elagos you will be right there with me. A Lady can't possibly go without her handmaid!'

The two laughed, but both were thinking of the implications of future travels. Alinor knew she would hardly be travelling with the retinue and ceremony that the queen of her country might be expected to do, though at some stage it would be appropriate. But that would only be a hindrance if she and Sirad were to pursue their destinies and finally find out the nature of the tasks that should be theirs. They both had much to learn still, and the development of their individual powers needed work; in her time back in Thorgiliad there had been no time for Alinor to devote to greater understanding of her skills. There was still that book that she had brought with her, the one they had found in Remon's house. She needed to allow herself some serious study time with that, but it would have to wait still until this business with Vixlan got sorted out. Semira's thoughts were about how soon Alinor would be satisfied with her new government to enable her to leave again with some peace of mind; and when Alinor did set out on her travels with Sirad and with Semira alongside too, she wanted to be capable of looking after herself, defending herself as well as not being a burden to the extraordinary couple and whoever else rode with them. Likely to be Benharad, she thought, he and the prince were very close; she knew that Ben was Sirad's foster brother and totally devoted. For a moment she pictured the tall Rider; not bad at all she thought, but then censured herself. The prince's brother, for goodness sake! He's not for you, her head told her; unbidden, she suddenly had a fleeting remembrance of the somewhat prickly conversation she and Rekar had that day in the city sprung into her mind. Certainly not him either, arrogant so and so, she thought. Anyway, what do I want with men? Forget it girl.

'I hear that you have made good progress,' Alinor interrupted the train of thought.

Semira frowned.

'Sorry, progress? You mean the household?'

'No you woolly-head, I mean your training with arms!'

'Oh, yes, of course. I have been trying, my Lady, as much as I could.'

That was a bit of an understatement. Alinor knew from Dhalen that her very proper Household Mistress had been working extremely hard in her bid to become a fit companion to her warrior mistress. Swordplay would never suit her, but she had become very proficient with a knife, and was making good progress with mastering archery. Though not as strong as a man would be in drawing a big bow, she had recently been working with a smaller, lighter weapon, and was quickly becoming exceptionally accurate.

'Not so self-effacing, my little friend,' said Alinor. 'Dhalen has told me of your efforts and I am quite impressed that you have come so far in such a short length of time. I know only too well how much effort it takes and I am proud of you.'

Semira hardly knew how to respond. Unseen, she had watched Alinor training with her elite guard and wondered at her exceptional skill. How could this young woman have become such an incredible fighter? She knew that Alinor and Sirad were possessed of some extraordinary power, but as yet hadn't found anyone who could tell her more. The more she came to learn about Alinor, the less she found she actually knew.

'Dhalen is a strict teacher,' Semira acknowledged, 'but he has been so generous with his time for me, I am so grateful. I really like him,' she added.

'He is an outstanding soldier and an admirable man. His loyalty to my father was paramount and I count myself fortunate to have had him as my teacher and now my friend and advisor. Such as he are the treasures of mankind.'

At that moment one of the guards rode up to say that they were approaching a small village and the people were anxious to pay their respects. Alinor acknowledged him and said that she would stop and speak with them.

So the day went on. Their overnight at Berman's beautiful country house was very enjoyable. He was an elderly man, and as Alinor had mentioned, no longer in the best of health. He managed well with a stout staff to support himself and was obviously thrilled to welcome Teleston's daughter to his home. Alinor had insisted that there should be no ceremony here – she was visiting an old family friend. Berman's wife had been extremely apprehensive that the new queen would be paying a call and had almost driven her staff mad with constantly checking everything; but the evening went off without a hitch and the young sovereign put her at ease almost immediately. She would be the envy of all her acquaintances and could be well satisfied that she would be the centre of attention at all gatherings for some time to come. As it was, Alinor made sure to share a few 'confidences' along the way, sensing that the good woman had felt cut off from their previous society lives and longed for something to brighten up her everyday life.

In due course the party returned to the capital and prepared for the next excursion, due the following week. This went much as the first one had, calling on various towns, passing through numerous villages and visiting loyal subjects of the crown.

Back in Thorgiliad Alinor discussed her plans for the next few excursions. In one of her regular daily briefings with the Steward she shared some of her intentions.

'I want to go up to Coranien-dulat for a few days,' she said, 'for it will be pleasant to see all my childhood friends there. But I also have in mind some plans for the future. I am considering finding a suitable property which I can use as a retreat from the palace, somewhere I can be a little more private, particularly after I am married. It strikes me that there is some excellent hunting country out to the east of here; maybe I shall find something suitable around there. What do you think, Steward?'

Vixlan was careful to maintain his composure. If this troublesome girl were to start exploring close to where he had his own secret hunting lodge some local peasant would be bound to mention it to her, despite the precautions he had taken to keep it from public knowledge.

'What an excellent idea, my Lady. The load you bear as our sovereign is heavy and you deserve to be able to leave it behind for a while. You can be assured of our diligent care in your absence; you need not worry that everything will be in safe hands.'

'Of course, Vixlan, and that is just what I was hoping you would say. However, I am not particularly familiar with that part of our country and it would help if some more knowledgeable people were to accompany me. What about yourself? I gather you have made a number of visits to that area and knowing how efficient you are, you must have picked up quite a bit of local information. After all, it will not be a very long trip at this time, more a small sortie to spy out the land.'

'You are most kind, my Lady, but I am sure I could find others whose experience of the area is far better than mine.'

The Steward was eager to avoid travelling with Alinor; his quick mind had already come up with a plot to ambush the young woman's party. No way was he going to risk her finding his hoard; he had been formulating plans to remove it and himself from Ancor for some time and he was desperate now to put them into practice. If she, the gods forbid, were to find his lodge, there was no telling what would happen. He had come too far now to give up.

'Yes, I suppose you might, but then I would value your assistance in finding the right place. I know you must have far more experience than I in such a matter.'

The irony of the situation was lost on the man. All he could think of now was how to stop this woman from destroying his future.

'You flatter me, my Lady, but it is as you wish. I shall go and oversee arrangements immediately.'

Rising, he bowed and hurried from the meeting chamber.

I'm sure you will, Alinor was thinking, and I know what those arrangements are likely to include, you murderous little rat.

She dismissed the other officials and strode off to find Dhalen. She needed some input from the veteran about the best way of being prepared for trouble but also not letting Vixlan know that she was aware of his intentions. No doubt he would want to go with her, but he would understand that his presence alone would raise the profile of the journey and make Vixlan suspicious.

As she expected, Dhalen was not keen for her to put herself at risk, but equally he respected her abilities and her interpretation of the situation. He recommended the men he considered most capable.

'That weasel barely knows one guard from another,' he scorned. 'I can have some of my best men in your party and he will be none the wiser.'

'I expected as much, old friend. I know I can rely on you to ensure that they understand the purpose of this little expedition and the importance of keeping Vixlan in the dark. To all intents and purposes I am on a scouting trip to find myself a holiday retreat.'

Dhalen nodded his approval – his young protégé was turning out to be quite a useful tactician, learning fast the devious ways that all rulers must master in potentially dangerous situations.

'You'll have to take that black-haired beauty with you,' he looked up at Alinor under raised brows from where he was sitting.

'No, I don't want to put her in danger.'

'You really think you can come up with a suitable excuse to keep her here?'

'She won't like it, of course, but she's so inexperienced . . .'

'But she's not going to learn unless you allow her to,' corrected Dhalen. 'Your Semira is not the delicate little flower you suppose her to be. Perhaps I didn't quite make it clear last time we spoke about her training.'

'If you really think so?'

'I do, my Lady, and besides, if you were to leave her behind that would certainly alert Vixlan that this would not be a pleasure trip.'

'You're probably right. Oh well, it's going to be an interesting few days, that's for certain. And Dhalen, you will appreciate just how much I want to finally confront that man and see that he gets his just reward for all the harm he has done.'

'I know it well, young Alinor, and I will finally rest a little easier once he is removed from power.'

'I'll leave the arrangements with you – you'll find Vixlan is already busy with his plans.'

Dhalen nodded, scowling at the thought of the Steward's meddling. As soon as Alinor had gone, he called for his fellow commander Herran to attend, at the double.

Chapter 14

It was hard to keep on going with no end in sight. What was the point? He had no way of referencing time anymore and to be honest, no longer cared. He had climbed hills, crossed river valleys, clambered along slippery rocky tracks beneath overhanging cliffs, sheltered in caves and under huge trees, but got absolutely nowhere. It went on and on, and for what purpose who could know. Why am I doing this, he wondered a hundred times a day. His body ached almost all the time now and every so often there were stabbing pains that made him gasp, collapsing upon the ground and writhing in agony. He had found himself desiring nothing more than to lie down and sink into oblivion.

Still he went on.

I know my name, but not myself. I remember the pain and Verun but I don't really remember why I was there in the first place. Why did Verun have that fearful gem and wield it with such destructive effect? He has sentenced me to a living death; I cannot wake up from this dream, nor can I end it. If I sleep it is not a true sleep for I will wake to the same eternal banishment. I can barely remember what my life was before this time and have no idea how this will end. Why do I know about Mnethar, but yet not know from whence it came or the reason for its existence?

What little memories he had were merely tantalising glimpses of who he had been. Try as he would, he had recalled little more than that day when he had first made fire again.

'I cannot go on,' he shouted at the overcast skies. 'It is enough, I have given all I can. Please, let this end.'

His anguished cries vanished into the air and he sank to his knees, sobbing in gut-wrenching misery.

After a while his tears stopped and he simply sat looking into the distance, his mind numb with grief, his eyes sore and his head heavy.

Gradually he became aware that the day – morning or afternoon he wasn't sure – had become a little brighter. The clouds had thinned a little and here and there were patches of sunlight filtering down. A movement off to his right caught his eye and he glanced over to see a small bird watching him from a nearby bush. Its head moved in sharp little jerks, its emerald eyes taking in the sight of a dishevelled man just sitting there. It flashed its wings a couple of times seemingly sending up sparkles of brilliant gold; its body was neither golden brown nor red but yet was both those colours and more. Every slight movement seemed to give off a different hue. It made no noise but simply looked at him.

Amiros decided he had never seen a bird like this one before and his curiosity was aroused. He moved his hand slightly and the bird flashed its iridescent wings again, but did not fly away.

'How lovely you are, little one,' he said, his broken voice hardly more than a whisper.

At this, the bird flitted from its perch to a branch further up the bush, still watching. It then flew several yards away along what could be described as a track, stopped for a moment and then returned. Again it studied him before flying away up the track with a final flash of brilliance. For some reason he decided to follow the path that the bird had taken, hoping to catch another glimpse of it. He was not disappointed, for he saw it again, some distance further on but easily spotted because of its glorious colour. It went on and so he followed.

Bird and man continued for maybe a couple of hours, the track taking them across a grassy plain and across the inevitable stream that fed the lush growth. He stopped for a break for his body still complained, yet there was something that urged him to continue again. Eventually he had to halt for the night and was able to rest reasonably comfortably until dawn. When he awoke he could hear birdsong, and there it was again, his little feathered companion.

'Why are you here?' he asked. 'Where are you leading me, or is this just wishful thinking on my part?'

The bird sang a few sweet notes and flitted off.

Amiros sighed.

One more day, he promised himself. Just one more day. And after that . . .

He shook his head, took up a slender staff to help him keep his balance on the rougher ground that he could clearly see ahead, and set off wearily.

The sun was warm but the breeze cooled as it became more fresh; the clouds were building again, rushing across the sky like a herd of wild horses chasing the wind. Fragile optimism was slowly giving way to an insidious depression again as he struggled to keep his footing on the scree of the hillside, forcing himself to just keep going long enough to reach the top of this outcrop. Probably it would only lead on to another hill. So tired of this, he thought, concentrating on where he was placing his sore feet, hunched against the invasive wind. It can't be far now, he thought and looked up to check. He blinked several times thinking that he may be imagining things, but there was something there, maybe even someone. As he stood trying to focus the shape moved and resolved itself into a person that started to come towards him. Confusion held him rooted to the spot; after all this time was he finally going to meet another human being, or was this just his tired mind creating an illusion of what he had wished for?

No illusion this, he found, as a young boy, maybe ten or twelve years old, approached him, calling out a greeting.

'Welcome my lord Amiros, I have been sent to guide you to safety. They have been waiting for you and feared you would not come.'

'I don't – ' he stammered and had to collect himself.

'Thank you,' he managed, 'I'm not sure where I am.'

'Don't worry,' the boy smiled at him. 'It's hard, I know, but here, let me help you. It's not too far now and you will be able to rest.'

Despite the boy's reassuring tones, Amiros was uncertain whether to believe his apparent rescuer or not. But then, the boy reached out and took his arm gently to help him up the last few yards to the crest of the hill. Amiros could see the tops of trees beyond, but the effort of putting one foot in front of another was proving too much. He felt totally drained of any strength; his vision blurred and he could no longer resist the waves of weariness that swept over him.

'I can't,' was all he managed to whisper before the darkness claimed him.

A woman's voice full of love and sweetness, a touch so gentle it was as if it had been a feather, fleeting impressions that he could not hold on to. Three or four times the sensations penetrated his consciousness before at last the exhausted man rose above the sea of his weakness; it was obviously daylight, but the brightness was dimmed where he lay upon a bed, warm and drowsy, pain forgotten for the moment. He lay staring up at the ceiling, its pale colour complementing the soft tones of the walls of the room. He moved his head slightly to explore his surroundings. A comfortable room, he thought, the sunlight filtering through silken drapes onto a patterned floor; a couple of tables, elegant chairs and an ornate cabinet against one wall. The panelled door opened quietly, a slim figure silhouetted against the brightness for a moment before entering.

'It has been a long time, my dear friend,' the well-remembered voice said. 'I rejoice to see you, but grieve that it must be under these circumstances.'

Amiros' heart missed several beats and his eyes filled.

'How can it be you? I don't understand.'

The Lady Meriona-en-resaan approached and laid her hand gently on his.

'It is really I, dear Amiros, but as for how this has come about, well, that is somewhat more complicated and a matter we should perhaps not discuss quite yet. You were very weak when we brought you here and you will need time to regain your strength. There is still a long road ahead of you before we can bring about an ending to this unnatural predicament.'

He grasped her hand, rejoicing in the warmth of her touch; he could feel the unmistakeable flow of energy coming from her to ease and restore his troubled soul.

'I missed you,' he whispered, 'and have grieved all these years. My love for you remains true, as you well knew, although we were never destined to be together.'

'You know that I have always loved you, my dearest friend, but you always also knew that my love for Teleston was greater. His cruel death was a savage blow, but I can rejoice that he is free – no, I cannot explain more than that for you are still alive, even though you are caught in this limbo.'

The man sighed deeply; his mind struggled to comprehend what was happening, how it was that the beautiful Meriona could be here with him, wherever here was.

'This is E'shariya, Amiros, the place of healing and knowledge,' she answered his unspoken question. 'Very few who are lost ever manage to reach it, but I am so glad that you have come and I hope with all my being that you will find the answers you need.'

She smiled at him and it was as if the sun which had been hidden was suddenly revealed.

'Sleep now and eat when you awake, you will feel better. I shall be waiting when you are ready.'

She rose, so elegant and lovely he felt his heart melt all over again as it had when he had first set eyes on her so many, many years before. He had thought her the incarnation of magical beauty and adored her from a distance until Remon had tasked him with the guardianship of her daughter. Alinor, he suddenly thought, I had forgotten Alinor. So like her mother in many ways, but yet so different. His thoughts tumbled as he tried to put the pictures together.

Meriona gently touched the man's brow and he found himself drifting as if on a lazy river boat, peaceful and relaxed. He slept.

He hadn't dreamed at all, he thought when he finally awoke. Slowly he eased himself up and sat on the edge of the bed. He remembered the boy meeting him on the hill-side but nothing of how he had got here. He remembered too that his clothes had been filthy, his hair dirty; someone had obviously washed him before putting him to bed in a clean robe. He was hungry for he had eaten little since his exodus from that strange illusion of paradise.

There was a selection of appetising foods on the table – not too much to overwhelm the recovering patient, but enough to provide appropriate nourishment to start to build up his strength again.

As he was finishing there came a soft knock on the door and a young woman entered.

'Would you care for anything else, my lord?' she asked.

'Thank you, no, that is more than sufficient,' he responded. 'Can you tell me where the Lady Meriona is?'

'Of course, I will take you to her now,' she nodded and indicated that he should follow her.

His door opened onto a stoned pathway leading around a little square garden area. It was pleasantly bright and he could feel the warmth of the sun penetrating his bones. The woman led the way around the garden and through a stone archway into a big courtyard containing a decorative fountain in the centre and surrounded by a colonnaded walkway. The woman bowed and pointed across to the far side where he could see Meriona seated, a basket of flowers at her feet.

She smiled up at him as he approached.

'I can tell you are feeling a little better,' she said. 'Hopefully it will not be too long before you are back to your usual self.'

His eyes drank in the sight of her beauty, his heart warmed at the sound of her voice; his eyes filled with tears of joy to be able to see her again.

'Thank you, I am definitely better after such a long rest. Food helps!' he added, trying to distract from his emotions.

'It is not going to be easy for you.' Meriona shook her head slightly and looked saddened. 'The effect of Verun's anger directed through the gem was fairly devastating, but the fact that you have come this far is in your favour.'

Amiros blew out a short breath.

'I'm really quite lost with all this,' he started, 'it was some time before I even remembered who I was and although

I did recall when Verun . . .' he tailed off, the remembered pain still sharp.

'It will hurt, and continue so for some time, I think,' Meriona said. 'But you will master it in time.'

'But I still don't really remember that much about my life,' Amiros frowned and grimaced. 'Yes, I remember you of course, and that led me to Alinor. You would be proud of her, she is an exceptional young woman.'

Meriona smiled.

'I know,' she said. 'The legacy she carries is a huge burden; Teleston and I were both aware of the implications but I had confidence that with your protection and guidance she would grow into it.'

'She's quite headstrong you know.' As he spoke, memories of Alinor's childhood were returning and he laughed as he now shared some of her escapades with her mother.

'Her father had to be quite strict after I was gone,' Meriona said, 'Oh, I do know a few things. I have been able to watch her sometimes, though not as much as I would have liked.'

Amiros wondered about this strange existence, about how those who had left this life, or rather the life that he had known, could still somehow watch over the ones left behind. He could barely take his eyes off the beautiful woman sat beside him, her voice, her very presence breathed life into his soul.

'It's not easy to explain, dear friend. Perhaps as you progress here you may come to some understanding, but that is as maybe. For now it is important that you regain your own memories before you may learn what could be. Learn to walk again before you start to run and jump!'

'You are right, of course, but it is hard when there are so many gaps. I just want to – I don't know – get back to how it was, I suppose. But then, that can't happen can it? I cannot undo what has been done to me.'

'No, you cannot undo it as such, but you can go beyond it. You need to come to terms with what has happened before you can even start to think of what is to be after that.'

Amiros was thoughtful. First things first, he supposed, but is there a future for me?

'Only you can answer that,' said Meriona.

Of course she knew what he was thinking, she was Ben-Neteru after all. More to the point and more confusing, she was dead, wasn't she? She had passed on from her life – was that death?

Meriona rose and picked up her basket.

'You need to be on your own,' she said, 'I will see you again when you are ready.'

He took her hand and laid his lips gently on it.

'If I can find one point of joy in all this,' he said, 'it is that I have seen you again.'

'Be strong, my dear, I believe in you – always have done – and trust that you will be able to choose the right way.'

She turned and went off down the shaded walk, disappearing through a small doorway at the far end.

Amiros watched her go, taking some of the brightness of the sun with her; she hasn't changed at all, he thought, she is just as I remember her. But, he sighed, I need to remember everything else as well. He started to walk around the courtyard, barely seeing it, engrossed in trying to form his thoughts into a coherent pattern. It was difficult to know where to start, images arose randomly, some from early in his life, many from later, then back again. Voices talking to him, places he had been, so many people whose names he couldn't recall; some he knew he should know well, others not so much. He stepped out from the shade of the columns and wandered over to the fountain. The water was cool and clear, its gentle splashing soothing the tumult of his mind.

There was a fountain not unlike this, he thought. Where was it? Yes, in Pelamir it was, in the palace. Alinor was showing him how she had first learned to create an illusion – the wonderful horse which grew wings. He smiled. She had been so pleased with herself, it was shortly after she had learned to use The Firestone and they had spent useful time in the great library. Early days for her it had been, before she had met Remon.

There, another breakthrough. Whilst he had recalled that the great Mind-Master had sent him to watch over Alinor the thought had been connected with the lovely Meriona. Now he started to think back over the years he had spent studying with Remon, his acceptance as a student and progression into the Brotherhood. How many decades had he toiled over the books and struggled to perfect his magics; and how careful Remon had been to keep certain knowledge from him in order that he could protect Alinor and Sirad so that if the worst came he could not betray what he did not know. The worst had come in the shape of Verun and the years of care had paid off. Despite all Verun's attempts he had been unable to extract the information from him and had thus vented his anger by the use of the Stone of Power.

It was slowly falling into place now.

He felt tired, his head throbbing with the effort to trying to marshal the wayward memories. I really don't want to think about this any more today, I've had enough, it's too much.

He made his way back out of the courtyard and to his room. He poured himself a little wine and sipped slowly. After a little while he simply lay down on the bed; within moments his eyes closed and he drifted off.

The next morning saw the start of how his days would to follow a pattern; after breakfasting he would meet Meriona in the courtyard to talk for a little while but would then spend time wandering through the gardens to let his mind work on remembering and adjusting. A couple of hours later he was taken to see one of the healers.

'Your body as well as your mind has suffered punishment,' Meriona told him. 'Although you may not be aware of exactly what happened I can see how the power of the stone exacted an awful toll. Alinor and Sirad were able to mend much of the physical damage when you were returned to them, but as you have never regained consciousness in that life, you fortunately cannot appreciate just what occurred.'

'But I seem to be fine now,' Amiros protested.

'That is your perception, certainly, but this plane of being which you currently inhabit alters your perceptions and thus you have not yet recognised the damage to your physical body in the real world.'

That took some thinking about for Amiros; however, he bowed to Meriona's superior knowledge under the circumstances and agreed to let the Healer see him.

He was directed to a quiet room wherein the Healer was waiting. It was a woman neither old nor young, some indeterminate age but with an unmistakeable aura of quiet power. She bade him sit and simply gazed into his eyes for a while; he could feel the soft probe of her mind seeking whatever was wrong with his body.

'The Lady Meriona was right in what she has told me about your experience,' she said. 'I have not seen one with such extensive damage before and I wonder that you survived at all.'

Amiros tried not to show his dismay at her words. Even though Meriona had warned him, he had found it hard to believe until the healer herself had confirmed it.

'No, do not be upset,' she said, well aware of his feelings, 'you have been fortunate to have received the attentions of very skilled healers even before coming here. Were it not for the work they did, it could have been a different matter.'

She busied herself setting up aromatic candles and filling bowls with various herbs which she placed around the room before directing him to a low couch.

'Please, lie down and calm yourself. I shall not cause you any pain, indeed, you will find our session quite relaxing.'

He did as he was bid, curious now and interested in her actions. He had never studied healing to any great extent, though was quite proficient when needed. The healer walked around him twice, stopping now and then to hold both her hands a few inches above his body, concentrating on his legs, arms and hands. He could feel a warmth seeping into his limbs, not at all unpleasant; but then she stopped at his head and rested both hands over his eyes. He felt a shock; hard to describe, it didn't actually hurt, but was very strange.

She moved away and stood with her eyes closed, breathing deeply.

'This will take time,' she said finally. 'Even though I was warned I did not expect the damage to be so deep.'

'But you can do something?' asked Amiros.

'Yes,' she replied slowly. 'But I must tell you that in life your eyes have been burned extensively.'

'But yet I can see,' he frowned.

'While you are here, yes. But if you were able to return, and that is not yet certain, I do not think you would still have that sight.'

He left shortly after this pronouncement and spent the rest of the day considering his strange circumstance.

When he saw Meriona the next morning he didn't have to tell her of his anxiety as a result of what the healer had told him.

'I find it so – difficult - ,' he started, 'to understand how I am here in this place, on this plane, in this state of being, which is and is yet not life. This body I have,' he opened his hands, palms facing upward, 'seems real enough, and yet the healer has told me that my *real* body was, is, damaged. How can this be?'

'You had already remembered about your encounter with Verun before you arrived here, and I know that you experienced a shadow of the pain he inflicted upon you. The effect of Mnethar was to tear your inner being, your very soul, from your earthly body, and cast it into this existence. He intended it to be an eternal punishment, for your body would remain trapped, alive, but without its essential essence.'

'I knew that this between life and death was supposed to exist, but I suppose that in a way I treated it as a myth, half believing but not convinced. I have no choice now but to believe, it seems, as I am apparently here.'

Suddenly a wave of confusion swept over him, a chaos of emotions: despair, loneliness, desolation and helplessness. He wanted to rail at whatever powers had reduced him to this state. Meriona sat quietly watching as the turmoil raged through her beloved friend, powerless to intercede. Eventually she sensed the worst of it had diminished.

'I am sorry my love, and I wish I could do more to help you, but even I do not fully understand what has been done to you. I do know, however, that you must come to accept it, even if you do not know the extent of it, before you can move on.'

'Move on how?'

'You must re-learn yourself, what you are, what you know and what you can do. When you have done that it will be time to fill in what you were not taught and pave the way for your full development, if that is possible.'

She would say no more about it, but merely told him that understanding could only come from within himself.

So the days passed, walking and thinking, spending time with the healer and then just more thinking; gradually building his strength up along with the memories of his life, the studies he had undertaken, identifying again the scope of his own skill.

Above all he enjoyed the limited time that was spent with Meriona. Her very presence instilled a calmness in him and helped to ease the discomforts that some memories engendered. When she perceived the time was right she directed him to a building that housed a number of books. He had passed by it several times on his way around what seemed to be in effect a small town. People went about their business, what that may have been, as they would have done back in what he had to call real life. The difference was a total harmony and lack of any want or hardship. It wasn't the same as the mysterious paradise he had managed to escape, but yet it was a place of peace. As the days passed he felt more relaxed and resigned to his condition. The library building was not large, nor did it appear to house the vast collections with which he had worked whilst in Pelamir or Ancor or even Remon's mansion. Everything he looked at was new to him, an immense wealth of arcane instruction. The first volume he chose fitted as an appropriate follow-on from his existing knowledge, filling in some gaps in his understanding of the ancient myths, and introducing previously unknown information. Gradually he could start to see how the ancient lore had taken shape, reflections of the way of life under the Ben-Neteru from centuries uncounted. There were accounts here of the conflict from time immemorial between forces of good and evil and how Rakep-thos in his youth had been instrumental in banishing the baleful entity that was the source of this evil. Banished, but not eliminated. The destructive influence would still be felt and it had eventually led to the Scattering Wars, an attempt to destroy the harmony of the peoples of Sakor. To an extent it had succeeded, and as Amiros was aware, almost all of those beings who possessed the Power had been lost. But Rakep-thos had toiled to restore the kingdom to some of its previous glory, but by the time of his passing the Powers and lore had become more myth than reality.

He remembered chiding Alinor that she had not considered that her bloodline as a descendent of Rakep-thos had made her a recipient of some of the powers of the ancients. The time he had spent in the library in Pelamir helping her to learn had been a time of learning for him as well; he had willingly undertaken the role of guardian and teacher for Alinor and Sirad and had not allowed himself to regret that this had prevented him from completing the training that Remon would have provided his successor. It did not occur to him now that in some way this was being remedied. Instead he simply indulged his natural curiosity and desire to study with this opportunity he had been given.

It was a strange period; there were times that the almost inconceivable nature of his present state prevented any coherent thought and caused heart-wrenching distress, but at other times he could forget that completely and feel totally comfortable with his sojourn in this peaceful haven.

He and Meriona sat one lunchtime in the dappled shade of the courtyard, listening to the drowsy sound of bees and insects amongst the flowers, birdsong and the quiet splashing of water from the fountain.

'It is good here,' said Amiros, 'I had not expected to feel this way.'

'Go on,' said Meriona when he seemed lost in thought.

'When I first arrived you said that I needed to recover before seeing what may come later. I know that I am as well as I can be – the healer has helped with that, although she won't talk about my eyes which is perhaps a little annoying. However, having those books to study is a great joy – they will give me years of pleasure, and I have your company again.'

The lovely woman took a deep breath, shook her head and looked sadly at him.

'Amiros, dearest friend, I am sorry but you must realise that this will not continue. There are decisions you must make and I don't know that I could stop you if you were to try to stay. But you need to understand that I will not be here much longer. I do not know how I came to be here, but I was sent to help you if I could, to be a part of your healing and an instrument of your development.'

His shock registered plainly, followed by an empty feeling deep within his heart.

'Must I lose you again?' he murmured, controlling the urge to take hold of her hand. 'I must have been a fool to think that there could be joy after such pain.'

'You are no fool, do not ever think that,' she reprimanded him. 'You never were and never could be. It was almost inevitable that you would reach this point. Others who are less strong than yourself might give up, but you have always faced up to the challenges that your destiny created and I don't believe that you have changed so much that you would now abandon the role you committed to in life.'

There was silence between them for several minutes.

'I don't know,' he said, 'I cannot make that choice. How can I go back if it means a return to the pains and anguish of before when it was just so hard – so hard?'

He covered his face with his hands, everything that had hurt him in life once again overwhelmed him.

'My daughter needs you.'

He shook his head several times and grimaced as if in pain. He had promised, he had sworn to protect Alinor and now her beloved mother was calling on that promise.

'Without your help she and Sirad will likely fail. Can you really let that happen?'

Amiros looked into her eyes, the eyes of a mother full of love for her child, pleading with him to fulfil his oath.

'You know that I cannot deny you,' he said, his voice breaking. 'I cannot deny what is in me and the love I have always carried for you in my heart. If it must be, then so be it.'

She smiled sadly and took his hand.

'I am so sorry. I know that what I am asking I would not ask of any other but you. I myself do not fully understand how this is to come about, but only what is required of me to help you progress.

'When, if, you are released from this level of existence, you will need to be prepared for what may happen. As it is with Alinor and Sirad you must be given the knowledge that will enable you to develop the skills that are necessary for you to progress. The Power is there for you, and in time you will draw upon it and learn its worth. In Remon's time you made use of the crystal to harness the energies that shaped your mind. Now it is time to go beyond that.'

He nodded.

'You remember that it was not an experience without requiring considerable effort; stress is a somewhat feeble way of describing it.'

Amiros nodded again, clearly remembering just how 'stressful' it had been.

'Tomorrow morning I will take you to the sanctuary and there we will begin.'

'How - ?' he started but she interrupted.

'No questions now, dear friend. Take time to prepare yourself and we will meet after breakfast.'

Chapter 15

After a cold and misty damp start the day gradually improved and by mid-morning there were fewer grey clouds scudding across the skies, although the temperature stubbornly refused to rise very far. It was a route Alinor knew well, though even after a couple of years there were many changes; trees had grown bigger, some had been felled or lost to bad weather, some old farm buildings abandoned or fallen into decay, some homesteads improved slightly, others looking the worse for wear.

Was it only two years or so since she last came this way, when her father had requested her return from Coranien-dulat? Time was a strange thing, she thought, for it seemed both like an eternity and yet so recent. I was so young then, so naïve in many ways, and like all young people thought that things would never really change. How wrong I was! I had expected my father to reign for many years to come, he was invincible, the valorous and noble warrior king, respected amongst all other rulers and loved by his people. And yet, within six short months of my return to Thorgiliad he had been murdered, butchered by wicked men driven by an enemy the depths of whose evil I cannot not yet comprehend. The pain of his loss still left her heart aching and today was one of those days when she felt it strongly. It was bearable, of course it was; life does not stop when you lose one you love, you have to carry on, no matter how much it hurts or how much you would wish it to all go away.

Elkana tossed her head, reminding Alinor that much good had come into her life despite the hardships and agonies of those past two years. Stroking the silky neck of the beautiful mare she was reminded that the horse was Sirad's first gift to her. Thinking of him warmed her heart and helped to heal the hurts in her soul. Whatever happened they would have each other; however dangerous the way ahead would be they could rely on the support and love that bound them each to each.

Semira saw how Alinor's face relaxed when she stroked the mare. Riding off to one side she had watched unobtrusively as her friend's demeanour had saddened for a while, recalling what memories she could not even guess at. She knew better than to intrude on Alinor's opportunity for personal moments – goodness knows there were few enough of them except in the dark hours of the night when she was aware that the young queen spent too many sleepless hours. She felt a bond of friendship with the extraordinary woman that surprised her with its intensity; even in the short time they had known each other they had become very close and Alinor would talk over many things in her daily life, not that she was expecting Semira to advise her on matters of state, but inviting her opinion and impressions as a valued companion. For that Semira felt honoured and daily more determined to support and defend her royal friend.

Just then Alinor turned and smiled at Semira.

'I think that Coranien-dulat will perhaps remind you of Elagos,' she said, 'though not with the same magnificence by some margin, but the mountain country has great beauty and it is a city of which I am very fond.'

'Are you looking forward to seeing your friends?' asked Semira.

'Yes, I am. I had many good years there and it will always hold pleasant memories for me. I remember one day . . .'

For a couple of hours Alinor regaled Semira with stories of the games she and her companions used to enjoy, and of the tricks they would play upon gullible adults charged with their care. Their talking was punctuated regularly with happy laughter as the miles slipped by.

The trip was to be a low-key, semi-private one, to allow Alinor a bit of breathing space after so many weeks of intense work. She was still tired, but was starting to sleep better now that she felt things were more under control. The pressures she had felt to continue the fight against Verun had diminished, and although she knew that the battle was far from over, she had managed to get some perspective back. The worry that hurt most was the continuing state of the Lore-Master. There had been no word from Sirad about the arrival of Eldren and Mirantha which was disturbing, but she forced herself to accept that there must be a good reason for the delay.

Coranien-dulat did not disappoint either woman. Alinor was welcomed as a long-lost daughter, albeit with the deference and pomp appropriate to the new queen. Alinor swiftly made it clear that she was not there to stand on ceremony and wished to enjoy a few days amongst old friends away from the burdens of rulership. Hence the time passed easily, and alas, all too quickly. Alinor appreciated the break and enjoyed being able to relax in a place so familiar to her. The mountain air, cold as it could be, was refreshing, and she enjoyed introducing Semira to her childhood friends, some of them now happily married with young children in arms. There were occasional mentions of Vixlan's mismanagement, but most had heard of how Alinor had made many changes and knew that it would not be too long before the greedy Steward got his well-deserved come-uppance. Not a few would be more than happy to see the man come to a permanent end.

Alinor and Sirad talked – not every day, but often enough so that each were aware of what was happening. Alinor felt confident enough now to tell him her thoughts about her coronation and that the mid-winter festival seemed to be the favourite date. It wasn't too far away now, he pointed out, in view of the time it would take for the necessary preparations. Don't worry, she said, it will be fine. When I get back to Thorgiliad I will start the ball rolling, send out invitations, and all that sort of thing. I've got a brilliant woman to oversee arrangements . . And who is that, interrupted Sirad. Not sure if you know her, joked Alinor, a young woman from Elagos, goes by the name of Semira.

They laughed together at that. Always thought she was a capable sort, said Sirad. And you were right, my love, Alinor responded. She has taken the palace by the ears and given it a good shake-up. Although, she hesitated, Semira doesn't actually know yet about the coronation! But, there are some excellent people to assist who know all about the correct protocols and traditional stuff so she won't be on her own.

Just as well, said Sirad, for I would have thought it a totally overwhelming task to take on.

This is the start of a new era for Ancor, said Alinor thoughtfully, and I do want to make some changes – not to upset anyone, but because this is now my responsibility and it will be done my way.

And I am sure that you will succeed, my beloved. I look forward to receiving my own invitation to the ball!

I miss you so much, my darling prince, I long to have you here with me so that I can really touch and hold you.

You have no idea how I long to be there, responded Sirad, but it won't be long now.

Through Alinor's eyes Sirad was able to look out across the mountains surrounding the city and could feel her pleasure at being there. He could feel too her longing and her love reaching out to him. For a moment he wondered if their parents had shared the same sort of rich emotion that forged such a remarkable bond between those who truly loved. They must have done, he decided, or we would not be here.

Try not to take any unnecessary risks; that had been Sirad's warning when Alinor set out on what would be a crucial trip to search out Vixlan's secret lair. Knowing that the deceitful man had instructed his minions to ensure that the meddlesome new queen did not reach his treasure trove before they had had chance to remove it all to somewhere safer, Alinor was aware that it would be a potentially hazardous venture. Even with her enhanced skills, she could not watch everyone all the time, but every precaution that she and Dhalen had put in place should be sufficient to forestall any attacks that Vixlan's men could make.

The Steward himself had been uneasy for several days prior to their leaving Thorgiliad and Alinor had enjoyed the man's discomfort at the thought of losing everything he had managed to steal from her people. He had worried less for his own safety, his arrogance assuring him that he would somehow be safe from any actions she could take. How little you know you miserable rat, was her thought.

For the first week on the road things went along smoothly, but once they got nearer to their goal the tensions rose. Alinor maintained her air of innocence in her search for an ideal retreat, somewhere she, with or without her consort, would be able to relax, hunt perhaps and simply get away from affairs of state. In contrast, Vixlan was trying, not completely successfully, to intercept any of the locals' suggestions about suitable properties. He tried to convince Alinor that it would be much easier for her to choose a site and build a villa for herself – something suitable for a queen. He was less than happy to be assured by that lady that she didn't want another palace, only a more simple lodge – hence finding an existing property rather than start from scratch.

'I'm pretty certain that today will see some action from Vixlan's supporters,' she quietly told Mikeln, the captain chosen by Dhalen to command her protection party. 'Likely an ambush of some kind. He wasn't able to bring too many of his minions with him, but you do need to keep an eye on them – I know you have been all along, thank you.'

'Don't worry, my Lady, we are well prepared. No harm will come to you from anything that man can do.'

'No, I'm not worried for myself, Captain, but I would not like any of *my* entourage to be hurt.'

The man nodded, fully understanding her meaning, and then strode off to oversee the party's breaking camp and setting off.

It was wet underfoot, but not enough to slow the party and the wind was blustery and cold. Not the most pleasant of days, thought Alinor, but this trip is important. I want Vixlan finally brought to justice; I want him to answer for his greed and cruelty; I want my people to have what is rightfully theirs. This needs to end today.

It was shortly before they planned to halt for their midday break that one of her party approached, bringing a local man with him.

'My Lady,' the courtier said, 'I asked this man if he knew of anywhere suitable in the area, the same as we have asked all those we met, and he has a suggestion.'

Alinor looked down and noted a middle-aged man, weather-beaten and accustomed to the hard work of eking a living off the land. He held his battered hat loosely in one hand and seemed not in the least awed that he was in the presence of his sovereign. He met Alinor's piercing look with openness and confidence.

'Good day to you, woodsman,' said Alinor, 'I appreciate your coming forward and sharing your knowledge. This time of year must keep you very busy preparing to see out the winter with your family. Your son still lacks the years and strength to be of much assistance to you.'

The man's eyes registered some surprise, but then he nodded.

'Indeed, but he works hard and is very good at draying the wood back to our farm.'

'A son to be proud of, I am sure,' responded Alinor, 'but what of this property that may suit my purpose?'

'A long day's walk from here, your Ladyship, east until you can see the river coming from the high ground to the northeast, then north to where the forest thins out. Moons back it belonged to a wealthy lord, but when he died it fell into disrepair and remained so until the summer before last. Then new folk came and repaired it all, secured it against the elements and all comers. I don't rightly think that anyone lives there much, but there is coming and going quite regular.'

'That sounds interesting, woodsman. If it is not someone's full time residence, then it may indeed be just what I am seeking.'

Alinor signalled to one of her entourage who handed her a small purse of coins which she passed to her informant.

'Thank you for your information, I am grateful to you for your time.'

The surprised man looked at the purse, judging its weight and realising that it would considerably ease the hardship of the coming winter.

'It is I who is grateful, my Lady. If you ever have need, just ask for Evin. I would be glad to be of assistance.'

'Thank you Evin, I shall not forget.'

Alinor nodded to the man and the party moved off, but she made sure that Captain Mikeln ensured that no-one from Vixlan's group followed the woodsman as he returned to his work.

Vixlan was trying to stay as far away from Alinor as possible; surely his people would make their move very soon, especially after that annoying local had so clearly identified his formerly secret treasure store. He had taken months to prepare the place, with every precaution possible to prevent anyone suspecting that it was more than an occasional place for some well-to-do to visit. If his instructions had been followed, some of his ill-gotten gains should already have been moved temporarily, but he had the uncomfortable feeling that his hitherto reliable servants were perhaps less to be relied upon than before. Of course, Alinor chose now to talk with him and tell him what the man had said.

'It sounds as if it may indeed be what you seek,' he said to her, the words sticking in his throat. Even in the cold air he could feel a trickle of sweat starting to run down his back and fought to maintain a calm demeanour in the presence of this young woman who sometimes seemed to see right through him. Was he about to lose everything he had gained since the old king was murdered? Although he hadn't been an active participant in the ambush of Teleston – indeed it had come as a bit of a surprise – he had not hesitated to turn the situation to his advantage. He had believed that the removal of Alinor would serve his purpose; whilst the king had trusted him enough to confide that it was necessary for him to take his daughter to Elagos, he had not revealed the actual purpose of that proposed visit. Easy enough for Vixlan to have passed on that information to his mysterious contact who had first approached him nearly three years ago. Without the Steward being aware of what was happening, he had been systematically indoctrinated, his former loyalty to his king eroded – not a difficult task in view of Vixlan's innate greed – and the way was paved for the destruction of Ancor's ruling family.

Now the Steward could feel the walls closing in around him. All his efforts, for he did not credit any others with their part, could be brought to nought if this meddlesome female was not stopped.

'Perhaps now would be a good time to halt for some refreshment, My Lady,' suggested the Steward. 'All this travelling gives me an appetite.'

Alinor knew the ruse for what it was. If they stopped now, it could be an ideal opportunity for the proposed ambush to take advantage of the situation with everyone less on their guard perhaps.

'A good suggestion,' Alinor responded and signalled to where Mikeln was riding a few yards off to one side.

As Vixlan endeavoured to move away as quickly as he could, Alinor murmured a few words to her Captain, ostensibly simply requesting a halt, but in fact advising him to alert his men to be ready for what was surely about to happen.

Alinor called Vixlan back to her as they all dismounted; Semira had ridden up from where she had been chatting with a couple of the palace servants and Alinor passed Elkana's reins to her with a smile.

'If you don't mind?' Alinor said.

'Of course not,' Semira replied, knowing that there was an ulterior motive. She's expecting something to happen, I can tell, Semira thought, and wants me out of the way. Warning understood.

The area where they had stopped was bordered by mature trees set a little way back from the track they had been following. The ground was covered with rough grass, somewhat uneven in places with the occasional large moss-covered boulder. As servants unpacked food and drink from the spare horses as started to set out a place for them to sit, Alinor was asking Vixlan some harmless questions about the area and the best way for this new lodge, should it be suitable, to be prepared.

The conversation didn't last long.

In a moment, uncannily like the day in Mindros when Sirad and his friends were attacked, armed men attacked the queen's retinue, coming at them from three sides. Had it not been for Alinor's warnings, perhaps her guard would have been slightly less prepared. As it was the fighting was bloody. Alinor had drawn Shenbran in a split second and dispatched two attackers before they had chance to defend themselves. They were perhaps outnumbered, but the attackers did not have the training and discipline of Alinor's guards, though they were able to inflict some minor injuries on both the guards and the unfortunate servants. Alinor was a key target but Vixlan had drastically underestimated the young woman and thus his hired assassins were unprepared for the savagery of her counter-defence. For her part, Semira had readied her bow as she stood in the horse line, unseen by the attackers. A couple of well-placed arrows found their marks before she drew her knife to defend herself against a large attacker. He in turn was struck down by a guard as he advanced on the slight woman.

Vixlan had dropped to the ground the moment the fighting started and tried to hide behind one of the boulders, not completely trusting his hirelings to make a mistake and take him out as well.

Alinor took in the scene; the would-be assassins were nearly all dead with the remaining couple out of action, the ambush an ignominious failure. Vixlan hurriedly got up and rushed to Alinor's side, asking if she was all right and condemning the outrageous assault on her person.

She had chance to respond that she was totally unhurt but before she could say anything else she felt a stab of heat from where The Firestone hung around her neck and clearly heard a loud neigh of warning from Elkana.

An unearthly, deep rumbling growl from behind where Vixlan had been hiding caused Alinor's blood to run cold. There was no-one within twenty feet of her other than Vixlan; it would take barely a few seconds for the *bahlam* to reach her. The enormous cat seemed to materialise from the dark shadows, its strange eyes glowing as it focussed on her, its mouth partly open revealing huge teeth. She still held Shenbran in her hand, the fateful sword glowing with its unearthly power as she stared back at the creature. With her other hand she tried to push Vixlan out of the way, but the man was petrified and clung on to her, babbling that she must save him. Before she could release herself from his grip the cat launched itself with frightening speed. Vixlan was in the way.

The cat closed its jaws on the hapless Steward's throat and tossed him aside like a leaf, blood spraying from the ruptured arteries. Alinor stumbled on the uneven tussocks of rough grass dropping to one knee. With barely any hesitation the cat prepared to take its intended victim. Almost before Alinor could raise her precious sword an arrow whistled past her head, striking the cat in the shoulder. The cat howled but was not stopped; the moment's hesitation allowed Alinor to strike the creature directly in its chest, missing the ribcage and entering its heart. The weight as it dropped almost took the sword from her grip; for a moment the cat lay with heaving sides as its life blood poured from the fatal wound into the waiting earth. The cat's eyes looked straight at Alinor, the unnatural glow fading; she had the strangest feeling that the animal was somehow thanking her for releasing it from the evil under which it had been constrained.

She took a few deep breaths and looked around to find who had let loose that timely arrow. Her dark hair flying, Semira came rushing over to where Alinor stood over the body of the *bahlam*, still carrying her bow.

'Are you hurt, are you all right?' her breathless questions came quickly.

'I am fine, thanks to you my friend,' Alinor smiled and reached out to touch her companion. 'Your arrow was timely indeed – I can see that Dhalen was right about not underestimating your growing skills. I owe you.'

Semira blushed, relieved beyond words that her mistress has escaped unscathed. She looked down at the cat in wonder at its sheer size, amazed that such an animal existed, and very much in awe at the undoubted power it had possessed.

The pair were surrounded now by the guards as Mikeln anxiously sought Alinor's reassurance that all was well. Satisfied as he was by the way the ambush had been thwarted, the appearance of the cat had unnerved him and he felt guilty that he had not been able to protect his sovereign in such a perilous moment.

'You have carried out your duties well, Captain; please do not feel any guilt, the cat was after me alone and there would have been little you could have done to protect me from such a creature. It did, however, claim one unintended victim,' she indicated where Vixlan lay, still as death.

'Quickly,' called Mikeln to one of his men, 'help the Steward!'

Alinor reached out a hand.

'It is too late, Captain. He didn't stand a chance.'

A closer look told Mikeln she was right. Swiftly he ordered that the body be taken up, and checked on any of his troops who had been hurt in any way.

'We will press on and find this property. We'll stay there tonight before we make a return to Thorgiliad tomorrow. You will have chance then to have Vixlan's body tended so that he may be returned to the capital. As for them,' she indicated the remaining assassins, 'patch them up and we will take them back as well.'

The man nodded his understanding and proceeded to organise a clear up of the area, bodies were buried and horses retrieved. Alinor instructed that the cat be buried separately, and herself placed a small cairn of stones over its grave. You were not to blame for how that magician used you, was her thought, as she remembered the dying look in its eyes.

Brief refreshment was taken before finally setting off again. They moved at a fair pace and were able to reach the property before it was fully dark. It wasn't possible to get a good look at the outside, but the refurbishment inside was reasonable and enabled the party somewhere comfortable to stay for the night. The interesting development was when they accessed several rooms which were packed with monies and valuable items acquired by the late Steward.

Alinor's captain whistled as they broke the door down on one of the rooms. There were trunks of rich fabrics, jewelled lamps, statues, carvings and furniture that would not have been out of place in the palace itself.

'I remember some of these items,' Alinor said through gritted teeth. 'That man has systematically looted our family's treasures. I can hardly believe how he managed to get away with it.'

If Mikeln was thinking how appropriate it was that the Steward had met a grisly end, he managed to hide it, although Alinor didn't need any sixth sense to recognise his anger and disgust.

'After we get back to Thorgiliad I would ask that you take charge of returning all this to its rightful place, Captain. We can leave a guard here, can we not, until that happens?

'Of course, my Lady, that will not be a problem. And I shall be glad to oversee its return.'

After a night's sleep Alinor allowed herself to feel a relief that the problem of Vixlan's punishment had been unexpectedly solved. Ironic really that it had been as a result of Verun's machinations. His death, not at her hands, would still allow her to present his criminal activities to the people. They would not be sorry that he was dead, that was certain, although some would perhaps prefer him to have been publicly tried and convicted in order to visit a suitably painful punishment upon him.

It was with a huge feeling of relief that Alinor returned to Thorgiliad. At last she felt that she had made real progress in rescuing her beloved country from the tyranny that Vixlan had visited upon it. Although there was still much to be done, now she could feel that with the help of the good people she had gathered around her, the government of Ancor could finish the task of dismantling the controls and restrictions that the Steward has introduced and her people to look forward to a return of freedom and prosperity.

Word of Vixlan's demise spread like wildfire through the palace and city; within a few days it would reach the borders of Ancor. Many a cask of ale was breached in the taverns as people celebrated – not too obviously, mind – and raised toasts to their new ruler.

Alinor returned to her apartments following a brief meeting with various key ministers and spent a few minutes going through some paperwork, fortunately nothing particularly urgent, but she wanted it out of the way. Summoning one of the ever present footmen outside her door she sent him to find the Mistress of the Household and request that she attend her Lady at her earliest convenience.

It wasn't long before Semira arrived, wondering what was so urgent this morning. An hour earlier Dhalen had privately sought her out specifically and commended her actions during the confrontation with the late Steward's assassins and the attack by the *bahlam*.

'Your diligence in training has paid off, young lady,' the doughty warrior said, 'and I am grateful that you were able to intercede. But for your timely shot, things may have turned out differently.'

Semira shook her head.

'I am sure that Alinor, I mean, Her Ladyship, would have been all right really,' she said.

'That's as maybe,' responded Dhalen, placing a kindly hand on Semira's shoulder, 'but I have no doubt that you prevented possible injuries.'

'Thank you, Commander, I do appreciate your words. And I have to thank you for all your help in teaching me. I know I still have much to learn and need to keep working to improve, but without you I may never have realised what I could do.'

Dhalen looked down at her and smiled.

'You have proven to be a well-chosen companion for Alinor, Semira. I am glad she has such a one as you for a friend.'

Still basking in the glow of his words, Semira entered Alinor's rooms and approached the large table where the young queen sat, compiling a list of – she didn't know what.

'Oh good, there you are,' said Alinor cheerfully. 'Do sit down, we've got a lot to sort out.'

With a slight frown, Semira did as requested.

'Is this about the stuff that Vixlan had in the lodge? I thought Mikeln was going to –'

'No, no, no, no,' interrupted Alinor, 'that's all in hand, you don't need to worry about that at the moment. This is something else entirely.'

That's a relief, thought Semira, because I wouldn't have the first idea about what to do with it.

'Now that Vixlan is finally out of the way I must accede to the demands being made by my ministers about the coronation.'

Semira couldn't stop herself.

'Oh wow, this is wonderful!' she exclaimed. 'I've heard stories from some of the older folk about your father and mother, and I must admit I am really excited about it.'

'I would never have guessed.'

They both laughed at that.

'Seriously, now,' said Alinor, 'there is a lot to do as I have decided that the mid-winter festival is probably the best date, but, as you know, that is not so far away now.'

'Good grief, that's only, what, less than three months? How on earth are you going to manage?'

'I am well aware of the timing,' Alinor chided, 'and I am also aware that within the palace people have had this in mind and have been making their own preparations ever since I came back from Elagos, so it won't be such a surprise. And as for *me* managing, I rather thought that the task would benefit from the attentions of the Mistress of my Household.'

'What! Hang on a moment. We're talking about a coronation, not a banquet or, or, whatever.'

'Slow down, Semira, and just take a few breaths to calm down.' Alinor was trying not to laugh out loud at the expressions on her friend's face. 'I am not suggesting that you will be solely responsible for everything – remember there are a lot of people in the palace, and there are a number of very experienced folk whom we can rely on to provide assistance, information and knowledge. There are a couple of people with whom I will set up a meeting; they are steeped in the traditions of Ancor and I want to see what they have to say. I have a mind to break with some of the old ways; this is not out of disrespect, but because we are in a new era and I want to do some things my way, and not just because it's always been done like this or that.'

Semira nodded her understanding. She didn't think there had ever been a sovereign quite like this young woman and it made sense that she would want to start as she meant to go on.

'All right, I can see that is a good point to start from. But I have no experience with anything even remotely like this. I can admit that the thought simply terrifies me!'

'Well, my friend, you can put that feeling away right now. Yes it is an occasion of pomp and significance for both Ancor and all our allies, but it is also a day of celebration, of looking ahead, of starting a new reign in new times. It must not be so overshadowed by formality as to detract from that celebration. If I were really honest, I would just have a very small ceremony, a bit of a party and that's it. However, I don't think that would be allowed!'

Semira had to laugh.

'You're right there, m'Lady! As if we could let this day go past without making the most of it. I won't let you do that, let alone what everyone else would say.'

'Thought as much,' said Alinor wryly. 'So, faithful friend, I think we'd best start looking at making some plans.'

Semira's quick mind moved into top gear.

'Firstly we need to send out invitations, in view of the timescale. Those coming from far afield need time to prepare themselves and travel. We need to have some idea of how many people you are inviting and what we shall be doing with them when they get here. When are they likely to arrive, how long will they stay, and all that sort of thing. Then logistics: we need to feed and house them all, together with their retinues. All that is apart from the actual ceremonies, which I don't yet have any information about.'

Alinor could smile to herself; she knew that Semira would soon get to grips with the occasion and despite her actual inexperience would use her natural ability as an organiser to itemise the tasks – with input from others of course – and ensure that all eventualities would be covered.

Semira was talking quietly to herself.

'Ceremonial robes – need to find out about those. Robes for all the palace attendees, some really stunning outfits for the centre of attraction. Décor. Hangings in the Great Hall, they'll need to be replaced. Then what about where the ceremony itself takes place, will that be in the Great Hall or the Throne Room? Not sure, need to ask about that. Flowers of course, lots of flowers.'

'I think you're getting the idea now,' said Alinor. 'Told you it would be all right.'

Semira dragged herself back from an ever-increasing mental list.

'What I suggest you do now,' Alinor continued, 'is to go back down to the kitchen, speak to Maesie and ask her to start considering which special cooks, bakers and other culinary artists she wants to call on to assist her. I'm sure that those who were obliged to leave will not miss the opportunity to return for this occasion! I'm going to ask a few people to meet with us later this afternoon just to start the ball rolling.'

Semira nodded.

'Of course, a ball or two – or even more, musicians and all that. Mmm, yes, Maesie will have ideas for how to cater for that as well.'

'One thing at a time, Semira! We'll draw up a timetable this afternoon, work out some priorities and identify the people we need.'

'Yes, this first meeting will help to clarify matters,' said Semira eagerly. 'We'll probably need to have quite a few meetings in quick succession at the beginning.'

'Go on, get out of here before you get ahead of yourself,' urged Alinor, trying not to laugh at Semira's seriousness, 'and I'll see you down in the Blue Chamber later.'

No going back now, thought Alinor as Semira hurried from the room. There was a great deal to think about and although she had entertained a few ideas over the past few weeks, she had not actually made any real kind of decision about what she wanted to do. What was the most important thing, she wondered. What will be the future of Ancor? Verun may be out of the way at the moment, but we haven't seen the last of him, that is certain. So much unfinished business, so much that is still hidden, mysteries that may well be far more important than me being crowned ruler of Ancor. Power. And Tokens. All the things that Remon hinted at but did not explain. What of Sirad and myself and our heritage?

Amiros. What about Amiros? We need him, I just know that he is important and oh, I miss him so much.

For a while Alinor simply sat remembering all the time she had spent with the Lore-Master. He had told her such wonderful stories, many of which she now knew to be true. From the little that Sirad had told her after his meeting with Eldren, she now realised that neither of them had even come close to imagining the truth about their former teacher. She wondered how it was that Amiros had been happy to forego his further learning in order to become their protector. That had been an extraordinary commitment to make she thought. And look where it has got him – beyond their reach, trapped in a strange existence. She daren't dwell on those thoughts – too easy to become depressed and overwhelmed by her whole situation.

The book. The one she and Sirad had brought from Remon's house in Elagos. She hadn't really looked at it all since returning to Thorgiliad. *I need to find out what it contains,* she decided.

A knock at the door brought her back to her present duties. A maidservant enquired if the Lady needed anything and was told to send a footman in about five minutes to deliver various messages. There were meetings to set up, she reminded herself, and set about doing just that.

Chapter 16

Sirad was following the herd of horses as they returned to their winter home. The days had drawn in, the summer well past now and autumn would soon give way to the chills of winter. It wouldn't be that long before crisp frosts would sharpen the early mornings. It was a time that Sirad had always enjoyed – the clarity of the fresh air rather than the haze of hot summertime, the way that frost seemed to put springs into his horse's feet with a new eagerness to gallop out across the meadows.

As always, his eyes roamed over the fine animals, noting how the youngstock were rapidly maturing. Time for many of them to start their training, he thought, not only to maintain the number of mounts available for the Riders, but in this time of need to increase the number of troops available.

Since returning from Elagos, Sirad had initiated a recruitment drive. True, Pelenin had a good standing military force, but there would be battles to fight in the not too distant future and he needed to be sure that he could call on sufficient numbers to ensure that they could meet whatever enemies arose with a level of confidence.

He had made a few journeys in the weeks since returning from Elagos, strengthening the bonds within the Alliance, explaining as much as possible the dangers which they all faced. It was not yet time to reveal his and Alinor's secret about their inheritance, but he guessed that it would have to come out fairly soon. As their powers had increased, so it became difficult to hide. He was still learning about his own skills but as time passed he had begun to feel more comfortable about them. Still so much to learn, he thought, and no idea where it will take us.

A dark shape suddenly appeared beside him – Taukhet. The colt had grown unbelievably quickly and had developed into a strong and very handsome creature. Whenever Sirad had been anywhere near the horse pastures, the lively youngster would find him, galloping at break-neck speed to be at the prince's side.

'Steady on, young chap,' laughed Sirad, 'you'll have me off one of these days!'

The colt tossed his head, the long dark mane flying as he bucked and pirouetted.

'You're too young yet,' Sirad told him, ' though the way you are growing I think I may have to put you to work before too much longer.'

Taukhet came to a halt beside him and looked hard into Sirad's eyes as if to somehow convey a message. Another toss of his head and he galloped away.

The odd encounter left Sirad thoughtful. Yes, he was used to having a close bond with his horses, but with Taukhet it seemed to be something more than that and the creature was still so young. It was strange indeed.

'Patrol reports a couple of riders not far from the city. It sounds like it could be Eldren and Mirantha.'

Ben had hurried to find Sirad to tell him the long awaited news.

'At last!'

Sirad chucked the papers he had been studying onto his desk and grabbed Ben by the arm.

'Come on, Ben, let's go and find them.'

The young prince had been chafing at the delay of the arrival of the two healer-magicians. Every day he had visited Amiros' bedside, hoping to see some kind of change that would suggest the old man would re-awaken but there had been almost nothing. A couple of times the skilled women caring for him had reported that Amiros had been restless, and had even cried out, but then he had settled again. They shook their heads at his repeated questions – no change, no change.

If Amiros was to be Remon's successor, they just had to get him back, Sirad kept telling himself. There has to be a way. Like Alinor he too had fond memories of the old Lore-Master and how he strove to teach the young prince, not always successfully, Sirad thought. *I think I tried his patience sometimes.* But as the years went on, Sirad's respect had grown for his mentor and he missed being able to share his concerns with someone who listened and understood him and whose advice was always sensible. *We need him*, was Sirad's ever-present thought.

The two men quickly made their way down to the stables and within minutes were heading out from the city to intercept the new arrivals.

Eldren was looking a little tired, he'd said he wasn't much of a one for riding and it showed. His companion was something else. Dressed in a flowing dark green robe, Mirantha sat easily on her horse, long dark red hair spilling out from under the hood of her cloak, green eyes gazing out from her pale fine-boned face.

'I'm sorry we took a little longer than expected to get here,' Eldren's rich voice greeted the Riders. 'A few things that had to be done, you know how it is.'

He turned to his companion.

'Mirantha, this is Prince Sirad of Pelenin and his brother Benharad. Gentlemen, may I present the Lady Mirantha.'

'Welcome to Pelenin, my Lady,' Sirad bowed his head to acknowledge the introduction. Ben bowed, not taking his eyes off her.

'I have heard much about you, Sirad, and I am pleased to finally meet you, although I wish the circumstances had been otherwise. Still, we are here now – and I'm sure Eldren will be very glad not to have to ride another day!' Her voice was musical, rich and vibrant but gentle too.

She smiled then, her eyes sparkling; she was stunningly beautiful with the most extraordinary aura around her.

Ben finally found his voice.

'It isn't far now, your Ladyship, and then you may both rest.'

Sirad looked at his brother. *Oh dear, I think he's smitten*, was the first thought that entered his head as he tried not to smile at Ben's obvious reaction to this gorgeous creature.

When he and Eldren had discussed their plans with Ben after returning from Mitos, they had not mentioned that Mirantha was Ben-Neteru. Having now met her, Sirad could sense the kinship between them, but of course, Ben was totally unaware. I hope this does not get difficult, he thought, when Ben finds out who she really is. It's bad enough him still trying to accept Alinor and I.

Mentally shrugging his shoulders, Sirad wheeled about and the party made their way as quickly as Eldren could manage to Pelamir. Once there Mirantha and Eldren were shown to their rooms so they could freshen up after their long trip.

Mirantha insisted they visit Amiros before doing anything else so she could get a better idea of how desperate the situation was.

Word of their arrival had reached the palace Healers and the three senior women were awaiting them by the door to the Lore-Master's rooms.

'Welcome, my Lady,' said the eldest, curtseying as best as her advanced years would permit. 'It is an honour to welcome you.'

The other two women made their obeisance, all three obviously in great awe of this extraordinary personage who now graced them with her presence. Mirantha's reputation amongst the healers was in the realms of legend, and it was said that healing was not her only skill.

'I am reassured that the Lord Corrbel has been in good hands, mistress Nashira. Over the years I have heard good reports of your work, together with mistresses Helna and Petral.'

Almost overcome by the unexpected acclaim the three barely managed a response.

'Tell me what you have observed,' said Mirantha as Nashira led the way towards where Amiros lay unnervingly still.

The old woman provided a concise background to the man's condition since arriving in the palace before stepping back a few paces to observe Mirantha's actions.

Placing a hand just above Amiros' forehead she closed her eyes and seemed to withdraw into herself. For several minutes she simply stood there, the others almost holding their breath, trying to sense whether anything was happening. Sirad understood that she was searching deeply into the comatose man's mind and also studying the damage that had been inflicted on his body. He could recognise that her power of perception was considerably greater than his own or Alinor's and wondered anew at the abilities of the Ben-Neteru – and that as both he and Alinor were of the same heritage they too may in time possess similar skills.

Finally Mirantha opened her eyes again and sighed deeply.

'I did not expect things to be so severe,' she said. 'I need time to think about this.' She looked over at where Eldren was gazing down at his fellow magician.

'We must talk,' she said.

The little herbalist nodded.

'I knew it was bad,' he said, 'but even so I find it hard to accept what has happened.'

He placed a gentle hand over where Amiros' fingers lay unmoving on the light coverlet.

'How has it come to this, my brother and my lord? There must be some way that we can bring you back to this life.'

Mirantha turned to Sirad.

'I can do nothing for him at present until I have had chance to discuss this with Eldren and yourself. There will be no quick cure, I'm afraid.'

If he was honest, her words came as no surprise, even if he couldn't help but be disappointed. Alinor and he had tried many times to reach Amiros with no success, but it was unfair to expect Mirantha to perform some kind of instant miracle within minutes of her arrival.

'I had expected as much,' the young man said, 'but now, both you and Eldren deserve some refreshment after your journey and we can perhaps discuss what may be done later.'

Mirantha nodded.

'Thank you, some food would be welcome and a chance to gather my thoughts. I know my friend here –' she gestured at Eldren, 'has been longing for a decent meal for the past couple of days!'

The little herbalist grinned at her remarks.

'Travelling is hard work,' he assured them, groaning for good measure, 'and a body needs nourishment after all, as well as a break from being bounced around on four legs!'

With a brief word to the palace Healers, Sirad led the group away.

A couple of hours later, Sirad, Eldren and Mirantha were sat in a pleasant room overlooking a small courtyard garden.

'If you don't mind,' began Mirantha, 'I would like to understand a little better exactly what happened after our comrade's body was delivered to you.'

Sirad realised that his words alone could not supply all the information that she sought. Her exceptional mind reached out to him, her power held in check so as not to alarm him, but nevertheless sharply clear. He was aware that she had somehow involved Eldren and that the little man was clearly affected by what he now understood about the torture that Amiros had suffered at the hands of the deranged and highly dangerous Verun.

Up to now the only being that Sirad had shared a mind-link with had been Alinor; neither of them had explored exactly what their mysterious Bond entailed, or what it may do. With Mirantha it was a totally new experience, a little unnerving, but intriguing and exciting too. It took him a moment or two to focus on the matter in hand rather than become distracted by the extraordinary possibilities, but then it was so simple to provide a complete background to what had happened, how Alinor and he had struggled to reach the stricken mage and together had done all they could to try and mend his damaged body.

'You have done exceedingly well, Sirad,' said Mirantha eventually. 'I doubt anyone other than the pair of you could have done as much – no, I am serious, I believe it would have been beyond even my skills. In all my years I have never seen such a case, and certainly there has never been any hint that a person, no matter how magically protected, could withstand the power of Mnethar used against them. Amiros was destined to survive, I am sure of it.'

'But we still need to get him back,' said Sirad.

'She is right,' Eldren said quietly, still shocked by what he now knew. 'There is purpose in this, somehow, the nature of it not yet clear. To attempt to bring him back is fraught with danger, I fear.'

He looked at Mirantha who nodded, her green eyes darkening.

'I will need to try and see if I can identify the path that we must travel in order to reach him. That much I can do and once I have done that, we must talk again.'

The two men accepted her guidance; Eldren obviously understood far more about the situation than Sirad, but the young man realised that Mirantha was far more than just a healer. The contact with her mind had been limited by her, he realised that, but he had been aware of just fleeting impressions of extraordinary knowledge and abilities beyond his present understanding.

We are Ben-Neteru, came a thought from Mirantha, directed purely at him. Long have we waited for this time to come.

What do you mean? Sirad responded.

I am sorry but it is not for me to say further. In time matters will become clearer, even for me. The lore was not specific and so much of our knowledge is mere speculation.

But you must know something, insisted Sirad.

Patience, I'm afraid, is a quality you must learn.

It was obvious that Mirantha would not expand on her original enigmatic words so Sirad had to be content with adding another question to the multitude already awaiting enlightenment.

Mirantha returned to Amiros' bedside, telling Sirad and Eldren that she would speak with them later. It would take some time, she said, and she needed quiet so there was no point to either of them being there. Eldren said he would be happy to consult some of the tomes in the library now he was here; Sirad showed the little herbalist the way and left him gleefully studying a large stack of books covering almost every plant known to man.

Sirad felt restless. Knowing that there was nothing he could do immediately to help left him feeling dissatisfied. He didn't want to talk to Alinor until he had something more to report about Amiros; she was worried enough about the old man and besides, he knew that now Vixlan had met his end – how fitting that was! – there was more than enough for her to do with finalising the restructuring of her government, not to mention the small matter of the long-overdue coronation. That was something he was happy to leave to Alinor and her talented companion; he was, truth be said, rather looking forward to that occasion. Even more, he really just wanted to see her again, hold her in his arms and, at least for those precious few moments, forget the rest of the world.

He needed to work off a bit of frustration, he decided. Best place for that is the training yards. Briskly he strode down the levels and out to the barracks area where, as usual, Riders were doing their drills and engaging in serious sword-play.

'Hey Fehlen,' Sirad called, 'how about a few rounds?'

'Any time, Commander,' came the immediate response.

Both men put on some protective breastplates and took up their stance in an area suddenly vacated by the other Riders who now gathered in a large circle to watch their prince put some moves on one of their favourite Captains. It's not that they were unevenly matched, for Fehlen was a highly skilled fighter; it was more a case that Sirad's skills were far more than simply brilliant. Recent months had somehow taken him to a level that other men could only marvel at and dream of achieving, even though they knew it could never be. Sure enough, Fehlen had to admit defeat as his sword flew from his grasp following a lightning flick by Sirad. By that time the audience had grown; Osan was next into the arena, but he too met a similar fate. Sirad was beginning to enjoy himself now.

'Come on, let's have two of you in here,' he called out. 'See if all your practising has been worthwhile.'

Two tall Riders stepped forward, keen to take him on but sensibly wary of his uncanny speed and skill. Calmly Sirad took a few steps towards them, daring them to strike out; they didn't fall for his ploy and moved apart to try to make it more difficult for their target. Swords clashed, bodies whirled in skirmish after skirmish. Sirad was testing them, they knew, and they tried to anticipate what his next moves would be, but they were not making much progress.

'You can do better than this, lads,' taunted Sirad, driving them both back, 'put some real meaning into it.'

With renewed efforts the two responded and finally gave Sirad some real opposition. Of course, it still didn't win them the battle but Sirad was generous as he collected their swords and handed them back.

'Much better that the last time we worked together,' he said, 'your hard work is starting to pay off.'

There were grins and breathless thanks at this and applause from their audience.

Sirad splashed his face and head with some cold water from the nearby trough and returned the spare armour to the pile. Ben came out from the shadow of the overhanging roof to ask:

'Any news, from the Healer Lady?'

'Not yet, Ben. She went back to see him again and I hope that perhaps she can come up with something that we can do. I'm trying not to get my hopes up too much, but it's not easy.'

'She's quite – lovely, isn't she?' said Ben, in what he hoped was a conversational tone.

Sirad pretended to think about it.

'Mmm, now you come to mention it, she is rather easy on the eye.'

Ben looked slightly embarrassed.

'It's just that I didn't expect her to be like that. I mean I don't really know what I was expecting, but, she's – rather – you know what I mean.' He finished lamely.

'Yes, Ben, I think I do. But she is, shall we say, not like the rest of us.'

Ben glanced at Sirad; he understood that his brother was trying to tell him something in not so many words but wasn't too sure he wanted to work out what he meant.

'Come on Ben, there's a few things I'd like your opinion on.'

Together they went off, deep in conversation, not returning to the palace for several hours. Ben was still with Sirad as he headed for the Lore-Master's rooms, curious to hear if there was any news and quite looking forward to seeing the lovely Mirantha again. As they approached they could hear her talking to the three palace women, offering advice on the care of their patient. Hearing their soft booted footsteps approaching, Mirantha took her leave of the three and came to meet them.

'His overall condition is intriguing,' she started, 'and under the circumstances I can only describe it as very positive. I would have expected far greater debilitation after this period of time, and yet he maintains a surprisingly high level of condition. Most peculiar. But then, I have never come across someone in this predicament before.'

'That first night,' said Ben, his face reflecting his memories, 'when he was brought to the camp; it was awful. I never thought he would live to see the dawn.'

'No, that I can understand,' Mirantha said, a gentle smile on her lips as she regarded the Rider. 'It must have been particularly difficult when you have known him so long.'

Ben nodded. He wasn't sure what to make of this beautiful, strange woman; she seemed to look into him, a bit like Alinor did sometimes; slightly uncomfortable, and yet not threatening or intrusive. Just strange.

'I think we should talk about this in the morning,' she turned to Sirad. 'There are a few things I need to ask Eldren to think about, but a decent meal and a good night's rest would be in order.'

'Of course. I will send someone to direct you to the dining hall shortly - it's nearly time .'

They walked back towards where Mirantha's and Eldren's rooms were located and parted, both men bowing instinctively in response to the woman's dignified presence.

The king was not at dinner that evening; Sirad had seen him earlier and he simply said that he was feeling rather tired and would prefer to take an early night. Sothan was interested to hear that Mirantha had arrived and asked that she visit him the following day. Sirad duly passed the message on and Mirantha enquired after the king's health.

'I'm not sure when I last saw your father,' she said, 'but it must have been many years ago. I would be delighted to renew the acquaintance, slight though it is.'

Many curious eyes were focussed on the two visiting healers; various stories had circulated amongst the palace staff, some highly speculative, and their presence did not disappoint. Mirantha's lovely smile made each feel special, and Eldren's rich dark voice entertained many with tales of far-off places.

It was mid-morning before Sirad joined Mirantha and Eldren to hear what they had to say. He was trying not to be too optimistic and scanned their faces as he sat down with them; it did not seem that good news was the order of the day.

'As I mentioned yesterday,' Mirantha began, 'I have personally never seen this strange condition before, though both Eldren and I have heard that souls could be trapped in this otherworld. Old stories say that such a person may be brought back only if they desire to do so, but the means of persuading them to return is not clear.'

'From my understanding,' Eldren spoke now, 'the one seeking the lost soul is obliged somehow to travel to where it is through an induced trance. Whilst it is not unusual for a healer to enter a trance state in order to address various ills that may befall their patients, this enterprise goes far beyond that which is usual.'

'Indeed Eldren, you are correct,' Mirantha nodded. 'I have thought deeply and searched my memories – which are considerable – to try and bring forth the information which we need. What I have found does not fill me with great hope, but –' seeing the dismay registering on Sirad's face she gently put her hand on his '- I believe there may be a way to reach our friend. It will not be easy, and indeed the undertaking is not without risk. During the time I spent with him yesterday I was able to identify what I believe will be the pathway to his location. Alone it was not possible for me to do much more than that, besides which we will need to make very particular preparations in order to protect us on that journey.'

'You and Eldren have only to ask and we will do everything to assist; I am sure that we will be able to find whatever you need, ' Sirad could not keep the eagerness from his voice.

'Not so fast, young man,' said Mirantha, 'this will be no simple matter. It will be necessary for two of us to enter the trance state, but it is essential that strong minds remain to anchor us or we ourselves may be unable to return. I know what this means to you but it will be Alinor whose presence with me is required for this undertaking.'

For a brief moment Sirad was tempted to argue, but knowing their individual talents, he realised that this unusual woman was right; Alinor was capable of great mental perception and endurance whilst his own undoubted strength, together with Eldren, could serve to maintain the anchor that Mirantha had described.

'I do not for a moment believe that Alinor would allow us to proceed without her in any case. Although she is still new to her powers, she has learned much; her particular abilities will mesh with my own and together we should have a reasonable chance.'

'If she thinks there is a way to help Amiros there will be no stopping her,' Sirad said with a wry smile. 'As soon as I tell her what you have said she will be on her way here, regardless of whatever other matters she should be attending to at court. Her coronation is less than three months away, a ridiculously short time to get everything organised, although she has assured me that everything is under control!' he added as an afterthought.

'I have some of the essential herbs that I can blend as part of the protection they need when the two of them enter their trance, but Mirantha has explained to me exactly what is required for the trance potions. This includes plants with which I am not at all familiar,' Eldren looked a little worried. 'We cannot proceed without them.'

Sirad got up and paced the room.

'What can we do then?' asked Sirad. 'Do you know,' he looked anxiously at Mirantha, 'where they may be found?'

'I do,' she responded, 'but it means that I must go and seek them out myself, and that may take a little while.'

'How long are we talking about? Days, weeks?'

'Probably around three weeks or so, if I am fortunate enough to find them quickly. And if you are prepared to lend me a horse, it would make the travelling a little easier.'

'Anything you need, just ask,' Sirad immediately answered. 'I think we all know that it is of great importance that Amiros is restored to us, even though we have as yet little idea of what lies ahead.'

'I do understand and therefore I will be prepared to leave tomorrow at dawn. Alone, I must travel alone Sirad, but do not concern yourself about my safety. I am not a target, and I doubt that Verun is even aware of the possibility of our reaching Amiros so he is hardly likely to be wanting to watch over him, even if he is actually yet able to. Both Eldren and I have sought to locate any trace of Verun's power without success, I am glad to say. Besides which you have sufficient other matters which require your attention, so let those occupy you whilst I am gone.'

The young prince knew that there would be no point in arguing with her and accepted that she was more than capable of protecting herself. Exactly what powers she had he couldn't tell, but it was enough that she was Ben-Neteru with more than enough magic to deal with whatever came her way. He looked forward to when Alinor and Mirantha should meet up – two exceptional women, a truly awesome combination he thought. If anyone can save Amiros it would be those two.

'If you would be kind enough, Sirad, I should visit your father now.'

'Oh, of course, I had nearly forgotten. I'll take you to him straight away. I know he is looking forward to seeing you.'

Mirantha inclined her head and rose to follow Sirad from the room.

'I will make a start, Mirantha,' said Eldren, 'and carry on having a look at all the possibilities in Amiros' treatment.'

'Thank you, Brother,' she replied, 'all information is potentially valuable under the circumstances.'

'Your father has been unwell recently, I understand,' said Mirantha to Sirad as they walked the long corridors of the palace.

'Yes, he has rather. And I don't think it is just his age,' replied Sirad thoughtfully, 'he's not so old. But something, maybe the old injuries, seem to bring him down every now and then; and then when it's like that, he cannot help but feel depressed, which doesn't help the situation.'

'That is always the way,' observed the woman, 'and if you are not careful, it is easy to become trapped in a cycle where pain brings on depression and saps the will to defeat it.'

'Do you think you may be able to help him?'

'It is always possible to help, young man, as long as the patient wishes to be helped.'

They reached the king's apartments and were admitted to a spacious and comfortable room when Sothan was accustomed to spending much of his time.

Upon seeing his visitors, the weary king rose to his feet, stretching out his hands in greeting.

'You are most welcome, Lady Mirantha. It has been too many years.'

Mirantha curtseyed elegantly and took both his hands in hers.

'Indeed it has, your highness. It is good to see you again.'

Sothan gestured to her to take a seat and signalled his page to bring refreshments.

'I will leave you two to talk,' said Sirad, glad to see his father's animated face.

'Yes, do go on, son. The Lady and I have much to catch up on!'

Sirad bowed, smiling, and left them to it.

Chapter 17

The air was pleasantly cool but the man was sweating and obviously in great distress as he turned his head this way and that, eyes tightly closed against the pain which felt as if his whole self was being ripped apart and twisted about. He let out a muffled cry and sank back onto the low couch, totally drained.

A period of blessed peace lasted for some time before Amiros finally came to again.

He lay there for a while relieved that the pain had gone for the time being. He had suffered a similar experience a number of times in the past, though not to such an extreme; that had been at the hands of Remon the Mind-Master, his teacher for so many years. He knew that Alinor had undergone a much lesser trial when she had visited Remon in Elagos; it had been hard on her, but she had an inner strength which had enabled the Seer to accelerate her initiation at a crucial time in her life.

Although he had accepted that he had no choice but to undergo these ordeals, Amiros was still uncertain about what the future held. Did he wish to return to his previous life – assuming that possibility existed – or could he stay here, with or without Meriona to lighten his days?

The promise he had made weighed heavily upon him. Of course he couldn't ever consider breaking that trust. But this was a different reality now. Not dead, he thought, though I may as well be. I am no longer the person I was. If I were to return, what would I be like? These people here cannot tell me, only that I am damaged. I may be returning to a life of unbearable pain. Why go back? Surely Alinor and Sirad didn't still think that he would return from this cursed exile?

He shook his head. I just don't know.

The Healer entered the quiet of the sanctuary and approached Amiros, diverting him from his mental debate.

'You should return to your rooms now, my Lord, and rest. I will give you something to ease your sleep – no, it is for the best I assure you. Today was only the first of your trials. Tomorrow will be similar, I believe, although my understanding of what is happening is limited.'

Not sure I want more of this, was the man's thought as he slowly followed the Healer out into the afternoon sun, his body aching and reluctant to make the effort. I seem to have lost all sense of time. Surely I was not in the sanctuary that long?

Back in his rooms Amiros ate a small meal and drank the cup of delicate herbal tea that the Healer had provided. Within a few minutes it served to relax him to the extent that he lay on his bed and almost immediately drifted into a deep restorative sleep.

The following day, as the Healer had said, Amiros visited the sanctuary. There was nothing obvious within its confines to identify from whence the strange powers came that assaulted the Lore-Master's mind and body. Here and there, multi-coloured crystals glowed soothingly giving the impression of being immersed in a world of gentle light; was there some kind of sound, perhaps, nothing that could be described or annotated, that permeated everything, unobtrusive and yet pervasive. A sound you felt rather than heard. The ordeal he underwent defied description and whilst the experience caused undeniable anguish, it was not so extreme that he felt that it was beyond bearing. He could not say what was different about himself, but there was something deep within his being that was being released, as if it had been constrained and was now starting to take up its rightful place.

Again, the Healer gave him a draught similar to that of the evening before. However, this time the man slept right through the following day, blessed sleep allowing his mind to rest. When he finally awoke it was evening. He felt wonderfully drowsy and comfortable, and it was some time before he eventually got up. He bathed and on re-entering his room found the table laid for two. Before he could think to enquire the door opened and the Lady Meriona entered, smiling to see him looking so refreshed.

'Sleep is a wonderful restorative, is it not?'

Amiros smiled in response.

'Indeed it is, I am glad to say.'

Servants arrived with trays of dishes emitting enticing aromas which they proceeded to set upon the table.

Meriona moved to take a seat and looked questioningly at Amiros who was simply gazing with undisguised emotion at his dinner companion.

'I know this is hard for you, dear heart,' she said, indicating that he should take his own seat opposite, 'but I know that you will come to accept what must be. The love we share with those who are dearest to us, whilst painful at times, is in fact our greatest strength. It holds us true to who we really are and can never be taken away from us. The bonds we have between us can not be broken and will remain steadfast despite time and distance. Even though we must part again, we shall remain close, I am sure of it, and I believe that in the end we will all be together, however distant in the future that may be. So please my dearest Amiros,' she touched his hand gently, 'do not grieve or let the pain hold you back from what will be.'

The man looked into her eyes, aware that he could drown in their depths, and managed a rueful smile.

'What you say is true, no doubt, and I shall try my best,' he said quietly, 'but I shall cherish this time with you.'

The woman nodded sadly, hiding her sorrow at the thought of what the uncertain future may hold for both Amiros and Alinor; but then she smiled again sensing that there was room for great hope – for why else would they both be here in this strange existence?

They both raised a toast to life and love before doing justice to the delicious meal provided.

When Amiros had undertaken his role as guardian to Alinor and Sirad all those years ago he had ceased the further training with Remon which would have seen him become the old Seer's successor. Now it was necessary for Amiros' mind to adjust in order to fill in most of what Remon would have taught him in a somewhat shortened timescale. Abilities that had been denied could now develop. Knowledge needed to be unlocked. But it was never going to be a comfortable experience.

So it was that the former Lore-Master returned several more times in the following days to the mysterious sanctuary and underwent the indefinable transformative instruction that fate had finally laid out for him.

The new Mind-Master had now commenced his journey to maturity.

Chapter 18

Lanterns had been lit all along the corridors leading to the strong rooms, deep beneath the palace. Accompanied by the venerable Berendon, former Master of Ceremonies in the reign of Teleston, and his younger apprentices Alinor approached the huge door of the main vault housing the crown jewels. Guards snapped to attention as the party approached; normally they took their post at the entrance to this lower level, but today, their new sovereign was coming to inspect and choose the traditional jewels that would play such an important part in the forthcoming coronation ceremony.

Berendon, his advanced age slowing his footsteps somewhat, had been explaining exactly how the ceremony had altered over the years – not that much to be honest, but just small things that reflected the different natures of the rulers over the years. The elderly courtier had seen two kings crowned, with their queens, and was secretly delighted to be able to guide the preparations for this extraordinary new young sovereign.

'I can remember my father's crown quite well,' Alinor was saying, 'an impressive, though rather large example of the jeweller's craftsmanship, a magnificent symbol of power and majesty with all that gold and velvet and such wonderful gems. However, I cannot imagine it on my head – way too heavy, I wouldn't be able to hold my head up straight.'

Berendon chuckled.

'It can of course be re-made for you, but then I fear you may be right. It is not what I would have envisaged as suitable for a queen. On the other hand, though . . . Excuse me a moment.'

They had reached the door and the elderly minister brought out a set of large intricate keys which he proceeded to insert into the four locks sealing the vault. Silently the huge door was pushed open on well-oiled hinges and Berendon signalled for his juniors to start lighting the array of lanterns along the walls of the room. As they did so the room came alive as priceless artefacts reflected rays of golden and multi-coloured light all around.

Alinor gazed at the stunning display, realising for the first time that she was now the caretaker of this priceless collection – quite a responsibility.

She approached the large pedestal upon which was set the king's crown. It was truly beautiful and for a moment she found her head filled with memories of the limited occasions she had attended when Teleston had worn it. He had looked so regal, so commanding she remembered, and a smile touched her lips at how proud she had felt to be his daughter. There was no way that she would wear that crown, she had already decided. But there was another.

A second pedestal bore an extraordinarily beautiful item. An abundance of tiny glittering jewels were set into an intricate golden circlet, the design so delicate that it appeared incredibly fragile, though surely it could not be and still support all those gems. It seemed like a sinuous flowering vine circling about, its blossoms made from precious stones cut to reflect the light, interspersed with gold and silver leaves.

'Mother's crown,' whispered Alinor, hesitantly reaching out to take the unique masterpiece in her hands.

Carefully she turned it this way and that, studying the exquisite workmanship. It felt so special, it felt – she couldn't describe it to herself – it just felt as if it had been waiting for her to come and take it. It was meant for her.

'It is the most beautiful thing I have ever seen,' Berendon's voice was gentle, 'apart from your mother, that is. When she wore it, well, there were never words to describe how magnificent she was. We all miss her dearly.'

'Thank you, Berendon, for your kind words. I just wish that I had been able to spend more years with her.'

Alinor was unable to take her eyes off the crown, and as she studied it further noticed an oddness in the design. To her eyes there appeared to be an empty space, as if it had been intended to take just one final jewel to complete it. It hadn't been that obvious but now it intrigued her.

'I suppose that this is complete, nothing has been removed from it or anything?' she asked Berendon.

'Indeed not,' the man nearly sputtered with indignation. 'There has never been any question of that, or damage, or anything. It is as your mother brought it with her as a bride and always wore it thus.'

'Yes, of course, I didn't meant to suggest otherwise,' Alinor reassured him, 'please accept my apologies. I know that you have always been an excellent protector of this collection.'

'It is in safe hands, your Ladyship, and when it is time for me to stand aside, I assure you that you will be able to rely on those whom I have been training, and whichever one of them finally assumes my post.'

'I do not doubt that, dear Berendon. My father always spoke highly of you and trusted you implicitly, as do I. And I am very appreciative of your knowledge and experience in preparing for this occasion.'

'Your people are so happy that you returned to us for we had all but lost hope. Tragic though your father's loss was, you will bring new life to Ancor, I know.'

Alinor did not respond, but laid a hand gently on the old man's shoulder. The crown was replaced on its pedestal for the moment and attention turned to some of the other items that Berendon had informed Alinor would be needed for the ceremonies. Most of them would be taken now to the royal jewellers for cleaning and checking for any necessary repair work before the day.

The little party left the main vault and Berendon opened up a couple more rooms in which precious items such as the huge wall hangings had been carefully stored. These too would be brought up to be aired and examined carefully by the seamstresses to ensure that none of the intricate embroideries needed repair. There really was not a lot of time before the big day, and everyone would be putting in a lot of extra hours in order to be prepared for what was going to be a truly magnificent occasion.

Meanwhile, Semira didn't know whether to laugh or cry when she thought about everything that needed to be done. At first she had been overwhelmed; there is no way that I can take up this challenge, she thought. Alinor is expecting too much of me. But then her innate stubbornness came to the fore; no way she would let down the exceptional young woman who had become her friend. This *will* be the most impressive occasion Ancor has ever seen, she decided, how could it be otherwise?

And so it began. Semira had meetings with all the palace employees to set in motion all the hundreds of tasks that had to be done; artisans and specialists were asked to prepare their ideas to present at the next round of planning meetings. There was no time to waste.

Alinor, Semira and senior ministers met to finalise the list of invitees from all the nations of the Alliance; as expected, the number they eventually agreed on was somewhat greater than Semira had hoped it would be – how to cope with so many, her mind was in a whirl. However, everyone else seemed to think it quite reasonable and they should know, so she shrugged her shoulders and got on with the planning. The politics of who got on well with whom was really something she didn't want to get involved with, although she could appreciate that causing a diplomatic incident by not being prepared for potential cold-shouldering amongst the guests was to be avoided at all costs. Fortunately the minister concerned with foreign affairs was a fount of information and she gladly left the matter in his hands.

Seeing the glorious array of fabrics and items being brought up from the secure storerooms lifted her spirits. Those who took charge of them were experienced and skilled, a great relief to Semira who knew that she could trust them to do their jobs. She went from meeting to meeting during which she learned a great deal about their tasks and grew to respect their individual talents. The more she learned, the more confident she became in her role of overseeing and co-ordinating everyone's efforts.

With the initial burst of frantic activities, meetings and discussions, not to mention the ever-present government business that required attention, Alinor was beginning to think that she would never have a moment's peace again. I suppose that's not really true, she told herself, but some days just seem to be so crowded. Everyone is doing a good job, but they haven't got used to me yet so have to keep checking that they are right and that I haven't changed my mind about anything!

Finding herself miraculously on her own for a moment she decided to take a bit of time to just switch off from the current round of duties; a few minutes to rest her mind and put aside the busy thoughts. On impulse she made her way to one of the tall towers where she had used to slip away as a child sometimes, to look out over the city and surrounding countryside; she wasn't supposed to climb all the way up there for some reason, she couldn't remember why that was for it was not unsafe or anything. Now she made her way up the narrow winding steps, catching glimpses through the occasional deep slits in the walls. It seemed further up than she remembered, but having started she was eager to reach the top.

Eventually she reached the solid oak door that gave out into a small room at the very top of the tower. It was cold but dry and her feet crunched on some dry leaves as she went over to one of the windows to take in the vast panorama spread out beneath her. For several minutes she simply stood and gazed, picking out familiar sights, identifying buildings where merchants lived, the markets and bakeries, workshops and storehouses, areas where children were playing in the bright cold sunshine. Immediately below she could see one of the courtyards where there was a gate into the palace area, a bustle of activity, carts coming in and out with goods to be delivered, guards watching vigilantly, people bustling from one place to another or talking animatedly, probably about the coronation Alinor thought. Further away she could make out where roads led off in all directions, a bit of smoke rising from small villages nestled into the fold of the hills, here and there a rider coming or going, a farmer bringing his goods into market, just ordinary people going about their everyday lives.

It does seem so peaceful, so ordinary. They really have no idea, was Alinor's sobering thought. She turned to look around the room. Someone had obviously spent time in it at some point in the past. There was a low table, well-made but showing signs of neglect now. There were a couple of chairs that had obviously been comfortable and therefore well-used, but the formerly rich fabric on the seats and backs needed replacing; a good dose of beeswax wouldn't go astray, thought Alinor. A small chest stood against the wall behind the door. Curious, Alinor tried the lid; it opened, slightly stiffly, but was disappointingly empty.

As she turned away a shaft of light caught on a small leaf blown in by the wind making it look as if it had been gilded. Alinor reached down to pick it up but her eye was caught by a design carved into the wall, a design that flowed along the stones, stretching nearly half way around the whole room. How odd, Alinor thought, to place such pretty work so low down rather than where it could be more easily seen. I wouldn't have noticed it but for that leaf. Her fingers traced it along to where it stopped short. I'm sure I've seen this before, somewhere, but where? She wracked her brains, going over various decorations in the numerous places she had been, designs on materials or flags, emblems and carved furnishings. Finally her brain latched on to jewellery. Of course! It was a more simplified representation of the sinuous vine on her mother's crown. But why here?

Had this been a favourite room where her mother would sit and look out? Even if it was, what had been the point of putting in so much effort to produce a carving in the stonework? It stopped before it reached the last bit of wall anyway, did they just give up? She ran her fingers over the final piece. It felt warm to her touch, unlike the rest of the stone. How odd, how very odd. She became aware that The Firestone hanging on its silvery chain around her neck also felt warmer. What are you trying to tell me, she wondered. There must be a reason for this. A clattering by the window startled her as a bird landed on the windowsill causing her knuckle to strike against the stone. Instead of resisting her push the stone moved slightly, sinking back into the wall.

What on earth? She pushed it again and it slid all the way in to reveal a large cavity hidden in the depths of the stonework. It wasn't easy to see much, but Alinor could make out a small container of some kind. Carefully she reached in and took hold of what turned out to be a fairly plain wooden box. Bringing it into the light she studied it for a few moments; the wood was pale with a reddish hue, the graining close; on the lid there was a runic carving:

ᚱᛒᚲᚨᚲᛩᛞᛒ

'Legacy,' breathed Alinor.

There was no lock, simply a tightly fitting lid. Gently Alinor eased it off. The first thing she saw was a folded sheet of paper; the blank side was facing her as she picked it up, but it was not totally blank. One word was inscribed there: Alinor.

Her heart beat faster as she unfolded the paper to reveal elegant writing that flowed across the page.

My dearest daughter

As you are reading this it must be that you have now entered into your inheritance and your journey towards fulfilment has begun. That which was foretold so long ago – even before I was born – is now upon us and there is no going back.

I am so sorry that I was not there to be with you as you grew from childhood into the beautiful woman you always promised to be. You must understand that it was destined that I should pass from the life you know, and it was not without heartache that I left my beloved Teleston and the child I loved even more than my own life. It was my choice to go. I know the pain you must have suffered to lose your mother so early, but know that my love endures and will always enfold you.

The road ahead of you is a dangerous one but I have faith that you will succeed. You will not be alone on your journey, and there are those whose help you will receive along the way. Have courage, my beautiful Alinor-Merion, and trust where your heart takes you. Be strong and gentle in equal measure and above all be true to yourself.

This is my gift to you, that which was passed down to me to hold until the time should come when the Tokens would finally be brought together again. It is yours now. May it serve you well.

With eternal love
Meriona-en-resaan

Alinor had been holding her breath but now let it out with a deep shaking sigh, tears brimming in her eyes and blurring the words on the page she held in her trembling hands. She brushed them away, sniffed, biting her lip and raising her eyes to gaze unseeing at the room around her.

'Mother,' she whispered, her heart aching, overwhelmed with a yearning to go back to her childhood and be comforted in her mother's arms. She closed her eyes and hugged her arms around herself, her mind a jumble of memories and emotions.

For several minutes she remained thus, wrapped up in the past. Eventually she relaxed her arms, opened her eyes and took a few deep breaths to steady herself. Slowly she re-read the precious words, sensing the grief and love her mother had felt along with the incredible strength of a woman who understood her own destiny and who was unafraid to choose what she knew was right. The way the words had been written was odd – the tense was wrong. It was as if they were written after her mother had already died. How could that have been?

'That which was foretold . . '

Destiny again, thought Alinor, and it seems that it has come down to me to fulfil – something. The Tokens will be brought together again, her mother had said.

'But I still haven't found out what these tokens are,' Alinor said out loud, 'or how I should go about re-uniting them.'

'My gift to you.'

The box was in her lap as she sat there on the floor; placing the precious letter beside her she focussed her attention on what the box contained. Reaching in her fingers gently touched a soft padded leather pouch, the same colour as the wood of the box which was why she hadn't immediately seen it before. Carefully she withdrew it. There was no real weight to it, but there was definitely something solid inside. Curious, she teased open the pouch and emptied the content into her hand.

She gasped as a brilliant light flashed for a split second, so briefly that she wondered if she had really seen it. In her palm lay a beautiful gemstone the like of which she had never seen before. Its colour lay between a brilliant blue and delicate sea-green, neither one nor the other, or maybe it was both. Larger than The Firestone, yet seemingly weightless, it nevertheless radiated an unseen power which flowed from her hand into the whole of her being. She could feel an echoing warmth from The Firestone around her neck, as if it recognised the new jewel.

'How beautiful,' Alinor murmured. But more than just a jewel, she thought. If her mother had been holding it in order to pass to her, there must be something more to it than that. It would seem that there is a connection with The Firestone, so it is obviously another of the stones of power. What sort of power? For what purpose?

'May it serve you well.'

Serve me how, wondered Alinor. Just another mystery I have yet to understand.

She stayed sat there for several minutes, turning the precious gem this way and that, wondering what skill had shaped it, watching the light reflected from its depths, marvelling at its loveliness. She held it up to admire the play of light around its edges.

'Yes,' she said suddenly, 'I know where you should be!'

Her mind brought up a picture of the Queen's Crown and the odd gap she had observed in the design. This jewel is exactly the right size and shape to fit there, she thought; it is absolutely the right thing to finally make it complete.

For a moment she was tempted to rush back down the tower and into the vaults to unite the gem with the crown, but almost as soon as the thought was formed she dismissed it. Not yet, not just yet. I'm going to wait for the coronation, she nodded at her decision, sure that she was making the right choice.

Alinor stood and closed her eyes.

'Thank you, mother. I may not understand exactly how this precious thing fits into my life, but I know it is important, but even more important is that it is your gift to me. I know that no-one else has touched it since you placed it here for me to find and I can feel the warmth of your hand on it. I will not betray your faith in me.'

Alinor replaced the gem in its pouch and back with the letter in the box. She reached into the gap in the wall to see if there was a way to get the brick out. At the touch of her fingers, the brick slid back into place as if it had never been moved. Satisfied, Alinor carried her precious gift back to her rooms to lock it where it would be safe in a small chest along with her most personal items. As she placed it gently under cover of her favourite travelling cloak her eyes lit on the book she had taken from Remon's house. It was high time she had a serious look at it. When they had first come across the book she and Sirad had spent an hour or more reading bits here and there with the help of The Firestone's strange power, but much of it had eluded their understanding. What she really wanted to find now was information about the Tokens, and more specifically about this new gem her mother had left for her. Just as she was reaching in to retrieve the book she heard sounds of approaching feet outside her apartment. Bother, she thought, I could have done with a bit longer. I suppose another few hours won't make too much difference.

She closed and locked the chest, ran her fingers through her hair and went back to face whatever the rest of the day would bring.

Later that night when the palace had quietened, Alinor sat poring over the archaic script, looking for the part where she and Sirad had found mention of the Tokens. It was tempting just to skip through, but in doing that she may miss something potentially important, so she curbed her impatience and tried to read slowly but steadily. As before she came across words that she didn't understand, references to things – people? – which could be good or dangerous, it was hard to tell, the book didn't really elaborate. Her eyes were beginning to ache when she finally came across a section mentioning both Rakep-thos and Remon. As she read the concise account she felt chilled. It was only a short passage, lacking much detail, but it was enough. This was maybe the reason behind her mother's words.

She read it through twice, hoping that she had perhaps read it wrongly the first time. She didn't think so. She closed the book, not wanting to read any more, wishing she hadn't read it at all. It had been so long ago, maybe it wasn't that real. All things pass, she told herself, so perhaps this is more myth than fact.

She yawned, suddenly desperately tired. I need to tell Sirad about this, she thought, but not tonight. Just now, sleep is more important. Whatever else is in the book must wait.

Sirad was awake, just lying in the dark. He didn't know what had woken him, but he could sense that Alinor was upset about something. For a moment he was tempted to reach out to her, but something held him back. If she had wanted to share whatever it was, she would have done so, but he respected her privacy and judgement and was prepared to wait for such time as she decided was right. The bond between them was an extraordinary one, but they were still individuals with the need to be their own person. Neither would intrude upon the other unnecessarily; they had their own lives to lead with their own particular responsibilities to face. Much was shared, and the future held the expectation of an even closer bond, but for now they both had matters closer to home to deal with – though he wished they were not so far apart.

Eventually he got back to sleep but rose early, knowing that Mirantha would be leaving in a couple of hours and wanting to hear what she had to say after her meeting with his father. Sothan's poor health had been a source of worry for some time, but no-one seemed to be able to suggest its cause. He wasn't so old, and he had never suffered any truly grievous injuries or sicknesses, so why such a decline?

He caught up with the mystic Healer outside Amiros' room where she was in discussion with Nashira.

'Just maintain the routine as I have instructed and I will hope to return as soon as possible.'

She turned as Sirad approached and smiled a welcome.

'I had forgotten just how good company your father could be,' she started. 'He has lost none of the charm that drew your mother to his side!'

Mirantha led the way back to where Eldren was – as usual – engrossed in reading a large tome about herbal preparations.

'Do sit for a moment,' she said and indicated that Eldren should join them.

'You are concerned about your father, of course, and it would seem rightly so.'

For a moment Sirad feared the worst.

'No, no, it will not come to that – at least not for some time yet. He is getting older as are we all, but he should have good years ahead of him. He has,' she paused thoughtfully, choosing her words with care, 'what I can only call a darkness that has infected him. Whence its origin I cannot tell, but I have seen such a thing before, many years ago. In his case it may have taken decades to reach the point at which it now affects his natural resistance.'

'Something can be done, then?' the young prince's voice was full of hope. 'Are you able to help him?'

'In the years since I first encountered this condition I have learned a great deal and, as Eldren is aware,'

The little herbalist nodded.

'. . have been able to develop and advance my own skills in order to recognise such an illness. Because your father has been carrying this infection for such a long time it may be a while before he can be fully rid of it.'

'But it is possible?'

'I believe that to be the case,' Mirantha smiled gently at the young man's obvious delight. 'There is not time this morning to explain exactly what I have done, but you have a healing talent yourself and I would be pleased to talk with you about this on another occasion. In the meantime I have given instructions to Mistress Nashira about what treatments he should be given which my esteemed friend here,' she indicated Eldren, 'will shortly be preparing.'

'Indeed, indeed,' said Eldren enthusiastically, 'I am more than pleased to be able to assist. It will be a great pleasure to help this noble man to return to health.'

Sirad was silent for a couple of minutes, taking in the unexpected news, a welter of emotion running through him. It would be so good to have his father back to strength instead of being almost trapped within the palace. He could get out and about again, see and be seen by the people of Pelamir and the surrounding countryside.

'It can't be rushed,' Mirantha cautioned him, 'although I suspect that your father may want to push himself once he starts to feel better!'

'I cannot find the words to thank you, gracious lady. I had almost given up hope of any improvement.'

'I know, Sirad, and I am indeed thankful that circumstances allowed for me to be here at the right time for him. The outcome may not have been so promising had his condition continued for many more months.

'But it is time to face our next challenge, one that is equally important for all of us. We have to try and reach Amiros and hope that he will indeed wish to return to us.'

Mirantha rose and reached for her travelling cloak.

'I must leave now for time is of the essence and I have a way to go if I am to gather what I need.'

Sirad and Eldren escorted Mirantha down to the courtyard where a horse had been prepared for her. She took very little with her and it only took a moment to attach her remaining small pack, a task that Ben undertook willingly.

'Perhaps it would be safer if you had an escort,' the young Captain said hopefully.

'Thank you, Benharad, but no, this I have to do alone.'

Mirantha favoured him with a sweet smile, causing his hands to tremble slightly as he held the horse for her to mount. She turned her attention to Sirad, silently telling him not to worry too much while she was gone. Destiny would be fulfilled.

Then she was out of the gates and cantering away from the city and their sight.

Chapter 19

Busy was barely even close to describing the activities of all within the palace of Thorgiliad.

'A coronation, at last,' was on everyone's lips, smiles in equal measure to the declarations of perceived impossibility at getting everything done on time. It was usually the younger, less experienced members of the household who found it hard to grasp exactly how the myriad tasks could be done, but unhesitating assurances from those of longer standing kept them in line and, against all the odds, matters were proceeding in splendid order.

Semira was in her element now as her own confidence in the staff grew. With the guidance of the most senior palace ministers and servants, whose experiences during the reign of Alinor's father enabled them to appreciate every possible aspect of the forthcoming ceremony, she was able to interpret the changes that Alinor had instructed and pass them on to those responsible for each element of the preparations.

Down in the kitchens Maesie was in her element; one morning when Semira went down for what had become her usual break, she found the huge table covered with pieces of paper listing menu suggestions and plans to cover all the days surrounding the celebrations. There were lists of various meats to be sourced, vegetables available, fruits from within the palace stores and other preserved items from further afield. Semira glanced at some of the lists in amazement.

'I didn't realise that you would be able to get these,' she exclaimed to Maesie.

'Oh yes, my dear, a banquet must have a decent selection,' the old cook replied. 'It's going to keep us busy, but I can promise you feasts to remember, such as have not been seen for many a year!'

'I can see that,' agreed the younger woman.

'And,' she said in a portentous voice, 'I have been able to get Alessandron back – though he didn't need any persuasion at all.'

'Who is he?'

'Only the very best sweet maker in the country, or indeed for hundreds of miles around!' responded Maesie, 'and he has his son with him who looks certain to be every bit as good as his father. Between them we can expect the most glorious masterpieces of confection and dessert.'

'Gracious, that does sound exciting,' Semira laughed, infected by Maesie's obvious delight.

The old woman then advised about all the other help that had been recruited; the kitchens would be full to overflowing with people, thought Semira, so where would all the food be? She didn't actually say as much to Maesie knowing the cook would have everything under control.

I really believe that this is all going to work, was Semira's thought as she returned to the upper floors of the palace to visit the seamstresses and admire their intricate stitchwork. Later she would again do a round of the various accommodations allocated for all the noble guests; preparations were all going smoothly – unless of course the retinues for these visitors exceeded the norm! Oh well, no doubt we'll manage somehow, she sighed to herself. I'm not necessarily convinced that my imagination has done justice to the situation. Never mind, she told herself, just get on the job!

Alinor meanwhile was sat cross-legged on her big bed, the ancient book brought from Remon's house on her lap. She had reached the point where her ministers, both new and old, had got to grips with the various matters of state and she could feel confident at last to let them get on with their jobs without permanently needing to check on progress. Since her return to Ancor she had been working non-stop apart from the brief visit to Coranien-dulat; but of course that too had also had an element of politics to it.

Now however it was high time to return to that which was of the utmost importance. During the maelstrom of activity of the past weeks she had allowed more immediate concerns to push thoughts of her real task into the background, surfacing only occasionally. Hearing from Sirad that Mirantha had left Pelamir in her search for strange herbs brought Amiros' plight to the fore.

I really need to find out more about the Tokens, she thought. Mother implied that when they were brought together again it would be for a purpose, which of course she did not explain. Did she know herself? It was long-awaited she said, but perhaps even she did not know the details. The letter that Remon left for Sirad mentioned the Tokens but again, there was no detail. What are they? How many are there?

Some things we know, or can deduce.

Firstly, there are the Swords of Bran; Shenbran I have already, and Tauenbran is its counterpart. We found that mentioned in the book when we were together in Remon's house.

Secondly, I have The Firestone; we know that it is a jewel of power and I am its Guardian.

Next is the gem that mother left for me; I'm sure that it will play a part, but don't have any idea what power it actually has.

Then there is, possibly, Mnethar.

Alinor felt her insides churn at the thought of that deadly jewel. Remembrance of the unspeakable pain that had been inflicted upon Amiros that she had encountered through her contact with his mind brought tears to her eyes and it took a few moments for her to regain control of her emotions.

Could it be that it too is one of the Tokens?

I need to know more about what has happened to Amiros. What is this strange existence to which he has been banished? Mirantha has said that it should be possible that we can somehow travel to where he is and bring him back. From what Sirad told me, she describes it as a very risky enterprise, with no guarantee of success. But we have to try.

Alinor's thoughts were almost shouting at her.

'We have to try,' she whispered aloud, 'we have to.'

She opened the book, letting it choose itself which page to show her, and started to read.

An hour later she finally looked up and rubbed a hand over her eyes. The quiet light of The Firestone around her neck slowly faded as she closed the book and put it to one side. She let out a deep breath and got up, stretching her neck and easing the mild stiffness from her legs. What she had read cast a light on the situation that Amiros was in, but was not reassuring. It had been long, complicated passage with references that she could not at present understand. Whilst it did hold out the possibility of the Lore-Master's return, the means of achieving it were fraught with danger, and there was no definite promise of success. Obviously, Mirantha had an understanding of how the seeker of the lost person may employ arcane skills in order to cross into the strange existence wherein they may look for their comrade. However, the book did not go into much detail about what to expect. According to Sirad Mirantha had said that she had located the pathway to Amiros' location, but that was not to say she knew his actual whereabouts. Unnervingly the book had noted that it was not unlikely that the one undertaking the search could also become lost and trapped within the same existence. The book mentioned possible challenges to whoever undertook travelling such a distance whilst in a trance, though again gave no details or even hints as to what they may be.

Amiros had to choose whether to return; after what he had suffered, would he want to? Alinor knew that she and Sirad had managed to alleviate much of the pain he had endured, but his body had been so badly injured. She shuddered anew at the memory of the night they had found him. After all the years that he had watched over and guided both she and Sirad would he now leave them to face whatever their destined task was alone?

It was a question that would not, could not, be answered until such time as she and Mirantha were able to find him.

Alinor was curious about Mirantha. She is Ben-Neteru, like us; I wonder how many others there may be. The thought that there was at least one other sharing their ancient and mysterious bloodline was some comfort for the young woman who still found it difficult to comprehend, let alone accept, that she and Sirad were so far different from everyone else as to make comparison impossible.

Enough for now, she decided, besides I need to have a word with Dhalen and a few others about my returning to Pelamir for when Mirantha returns. I've got a week or so before she's likely to be back; if I travel alone I would be there very quickly but it could be difficult persuading the others to let me do that! Oh well, I can but try.

For the next week Alinor carried out the necessary duties of her sovereignty, now far less onerous with Vixlan removed from the scene. The wheels of government were turning easily as her new ministers and courtiers happily adjusted to their new ruler's instructions. Coronation preparations were well in hand; she had no qualms about leaving on-going arrangements in the capable hands of others. There were still two months, well, nearly two, so there was time for her to go to Pelamir.

I shall set out the day after tomorrow, she told Sirad, I can't wait to see you again!

And I you, was his heartfelt response. I have missed you so much. Everything still going along smoothly?

Well, yes it is, I'm glad to say. Preparations for the coronation are pretty hectic, but in an organised way, if that isn't too much of a contradiction.

It could only happen for you! Sirad was laughing at the pictures she conjured up.

How is your father, she asked. Has there been any improvement since Mirantha saw him?

I think there has, Sirad replied. It's very slow, but she did say that it would be to start with. He seems happier in himself than he has been for a while, and he's getting a bit more active every day. That in itself makes him feel better, so it's all part of the process.

I'm so glad. I do like your father very much, Alinor paused a moment. I've just realised, she continued, I'm going to be, sort of, on the same standing as he is. I mean, I going to be a queen, and he's a king.

Sirad couldn't help but be amused by her tone of surprise.

You already are a queen, he pointed out, coronation or no coronation. In a way, nothing's changing, but I suppose I'd better mind my manners now and be careful not to offend this particular sovereign or I could find myself in the dungeons.

Idiot! Alinor responded with a wave of warmth that filled his whole body.

It will be so nice to actually talk to you again, she continued, instead of being so many miles away.

At least we have that, he pointed out, I don't know that I could have stayed away from you for so long otherwise.

Yes, I suppose I should be more grateful. But thinking of how our minds can be so close only reminds me that we have so much still to learn.

I know. Or rather I don't know. That's the problem isn't it? We have no idea of what we should do next, but perhaps we should concentrate firstly on Amiros and then see what happens.

Mm, it's hard to think beyond that.

Sirad could feel Alinor's concern for the Lore-Master and so changed the subject, enquiring about various preparations for the coronation until she brightened up again.

As planned Alinor left Thorgiliad in the weak light of early morning two days later. If she could have got her own way she would have travelled alone, but she had bowed to the expected pressure and was accompanied by half a dozen of her

Elite Guard, having put her foot down firmly at the suggestion that the party should be larger. Their route would allow them to change horses regularly, except of course for Alinor herself. Riding Elkana meant that she could have travelled far quicker than on lesser, albeit quality nonetheless, mounts but keeping the group at a reasonable pace the fey horse of Pelenin would comfortably cope with the effort involved in traversing the miles to Pelamir.

The first couple of days were cold and unpleasantly damp but by the time they were south of Harfeld it had brightened and dried up considerably. Even though it had been essential for Alinor to be in Thorgiliad to address the wrongs that Vixlan had inflicted on her country, she felt a sense of relief as well as an eager anticipation to be back on the road again, facing further challenges directly related to her apparently long-awaited destiny.

Elkana was obviously feeling enthusiastic too, perhaps looking forward to being with her own family again. Did horses feel the same sort of kinship, wondered Alinor.

The mare snorted in response, a definite rebuke to Alinor's doubt.

Of course you do, the young woman directed at her silvery partner. I must apologise – I still haven't got used to the idea of talking to an animal and actually having it answer!

Velvety ears flicked back and forth to remind Alinor that there was likely more to this relationship than met the eye. Alinor could sense the controlled energy in the mare, a longing to simply take off and gallop faster than the wind, to leave these other mortals behind.

Not yet, she sent out her thoughts, but when we get to Pelamir it will be a different matter. Then you can find your kin and gallop to your heart's content!

Elkana gave a small buck of appreciation making Alinor laugh aloud with the sheer pleasure of riding such a wonderful creature.

The journey to Pelamir was accomplished remarkably quickly; changing horses regularly at pre-arranged staging posts en route enabled the party to push on. Alinor enjoyed talking with her bodyguards, learning about them and their families, and also hearing more about their feelings towards the late Steward. The depth of the man's greed and the extent of his betrayal of her father still made her feel angry, but the words of support from her men buoyed her up and she knew that as far as she could control the future for her people was positive. She tried not to think too much about the unsettling and currently still undisclosed destiny for which she and Sirad had been watched over and guided since childhood. Knowledge was the key, she thought, and we need to continue our search in earnest. It's ridiculous that there are so many gaps in our information; it's almost impossible to work out where we need to go next or what our first aim should be. It will be so good to talk things over properly with Sirad again, but it's Amiros we need. If he really is the successor to Remon he surely knows more than he ever told us.

Crossing the border into Pelenin Alinor felt her spirits lift, assisted in no small way by Elkana's obvious pleasure at travelling the land of her birth again. They had met several parties of Riders patrolling the furthest boundaries but Alinor had told them not to bother sending a Rider to the capital as her party would be right on their heels. Besides, Sirad was aware of exactly where she was and had already set out with Ben to welcome her back to his home.

Some thirty miles out from the city, Alinor called a halt to her party. Telling them to wait for her, she urged Elkana into a gallop and literally flew across the grasslands to where she knew Sirad would be. Seeing her approach, Ben held his horse back, allowing the couple to meet some distance away, not wishing to intrude upon a very personal meeting. Sirad's arms enfolded his beloved lady, their kiss sending shockwaves of deep pleasure though them both. Ben could have sworn that there was an actual aura of energy shimmering around the extraordinary couple, even at a distance; what can it be like to have such a bond of love, he thought. If I ever experienced even a tiny part of what they have it would be amazing.

Several minutes later, Sirad waved to Ben to join them and they returned with Alinor to where her guards were patiently waiting. Sirad thanked them for taking good care of his betrothed before they all made their way on to Pelamir.

Almost before they had even dismounted, Alinor told Sirad she wanted to see Amiros.

'Not much difference to see, I think, but I quite understand.'

The two made their way quickly up through the palace to where Amiros was being tended by the wise old Healers. As they approached, Nashira made a slight bow.

'Welcome, Lady Alinor. It is a pleasure to see you again.'

Alinor smiled.

'Our patient is in surprisingly good health in spite of the persistent comatose nature of his illness. The advice of the Lady Mirantha and the wise Brother has been of benefit, even though the condition stubbornly remains.'

'I am sure that you have done the best that could be done under the circumstances,' said Alinor. 'I know you have already realised that his condition is not natural and I appreciate your reticence in not making it a talking point amongst you. I, we, are hoping that very soon it will be possible to somehow break through the barriers of his affliction, though there is no guarantee that we shall succeed. We must all just pray for his recovery.'

'We have always held the Lord Amiros in high esteem,' Petral said, 'and pray constantly for his return to us.'

'Thank you all,' Alinor smiled at the three Healers. 'Your loving care is a comfort to us all.'

As the Healers left, she moved quickly to Amiros' bedside and laid her hand gently upon his, motionless upon the soft coverlet.

'Oh Amiros, it is so good to see you again. Please, dear friend and teacher, you must come back to us. We need you so much.'

She and Sirad stood silently looking down at the pale, gaunt figure. The awful burning around his eyes had mostly healed, but fine scars remained and both were aware that under the eyelids there remained awful damage. The Lore-Master's damaged limbs had knit back well, even his hands which had been twisted and burned appeared much restored.

'He looks much better that I expected,' murmured Alinor.

'They have worked wonders on his physical body,' acknowledged Sirad, 'he has improved greatly. It is just this malevolent curse that has been inflicted on him that we have to find some way of lifting.'

'You must tell me again everything that Mirantha said,' Alinor said, 'and we can look at what I found in the book about it, even though it wasn't really enough to provide any kind of answer.'

'Come,' Sirad took Alinor gently by the arm, 'you should at least freshen up after your trip. Then we can have something to eat and talk as much as you like.'

'That would be good, thank you. And I should pay my respects to your father, too,' Alinor added, conscious as always of the office she now held as a sovereign in her own right.

A few hours later, wrapped in a warm fur cloak, Alinor walked with Sirad in the quiet of one of the gardens. The clear, dark blue sky was peppered with stars and a moon, some days off full, cast a silvery light on the trees and shrubs.

'Frosty tonight,' observed Sirad, 'the seasons are moving on.'

'Mmm, you're probably right,' responded the young woman and yawned.

'Time you got to your bed,' admonished Sirad, 'get a decent night's rest. We've still got plenty to talk about tomorrow.'

'Bully,' was the response, 'but you're right – again. I suddenly feel really tired, so bed will be welcome indeed.'

Sirad leaned over and kissed her gently.

'Come on, let's get you inside. Tomorrow is another day.'

The morning was bright and frosty as expected. For the first time in weeks Alinor had slept dreamlessly and awoke feeling wonderfully refreshed and optimistic. The previous day had seen her pay a brief visit to Sothan and she was really pleased to see that Sirad's father did indeed look better than in all the time she had known him. They had talked briefly and the king had intimated that he was intending to make the journey to Thorgiliad for her coronation. Alinor was astonished by his announcement and humbled to think that this man, after so many years of poor health, would willingly put himself under such stress to attend the ceremonies. It would appear that Sirad too had been taken by surprise; he didn't say very much, but it was obvious that he was both impressed by his father's new-found vigour and delighted that the king was once again going to be undertaking public duties.

'I never expected that!' the two young people said in unison and laughed.

'It's early days yet,' Sirad pointed out, 'I don't know what Mirantha did, but it certainly seems to have succeeded.'

'I'm really looking forward to meeting her,' said Alinor, 'another Ben-Neteru like us – what is she like?'

Sirad blew out a quick breath.

'Well,' he said thoughtfully, 'she has a very powerful mind, but that's only to be expected. We shared thoughts when she wanted to know about Amiros, but she really didn't reveal anything much of herself. I suppose I should also add that she is quite a stunner.'

Alinor eyes widened and she gave Sirad a hard look.

'No, don't get the wrong idea,' he laughed at her expression, 'but you should know that our Ben seems smitten. He can hardly get a word out when she's around.'

'Gracious,' said Alinor with a wry smile, 'that sounds serious. But what does she think – do we know?'

'She's very gentle with him, doesn't give him any encouragement at all, but I would think that she's had this happen before. I've tried to just give him a bit of a hint that she's not for him, but I doubt that he heard it.'

'Oh poor Ben. I am very fond of him and it would be so good if he were able to find someone. But then, she's Ben-Neteru and he wouldn't understand.'

Sirad was silent, looking down.

'All right then, out with it,' demanded Alinor.

'He knows. That is, he knows about us. He guessed, I suppose, and he came right out and asked me straight.'

'Oh!' Alinor was silent a moment. 'You never mentioned that.'

'I know. It was, you know, a bit awkward at the time. It was when we were down south and we found this cave with a passageway and runes and that sort of thing.'

'You never mentioned that either.'

'No, I'm sorry. But I needed to think about it before we discussed it and with you dealing with all the problems that Vixlan caused I felt it wasn't the right time.'

'Well, I'm here now and perhaps it is about the right time to tell me!'

'Tomorrow, my love, tomorrow,' Sirad said firmly adding that they should go and eat as the evening was drawing on.

Now in the light of a pleasant morning, Alinor and Sirad sat down to break their fast and were joined by Eldren. Alinor had been introduced very briefly the previous evening but hadn't had much chance to form an opinion of the little herbalist magician. Within minutes they were chatting easily, Alinor finding him an amusing companion and keen to find out more about his life hidden away on Mitos. That he was an absolute fount of knowledge soon became apparent, as did his heartfelt love and respect for his colleague of the Brotherhood. They talked briefly about Remon and his passing and Eldren emphasised the importance he placed on Amiros succeeding the ancient seer as the latest incarnation of the Mind-Master.

Alinor recounted the information she had found in Remon's book about the obstacles to reaching and hopefully saving a soul banished to the mysterious existence.

'The book mentions possible difficulties, but fails to shed any further light on what they may be,' Alinor said.

'Mirantha may know a little more,' Eldren's rich voice was low, 'but she tends to say little at the best of times.'

'You know her, obviously,' said Alinor, 'can you tell me more about her?'

'How does one describe the quality of air, water and earth? She has the way of the Ben-Neteru but her chosen path is that of healing. Her knowledge is so far beyond my own, which is not so insignificant,' the little man was not boasting but merely stating the truth. 'I've known of her all my life, long before we ever met. I would not hazard a guess as to her age, but that is only to be expected of one of your race,' he smiled at the young couple. 'She is her own master, and answers to none that I have ever heard. Even Remon treated her with great respect.'

Alinor shared a look with Sirad. *She must really be something*, she thought at him.

She is, confirmed Sirad. *I think you will like her.*

Alinor continued aloud.

'I just hope that she will be able find where Amiros has gone and that we can persuade him to return to us.'

'I don't believe there is another who has the knowledge and ability,' said Eldren, 'so we must do everything in our power to make that happen.'

Grabbing an apple, Eldren stood up.

'Back to my books,' he declared. 'I shall see you both later, I think.'

'Well, yes,' said Alinor, as the little healer bustled off. 'Is he always like that?' She turned to Sirad.

'Pretty much,' he responded. 'He absolutely lives for books about plants and medicines. The Chief Librarian is in his element searching out volumes for him that no-one has even glanced at for decades!'

'I like him,' said Alinor smiling. 'He's full of energy and radiates a wonderful sympathy.'

Sirad agreed with her and then indicated that they should leave the dining hall.

'I'd like to have a look at the book this morning, but I know you would like to catch up on some other happenings first.'

Alinor nodded.

'I think it's about time, don't you?'

'We can check in on Amiros first and then we can get away and talk.'

'I promised Elkana the chance to really gallop once she got here so perhaps this morning would be really nice for a ride.'

If Sirad thought it odd to make a promise to her horse, he didn't remark on it but agreed it was a fine morning for the exercise.

So it was that an hour later they pulled up after racing each other across several miles of rolling countryside. Their horses were not even blowing despite the speed and distance covered, and both Alinor and Sirad were grinning with exhilaration.

'I just love it when Elkana really stretches, but it's so much more fun when you're here as well and the horses can race each other properly.'

'Not bad, is it?' Sirad laid a hand on his horse's neck. 'It seems ungrateful, but I do miss my old boy. He was a real companion.'

Alinor could remember Sirad's grief at losing his horse in the dreadful fighting at Elagos.

'Hey, what about that colt of Lightstar's? He must be growing on a bit by now.'

Sirad nodded.

'Yes, he is – amazingly so. I've never known or heard of one that grew so quickly, to be so mature, at this young an age. He, um, is quite a character. Not like any of the other horses at all. Very, sort of, odd.'

Alinor chewed her lip thoughtfully. That day she had gone with Sirad for him to see the colt for the first time, she had recognised that the young creature was something special. Sirad had asked her to name him, a singular honour, and she had felt a strangeness come over her. Sirad told her afterwards that she had described qualities with words from an ancient language and decreed that the name should be *Taukhet*. With what Alinor had learned in the months following, she now knew that, just as Elkana was destined to be her horse, so Taukhet was inextricably tied to Sirad. She knew too, that these horses held an important place in their future ventures, though what that would be was not yet obvious.

She hadn't told Sirad about her amazing bond with Elkana, unsure how he would take it. But now, if the same thing were to come about with him and Taukhet, then he would come to understand it.

'Why don't we go and see him now?' she said, Elkana prancing at her suggestion and generally behaving more like a fresh-broken filly than a mare of more mature years.

'Why not?' responded Sirad, wheeling about and heading off to the winter pastures.

Alinor could feel her mare's increasing enthusiasm as they approached Lightstar's herd, and Sirad's horse was equally buoyed up. As they approached, a dark shadow split from the quietly grazing animals and hurtled towards them. There was no doubt about what it was – the magnificent young stallion positively flew across the grass, mane and tail streaming out and eyes sparkling, and almost skidded to a halt in front of them. Tossing his fine head, he snorted loudly in welcome and gently touched noses with Elkana, his sister.

'Wow,' was Alinor's amazed reaction, 'he's grown so much! I can hardly credit this is the same colt I saw earlier in the year. He's filled out a lot and muscled up, and what a turn of speed!'

'You see what I mean,' said Sirad, 'he really is something else.'

They both dismounted. Taukhet came straight to Sirad and rested his head on the man's shoulder as he ran his hands down the rippling muscles of the horse's neck.

'He's more like a four or five year old already,' said Sirad, 'I can't understand how that could be.'

'I knew he would be special, that first day that Ben brought me out to see him, you know, when you had gone up north.' She didn't need to add that he had been urgently seeking out any trace of her father's murderers. 'He really is quite extraordinary – so beautiful and so full of power and energy.'

Taukhet rubbed his head against Sirad and then reached out to touch Alinor gently on the cheek with his amazingly soft velvety nose, blowing gently at her with sweet meadow scented breath.

She stroked him in wonder and looked across at Sirad whose eyes were taking in the quality of this striking animal. Without question this horse had been destined for him; immediately his mind began looking forward to the day, which would not be long postponed, when he would ride him for the first time and create the lifelong bond of a Rider and his horse.

'Perhaps I should let Elkana have a few days out here with them,' suggested Alinor, 'once we're back in the palace I get someone to bring her back to the herd. I know she would enjoy spending time with her family.'

Sirad looked slightly askance but realised that Alinor had not spoken in jest, but more as if a friend of hers had told her she was visiting home to spend some time with her mother and siblings.

'Yes, of course, I'm sure you're right,' he said.

Taukhet stamped and snorted.

'Of course I'm right,' responded Alinor, 'even Taukhet is looking forward to learning what his elder sister has been up to.'

Sirad couldn't think of a suitable response to that statement.

Elkana whickered softly to her young brother as Alinor and Sirad remounted and headed off back to the city. With a toss of his head the gleaming black horse turned and galloped away.

Chapter 20

There was an indefinable tension in the air this morning, something that he had not felt in all the time he had spent in E'shariya. Amiros left his rooms and made his way to his favourite courtyard where he had been accustomed to meeting with Meriona - not every day, but fairly frequently, although since they had shared dinner that night, she had not graced him with her presence.

Hoping to see her, but expecting another disappointment, he smiled as he realised that today she had returned. Trying not to hurry unduly he walked briskly over to where she sat on her usual seat, tying bunches of fragrant herbs and placing them gently into a small basket.

'I missed you these last days,' he said, taking his place opposite her.

Meriona smiled and nodded, observing him closely.

'I see a change in you,' she said quietly, 'I sense a power that was not there before.'

Amiros hesitated before replying.

'Perhaps,' he said, 'I suppose that could be it. I know that there is a difference in me since going to the sanctuary, although I cannot quite work out exactly what. I have been – stretched – I suppose you could say. I feel that I have been pulled apart almost, my mind pressured and then squeezed before being eased again. It has not been an enjoyable experience,' he finished ruefully.

'I am sorry for all the pain you have endured, dear friend. It sounds so callous to say that perhaps it was necessary. Was this always your destiny? – I don't know. Who are we to understand?'

'You said, that evening, that you were confident that I would come to accept what must be.'

She nodded.

'I think that perhaps you may be right in a way, that I have finally come to some acceptance, even though I am not totally sure of what it is I am accepting! If that makes sense?'

'Perfectly,' the beautiful woman responded.

'Mm, well, I don't know that I am quite convinced about this leap of faith in my destiny,' the Lore-Master pointed out. 'I am, shall I say, uncomfortable. I – I believe you already know that I have an anger in me at what has happened. Many have suffered and died because of the greed of one of my Brotherhood, and yes, I am angry about what has been done to me. It is a cruel destiny that robs people of those they love and inflicts so much pain. It makes me want to strike back, to take revenge.'

He did not shout, but his voice radiated powerful emotion.

Oh yes, he has changed, thought Meriona to herself.

She reached out her hand to touch the mage on his arm.

'Vengeance must be controlled, my love, or it will destroy not just you. Of course you wish to take revenge, as anyone would, but not with fire in your soul. You must be the master of yourself or lose everything. This has all happened so quickly it will not be easy for you, but I beg you to be careful.'

Amiros rubbed a hand over his eyes. She was right, he knew, but he also knew that the rage he felt was a fierce beast to overcome. At least I am aware of the beast, he thought, I suppose that is a start.

Sitting there, all these thoughts and emotions fighting for supremacy in his mind, he suddenly realised that he did want to return to his real existence. He wanted to continue with whatever quest had been set in motion regardless of the danger. He could not live with the thought that if he did not, then he could be allowing Verun to succeed in whatever diabolical plan he was embarked upon. Yes, he might fail, but his whole life had been a preparation for this time. Alinor and Sirad existed for this quest, and he could not, would not, let them down.

But how? Whatever the intention of Verun had been when using Mnethar as a weapon against him, the truth was that he was trapped in this strange parallel existence with no clue as to how he could break away from it.

'There must be something I can do,' he took Meriona's hand, but she shook her head.

'I am sorry, I have no idea whether it is up to you or not,' she said. 'The only knowledge that I have gleaned has all stressed that it is necessary for someone from the real existence to make the journey to find the soul that has been lost and persuade that soul to return.'

'I would need no persuasion,' Amiros said quietly, 'I only know that I must return.'

'I can only hope that someone will find their way to you, and soon.'

'I am torn though, for if I leave here, then I shall leave you too.'

Meriona hung her head.

'It is inevitable that we must part. Shortly after you first came I warned you that I would not be able to stay here with you. I found myself here by some strange means and I knew that I would have some part in helping to heal your mind. But I know that it is time for me to go and for you to finish that for which you have been sent here. It is not within my power to alter this,' she put a finger to his lips to prevent him speaking, arguing that it should not be so.

'Do not ask any more of me, for I cannot answer your questions. What has been decreed must come about, although what the final outcomes may be is not for us to know. There will be a time of reckoning, but there is nothing to give any indication as to when that will be, or even who will be involved. No, my beloved Lore-Master, we can only do what we believe to be right, whatever the dangers and heartaches. Your heart has always been true. Listen to it and be guided by the unassailable integrity of your soul.

Amiros groaned loudly and stood up abruptly. Shaking his head he walked away a few paces.

'No, no,' he breathed, 'you are making me out to be a far better man than I really am. I have made so many mistakes, been blind to situations – and look where it got me! What use can I be without putting your daughter in peril of her life?'

'Her life will be in more danger without you,' Meriona said very quietly.

Amiros stood with his back to her and took several deep breaths.

'I suppose you could be right,' he said at last, 'but I think this just proves that I am far from being ready to take up the role that Remon Mind-Master had intended for me.'

'On the contrary, I think it proves that you are well on the way to a far better understanding of your own self, and in that lies your strength.'

He turned back to her as she stood and came towards him.

'It is time,' she said. 'I must leave now. Do not grieve at our parting for we have been fortunate indeed to have had this time together, despite the awful events which led up to it. I have to believe that you will find your way back or there would have been no point to any of this. Know that I have faith in you. I cherish our friendship and love and I am certain that we shall all meet again.'

She embraced him then and kissed him gently on the cheek.

'Be strong my love,' she murmured.

He nodded, unable to speak, tears burning his eyes.

With a final loving touch, she turned, retrieved her basket of herbs and silently disappeared from the courtyard.

The man could only stand there and gaze after her.

'I suppose we should get round to that talk we were going to have yesterday,' said Sirad.

Alinor laughed.

'Yes, we did get rather distracted didn't we, what with the horses and everything,' she glanced at him, her eyes sparkling.

'It was interesting, to say the least. But, I think we need to focus a bit more for the moment. You said you had been thinking about the Tokens – have you discovered something new?'

'Actually yes, in a way.'

'Go on.'

'Well, you can guess what it's like with all these preparations for the coronation and such, so I just decided to try and find a bit of peace for a few minutes. There's this tower – one of a number as you remember – but this particular one was where I used to sneak off and climb up to enjoy the fantastic views. I wasn't supposed to for whatever reason, but that never stopped me.'

'Why am I not surprised?' murmured Sirad.

'Oh hush! That doesn't matter now. Anyway, up the tower I went. There's a small room at the top and it was obvious that it had been used by someone – I know now that it was my mother – probably as a retreat from the cares of the day just as I was doing. There wasn't much to see in the way of furnishings; a small chest, empty; a table and a couple of chairs; that was it. But then I caught sight of some lovely carving in the stonework. It was very low down, quite a strange place to put it. I thought that the design looked familiar and then I remembered: it was very like the designs on my mother's crown – I told you about that didn't I?'

Sirad nodded.

'So, I was just following this design around the wall to where it stopped. No sign of anything else. I had my hand on the stones which felt a bit warm, and just then there was a noise, a bird by the window I think, and I accidentally pushed on one of the stones and it moved inwards. There was a box hidden in the cavity in the wall, so of course I took it out.'

Alinor paused in her story, Sirad watching her closely.

'And?' he said.

'The box had runes on it – they said *Legacy*. So, I opened it. There was a letter inside with my name on it. It was from my mother.'

Sirad could see that Alinor had become quite emotional.

'That must have been quite a shock,' he said gently, taking her hand and stroking it.

'It was, rather,' she replied, 'I didn't know quite what to think. After all this time, I could almost hear her voice as I read it, but it was so strange. The way she wrote was almost as if it were recent, and she was aware that I had started on this awful challenge. It had been foretold, she said, and was now upon us but that I must be strong despite the danger. She was leaving me a gift which had been passed down until such time as the Tokens should be brought together again.'

Alinor had hung the small pouch containing her mother's gem around her neck and she brought it out now, emptying the jewel onto her palm. It didn't flare as it had the first time she touched it, but seemed to glow deep inside.

Sirad stared at the gem, mesmerised. He could feel its unearthly aura, a magical power contained and concealed within it. He could almost see it expanding to encompass Alinor, and then unexpectedly reaching himself.

'It's like The Firestone, isn't it?' he said quietly, 'but so much more.'

Alinor nodded.

'That was my first thought,' she said, 'but the strange thing is, I believe that it fits into mother's crown, or can do. I'm not sure if that is where it is supposed to stay, but it would definitely be in keeping with the design.'

'On the grounds that as yet we have no idea of what the Tokens actually are, it may be that this is one of them,' Sirad said thoughtfully. 'If so, then we are indeed on the road to finding them. Of course, if Mnethar is one as well, it is out of our reach. Verun is hardly likely to let it fall into our hands when he is set on getting them for himself.'

'True, but as we already have three in our keeping, Shenbran, Qanoor and now this, I am hoping that we have the advantage. We have to find some way of identifying what the others are. Remon's book told us that the other great Sword is Tauenbran, but, like everything else it is supposed to be lost. Is there anything which we have read that gives us any clue as to where it could be?'

'Not that I can think of. Still, we haven't plumbed the depths of the latest book have we? There must be something in there to lead us on to the next step. I reckon that is our next move; to go through that book completely – yes, I know, it's slow going, but I just feel that it contains important information. We have some time available to us, a few days at least, and between us I'm sure we can make some progress.'

Alinor nodded, her eyes narrowed as she thought.

'Good idea,' she said, 'I feel I have to do something while we're waiting for Mirantha to get here – I can't stand this waiting!'

Sirad kissed her forehead and smoothed away the lines of worry there.

'Let's just do what we can for now,' he said, 'she'll get back as soon as she can, I know, so we have to be patient a little longer.'

'Mm, I know, but that doesn't make the waiting any better. I'll get the book so we can make a start. Oh, can you get me something to drink? I'm so thirsty I can't concentrate!'

Whilst Alinor went to fetch the precious book Sirad arranged for some refreshments and instructed his staff that they were not to be disturbed for the rest of the morning. Once she returned they sat at a small well-lit table by a window affording a pleasant view of one of the courtyard gardens. Sirad armed himself with writing materials and paper to make odd notes; they set the ancient book on the table, linked their minds and opened it to the first chapter to commence their study.

The shock of being able to read the archaic language was not as great for Sirad as it had been that first day when he and Alinor had found the book in Remon's house. In fact, it seemed far easier than before.

You could be right, was Alinor's thought in response to Sirad's suggestion that maybe her mother's gem was complementing the known effects of The Firestone. The bond between us seems stronger than before.

It does, you are right. Still, there are quite a lot of names or descriptions here that mean nothing to me – rather like the reader is expected to know. I hope that by the time we've read a few hundred pages we might understand it a bit better!

Alinor shrugged.

We can but try. Some of these happenings written here must have been eons ago, well before the time of Rakep-thos; it's hard to put it into perspective.

Perhaps we should just both read a few sections and then take a break and try and work out what each of us think it means.

Worth a try, Alinor thought at him, see what happens.

For nearly a couple of hours the young couple pored over the pages, riveted by the complexity of the narrative and intrigued as much as by what was not recorded as by what they read.

Eventually Alinor dropped her head in her hands.

'Enough,' she groaned, 'I'm getting dizzy with all of this!'

Sirad leaned back and stretched.

'You're not alone there,' he said, 'I had absolutely no idea about any of this, and I thought Amiros had drummed enough history into my head to last me a lifetime.'

'I know just what you mean,' she laughed, 'but I never really started to get to grips with the past before Amiros set me to work in the library here. That was when he first told me about the Sight . . .'

Sirad nodded. He well remembered when he had brought an unconscious, possibly dying, Alinor in her guise as the young traveller Elukar, into the palace. Amiros had arrived – summoned as he said by Alinor – and had been able to bring her back to life. As soon as he had known she would be safe, he had left in what turned out to be a fruitless search for the man who had murdered her father. Neither of them had known at the time that they were both Ben-Neteru; neither of them had even now come completely to terms with their legacy, and neither were yet aware of the extent of their abilities, nor would be for some time to come.

The young man rose and reached out a hand to bring his beloved into his embrace.

'It is so good to feel you here in my arms again,' he breathed into her soft hair. 'Even though we can be close in our minds, it's not nearly as good as holding you.'

Alinor didn't reply, didn't need to. She just held him, his warmth enfolding her, giving her a feeling of such security she could almost cry with happiness.

'A shame we can't stay like this,' he said, 'but I hate to say it – I'm hungry! All this studying has worn me out!'

That did make Alinor really laugh. She punched him on the arm, 'Typical man, always thinking of his stomach,' she chided. 'All right then, you win. I won't say I wouldn't like a bit of something too.'

'Then we can have a bit of a brainstorm about what we've found so far.'

'OK, fair enough.'

They ate, then talked, took a walk out on the palace battlements and talked some more.

'Background stuff really, isn't it? Though there is a mention or two of some unidentified power or being in the background.'

'Yes, I got that,' said Sirad, 'not really enough information to put your finger on, but I have the impression that whatever it is is extremely important. It always seems to be on the periphery of everything, nothing obvious, but it is malevolent I think.'

'Yes, that's it. Nothing overt, but insidious. Important, I agree.'

'We need to find out more about this – influence. Hopefully the book will give us more information as we go on.'

'Another hour or so this afternoon, and then I think I would like to spend some time with Amiros,' said Alinor.

'Agreed,' said Sirad, 'and I want to have a talk with my father. Perhaps you would join us later?'

'I'd be delighted,' smiled Alinor, 'it's good to see him looking so well.'

The pair returned to their study of Remon's book.

The king was not in his apartments when Sirad went to visit, nor was he walking in his favourite garden. The prince had to enquire of a number of servants before he finally located his father down in the Riders' training yard talking with some of the officers.

'Ah, there you are,' said Sothan, catching sight of the tall figure of his son, 'I thought it about time I came to see how things are progressing with the troops.'

Sirad had a great smile on his face as he replied, 'Good day, father, I never expected to find you here.'

'Well yes, I know I've been neglecting matters for too long now. But I am feeling so much better it is a real pleasure to be able to get out and about – catch up with matters a bit more.'

Sothan led the way back into the palace.

'I hadn't realised,' he continued, 'just how out of touch I was becoming. Though I tried to maintain appearances, obviously with some success, I don't think I was really achieving much. It wasn't until Mirantha came to see me that I recognised that I had been – I don't know how to describe it – losing myself for periods of time.'

It was a reluctant admission; Sirad could detect his father's unease, a kind of shame.

'It was not your fault,' he said gently, 'don't blame yourself.'

'Hard not to, my boy, we none of us like to admit to our shortcomings. But Mirantha told me that I had been affected by this sort of darkness, as she described it, that served to create an insidious dampening on my mind. The past few days I have found myself suddenly remembering things that I had completely forgotten – important things. Whilst I did tell you some things about your mother and the past, I had left out much which needs to be said.'

They had reached the king's apartments and Sothan indicated that Sirad should take a seat, but he remained standing, and then paced to and fro across the room.

'I have not yet recalled everything,' the king started, 'my memory is not what it was. Improving day by day certainly, but it does require effort.'

'If Mirantha had truly managed to lift that darkness, then surely it is only a matter of time,' offered Sirad.

'Yes probably. I just hope that there is enough time.'

The king came and sat down, reaching out a hand to clasp his son's arm.

'I am proud of you, my son, and your mother would be too. She and the Lady Meriona knew that you and Alinor would be faced with a challenge so great as to defy description. She, they, believed that you would be up to it, but it would be hard, painful. She would not, or could not, tell me all the details; indeed, she said that she herself did not fully understand the prophecies of destiny. You and Alinor must re-unite the Tokens, that is the first part of the quest. I don't know what all the Tokens are, but the Swords of Bran are important, and are key to moving forward. You know about Bran?'

Sirad nodded.

'Alinor and I have been working on the book that we brought back from Remon's house. There was quite a bit about Bran, how he had been a mentor to Rakep-thos in his younger days. He was the ultimate warrior, none could stand against his swords – Shenbran and Tauenbran – and all believed that he would never be defeated. But then came the Scattering Wars, or at least the evil that gave rise to them. We've come across references to some power, some being that appears to be the root of all this evil, and it is that which caused the downfall and death of Bran.'

'Quite right, Sirad, that was so. Somehow, Rakep-thos managed to overcome that power, but he could not destroy it. People believed that the evil was contained in some way, cast out and banished from our known world. That may have been so, but the prophecies said that it would return to threaten our lives again and that unless the Tokens which had been lost, scattered and hidden, could be found and brought together again, the power would be triumphant.'

'Alinor has Shenbran,' said Sirad, 'as it had been passed down through the House of Thormeyern, as was Qanoor, The Firestone. And now there is another gem.'

Sothan's glance was questioning.

'The Lady Meriona left a gift for Alinor. She only found it by chance – or perhaps that was meant to be – with a letter. It is a gem, bigger that The Firestone but somehow related to it. I did wonder at first if perhaps they were once part of a bigger stone but the colouring is very different so that probably is not right. It has great power – I have felt it myself.'

'Yes, I remember it.'

Sothan thought deeply for several moments, one elbow propped on the arm of his chair, chin resting on his hand.

He continued quietly.

'It was part of her collection, Meriona's that is, and when she married Teleston she placed it in her crown. The most beautiful example of the jeweller's art that I have ever seen – I doubt that such a creation could be made today. It was known as Eletha, the Heart. And you say that Alinor now has it?'

'She does. She showed me yesterday and we rather thought that it may be one of the Tokens.'

'Indeed it is.' The king nodded. 'It does belong with Qanoor, in the way in which all the stones of power do, but together they comprise a pair of the Tokens.'

'From what you have said, and following on from what we have found, we must search for Tauenbran.'

'Yes, I think that is probably your best move. I have been giving it some thought and trying to see if I can remember anything about where it is thought to be. It's all legend of course, but there's always a grain of truth in the old stories if we can just get down to it.'

Sirad and his father continued to talk for another hour or more.

'I've asked Alinor to join us, father, if that's all right. She wanted to spend some time with Amiros, even though there is nothing either of us can do until Mirantha returns.'

'Of course, of course. We only had a few minutes the other day. I'll get them to send our dinner up here and we can continue our talks in peace.'

'I like your father very much,' said Alinor as Sirad walked her back to her rooms later that night. 'I love the stories of him and my father when they were younger – they must have been quite a pair.'

'Yes,' mused Sirad, 'he came out with some tales this evening that I certainly haven't heard before. He's always been so, modest I suppose, but I am coming to understand just how instrumental he has been in making Pelenin the country it is today.'

'It looks like both our fathers are going to be hard acts to follow,' said Alinor. 'I just hope that I won't let the side down – I have so much to learn.'

'Me too, though I have had more time than you and still have my father to guide me.'

Alinor paused and turned to her prince.

'I shall need your help, you know.'

'I will always be here for you, you know that. But I think you understand very well what Ancor needs, and I have complete confidence that you will be a great queen.'

'There are moments, though,' she said quietly, 'that I feel so unprepared, not nearly ready to take the crown. When I do, well, I can't ever go back to being just Alinor again, can I? All of this – we can't undo it can we, can't ever go back and unlearn what we know, who we are?'

Sirad held her, willing away her uncertainties and doubts.

'We have each other, whatever happens. Nothing can ever take away what we have between us. We have been chosen, willingly or otherwise, and together we will face this destiny.'

Alinor sighed, partly in resignation but partly also with satisfaction at the feeling of deep contentment that she felt in his embrace.

'We are truly blessed in each other, are we not? No matter what happens, I cannot forget that.'

She reached up to run her fingers through his dark hair and laid her lips gently on his, their kiss deepening with the powerful emotions that swept through them both. It was many minutes before they parted to return each to their own rooms.

Chapter 21

The following morning Alinor went to visit Amiros as usual whilst Sirad attended to a few regular matters with the Riders. They then spent another hour or so working through the book, hoping to find some indications about where they should commence their search for the missing sword, but with little success.

'This is ridiculous, we're just not getting anywhere.'

Alinor was feeling frustrated and angry; her worry about Amiros, coupled with everything else that was going on in her life had, for the moment, got the better of her. She paced around the room, picking up cushions and throwing them back down, not knowing how to vent her emotions. She was tempted to just pick up a vase and break it, but then couldn't do that and expect someone else to clean it up after her.

'I'm sorry, Sirad, all this uncertainty is getting to me. I want to do something, but don't know what.'

The young man watched her pacing, understanding her frustrations. He felt it too, but when he felt like that he tended to go down to the training yard and work out.

'Why don't you come down with me and we can just work out for a while? Get rid of that restless energy.'

Alinor stopped and looked at him.

'Mm, that's a good idea. You know, we've never actually tried out against each other. . .'

'Whoa, hang on a minute. I didn't mean that. But . . maybe it would be interesting.'

'Come on, let's go!'

With a laugh Alinor punched Sirad lightly on the arm and set off, bubbling with enthusiasm. Shaking his head he could only follow. This could be fun, was his thought.

There were only a few men practising at this hour as the pair chose a space and drew their weapons, not bothering with putting on any protective clothing.

For a few moments they simply circled each other, taking note of each other's stance, how they held their swords, how relaxed was their posture. Sirad had, of course, seen Alinor in battle and knew her for a formidable swordswoman, but he had never studied how she achieved her exceptional speed of reaction. On their way down they had agreed not to read each other's minds but to make it a proper challenge. So he feinted, she parried almost before he made the attempt. She in turn raised her arm as if for a head blow but immediately twisted her wrist and turned it into a slice from the side. He met it with his blade. She was quick, he acknowledged, and not easy to read.

They traded blows for some time, not too hard, but had they been intended would have wounded another opponent quite seriously. Both light on their feet, Sirad had a height advantage, but Alinor was extremely athletic and able to twist and turn with remarkable ability.

Their concentration completely focussed on each other, neither noticed that they were gaining an audience. Word had spread about this unheard of bout between the Lord Commander of the Riders of Pelenin and the Lady of Ancor, and men were putting aside whatever they had been working on and gathering round the edges of the yard. Wagers were being laid, but very unobtrusively.

'You can't catch me that easily,' jested Sirad, but in truth she was a more than worthy opponent and he had to work hard to prevent her getting the upper hand.

Breaking apart following a very rapid exchange of blows there were loud calls of admiration from the onlookers as it was patently obvious that the pair were so evenly matched the competition could go on for hours before either side gave in. The pair glanced round in surprise, then looked at each other and laughed, puffing from the exertion.

'That was fun,' gasped Alinor, 'I really enjoyed that. We'll have to do it again!'

'Not bad,' responded Sirad and added in a low voice, 'I'll teach you a lesson next time!'

'In your dreams, dear prince,' she responded in an equally low voice, 'but maybe it will be me teaching you.'

'All right you lot, the show is over. Back to work!'

With good-natured groans the Riders dispersed and Sirad took Alinor's arm to lead her back inside.

'Better now?' he asked.

'Yes, thank you. The uncertainties are still there in my mind, but at least I can keep them in proportion a bit easier. I haven't had much chance to practise recently and I realise that I do miss it.'

'It's good for both of us. In the same way we both have to work on what abilities our minds have, so too we cannot neglect that we need to be physically fit to face whatever comes our way. We saw only too well the punishments that we can receive in a pitched battle, let alone anything else that Verun had in mind. We've not seen the last of him, you may be sure, so we must be prepared.'

'Don't worry, I haven't forgotten about him.'

'I don't know how you do it,' sighed Sirad, 'here you are juggling warrior training and organising a coronation!'

'Never underestimate a woman,' laughed Alinor, 'we can run rings around you men! But, enough for the moment, I'm going to take a shower before lunch.'

'I wonder how much longer before Mirantha returns?' Alinor asked in between mouthfuls of apple. 'The time seems to be flying by and I won't be able to leave it too many days before I have to get back to Thorgiliad. And of course, you and your father will be making plans to leave to travel up to Ancor before long. Some of the other guests from further away will be setting off – they don't have the luxury of using horses like the Riders have. I don't suppose there's any way we can make contact with her is there? She is one of us after all.'

'It hadn't occurred to me,' said Sirad, 'but you may have a point. Perhaps we could send out a thought and see if she responds.'

The pair were standing on a balcony looking out over the city walls. Alinor linked her mind with Sirad who could clearly picture the red-haired mystic and who had the experience of previously sharing thoughts with her.

Within seconds they could hear her voice quite clearly.

Greetings Sirad, and greetings to you Alinor. It have some good news fortunately. It has been a difficult task and I have been obliged to travel further than I expected, but thanks to the efforts of this lovely creature (she pictured the handsome horse she was riding) I have managed to achieve my goal sooner than might have been.

How long before you return? Alinor asked eagerly, and then mentally chided herself. I do apologise, that was rude of me. Greetings to you Mirantha. I can only say that this is the first time I have met someone by means of a linked mind!

Understandable, came the response and Alinor could sense Mirantha's amusement. To answer your question, I am already on my way. Zaruk here has an excellent turn of speed and has promised to get me back before sunset tomorrow.

Both Sirad and Alinor were astonished, realising that Mirantha was in fact over two hundred miles from Pelenin. Yes, they knew the fey nature of their horses was crowned by their uncanny ability to travel faster and further than any other four-legged creature, but that distance in so brief a time was indeed unexpected.

Tell Eldren to make the necessary preparations please, continued Mirantha, for we cannot afford to lose any time if we are to succeed in our quest to save Amiros.

The link broke and the pair looked at each other.

'Gosh,' said Alinor, 'she really is quite daunting. Her thoughts were so clear, so powerful, and she seems so assured.'

'Wait until you see her for real,' said Sirad, 'she is quite special.'

But not as special as you, he sent the thought to Alinor.

Her lips curved in a slow smile.

'We'd better go and find Eldren and see if there is anything we should do to help get ready,' she said. 'Mirantha obviously is concerned and wants no delay.'

'Absolutely, I am with you there.'

They hurried down to find the little man and set things ready for Mirantha's return.

True to her word, before the sun had disappeared beyond the horizon the next day, Mirantha galloped through the main gates of the city and on up to the palace entrance. Both Sirad and Alinor were nearby having been waiting expectantly for the past hour, never doubting that she would be on time.

Zaruk's hooves clattered on the stone as he almost skidded to a halt; the bay horse was sweating and breathing hard, although not distressed.

Mirantha slid from his back and laid her hand gently on his forehead.

'Rest now, good friend, you have done well.'

The horse seemed to bow his head to her and then watched as she joined the young couple on the steps. A young groom took the horse's reins and led him away, murmuring words of admiration to his charge.

'Welcome, my Lady,' Sirad bowed to the Healer.

Alinor started to curtsey, the other woman seemed so regal somehow, but Mirantha reached out to her and embraced her.

'I am pleased to meet you at last little sister,' she said, her musical voice completing the embrace.

'And I you,' Alinor managed to say, quite overwhelmed by the aura of this strange woman.

'We have done everything that Eldren advised,' Sirad started, but was interrupted by the arrival of the plump little mage himself, his short legs carrying as fast as possible to join them.

'I am glad to see you safe returned,' he said, 'I admit to some concern for your welfare.'

'You need not have worried for me, old friend, you should know that by now.'

Eldren chuckled.

'Still,' he continued, 'these are bad times so you will permit me my little foibles.'

Mirantha touched him lightly on the arm and handed him her small pack.

'Everything we require is in here if you would please take it up for me.'

Eldren nodded and bustled off. Mirantha turned to Sirad.

'I need a while to refresh myself and gather my thoughts before we begin. I trust you are both ready?'

He nodded and she looked at Alinor, who also nodded.

'We have arranged everything in the room adjoining where Amiros has been lying. The Healers and staff know that once we embark on this ritual we must not be disturbed. I can trust them all. Please make use of the rooms you had before.'

'Thank you. Now, I suggest that you too have a little something to eat – there's no telling when Alinor will next get the chance. As I already warned you, we have no way of knowing what to expect, only that it could be dangerous. So, I suggest we gather together in one hour.'

With those words Mirantha walked purposefully off to prepare herself.

'Well,' Sirad turned to Alinor, 'what do you think?'

'I, um, can't really find the words to describe her. She seems to have this sort of power just simmering under the surface; I almost feel as if I know her, but I don't. Silly isn't it?'

'No, I know what you mean. I suppose it's because she is Ben-Neteru like us and there is a kind of kinship.'

'I suppose so,' said Alinor lost in thought.

'We'd best do as she said,' continued Sirad, 'you need to be ready for whatever happens.'

'Are you afraid?' the young woman asked quietly.

'A little,' he responded, 'more for you than for Amiros.'

'I do so want to help him, but, if I'm honest, I have to say I am a bit scared too. I don't like the possibility of being trapped and lost just like he is.'

'That's why Mirantha insists that Eldren and I are there to act as some kind of anchor, to help bring you back if you run into trouble.'

'I don't quite understand, but I suppose we just have to believe that it will be all right.'

They were alone in one of the corridors and Sirad just pulled Alinor gently into his arms.

'It will be all right, I believe in you and I believe that what we are doing is for the best.'

'When you hold me, I can believe too.'

'Hold onto that feeling, my love, it's the only thing we need.'

Sirad took Alinor back to her apartment and sent a servant to get some food for them both. Alinor didn't feel at all hungry but managed to pick at a few things, knowing that Mirantha's advice was good. They said little to each other, so many thoughts going round in their heads. At last Sirad stood up.

'It's time we went up. Mirantha will be coming soon.'

Alinor looked up at Sirad.

'Thank you,' she said, 'thank you for everything.'

'No need,' Sirad shook his head. 'I love you. I can't do anything different.'

'I love you too,' Alinor whispered, her eyes misting. 'I couldn't do anything different either.'

Eldren was going round the room he had picked as suitable for their task checking again that all the various crystals, candles and herbs were still in exactly the correct places. A faint incense permeated the area where Amiros had been brought in and laid on a narrow bed. Two couches had also been prepared for Mirantha and Alinor; a couple of comfortable chairs were available for Eldren and Sirad.

A small table was laid out with bowls of varying herbs and potions. On a tripod was placed a bowl of hot liquid, a potent steam arising from it, wafting a strange aroma into the room as Eldren passed to and fro.

'She will be here in a moment and then she can explain exactly what we have to do,' started Eldren.

The door opened quietly and Mirantha entered. She had changed from her travelling clothes and now wore a long sage green gown shot with flashes of muted gold. Her hair was loose and curled gently over her shoulders, the colour of a rich red wine.

The others watched quietly as she went to Amiros' side and laid her hand gently on his forehead. Turning to the other she spoke.

'The time is right and I have a sense that he is ready. In a moment or two Alinor and I will drink the potion that Eldren has prepared. This will induce in both of us a deep trance which will release us into the realm to which our friend has been banished. We may still be together, or perhaps we have to travel its road alone, I don't know. We will rely on the two of you,' she indicated Sirad and Eldren, 'to hold us in your minds, to provide us with strength and purpose. Whatever happens, you must not give way to doubt or we shall be lost.'

The men nodded.

'You know what to do whilst we are travelling,' she continued addressing Eldren, 'you have added the ingredients I gave you?'

'Yes, as you instructed.'

'Good. I know your skills, Eldren, and am grateful for them.'

She walked slowly around the room reciting ancient words in a low voice, creating a circle of protective power. Returning to the table she passed her hands over the bowl on the tripod several times using a series of incantations. Lastly she cast some more crushed leaves onto the burning incense resulting in a pungent aroma which filled the room. It wasn't unpleasant, but Alinor thought she was starting to feel a little light-headed.

Mirantha took two cups and filled them from the bowl, handing one to Alinor.

'Drink this, all of it, and then lie down on your couch. You will feel some strange sensations before you lose consciousness and drift into the other realm. Don't fight it. I shall be with you, even if we cannot see each other.'

Alinor took the cup, looked at the others, took a deep breath and then a tentative sip. It was strong, herby and a bit sharp. Mirantha nodded her encouragement and she finished the draught with no further hesitation. Sirad guided her to the couch where she laid down, blinking her eyes rapidly as her head seemed to swim.

Mirantha swallowed her own cupful and laid down, closing her eyes and relaxing to allow the draught to take effect.

'I'm here,' whispered Sirad as Alinor drifted into unconsciousness, 'I'm here.'

Alinor could hear Mirantha's voice.

'Get up, Alinor, get up.'

She opened her eyes but couldn't see the other woman. What she could see was a grey fog. She was lying on a gravelly bank by a rough track; sitting up she looked around to try and get her bearings.

'Follow the track,' came Mirantha's voice.

'Where are you?' asked Alinor, but there was no reply.

I can remember tracks like these, thought the young woman, and fog like this too in the marshlands. Just so long as the Marsh Wolves don't turn up I shall be all right. She set off along the track. The fog was swirling, though she could feel no wind, and the track came and went. Eventually it lifted slightly and she found herself scrambling over rougher boulders with bits of vegetation dotted here and there. Then with a sudden huge gust it started to rain, not gentle but a positive deluge which soaked her to the skin in moments. It was bitterly cold too and she shivered, unable to see anywhere to shelter from it. By now the wind was howling as if in laughter at her plight.

'What is this?' she shouted. 'What are you trying to do to me?'

In response all she got was another gust of wind which nearly took her off her feet. Drenched and cold all she could do was to keep moving. I've come to find Amiros she told herself, I have to keep going.

She struggled on for what seemed like hours and then, as suddenly as it had started, the rain stopped and the grey fogginess disappeared. The rocky surroundings were replaced by miles of sand with occasional dark outcrops sticking up into the burning sky.

This is weird, thought Alinor, I know Mirantha couldn't say what we would encounter, but all the same . . .

Instead of being soaking wet and frozen, Alinor was now stiflingly hot as the sun blazed down upon her. She stared out across the plains uncertain which direction to go in. The only shelter would be by the outcrops she decided and started walking towards what she hoped would be the nearest one. It was not easy going as the sand was very soft in places, and it took a lot of effort to even put one foot in front of the other.

Looking up after one particularly awkward scramble over a low dune, she thought she could see someone in the distance. A mirage was her first thought, but then – sigh of relief – she caught the sound of Mirantha's voice.

'Keep going, Alinor, I'm over here.'

The young woman renewed her exertions and started to cover the distance between them.

'Do you know which way to go?' Alinor called as soon as she came within range.

'To the cliffs,' Mirantha responded, 'but I don't think I can . . '

The reply was cut off and to Alinor's consternation the other woman's image seemed to shimmer and fade and was then gone completely. An illusion of some kind, the young woman thought, but as she drew near to where she had seen her companion she could see some tracks in the sand where someone had been walking.

Not an illusion then, it was real. But where had she disappeared to?

To the cliffs, she had said, so that is where I must go too.

She struggled on, the heat taking its toll of her. No water, thought Alinor, I can't go on indefinitely without water.

Brushing the sweat from her eyes Alinor was aware of an insidious thought creeping into her head. I'm going to burn up out here, I'm just going to lie down and the heat will dry me out and I'll end up as a desiccated corpse, my bones bleaching in the sun.

She fought to keep the awful pictures from her mind, but unexpectedly she felt a gentle cool touch of comfort.

This is not the real world it seemed to be suggesting. A fleeting moment, but it was enough to give her the encouragement she needed to carry on. The outcrops she had been heading for were much nearer now and she started to make out where there were huge rock faces rising vertically from the sandy floor, carved by wind and sand. Some shade would be good, she thought, doggedly continuing to put one foot in front of the other, really starting to get wearier the nearer the rocks came.

When she finally got there, it was as if the cliff face has been placed there by some giant hand. There was a bit of rough stone and small boulders at the foot, but not much. The rock had simply just pushed itself up out of the sand. She moved slowly along the base of the cliff hoping to find a cutting where she could get out of the sun. A small movement in the sand ahead of her caught her eye and she realised it was a bird, a little falcon of some kind. It lay with one wing outstretched but clearly broken. As she stooped to see it closer, it struggled to move.

'Oh you poor creature,' said Alinor and reached to take it carefully into her hands. Perhaps she could make use of her skills to heal it. The falcon quivered at her touch, but before she could even start to explore the damage, it let out a piercing cry and went still.

Alinor was horrified.

'I didn't want to hurt you,' she cried, cradling the warm lifeless body. 'I'm so sorry.'

Gently she scraped a hole in the sand and buried the bird.

She got up from where she had been kneeling, brushed the sand from her hands and continued her exploration of the cliff face.

Want to rest, she thought, just need to stop for a little while out of this wretched sun.

As if in answer she caught sight of a gap where the cliff face was broken. She quickened her pace and was heartened to see that it was quite a deep fissure that seemed to stretch quite a way back. Eager to get out of the heat she did not hesitate to step into the blessed cool of the dark shadow, finding it to be the entrance to what appeared to be a long tunnel disappearing into the depths of the rock.

This will do for now, she thought, sitting down on the sandy floor with her back to the wall. I'll just take a break for a while to get my strength back and then see if I can find any water.

She must have closed her eyes and slept. When she opened them again she was lying down but it was dark, totally, utterly dark. She couldn't make out the entrance to her tunnel, even though she waited several minutes to give her eyes chance to adjust.

It shouldn't be totally dark outside, she thought, there should be stars enough to give a bit of light. But there was nothing. She thought she knew which way she had come in, and tried walking back, keeping her hand on the wall, but all she could sense was that the tunnel was turning slightly, and the air was getting colder.

Carefully she tried to find out how wide the tunnel was, kneeling down and making her way across the sand scraping a gully with one hand to guide her back to where she had started. As it happened it was not more than about eight feet wide. She tried to retrace her way back to the entrance using this wall as a guide, but it didn't seem to work. Now she felt frightened; this darkness was somehow unnatural, but she supposed that in this strange existence everything was unnatural anyway.

Perhaps I am blind, perhaps the sun did this to me, I've heard of it happening. What if my sight doesn't return – what if I have been damaged as Amiros has been?

How can I find Amiros if I am trapped here in the dark, a feeling of panic forming. How can I even find my way back?

She reached for The Firestone which still hung round her neck, hoping for its light to guide her, but to her dismay it lay quiescent in her hand, only the tiniest of glimmers deep in its core.

At least I have not gone blind, she consoled herself with the thought.

I have to believe that this is just night, and that there will be a sunrise and the hope of some light reaching me.

Sleep, she told herself. That is your only option. Just try and sleep and wait for the day.

Not expecting that sleep could come to her she stretched herself out on the soft sand and closed her eyes.

There was light when she awoke from an unexpectedly deep sleep. But it wasn't the sun. A pale bluish gleam showed between the rocky walls and Alinor could hear a faint susurration in the background. Hopefully she made her way along the tunnel, the light growing a little stronger with each slight bend she came to. She passed a couple of smaller openings to each side, but they were dark and uninviting. Finally she came to where her route turned sharply to the left. Now the source of the blue light became obvious. She gazed in wonder at the sight of a huge cavern that stretched way out of sight before her. The walls, floor and ceiling seemed to be made of ice, with enormous icy stalactites depending from the roof. It was a truly amazing sight. The sounds she had heard were coming from a tiny crystal stream that came trickling down from an icy rock cluster a little way in front of her. Wonderful, she thought, and carefully she made her way to it and cupped the clear water in her hands to slake her thirst. Though her surroundings were frozen, the air was not cold at all, something Alinor couldn't understand.

There were a number of pathways leading across and around the vast space. She took the nearest one off to the right and made her way past fascinating ice shapes, marvelling at the way the light caught the angles and planes to lead her gaze to further wonders. She walked on and on, her mind somehow telling her that this was the way to go. All of a sudden the ice came to an end. The cavern now shrunk to the size of a large cave; at its far end were several openings, not dark this time but lit with a warm glow. Curious, Alinor entered the first and within a few paces saw a series of lamps set into the rock of the walls providing the light. The way was fairly wide, like a road smoothly cut by skilled craftsmen. A little further on she could see some indentations on each side of the road. As she neared them she was taken aback to see that each space contained a burial of some kind, some shapes still wrapped in linen but others merely a collection of bones.

The sight was unnerving; this was no place for living beings, she thought, starting to feel slightly nauseous. She turned thinking to retrace her steps and take one of the other tunnels, but the way she had come was now a blank wall of stone. With no choice but to go on, she took a deep breath to settle herself and walked on, keeping to the middle of the tunnel to avoid being too close to the remains. At intervals the roadway branched, each new road containing more remains, carefully laid out in their niches.

Alinor entered a larger space, like a room. No remains to be seen there, but there was a deep shelf along one wall upon which had been placed several bowls. Alinor started in fright as she heard footsteps entering from the far side of the area where two passageways led out. A tall figure entered and stopped, motionless as Alinor hurriedly backed away.

'Have I changed so much?' the figure asked, its voice echoing around the subterranean room.

Alinor thought her heart had stopped beating for a moment, but then it began thumping wildly.

'Father?' she almost stuttered, 'Is it, can it really be you?'

'Have you forgotten me, Alinor?' the voice was gentle.

'No, never forgotten,' she managed to reply, eagerly rushing forward and reaching out for her beloved parent. Before she could make contact, her fingers merely inches away, she became aware of an aura of coldness around the figure, and stopped short.

'But how are you here?' she asked, 'why now when I have so longed to be able to see you again.'

'I am here because you are being foolish. You should not have come here, Alinor,' Teleston spoke, 'you should forget this and return to Ancor.'

His words were totally unexpected and hurtful.

'But I have to find Amiros,' she pleaded, 'I can't just let him be lost.'

'He is not lost and so does not need your help.' The beloved voice sounded sharp and cold.

Something is wrong, thought Alinor, this cannot be my father talking, he would not abandon Amiros like that.

'I don't believe you,' she cried, backing away, 'you are not my father, you would not say that about someone you loved and trusted like Amiros.'

'Come now, daughter, that is not the way to talk to me. I have told you to go back. Do not disobey me.'

His harshness cut her to the bone.

'No. No. I shall not go back. Whatever you are you are not my father and I shall not do what you demand.'

The dark figure stepped towards the young woman, but she stood her ground, refusing to be cowed by the unnatural apparition despite the hammering of her heart.

It raised a hand as if to strike her. She didn't flinch but bore such a look of contempt on her face that it was as if she had struck first. There was an enormous noise like an explosion. The figure disappeared as the ground shook and chunks of rock fell from the roof. Alinor tried to cover her head and hurriedly retreated into the nearest passageway fearing the collapse of the roof more than that of the tunnel. She curled into a ball with her arms over her head to protect herself as best she could from the debris raining down all around and waited for the rumbling to stop. The lamps had all gone out and dust choked the air.

Eventually everything went quiet and the dust started to settle. She carefully started to brush herself off; a few bruises but nothing more.

When Alinor finally looked up again everything had gone. No room, no tunnels with their gruesome occupants, nothing. Instead she found herself huddled between a couple of fallen trees whose branches were keeping off most of the daylight.

Pushing them aside she took in the sight of a glorious valley, green with burgeoning grasses, bushes and trees, insects buzzing around fragrant wildflowers, birds singing joyfully from every point.

For several minutes she sat and gazed at the sight. One minute a desert, then ice, now this. And that *thing* trying to make me believe it was my father. For a moment she almost wanted to cry at the cruelty of the vision. What is this place? What is the purpose of these vindictive happenings? How is this leading me to Amiros?

She got up and walked down the slope of the hill where she had found herself. Where is Mirantha, she wondered. What has happened to her, and is it anything like what has been going on for me?

In the distance was what appeared to be a tiny cottage, right in the middle of nowhere, but then that was not unexpected in this altered reality. Alinor made her way there and as she drew near could see another figure, a flame-haired woman, also heading for the same place.

'Mirantha!' she called. 'Mirantha!'

They hastened towards each other and fell into each other's arms.

'You're safe,' said Mirantha, 'I've been worried about you.'

'And I about you too, though I have had some pretty horrid experiences,' replied Alinor. 'I was beginning to think I wouldn't find you again.'

The older woman sighed and shook her head.

'My perceptions of what this quest would entail were somewhat short of the mark,' she said. 'But we have come this far, so there is much to hope for. I don't suppose the rest of the journey will be without its trials, but with luck we can remain together and be stronger for it.'

The pair continued on to the little cottage, entering to find it cosy and welcoming.

'It's like being in a dream,' commented Alinor, 'when anything and everything is possible.'

'It is a kind of dream,' confirmed Mirantha, 'I have found this before when I have entered a trance world, that I would simply look for something and it would be there. One doesn't question the how and why.'

'But you said that you haven't been to this existence before?'

'Indeed not,' Mirantha said thankfully, 'this is some way outside my previous experiences. I think I told you that there is almost no information about how to complete this venture, even though the writings say it is possible.'

'I just hope the writings are correct,' said Alinor, rubbing her nose. 'I'm not exactly enjoying this adventure, much as I want to help Amiros.'

'Nor I, little sister. But we are well on our way I think, and cannot turn back now.'

'No, I don't want to quit. I just want to find him.'

Mirantha smiled and took Alinor's hand.

'You are a credit to your mother,' she said. 'I know she will be proud of you.'

'Did you know her?' Alinor asked eagerly. 'Did all the Ben-Neteru, I mean, well I'm not sure if this is a stupid question. Were all the Ben-Neteru able to link their minds like you and I and Sirad?'

'It's not a stupid question, Alinor, far from it. And the answer is yes, we can. In the latter days there are far fewer of us and we meet very rarely, but we are each aware of the others.'

'Are there many?'

Mirantha gave a little laugh at the young woman's surprise.

'Not so many, but enough. Time and circumstance has seen us spread far apart. We tend to keep to ourselves and people think of us as lost and legendary folk. Their hearts have largely forgotten us, and what knowledge they did have is turned into bed-time stories for their children.'

Alinor looked sad.

'I know what you are thinking,' continued Mirantha, 'you wonder if you and Sirad can be accepted by your people or if they will think of you as merely magicians, or worse, and drive you out.'

Alinor nodded.

'You will face many challenges Alinor, but the times are again changing, and I for one believe that the Ben-Neteru will be able to take their rightful places again. Oh, not as it was in the past when there were so many of us, but still we can be a source of good magic and power.'

'I do so want to believe you,' breathed Alinor, 'and I know that Sirad would agree. Although outwardly he seems to have come to terms with it, I'm not convinced. I know he worries a lot about Ben, his foster brother.'

'Yes, I know Benharad. He is a good man and devoted to Sirad. It has been very difficult for him and it is going to take quite some time for him to adjust. But he will be all right, I assure you.'

'Will you tell me about your life some time?' asked Alinor. 'I'd really like to know what it's like.'

'Being a so-called *immortal*, you mean?'

'No – well, yes I suppose I do. I wish I could have asked my mother, but without her you are the only one I could ask. I don't count Sirad because he doesn't know much more than I do, and anyway, it's not the same for a man.'

That really made Mirantha laugh.

'How very true,' she chucked. 'Men are a strange breed, are they not?'

Alinor heartily agreed. Talking with Mirantha was helping her put the disturbing nature of her encounter with the false apparition to the back of her mind.

'But Sirad is, well, you know how I feel about him I expect?'

'It's written all over you, hard to miss really.'

Alinor looked slightly abashed.

'Am I that obvious?'

Mirantha nodded.

'I'm afraid so,' she said seriously, 'but perhaps not quite to everybody.'

'That's a relief then. I never could stand seeing my girlfriends mooning over the boys!'

'When this journey is over and Amiros has been restored to us, we can perhaps talk a little more.'

'I would appreciate that.'

Alinor hugged her companion and then quickly changed the subject.

'I take it we stay here tonight and then continue this venture in the morning?'

'That is best I think,' said Mirantha, bringing out from goodness knows where a small bottle of wine which the two shared before settling down to rest.

Chapter 22

Nothing had changed when they awoke the following morning, but Mirantha cautioned that it was unlikely to last.

'Everything here is designed to confuse and upset as far as I can ascertain. It takes from each of us the things that we dislike or fear and uses it against us. It builds on any uncertainties and seeks to discourage us from our task.'

'I saw my father,' said Alinor, her voice subdued. 'Or it seemed to be my father, but something was not right. He – it - told me to go back. My real father would never tell me to abandon Amiros!'

'No, he wouldn't.' Mirantha was gentle, she could see how much it had hurt the young woman. 'Your father was a good man, a great king and he held Amiros in high regard. You were right not to believe what the vision said.'

'What do we do now?

'I shall need your help. Between us we should be able to sense the way forward. Although I did manage to identify this existence as the place where Amiros is, now that we are here I too am being tested and it is difficult to focus on his whereabouts.'

'Just tell me what you want me to do.'

Mirantha concentrated for a moment and then said, 'I think if you can recall times when you were together, happier times without any thoughts of pain or hardships, it will strengthen our minds and perceptions.'

The pair set off with Mirantha striding confidently across the dewy grass. After about half an hour they reached a roadway heading towards the nearby hills. It passed through small stands of trees, but as they came out from the shadows of a large forested area they were met with the sight of a broad river stretching for miles in either direction and apparently hundreds of yards across. The road itself stopped at the edge of the water there was no sign of any jetty or boat or any way of crossing.

'We have to get over there somehow,' said Mirantha frowning. 'Just another way to put us off,' she added.

Alinor walked along the bank upstream for some way, hoping to see something they could use.

'Nothing this way,' she called back.

'We have no means of constructing anything,' said Mirantha as Alinor returned to where the woman waited. 'We'll just have to follow it down and hope to find something we can use.'

Frustrated, they walked for several miles scouring the area for any signs of a boat or raft. Once or twice they thought they could see people on the far side of the river, but they were too far away and soon disappeared from view.

After what seemed like an eternity, Alinor shouted and pointed to where there was a small inlet.

'There's something there, it must be a craft of some kind.'

They hurried forward. It was as Alinor had seen, a small narrow boat, wedged into the reeds alongside the bank, a single paddle lying in the bottom.

'This will do,' said Mirantha, making her way carefully to the prow. 'Help me free this a bit and then get in, carefully mind you, as it doesn't look very stable.'

'I'm not too good with boats,' warned Alinor, 'not something we used much in Ancor.'

'Now is your chance to learn.'

'You sound like Amiros now,' said Alinor wryly.

'Good job,' nodded Mirantha. 'I suspect he would be pleased!'

Between them they moved the little boat out from the reeds and Alinor gingerly stepped over the low gunwale, picking up the paddle, and sat cautiously on the makeshift seat. The boat rocked slightly and Mirantha carefully joined her and took the paddle. Gently she pushed them out from the bank and turned the craft out into the main body of water. The current carried them downwards and Mirantha was content not to try and push against it, rather using it and deftly just keeping the boat straight.

'Here,' she said, and passed the paddle to Alinor. 'Just do as I did and guide the boat with the current.'

Alinor felt awkward but soon got the hang of it, shifting the paddle now and then to act as a rudder.

The open countryside gave way to hills and then increasingly large outcrops of rock which encroached right to the water's edge. Mirantha was studying the surroundings, her powerful senses attuned to catch any hint of Amiros' mind.

'We need to get off the water,' she said suddenly. 'I feel something bad ahead.'

She grabbed the paddle from Alinor, telling her to hang on.

The current had started to pull the boat quicker now as the river narrowed and they were being tossed about. Mirantha had to work hard to keep them from crashing into some huge rocks that had obviously tumbled from the sides of the ravine they now found themselves in.

'We won't make it,' shouted Mirantha.

Alinor tried to ignore a feeling of panic; although she could swim, her experience was limited to calm lake waters, not raging rivers. If they went in here, they would be dashed against the rocks and unlikely to get out alive.

Mirantha could see the ravine open out a little further on and desperately tried to keep the little craft facing forward knowing that at any second they could be turned over, but the river had it in for them. Unable to avoid a sudden vortex in the tumbling waters the little craft went into a spin and the waves poured over the side. Totally unbalanced Mirantha was unable to correct it and the boat was simply picked up and tossed carelessly to one side, breaking up on the rocks and hurling the two women into the churning waves. It swept them on with the debris from the smashed craft and they fought to keep their heads above water and not swallow too much.

It was over in only a few minutes, but it had seemed as if it would never end and Alinor was convinced that they would both perish.

Coughing and spluttering the pair found themselves in a calmer patch near the shore and struggled to clamber over the stones to where they could finally sit and get their breath back.

Alinor felt battered and bruised, her throat burned and any energy she might have had was gone. Mirantha was not much better.

They sat there for a while, relieved to have escaped.

'I don't think I like boats,' said Alinor eventually. 'I really thought that was the end.'

'But we are still here,' Mirantha squeezed the last of the water from her hair. 'I think we have Eldren and Sirad to thank for that.'

Alinor's look was questioning.

'That is why I said that we needed them to anchor us – some protection, even remotely, from the challenges that this existence is giving us.'

'We will be safe then?'

'There was no guarantee, but so far we have come through. We will need their strength to provide a focus once we have found Amiros so that we can return.'

Alinor was quiet for several minutes, thinking about Sirad, slightly reassured by Mirantha's words, but unable to completely overcome the feeling of being out of her depth. Yes, she had so far managed to get past – through? – the strange episodes in this weird and potentially dangerous world. How much longer would it last, and could they survive another episode like this, even if Elden and Sirad were supporting?

An image of Amiros came into her mind, nodding with satisfaction at something she had managed to achieve at some time, then it changed to little flashes of their travels. She remembered reaching Rekar's camp – he clearly knew Amiros from before. She had gradually learned that there was more to the old Lore-Master than met the eye, and now she knew that he was supposed to be the successor to Remon, well, that really put a different perspective on things. We must get him back, she told herself, we have to carry on.

Mirantha was aware of Alinor's thinking. Her many years' experience had developed her powerful mind, although in recent times she had avoided too much contact with others, devoting much of her time to the healing arts which were a great part of her abilities and an abiding interest. She had known of Alinor and Sirad since they were born and had tried to ensure that she had familiarised herself with any lores and writings which may be of use at a future date. The time had come, she knew, when these two young people would take up the pre-ordained challenge. What part she would play had not been obvious, but the terrible ordeal that Verun had visited upon Amiros was something that she was in a position to address and she had no intention of failing.

'We should go on now Alinor,' she said finally, 'I have a mind that our journey will soon be over.'

Alinor found it hard to feel particularly enthusiastic, although Mirantha's words gave her hope. She got up, wincing at the real discomfort engendered by her battering from the river, but followed Mirantha as she made her way purposefully onwards and led them away from the threatening rocks.

A couple of hours' steady walking found them climbing up from the river valley. As they progressed the vegetation became sparser and the ground beneath their feet more stony, with little outcrops of shale splintering as they started to scramble for footholds on a slippery track that wound its way up.

As she went Mirantha picked a few berries from a low-growing bush which had somehow found root between the stones, passing a handful to Alinor.

'These are good to eat,' she said, seeing Alinor's reluctance, 'they won't do any harm.'

There were good, Alinor found, quite sweet and very juicy.

'What are they? I don't remember seeing anything like them before.'

'No you wouldn't have,' replied Mirantha. 'They don't grow in your part of the world; I came across them when I was on Thetara.'

'Where?' said Alinor. 'I've never heard of it.'

'You wouldn't have. It's a very long way from Ancor; it's an island many, many miles to the south and not easy to reach. I haven't been there for years.'

The more time she spent with Mirantha, the more Alinor's curiosity about the woman grew. In some ways she was like Amiros, so much of her hidden, with just little bits hinted at once in a while.

Amiros. Focus on Amiros. He was here, she suddenly realised. We are getting nearer, I can feel it at last. Just when I was beginning to think we would never find him, I can really sense something.

'You are right Alinor, he is not far from us now.' Alinor could hear the how Mirantha's voice had lifted.

The ground was fairly steep now, and they found it hard going as they reached a crest. Pausing for breath at the top they looked down onto a distinct pathway winding its way off to the right, rocky ground giving way once more to green. It was difficult to make out anything more as the air itself seemed misty, tinged with a pale blue-green hue.

Alinor sat down and pulled off one of her boots to empty some annoying bits of gravel out.

'Looks like that's our way now,' she said to Mirantha, pulling the boot back on and standing up.

Without further hesitation, the two scrambled down to pick up the track and made their way down to the track with renewed energy. It was much easier here and they pushed on, knowing that they were approaching their destination.

The strange mist soon engulfed them, but it was neither cold nor damp as Alinor had expected. It was unsettling to simply be walking into the unknown, but then, everything was an unknown in this strange place. Focus, she reminded herself. Mirantha too was wondering about the nature of this *green-*

ness. She had experienced travelling in huge wetlands where the air was thick and moist, but this was quite different.

It seemed they had walked a long way before the mist started to thin and then vanish completely. They stopped in amazement to stare at the sight of an enormous gateway set into huge walls, the top of which towered fifty feet or more above them. The gate was constructed from a dark wood and inlaid with intricately cast metalwork.

'What do we do now?' said Alinor. 'There doesn't seem to be any access door or anything.'

Mirantha approached the gate and tentatively laid her fingers on it.

It sparked violently and she stepped back quickly.

'Well, that's different,' she said, looking at her fingers to check if they had been burned.

She approached again and this time placed both palms against the wood. Flames shot out, showering the ground with sparks, but then to Alinor's surprise a gush of water flowed out.

'What on earth . . .'

'Come Alinor, help me. Place your hands on the gate, don't be afraid, use your mind to see past it.'

With a deep breath she did so, trusting in Mirantha. The wood blazed; it felt hot but not burning and with a great effort Alinor cast her mind to try and look beyond the huge structure. Fire turned to water and the gate slowly moved, seemingly parting in half and sliding away to each side before both it and the walls simply melted away, leaving the pair speechless at the wonderful sight before them.

Beautiful gardens stretched into the distance with fountains and streams dotted here and there. Birds sang, insects buzzed amongst the flowers and the air was filled with a myriad perfumes.

There were buildings too, elegant in their simplicity, with colonnaded paths linking some of them. There was an overwhelming sense of peace and harmony inviting the newcomers to immerse themselves in its balm.

'If this is where Amiros has been,' said Mirantha, 'I can understand if he did not wish to return.'

'It's beautiful,' breathed Alinor. 'An absolute paradise. I can't believe that this is here after everything we've seen so far.'

Mirantha started walking, taking in the wonderful array of flowers and plants all around, subconsciously noting that they all held magical healing properties, some of which she had only heard about in half-forgotten tales. How can this be so real, she thought, Alinor is right, it is a paradise. With a great effort she pulled her mind away from the wonderful distractions.

'Come Alinor, we cannot allow ourselves to be lost in this place, marvellous as it is and no matter how much we would wish. We must go to Amiros now.'

There was urgency in Mirantha's words which penetrated through to Alinor, snapping her back to the real reason for their presence. Hurriedly she caught up with Mirantha and the two women strode on along the smooth roadway, ignoring the inviting little paths that meandered off to each side. Their route was joined by other roads, all seeming to lead toward a long low building, its walls a pale cream colour with arched windows dotted here and there. As they approached they found themselves in a large courtyard edged with small fragrant bushes and with a fountain in its centre, the clear waters splashing musically into the surrounding basin. On the far side of the courtyard was a shaded gallery supported by elegant columns.

The two women halted. They could see the shape of a man standing motionless in the shade.

'Amiros?' Alinor asked nervously.

The figure moved out from the shadows.

'So,' said the man. 'You have come for me.'

It sounded like Amiros, but Alinor stared, not at all sure that it really was him.

Beside her, Mirantha sank in a curtsey.

'Yes, my Lord, we have come.'

Alinor's head whipped round to look in amazement at her companion and then returned to the commanding figure as it approached.

Yes, she decided, it had to be Amiros, but he was not as she remembered, not completely. There were few signs of his awful injuries, this man appeared fit, almost younger; even his eyes showed nothing of the terrible burns. There was something so overwhelmingly majestic about him, a barely concealed inner radiance that made her feel totally insignificant. She couldn't help but imitate Mirantha's curtsey.

'Alinor.' The mere voicing of her name filled her with warmth. 'For some reason I did not expect to see you. In truth I was uncertain what to expect, only that someone would try to find me. And Mirantha,' he smiled at Alinor's companion, 'it has been a very long time.'

'Indeed it has,' she acknowledged, her whole demeanour one of courteous respect. 'I came seeking my fellow of the Brotherhood, but instead I have found one far beyond that.'

He reached out and took briefly took Mirantha's hand.

'I am still he, and will always be so, no matter what has now happened.'

Then he turned to Alinor who was wondering what Mirantha had meant.

'It is good to see you again, my child, although you have become a young woman to gladden your mother's heart.'

'Oh Amiros, I need you to come back to us,' said Alinor, 'we need you, Sirad and I. We cannot fulfil this destiny we have inherited without your help.'

Amiros took a deep breath and stepped back, turning slightly away from them. He tilted his head and gazed skywards, then lifted his arms, raising them high. The air around him shimmered and pulsed, waves of powerful energy radiated from his whole being, so much so that the two women shielded themselves from the brilliance of the light emanating from his hands.

'Why should I? Why should I leave this place of harmony and return to the chaos and unhappiness of the world?'

Alinor was shocked by his words, delivered as they were in a voice heavy with mixed emotion, including what she could only describe as pain.

'For my mother's sake,' she found herself saying, 'and because you know it is the right thing to do.'

The three stood there, silent. The manifestation of power had vanished and Amiros once more appeared to be the Lore-Master Alinor knew and loved.

'She is right, my Lord,' said Mirantha, 'you are needed. No longer the Hidden One, although I feel I was misled in my understanding of that title. We could never hope to understand how it is that you have been taken from your old life to become a Master with such ability as our world has not seen for since the times of Rakep-thos. This is your destiny too. You have to come with us.'

Amiros looked hard at the women who had taken such a risk to find him. He understood far more than they how they could be trapped. He let his mind encircle them and became aware of the link across time and space to where Sirad and Eldren waited, a tenuous mental hold on the two travellers who were now desperately urging him to return with them. He had told Meriona that he would need no persuasion to go back, knowing where his duty lay, but he couldn't stop himself from making a final attempt to fight it.

Meriona's voice came faintly to him.

Don't be distracted, my love, that thought is the product of the evil power that seeks to confound us. You are better than that. Help my daughter.

'So be it.'

Mirantha reached for Alinor with one hand and held out the other to Amiros. He joined with both of them creating a bond of mystical dimensions that erupted into a kaleidoscope of colours encircling the trio.

Alinor felt herself grow dizzy as the air seemed to start spiralling around them; she couldn't feel their hands any more, only a sensation of twisting and falling into darkness.

Chapter 23

It was fairly dark when Alinor opened her eyes and the first thing she saw was a small lamp. She let out a small cry and tried to sit up, horribly afraid that she had been carried back to the catacombs with all the bodies and bones.

'It's all right, you're back and safe.'

Gentle hands firmly eased her shoulders back onto the bed. She rubbed her eyes and looked into Sirad's worried face and then glanced around, recognising her own room.

His fingers caressed her forehead and she managed a small smile.

'Just take it easy for a little while,' he said, 'Mirantha said it may take a little while for your body to shake off the effects of the drug.'

Alinor closed her eyes and took a few deep breaths. Her head still felt a bit muzzy, and her mouth was so dry.

'Here, have some of this.'

It was Eldren who now came into view.

'I've prepared something which should help clear your head and prevent any uncomfortable after-effects.'

'Thank you,' murmured Alinor, propping herself up on one elbow, and took a few sips. It was a rather bitter and she grimaced.

'I'm sorry,' the little man said, 'I couldn't do much about the taste.'

Wrinkling her nose in distaste Alinor managed to drink most of the liquid.

She lay back and reached for Sirad's hand.

'What day is it?' she asked. 'I think we must have been gone maybe three days, but I'm not sure.'

Sirad shook his head.

'About four hours,' he said, 'but it did seem a lot longer. Time has no meaning apparently whilst you are in such a deep trance.'

'Amiros? What about Amiros?'

'He's all right, but still asleep. Mirantha had us take him back to his rooms but said that we must not try to wake him yet; it will be better if he comes round naturally.'

'But will he? How do we know that he's not still trapped.'

'Stop worrying, sweetheart. Both Mirantha and Eldren here are happy that Amiros is no longer comatose but merely sleeping. She has said that the darkness has left him, though she will not attempt to probe his mind at all and was uncomfortable when I asked her about it.'

Alinor bit her lip thoughtfully.

'It was so strange when we found him,' she started. 'The whole journey was more than strange, but I don't want to talk about that just yet. It's just that Amiros was different – changed in some way I can't describe properly – and Mirantha was really in awe of him.'

'I find that hard to believe,' said Sirad, 'she seems so at ease with everyone.'

'Well, she certainly was with Amiros. And he . . mm, wait until you have chance to see for yourself. I don't understand what has happened, but it's like he's had some kind of transformation. Though,' she paused momentarily, 'was it only in that existence, or will it be the same now back in the real world? Mirantha did warn us '

'Mirantha gave orders not to go near him for the next couple of hours at least. She didn't say why but was quite adamant about it.'

'Where is she now?'

'Eldren has gone to fetch her so she'll be here in a minute.'

As he spoke there was a sound of voices outside her room and the door opened to admit Eldren and her erstwhile companion. Crossing the room she came and sat on the bed and smiled at Alinor.

'How are you feeling, little sister? I know that the first time of travelling is not easy.'

'Better now, after that horrid concoction that Eldren came up with! It's hard to take in, but Sirad said we'd only been gone a few hours – it was days really.'

'Yes, it takes some getting used to, but in reality it was not that long. Had it not been for the efforts of Eldren and Sirad we would have faced far greater difficulties along the way and I am most grateful to them.'

'I was hoping to see Amiros, but I understand that you have said we must wait.'

Mirantha nodded.

'It is advisable. I'm sorry, I know how much this means to you. It won't be long now, but you need to be prepared for this is not the Amiros you knew before; the torture that Mnethar inflicted upon him is such that no other man could have endured it. In some way that we will never comprehend it is as if he has been – healed I suppose you could say, but we have but that is barely sufficient to encompass what has happened to him. Powers far beyond our understanding, beyond anything our ancestors ever even hinted at, have transformed his mind, even his being. How much of the physical damage remains, I don't know and I'm not sure what to expect. Destiny has brought this about, and we must follow the path upon which it has set us all.'

'We must thank you, Mirantha, for what you have done,' said Sirad. 'I know that we could not have got this far without you. After such a long time I know that Amiros will still need help to bring him back to health, so I hope that you will be staying with us for a little while – and you too Eldren.'

'Your hospitality is much appreciated,' the little man smiled and nodded, 'though I feel that I should not leave those who rely on me back on Mitos for too much longer. We left in somewhat of a hurry, you recall, and I would not have them think I have deserted them.'

'Of course not, we do understand and appreciate your concerns.'

Mirantha rose and inclined her head towards Sirad.

'Yes, I must be sure that our patient is set on the road to recovery and of course I shall be happy to stay for a while, thank you. I know Alinor would wish me to.'

'Indeed yes,' interrupted that young woman. 'There are many things I want to ask you about, but I am mindful that I myself will have to leave before too much longer to return to Thorgiliad.'

'Advisable,' said Mirantha with a smile, 'that you should be around to assist with some of the coronation preparations. It would be a difficult task for your staff to manage without the main protagonist being there!'

'You are right of course,' the young woman sighed, 'it would be asking too much for me to just arrive at the last minute! But, please, I would like you to come for the coronation. Will you?'

'I would be honoured and delighted.'

Mirantha gently touched Alinor's cheek.

'You will make a beautiful queen,' she said. 'I look forward to it.'

Alinor felt herself blush, an unusual sensation for her.

'I know it's getting late, but I'm feeling a bit hungry. I don't want much, but a bit of something before I think about sleeping again would be nice. There are so many thoughts whirring around my head I need to just try and relax a bit before bed.'

'I'll have something sent up and we can all have a bit of supper. This evening has been a bit of a challenge for all of us so perhaps we need to unwind for a while.'

Alinor got up, her muzzy head seemed to have cleared; a quick wash helped restore her and the four sat round the table to talk and eat. They avoided exploring any details about what had occurred whilst Mirantha and Alinor were in their trance state; better to wait until daylight for that. Mirantha described some of the strange places she had been in the past and along with Eldren created a warm and comfortable atmosphere where four friends simply enjoyed each other's company.

Alinor awoke early the next morning; it was barely light yet and the air was crispy cold outside her window. She sent a thought to Sirad and they met in the corridor outside Amiros' room.

'Have you seen Mirantha?' she asked.

'Not yet,' replied Sirad, 'but my guess is she will be up and about.'

'A lovely morning,' the musical voice of the mystic healer reached them and Mirantha approached. She had several dewy bunches of fragrant herbs in her hands, though where she may have obtained them the pair did not know.

'Go in,' she urged, 'with the new day I feel that he may soon awaken and it is good that we should be there.'

Quietly they entered the dim room, fingers of light gradually creeping through the window drapes to reach the bed where the Lore-Master lay. His chest rose and fell rhythmically.

'He seems comfortable,' observed Sirad in a whisper. 'He has moved in his sleep, which I don't think he has done much before.'

Mirantha placed her herbs around the room, their gentle fragrance slowly wafting about. She stood back by one of the windows and simply watched whilst Alinor and Sirad stood close together a foot or two from the bed.

The sleeping man's breathing changed and he started to stir, raising one hand to push his fingers through his hair. Not so long ago it had been a tawny colour shot through with the occasional silvery strand; now that was oddly reversed.

After a moment he weakly rubbed one eye and then the other, screwed them up and held his hand across them. A low groan escaped his lips.

Alinor had been holding her breath, but now she knelt by the bedside and took his other hand.

'Amiros, it's Alinor. You're all right, you're here in Pelamir.'

The man took his hand from his face and turned towards her. Slowly he opened his eyes and Alinor could see the fine lines of scarring across them, but she could also see that they did not focus on her. Closing them again he hesitantly spoke.

'It seems they were right. My eyes have not healed,' he sighed.

Alinor brushed away tears and looked up at Sirad beside her. He laid a comforting hand on her shoulder and shook his head, saying quietly, 'We knew that it was so when Czaten first brought him to us. We never expected that such damage could be undone, my love.'

Amiros eased his shoulders slightly as Alinor released his hand, then shifted his whole body.

'I sense that other than my eyes my body seems to have recovered well. You say I am in Pelamir – how long have I been away from you? What of Elagos and Verun?' His voice was growing stronger and clearer as he struggled to sit up with assistance from Sirad and Mirantha.

Propped up with several pillows he turned his head in either direction, his sightless brown eyes moving only slightly.

'We were only days away from Elagos when you were returned to us,' started Sirad. 'That city is free again and, for the time being at least, Verun has fled we know not where.'

Amiros was thoughtful.

'It would seem that I have missed quite a lot, but I am glad that at least Elagos has been restored.' He turned towards Mirantha.

'It has been a long time, Mirantha, but you seem well. I must thank you for what you have enabled.'

She shook her head.

'I need no thanks from you, my Lord, I could have done no less.'

'But you have my thanks nonetheless.'

He turn back towards Alinor and Sirad.

'Your time with Remon was obviously not wasted,' he continued, 'and your powers – both of you that is – have developed well.'

Alinor looked at Sirad, frowning. If Amiros was blind, how had he known just where Mirantha was standing? I suppose that could have been a fairly logical deduction really.

'Not entirely,' Amiros answered her unspoken thoughts. 'Although these eyes are no longer of use, I am very much aware of my surroundings. I shall need a little time to adjust, but do not for a moment consider me a blind man.'

Alinor eyes widened in surprise.

'No, er, I suppose I should have realised that such a thing could happen; I – we – could see that you were different.'

'That's one way of describing it,' Amiros actually smiled, although a little ruefully. 'I have changed, though it is still an uncomfortable realisation for me.'

'We cannot ever appreciate what you have been through,' said Mirantha, 'but I think we are all agreed on how relieved we are to have you back with us.'

The others nodded and murmured their accord.

'However, pleased as I am now that you are awake again, you are still my patient and I think that the first task is to feed your poor body. We don't understand how you managed to remain alive all these months, but I shall be satisfied once we get you back on your feet and fit again.'

Amiros laughed aloud.

'You always were the managing and capable one, Mirantha, and you don't seem to have changed!'

He looked serious again.

'I too have no comprehension of how this strange situation has come about. Whilst in exile from this world I could feel all the normal sensations – heat, cold, hunger and so forth – but not the injuries which had been visited upon me. Now, although I feel no actual pain, I am aware that my strength is perhaps not as it should be.'

'I am very surprised that you are not as weak as a kitten!' Mirantha said gently, 'but as everything that has happened is almost unbelievable I suppose that surprise shouldn't really come into it.'

'I would appreciate it if you would all leave me for a little while.' Amiros was firm. 'Then, indeed, I will take the opportunity to eat with you.'

'Are you sure . . .' started Alinor.

'Go, young lady, and the rest of you. Give a man a bit of peace – I have been on a long journey and would just like to sort myself out without interference!'

It was clear that Amiros would brook no dissension and so they left his room and went along to Sirad's apartments, voicing their various impressions of the former Lore-Master.

'You told me that when you eventually found him you were aware that he seemed to have great power about him – you're not wrong!' said Sirad. 'It's difficult to describe, but he has certainly changed – grown – and is not just the affable, sometimes irascible, talented magician/teacher that we knew before.'

'That he is not,' agreed Mirantha. 'I don't think we've seen anything yet.'

'You seem, excuse my saying it,' said Sirad, 'extremely respectful of him.'

'Ah yes,' Mirantha let out a breath. 'I realise that you are still thinking of him as your teacher and friend, but he is so much more than that, so far beyond what he was. Eldren already told you that Amiros was always destined to be Remon's successor. What he could not tell you, for he did not realise it himself, and I should add neither did I, was that Amiros would in some unaccountable way surpass his mentor. As your teacher and guardian, he had denied himself the opportunity to continue his development in order to protect you; he could never be forced to reveal what he didn't know. With Remon gone, Amiros is free to continue, but in some way far beyond my expectation or understanding, his development and skills have been accelerated beyond belief.'

'When I was with Remon I suppose something similar happened for me, but I was only a child at the beginning of my learning. For Amiros it must have been incredible.' Alinor could still vividly recall her experience at the hands of the ancient seer.

'Indeed,' Mirantha shook her head in wonder, 'we can never know what it must have been like.'

The three had been joined by Eldren now and related how Amiros seemed. They talked for half an hour or so, food was brought up and laid out in Sirad's private dining area.

'How long should we wait?' asked Alinor.

'Not long.'

Eldren rose saying, 'He has asked me to come to his room. He is ready to join us. Wait here.'

Sirad remembered how the little man had told him that he was not well versed in mind communication, but this seemed not to be a problem where Amiros was concerned.

Five minutes elapsed before they were aware of the approach of the two men. Eldren pushed open the door and stood back to allow Amiros to enter. Without hesitation Amiros walked over to where the three now stood. He seemed taller somehow, perhaps because he had certainly lost some weight, but his whole demeanour was relaxed, his movements easy, betraying no sign at all of the severe injuries he had received at the hands of Verun.

Alinor didn't know quite what to do. She was amazed and overjoyed to see him looking so well. She wanted to hug him but didn't dare.

'Don't be afraid – I won't break,' the much loved voice warmed her heart as he opened his arms and held her. 'I may have changed, but I will always cherish you, my child.'

He reached out a hand to Sirad to clasp him with a firm grip.

'And you too, young man. I have missed you both.'

They sat round the table to enjoy their reunion breakfast. Amiros prompted Sirad to tell him a little of what had happened at Elagos but said almost nothing of his own venture. Eldren and Mirantha listened quietly for their knowledge of what had gone on was very limited.

Immediate hunger satisfied Amiros addressed Mirantha and Eldren.

'I should like to speak with Alinor and Sirad for a while if you don't mind.'

'Of course. I think Eldren and I have some elixirs to concoct – not necessarily all for you,' she added.

Amiros raised his eyebrows and gave a half-smile.

The two healers left the room and Amiros focussed on the young couple.

'It would take far too long if I left it to you to just tell me what I have missed.'

The two understood immediately and with that became aware, albeit only on the edges of their perception, that the new Mind-Master was accessing everything in their memories that had occurred since the day he had left Alinor in Rekar's camp. He allowed them to see how Mekad had been fortified and manned by Verun's troops and the stranglehold that had been inflicted on the area.

Sirad was angry and Alinor distressed by the hardships of the local peoples, but it was a situation that would require careful planning and much time in order to rectify it. Although Sirad had travelled south with Ben and gained much useful information, he now realised the true extent of Verun's hold, and knew that his original ideas of taking the battle to him were totally unrealistic.

Amiros sat back and poured the three of them some wine, sipping his own thinking deeply.

'Interesting,' he said at last. 'It does seem that Verun's attempts to protect Elagos have backfired on him. Overstretched himself somewhat.'

'We've not been able to detect any sign of him since then,' said Sirad, 'we only know that he left by sea and hasn't returned.'

'We have breathing space for now,' said Amiros. 'I think he will need to take some time to recover and he will certainly be re-thinking his approach. I do not intend that he should find out that I have returned until I am ready. That in itself gives us a big advantage.'

He took another few sips of wine and then looked at the young pair.

'I must congratulate you on your betrothal,' he said, smiling at the slightly embarrassed expressions on their faces. 'It was only a matter of time, of course, but I am pleased for you.

The work you have done in Ancor,' he addressed Alinor, 'has been good. I would have expected nothing less from Teleston's daughter. Your coronation will put the seal on your country's recovery.'

'It will be so much better now you are back,' Alinor was brimming with enthusiasm.

'Ah no,' Amiros interrupted, 'I do not like to disappoint you dear child, but I cannot attend in person. I shall of course be with you in mind and spirit.'

Alinor's face fell.

'But why? I so wanted you to be there.'

'I am sorry but I will have to go back to Elagos as soon as I am able. I need time there; you will understand if you think about it. I have talked with Czaten and he has told me that it was Verun's idea to return me to my friends. I am grateful for all he did and suggested that he could now find a place here in Pelamir. However, he is quite adamant that he will not leave me, so he can travel with me back to Elagos. At the moment I am not sure what the future will hold for the little chap.'

Sirad reached for Alinor' hand and squeezed it.

'We do understand, Amiros, though I think Alinor is reluctant to admit it.'

She nodded.

'You will have a truly marvellous day, dear girl, and more importantly, your people will have a wonderful celebration to enhance their loyalty to the crown. Enjoy it!'

'I'm sure I will really, but I can't help but be disappointed. But of course I realise that you must do what is necessary for you. Although the coronation is an important day, it pales into insignificance when there is such evil that would destroy all of us.'

'Unfortunately that is true, 'Amiros concurred. 'It is good that you are able to celebrate this joyous event, for once the celebrations are over, you must return to your task. The Tokens have been well hidden, dispersed, with their existence slipping into legend. It will be no easy job to find them again; that was the intention and considering the abilities of those who did hide them you really will have your work cut out for you. No,' he forestalled their questions, 'I cannot help at the moment; not because I don't want to but because I simply do not have the information you seek.'

'But in the future?'

'Possibly, probably. But do not ask me to put a time to it. Your own powers are increasing, and you do need to spend some time in understanding them. I know there have been other things distracting you, but this is important and you need to be prepared and not caught unawares by developments.'

They both nodded, knowing that Amiros was right.

'I think that is enough for now,' Amiros said. 'l want some time to consider what I have learned from you and, though I don't like to admit it – and don't say anything to that lovely witch Mirantha – I am tired.'

'Of course,' Alinor rose and kissed Amiros on the forehead. 'We will let you return to your rooms; you can always let us know when you want to see us again.'

Amiros nodded. Masking his weariness he left the room and the young couple fell to talking over what had been said and how different their old teacher was, and yet still the same.

The day passed quietly; Alinor and Sirad rode out for a while, needing the distraction. Being outside in the fresh air relaxed them and they enjoyed racing each other across the open grasslands and meandering through the trees, the fallen leaves crispy underfoot.

Amiros was not ready to eat in the main hall just yet, so the group again used Sirad's apartments. When he entered the room it was clear to Alinor and Sirad that any likeness to their former Lore-Master had gone, for the aura that now enfolded Amiros was one of authority and strength. Aware of their discomfort his mind radiated reassurance and they found themselves once more at ease and they passed a pleasant hour.

Alinor spent some time with Mirantha the following morning.

'I must confess that I am amazed at his recovery, even knowing who and what he is,' Mirantha pushed a strand of wayward red hair out of her eyes. 'I would never have credited that one who had been in such a deep coma for so long could recover so rapidly, and show so few effects.'

'It is wonderful,' Alinor leaned on the wall overlooking the herb garden. 'I thought he would still need a lot of nursing, but he seems so fit already.'

'Certainly not much like an invalid! Not much that I can do for him now, other than the elixir Eldren came up with, though he seems to think he doesn't need it. Not my place any longer to tell him what to do, I can only offer advice.'

Alinor was quiet for a few moments.

'I'm sort of struggling to get used to him. One minute he's my old teacher, and the next he's some incredible being. I don't know how to behave or what to say.'

'Yes, it must be hard, for both you and Sirad. You'll adjust in time; he will always be the Lore-Master to you, the relationship you have with him is very special – I almost envy you!'

Alinor could appreciate that Mirantha was doing what she could to help her come to terms with everything and was grateful.

'I'm sorry he won't be coming to the coronation; I know he is intending to leave before too much longer.'

'And you too must leave soon, Alinor. Your poor people will find it difficult to sort some things out without you there to make decisions.'

'I suppose so,' Alinor made a face. 'Sometimes I'm looking forward to it, and then another time I just want to get away from the fuss.'

Mirantha laughed.

'You can't have a coronation without a bit of fuss, little sister. Let yourself enjoy it – it's any girl's dream.'

'I suppose you are right really. It's just that life is so up and down, sometimes I don't know what to feel. Sort of childish really.'

'Hardly that,' Mirantha chuckled. 'Well you've certainly not got a dull life, that's for sure. But I do understand that it has been difficult for you; your father's death, discovering your true nature and coming into some of your powers – it has been a bit of a tidal wave. But there is so much that is good and positive. For a start you have Sirad.'

Alinor turned and smiled at the other woman.

'Yes, I have. And I don't mind admitting to you that I love him so much it hurts sometimes.'

'And he loves you in return and would do anything for you.'

'I am really fortunate, aren't I? No matter what happens, no one could ever take away the love we have.'

'No, they couldn't. It is special, even without you both being who you are.'

'Why don't you travel back with me to Ancor? If Amiros no longer needs your presence, there is little point in your remaining here.'

'Well, I'm not sure about that,' started Mirantha.

'I want to wait another day,' continued Alinor. 'I'd like to talk with Amiros a bit more, but on the grounds that there is nothing I or any of us can say to make him do otherwise, he will be going to Elagos fairly soon I guess. I would rather not be here to say goodbye again as he goes. It's easier for me to leave first.'

'I understand. Let me think about it and I'll let you know later.'

Alinor had to be content with that.

The two wandered out into the main courtyard and out through the palace gate into the town. People there tried not to be obvious as they watched them chatting about goods on sale, pausing every now and then to pick up an interesting object. The women made quite a picture; one young, athletic and golden, the other a fey-looking red-haired woman with a distinctly mystic aura about her. They passed a pleasant hour before returning to the palace. As they entered a Rider came bounding up the steps behind them.

'My Ladies,' the man sketched a bow.

'Ben, where have you been? I haven't seen you since I arrived.'

'My apologies, I have been out on patrol.'

He turned his eyes to Mirantha.

'I,' he swallowed and gathered his thoughts, 'I understand that the Lore-Master has come round at last.'

'Yes, that is so, Benharad. He is remarkably well after his experience.'

'I am glad to hear that,' the Rider said, looking again at Alinor, 'I know just how worried you and Sirad have been. When I think back to that day . . .'

'I know, Ben,' Alinor put her hand on his arm, 'it was a nightmare that will remain with me always.'

'May I escort you anywhere?' he said hopefully.

'Thank you, no, we are fine. We've just been out in the town for a while.'

'Oh.'

Alinor hid a smile at his crestfallen expression. Sirad had been right when he said that Ben had fallen for Mirantha.

'Perhaps tomorrow.' Alinor took pity on him, and saw how his spirits perked up at the prospect.

'Please excuse me, I have a few things to attend to,' Mirantha smiled politely and continued into the palace, Ben's intent gaze following her.

With an effort he turned back to Alinor.

'Preparations for your coronation must be getting on quite well by now,' he said. 'There hasn't been such a big event for many years.'

'Yes, it is quite busy back home. To tell the truth it was nice to get away for a few days. Semira has been bossing everyone about, including me, and doing a tremendous job.'

Ben laughed.

'I find it hard to believe that anyone could boss you around! Excuse me, that was rather impolite.'

'Come on Ben, we are friends, are we not? Just because they are going to stick a crown on my head doesn't mean we cannot talk freely to one another. Nothing has changed, nor will it, I promise.'

To the Rider's total consternation, Alinor leaned forward and kissed him on the cheek.

'Friends, remember!' she said and strode off.

'Come with me, Sirad, I want to take Remon's book to Amiros. And I want to show him mother's gem.'

She had found Sirad coming back from seeing his father and took him by the arm.

'My father asked after you and if you had recovered from your journey to find Amiros. He had been very concerned, but is very pleased at the safe return of all of you.'

'That is most kind of him; I should have thought to visit him in person, but to be honest, I think I am still trying to adjust to what has happened.'

'When I spoke with Mirantha she did suggest that you may still have a few things to tell me, but that I should wait until you were ready.'

Alinor went and sat on a seat by the wall.

'I didn't remember everything immediately,' she started, 'then it just came back in fits and starts. It was like being in a dream, or rather a nightmare, and things kept changing, like one minute it was a grey stony landscape and the next was pleasant sunshine and greenery. Then it was a desert, for goodness' sake. But I think the worst bit was I suddenly found myself in a never-ending catacomb, with bodies and skeletons and stuff. Then I got to a room and my father appeared. Only it wasn't him at all. I knew it couldn't be him because he wanted me to go back and forget about finding Amiros.'

She hung her head and Sirad kept quiet, wanting to hold her but knowing she needed to finish her story first.

'I so wanted it to be him,' she whispered. 'I so want to be able to see him again, but I know it cannot be.

I thought he was going to strike me but I knew that I would be lost if I showed any fear. Instead everything exploded, literally, and he disappeared and I wasn't in the catacomb any longer. Oh Sirad, it was really frightening because it didn't make any sense.'

Then he did hold her; she was trembling so he just held her tight, kissing the top of her head and telling her it was all right until she finally relaxed.

Eventually she pushed herself away.

'I'm sorry, you must think I'm a real baby.'

'Don't be silly. That's the last thing I could ever think of you. It must have been an awful experience and I'm not surprised at how much it has upset you. The important bit is that you did not believe the apparition, or whatever it was, and you stayed strong. And because you are strong, Amiros has been brought back to us.'

Alinor sniffed and surreptitiously brushed away a tear.

'Mm, I suppose so. Anyway, it's over now and we've got Amiros again as you say. Now, let me get the book and we'll go and talk to him to see if he has any insights.'

The new Mind-master was very interested to see the ancient book. It was not one he recalled ever having come across before and he was curious to know what Alinor and Sirad had managed to glean from it's arcane writings. Sirad explained how they were hoping to find out more about the Tokens, particularly as to the whereabouts of the great sword Tauenbran.

'I do not think I am able to enlighten you any more than the information contained here,' Amiros said eventually. 'Yes, there were legends and I think . . .' he paused, frowning slightly in concentration, 'mm, yes, there was something about the swords could only be taken up by Bran's heirs, descendants, or so forth. So,' he spoke slowly, considering his words carefully, 'if the sword is to be found, it will only be revealed to his heir, one of his bloodline. Once found, should it be taken into the hands of another, it would almost certainly be fatal to that other.'

'But I have Shenbran,' Alinor was confused, 'I've had it for years, and I haven't come to any harm, in fact to the contrary. It has saved me a number of times.'

'Yes indeed dear child, you have. You do remember that your bloodline goes back to Rakep-thos, and so does yours,' he pointed to Sirad. But as so often happens, the complete family lines are not easy to piece together. I happen to know that you, Sirad, have a strong direct link to Bran, whilst Alinor's is slightly more obtuse. However, it is more than enough for me to know that the swords are destined for you and always have been. The awkward part is the lack of information about Tauenbran's location. Be aware that when you do find it, it will be protected and you need to take great care.

Finding the sword will likely make it easier for you to pursue your quest to re-unite the rest of the Tokens. They are your legacy as the writings have decreed.'

'Legacy,' said Alinor, her eyes lighting up, 'legacy is what was inscribed on the box that I found in the tower!'

Amiros made a questioning sound.

'I found a box that mother had left for me,' she continued. 'It was hidden in the wall of the tower where I used to like to hide when I was younger. She had put a letter inside to say that she had placed a gift for me in the box, something which had been passed down and destined for me.'

From inside her top Alinor pulled out the little bag containing her mother's gem. Placing it in her palm she felt its warmth as it seemed to brighten, casting a soft light around the three of them.

'Ah,' breathed Amiros, smiling, 'Eletha. She said . . .' he stopped himself for a moment. 'I knew that your mother had kept it for you,' he continued, 'and that she realised there would come a time when you would find it. May I?'

Alinor placed it in the old man's hand; it brightened for a moment with some flashes of brilliant blue deep in the centre. Amiros closed his fingers over it and sighed deeply before returning it to Alinor after a few moments.

'It is a wonderful jewel,' he said, 'and has the ability to bring much happiness to its rightful possessors. I am glad it is now in your keeping.'

'Can you tell us anything more about it?' asked Sirad.

Amiros shook his head.

'You will find out in time,' he said, 'from the little I know of the Tokens, they seem to behave differently in some circumstances.' He shrugged. 'Powers cannot always be forecast.'

It was a strange statement, but Sirad and Alinor knew that their mentor would not commit himself further and so did not question him.

'You are leaving tomorrow I think, Alinor?'

'Oh, er, I hadn't actually decided definitely.'

'A good idea. You have matters requiring your attention at home; it would be wise for you to be there, especially as there is nothing further to keep you away at present.'

Amiros had been making it quite clear that he didn't require any more fussing over and it was now Alinor's turn to be put right.

'Mirantha will go with you, it will be good for you both.'

Alinor looked at Sirad and made a face.

'No point looking like that,' Amiros picked her up immediately, much to her consternation. Being blind obviously didn't mean anything as far as her old teacher was concerned. He had said that he needed time to adjust, but it was pretty clear that in some strange manner he could see as well as any of them.

'Probably better,' came the immediate comment.

'No, as I promised you some time ago I will not intrude on your thoughts, but it is difficult to ignore you when you are so obvious.'

'It is so good to have you back, even when you are so disconcerting!' Alinor laughed. 'Mirantha did say she would tell me later, but no doubt you will be right. I suppose I had best see about making preparations for the trip, not that it needs much.'

'I will see you tomorrow before you go, child, but now please leave me in peace. I still find myself getting tired too easily.'

The pair took their leave.

Chapter 24

Alinor's party had left for Thorgiliad several hours ago in good spirits, knowing that Amiros was out of any danger and confident that his recovery would continue apace. The trip would not be made at the punishing rate that Alinor had employed when she came as she had agreed that the need for urgency had passed. Thinking of the timescale before her coronation reminded Sirad of the various arrangements he and his father were making before Sothan himself started on the long journey north. In deference to his recent return to better health, the king planned to make it a reasonably leisurely trip, allowing several days en route to rest. There was also the consideration of all the relevant extra luggage required when attending such a formal celebration, not forgetting the magnificent gifts that would be presented to the new queen. Sirad had more than enough to keep him busy for the next week or so before the royal party would leave Pelamir.

With Mirantha gone Eldren took over keeping a watchful eye on their former patient. Like his fellow healer, he had been struck by the transformation in his Brother, who, whilst certainly an accomplished mage, had always appeared to be simply that. Even knowing that Amiros should succeed Remon had not prepared the jolly little man for how the extraordinary hidden depths had been partly revealed. Sadness at the passing of Remon had been replaced with a level of curious expectation.

They spent a number of hours together catching up on what they both had been doing in the years since they last met and what had happened to others of the Brotherhood.

'In time,' he responded to Eldren's enquiry about when Amiros would seek to contact the others, 'there is no immediate rush to do so. I am more concerned about the future of those two young people and their safety. That has always been my task, and I feel that it will not be too long before they will be faced with dangers they cannot comprehend. I must be prepared so that they too may be ready for what they have to undergo.'

Eldren nodded. He had been impressed by Sirad when they met and seeing him with Alinor he had started to appreciate just how special the couple were. He remembered telling Sirad that his own skills with mental communication were not particularly good, but he was not really that surprised to find that Amiros could link thoughts with him with no effort at all.

'I will know if you feel the need to talk with me once you have returned to Mitos,' said Amiros. 'I have no idea, though, if and when I may need to request assistance from you and Mirantha, so for now it is right that you return home. People rely on your skills which is as it should be.'

Sirad himself accompanied Eldren and a small escort of Riders a couple of days later when he set off. Although Sirad would return after a day, the other Riders would see Eldren safely to the borders of Lefnan-ilos, not wanting to make their presence too obvious so far south. Before leaving Eldren had spent a while talking with Czaten about any care that Amiros still required on his journey to Elagos and described the dwarf as a versatile man who could turn his hand to many things.

'The most unnerving thing, though, is his all-consuming hatred for Verun and that has prompted his complete devotion to Amiros whom he sees as both another victim but also as a potential champion against the so-called Red Lord.'

'He certainly did well to bring Amiros to us; I don't think there is a better man to help him return to Elagos safely.

I must thank you, Eldren, for all you have done. Without you, and your being able to contact Mirantha, we may not have been able to save Amiros. I wish you safe journey home, but I think we shall meet again.'

The little healer shook his head.

'I need no thanks from you, it was the least I could do to save my fellow Brother. I feel hopeful for the future now, despite the warnings that Amiros has given us. You have great strength within you that I think you do not yet understand. With that strength, you and your extraordinary lady must succeed. But I think you are right and I look forward to our next meeting.'

Sirad had much to think about as he rode having taken leave of Eldren. The hours the two had watched and waited, their minds concentrating on Alinor and Mirantha whilst they were in their trance had created a bond of friendship with its purpose. Although he had been unable to see through Alinor's eyes as he was used to for the duration of her stay in that strange existence he could still feel her emotions and did as much as he could to comfort and strengthen her, holding on to their unbreakable bond. The link had been severely tested but that strength of which Eldren spoke had unknowingly enabled him to protect both Alinor and the others when they were finally able to return. The experience of Alinor being at such risk had frightened him; the danger had not been from some tangible enemy, but something almost beyond his comprehension. The thought of losing her had hardened his resolve and energized his innate power. He would not let her go, no matter what. The relief when she came out of the trance was overwhelming, though he had managed to hide most of it from her. Eldren had understood, he thought, and Mirantha certainly was aware.

He was not in a particular hurry and stopped before midday to let his horse drink and grab a few mouthfuls beside a stream winding its way through an area of forest of mature trees, beech, oak, hazel and birch. He knelt and cupped some of the icy water. It was quiet with little breeze, but suddenly his horse started, backing away to stand taught, ears flashing, nostrils flared. Instinctively Sirad reached for his sword and stood poised for whatever had spooked his mount. Looking all round he couldn't see anything, but then he sensed a presence in the shadow of a great beech. Silver grey fur blended well against the bark of the tree, but the baleful red eyes did not. Wolves did not normally pose much of a problem except in a really bad winter, so Sirad would not have expected it to attack. But this animal was focussed on him, a low deep rumble in its throat. They both stood motionless, staring at each other; the wolf took a stealthy pace forward, its body low to the ground, every muscle tensed to strike. Sirad made the smallest movement with his wrist, the sword glinting slightly in the weak light. It was enough; the wolf snarled, turned and disappeared back into the trees.

The man listened hard for a couple of minutes trying to detect if there were other wolves ready to join the hunt but he could hear nothing. It was somewhat unusual for one animal to be hunting on its own, but it could happen. Satisfied that he was safe, he sheathed his sword and remounted. Leaving the cover of the trees, he kept an eye out but there were no signs of any other predators in the area.

Amiros left Pelamir two days later with the faithful Czaten beside him. When it had come to supplying the pair with horses, Sirad had found a sturdy mount for the dwarf in keeping with his stature and offered Amiros a choice from the yard. As he and the mage approached where the horses were gathered a fine golden chestnut mare came straight to Amiros, halting in front of him and struck the ground a couple of time with her foreleg. She lowered her head and reached for his hand; in turn he ran his fingers down her forehead and she whickered softly.

'It looks like the choice has been made for you,' said Sirad, thinking that nothing that happened around Amiros should surprise him.

'Dhahari will suit me well,' the mage said, 'she has a brave heart and I shall take good care of her.'

That had not been the name by which the horse had been known up to now, but no one would question Amiros' decree. At a gesture from him the mare went down on one knee so Amiros needed no effort to set himself astride, declining the proffered saddle and bridle. Sirad followed as the mare quietly walked back to where Czaten had now finished loading their packs onto his mount and stood waiting for his chosen master.

'No, Sirad, I cannot say how long I will be away,' he answered what the man had wanted to ask. 'But I shall endeavour to keep an eye on you and assist where I can. You need not worry about me now, I shall be quite safe – I even have a bodyguard!'

'I won't let any harm come to him,' the dwarf's gravelly voice was adamant.

'I know that, Czaten, and thank you for your care of him,' responded Sirad.

Amiros reached down and laid his hand on Sirad's shoulder.

'Use your time well, Sirad, and make the most of what leisure you may have this winter. Matters may take a different turn in the spring.'

'You take care also. You know what Alinor would be like should anything happen to you en route to Elagos!'

The new Mind-Master laughed richly.

'I do indeed. But nothing is going to happen to any of us just yet – it isn't the time.'

The two rode out of the palace and out of Pelamir, Sirad smiling to himself that his old teacher hadn't lost his habit of dropping cryptic remarks.

Sirad was down talking to one of the craftsmen who was putting finishing touches to a new travelling carriage which was wanted on the king's journey to Thorgiliad. Whilst Sothan would want to ride all the way, Sirad was conscious that it would put quite a strain on him, and had therefore ensured that he would have a comfortable alternative available.

'That is fine work,' he was saying, running his hands over the polished wood, admiring the way in which the carpenter had accentuated the tones of the graining.

He could hear some raised voices coming from the Rider's stables and turned to see Ben crossing the way with a couple of other men, talking rapidly.

'What's up?'

Sirad had crossed the yard quickly sensing some urgency.

'A couple of merchants arrived about an hour ago and said that they had encountered a wolf pack last night when they were camped. Fortunately neither they nor their animals were hurt, but they were quite shaken up about it. I thought it a bit strange; it's not as if we've had bad snow or ice or whatever, so for wolves to be in this area is not a good sign. I thought that I would take some of the lads and go hunting.'

'I'll come with you, if you don't mind? I did have an odd encounter with a wolf on my way back the other day, but didn't think any more of it. Perhaps I should have done.'

'Happy to have your company,' Ben nodded.

Within a half hour the hunting party were well clear of the city and heading towards the place where the merchants had reported their skirmish. Once there they explored the area looking for any signs that the animals had left. They found a number of tracks criss-crossing between the trees and more open ground. Leaving their horses together, the men spread out in a circle around them hoping that the sound and smell of the animals would tempt the wolves to put in an appearance.

The light was beginning to fade before the horses themselves started to get restless, indicating that predators were nearby. Each man was on high alert, keen for their first glimpse of the wily creatures. They didn't have to wait long. Four misty grey bodies ran around the edge of the circle of men as if looking for a way to break in towards the horses. The pack were led by the red-eyed beast that Sirad had seen and it seemed that it was looking not so much at horsemeat for supper as a human feast.

Catching sight of its target the wolf homed in on where Sirad stood, armed and ready. The other three seemed to act in unison, trying to separate their intended prey, but not actually attacking the other Riders. This was not the usual behaviour of a pack. The shaggy beast hurled itself towards him, sharp fangs ready to pierce unresisting flesh, snarling angrily, it's eyes almost glowing with hatred.

In a split second Sirad recalled what Alinor had told him about the *bahlam* and knew that this wolf too was a victim of Verun's magics. The attack on the merchants had simply been a means to trying to bring Sirad to a location where it could strike.

Before the wolf could touch him, Sirad leapt to the side and struck out with his sword, piercing through the ribcage and into its heart. It dropped instantly. Sirad watched with pity as the glow faded from its eyes. But for Verun this would never have been necessary. The other wolves sped away and would not be seen in the area again.

'Shall we skin it?' asked one of the men.

'Not this time,' came Sirad's reply. 'We bury it.'

'What are you thinking?' asked Ben of Sirad as the party rode back towards Pelamir. 'That wasn't the usual way of wolves hunting, was it?'

'No Ben, it wasn't. That poor beast was looking for me under the influence of Verun. It was all too easy really and was not much of a threat unless it could have caught me completely unaware. To me it seems rather petty of Verun to go to the effort of setting it up. That said, it could also be a case of him trying to make me think that I can easily defeat whatever he sends, only to be faced with something a lot more dangerous and unexpected.'

'Even after you and Alinor caused him enough damage to warrant his hasty departure?'

'This may have been designed before that, or perhaps it was all he could muster after we turned his mental influences back against him. I don't know, but we can't dismiss the possibility of further attacks of some kind or another.'

Ben thought about it for several minutes.

'What about Alinor?'

'I'm sorry, although I told you that Vixlan had been killed, I didn't tell you that that the animal involved was another of Verun's victims. It had been stalking Alinor for several weeks without attacking, but on that day it did and the wretched Steward got in the way and in effect served to protect her.'

There was no point in Ben telling Sirad to take care; the young prince was the most capable man he knew, and no doubt his Ben-Neteru heritage served him well. Ben tried not to spend much time thinking about it; he was still more than uncomfortable with the discovery. Since their talk that night in the cave, neither had mentioned it again. Talking wouldn't change anything. It just was, and both would have to live with it.

'I heard about the incident with the wolves,' said Sothan when Sirad went to see him the following day. 'It wasn't a natural occurrence, was it?'

'No, it wasn't.' If Sirad was surprised at his father's perception he didn't show it.

'Be careful, my son. There is no telling what a man with Verun's abilities will try having been humiliated at Elagos by you. He may not yet know exactly what you and that young woman are capable of – no, don't give me that look, your mother told me enough and what I learned afterwards gave me plenty of room for thought. We have spoken enough already for me to be able to see that power in you, growing all the time.'

'It makes me uneasy, father, and sometimes I wish I could just go back to being an ordinary person.'

'But you wouldn't.'

Sirad shrugged.

'I suppose you're right. We cannot unlearn things, can we?'

'No man likes to admit a weakness, my boy, but the admission in itself is a sign of strength. If you do not know yourself, then you will not progress. One must be critical of oneself and positive about any failings so that we can work to overcome them. That is the only way.

Now, are you satisfied with how our arrangements are going with regard to this trip? I am really looking forward to it. It has been too many years since I was last in Thorgiliad and it will be strange to be there without Teleston. But, I cannot deny that his daughter is one to make any father proud. She will be a good ruler – oh, she needs time to adjust of course, but that will come.'

The two discussed various matters over the mid-day meal before Sirad went back to talk to some of the captains of the Riders regarding the time that he and the king would be absent.

'. . know yourself,' his father had said. Well, that was a task, thought Sirad. I used to think I did, but so much has changed. Amiros had also said that we have to understand our powers. A tall order, but he is right and I have been avoiding much since our return. Maybe I needed time to just relax a bit and let it all sink in, but then I have to be honest and admit that perhaps I have been avoiding the issue, not sure if I want to find out what I am.

Satisfied that his immediate tasks had been done, he slipped down to the stables and saddled his horse, escaping the palace before anyone could forestall him. He headed out towards the mountains, figuring that no-one would have expected him to go that way. In the far distance he could see the snow capped range and simply enjoyed the magnificence of it all. Systematically he began to go through everything that had happened to him; Alinor's 'treatment' when she returned from her time with Remon that had opened his mind to so much; his own visit to Remon's house and how the mysterious crystal had worked its strange magic, extending his abilities. He knew that, although not exactly what abilities they were. The Bond with Alinor that had created the energy to destroy the gates of Elagos had taken them both unaware; neither had had any expectation of such power existing. But he knew enough now to realise that it was just a beginning. Both he and Alinor had their own particular skills; she was an 'Imager', able to assume or create appearances, and great perception, as did he. Strength was an essential part of his make-up as Mirantha had observed and he knew that mentally he could inflict powerful coercive forces on other, less powerful, minds.

He remembered how Alinor used to enjoy creating little illusions, dragonflies, birds, magical creatures. That didn't appeal to him at all, but perhaps he too could do something similar. He had reached a deserted barn used to shelter stock in bad weather so he stopped and led his horse inside. There was a stack of dried hay, still sweet smelling, so he put the animal into a large pen and carried over a pile of fodder.

How does one learn to do these things? Focus. He could sense the word in his mind almost as if he were back with Amiros in the early days. Decide what you want and concentrate on it.

Fire. Alinor he knew could do that, and so could Amiros; when they were out somewhere in the wilds, he would gather wood and Amiros would create a flame. The man moved away from the barn for safety and found a few dryish sticks of wood. He knelt down and tried to concentrate on the image of a flame. Nothing. Heat, warmth, fire. Believe it, he told himself. So he focussed on it again and murmured the ancient words for fire. This time there was an immediate lick of flame, but it disappeared just as quickly. He tried again several times before he finally learned exactly what to do and managed to create a small fire.

So, I have fire, but I also need water. Not rain, just water.

He went back to the barn and found a couple of buckets. Taking one back outside he sat down and thought about it for a few moments. He closed his eyes and relaxed, breathing deeply. Opening them again he stretched out his hand over the empty bucket; fresh cold water streamed from his fingers until the bucket was full. He didn't feel elated or excited by this, but merely as if he had finally done something which had been expected of him all along. He didn't know if these skills were common to others of his heritage, but that didn't matter; the important thing was to understand that he had skills and abilities within himself which only needed to be called up. That knowledge gave him reassurance and a confidence which had perhaps not been there before.

Time will tell, he said to himself, time will tell.

'Do all Ben-Neteru have an affinity with horses?'

The party had been cantering along the road towards the river crossing and now eased up to a steady trot.

Mirantha smiled and stroked her horse's neck.

'Yes, we do. The horses of Pelenin are the direct descendants of those bred back in the days even before Rakepthos came to power. As you have already discovered, they are extremely intelligent and depending on the specific bloodline some have retained the ability to communicate with humankind.'

Both Elkana and Zaruk tossed their heads and whinnied as if to demonstrate.

'I nearly burst out laughing when they tried to give you a different horse for this trip and then Zaruk just pulled away from the poor lad trying to take him in and presented himself to you!'

'Well,' Mirantha made a face, 'we had an agreement, Zaruk and I, so I couldn't really not take him.'

'I can well believe it,' said Alinor, 'the Riders of Pelenin are just so fortunate to have these wonderful creatures. I know I would never part with Elkana.' She leaned down and gently pulled the mare's ears.

'And do you know that Elkana's little brother will be Sirad's new horse ? He lost his favourite that he'd been riding for years at Elagos and was very upset about it.'

Elkana was tossing her head at the mention, obviously wanting to give her opinion.

'Yes, someone did mention it. Lightstar's bloodline is quite a precious one and this new colt will, I am sure, be very special.'

'I went out to see the horses with Sirad only the other day. Taukhet is now so big, I couldn't believe it when he came galloping over to see us. He and Sirad already have a bond, that's clear to see.'

'Taukhet?'

'Yes, Sirad actually asked me to name him – a great honour I know – and I – it was a bit funny actually, as my mind was full of all sorts of strange things – I came up with that name.'

'The Fire Spirit. It is apt,' Mirantha said thoughtfully, 'he will be a great boon to Sirad.'

The party slowed to a walk and crossed the river a half hour later. A few days would see them back in Thorgiliad. As they travelled, Mirantha pointed out the properties of many plants and trees for healing as well as maintaining good health. Whilst Alinor knew some of them, she was amazed at the vast extent of uses to which they could be put, and questioned Mirantha extensively. She mentioned that Sirad had great healing skills which Mirantha was already aware of; the older woman was very complimentary and commented that the ability had probably come to him from his mother.

Alinor was interested to hear what Mirantha could tell her about the Lady Galena. Sirad very rarely mentioned her, and most of her knowledge had come from Sothan. That in turn led her to ask if Mirantha had known her own mother.

'Many, many years ago,' was her response, 'long before her marriage.'

Alinor had not given any thought to how old Mirantha might be; she knew, of course, that the Ben-Neteru aged very differently from the rest of humankind, but really, Mirantha looked not so many years older than herself. It was a sharp reminder of her heritage and was enough to cause a frisson of fear deep inside.

'You will come to accept it in time, little sister,' Mirantha's gentle voiced soothed her troubled thoughts. 'It is still very new to you, but don't fret about it. Let it rather be a source of strength, giving you the stability of time to achieve what you want.

And don't forget you have Sirad.'

'Thank you, Mirantha, you are right. It's just that sometimes I get – you know.'

'Of course, that is not surprising.'

'Tell me about when you were younger,' Alinor urged.

'What do you want to know?'

'Everything!'

'I don't know about that,' said Mirantha with a laugh, 'but perhaps some of it.'

They shared stories for the rest of the journey and Alinor felt a little of what it would have been like had her mother still been alive. Mirantha was so calm, worldly wise and understanding of the difficulties that a young woman faced without the benefit of a parent's guidance. Alinor could only be grateful at how destiny had brought this woman into her life at this time. She knew that once the coronation was over Mirantha would likely disappear again, but the bond between them would remain, and the ability to communicate mentally would always be there.

As they crossed into Ancor the soon-to-be-crowned young queen became thoughtful. Her country, her childhood home. She would honour the trust that people put in her. What did the future hold though, and would this remain her home? How could it not? But, she and Sirad were bound to each other, and he would in time become king in Pelenin. What would happen then? Destiny. What that destiny would be no-one could predict. We cannot see the future, but we do know that we have to face that evil, whatever it turns out to be. One day at a time, she thought, it will all come soon enough.

Chapter 25

The Lady of Ancor rode into the palace of Thorgiliad to find a happy organised chaos. There seemed to be far more people busily rushing about than when she had left, although they were all very purposeful and everything actually seemed to be under control.

She led Mirantha into the palace, giving instructions for rooms to be prepared for her guest and just nodding when told that the Mistress of the Household would attend Her Ladyship immediately.

Alinor made her way to one of the so-called small meeting rooms, a comfortably furnished retreat when the pair could take a few minutes to warm themselves after the last few miles when the temperature had dropped quite quickly.

Within a couple of minutes the door opened to admit a maid carrying a tray with wine and goblets, followed by the eager Semira who was delighted to see her mistress returned.

She was just about to rush over and hug Alinor when she caught sight of the tall elegant figure of the Healer and stopped to drop a brief curtsey. Whilst she had been told of the arrival of a guest, she was a little taken aback by the regal nature of the stunning woman.

'Mirantha, meet Semira, my Mistress of the Household, but more importantly my friend.'

'Welcome, my lady,' she glanced at Alinor.

'Semira, this is the lady Mirantha, a healer of some renown who has been instrumental in the return of my mentor Amiros. She will be staying with us at least until my coronation.'

'Then you are indeed more than welcome. I know how much it meant to My Lady to be able to save the Lore-Master. I will get a maid to show you to your rooms. Please do not hesitate to ask if there is anything you require.'

'I'm sure everything will be perfect, Semira,' Mirantha reassured her with a smile, instantly winning her over. 'I would not wish to burden you with any extra tasks – you already have plenty enough to deal with, but I am told that you are an excellent organiser!'

Semira dropped her eyes and blushed slightly at the unexpected compliment. She was saved having to respond by the arrival of a servant advising her that everything was ready for the new guest.

As soon as Mirantha had left the room Semira spoke excitedly.

'It's true then, the Lore-Master is returned to us?'

'He is, Semira, and I am so relieved and happy. I had almost begun to give up hope. It could not have happened with Mirantha's guidance; she is a truly amazing person.'

'I would like to hear more about her, if you are able to tell me sometime.'

'Of course, why wouldn't I?'

'Because she is like the Lore-Master, isn't she? I'm not so blind that I could miss that amazing aura of power all round her. Just like you, really.'

Alinor looked at her friend in surprise.

'You're rather alike in a way,' she continued, 'and the Lord Commander is the same. You're different from the rest of us. Oh I don't mean - don't get the wrong idea, please, it's difficult to explain and maybe not everybody sees it the way I do. It's not a case of you being born to royalty and all that; anyone would know you're a Lady through and through.'

She ignored a little snort from Alinor.

'When I first met the Lord Commander in Elagos, and then you, and saw you both together, it was as if there was a secret light shining within you. Everyone knows what happened, or at least what appeared to happen, at the gates of Elagos, and the word went round about how you and he have some powerful magic. But I don't think it's just the sort of magic that does tricks to entertain. It's deeper than that, and perhaps darker than that.'

'Are you not afraid, then?' Alinor asked gently, 'for if you are you have hidden it well, and I don't think you could hide much from me.'

'No, not really. I couldn't hide it from you even if that were the case, I know that. You have always been generous to me and allowed me to be your friend for which I feel both humbled and honoured. I know that you and the prince are worried about the future, although I still have no idea why. But I know enough to realise that it must be serious to affect you in the way that it does.'

'It is not yet time to talk about such things, Semira, but you will learn in time. You have become a good friend to me and I hope we shall remain that way for many years to come.'

'Unless I make a complete hash of these celebrations!' Semira lightened the seriousness of their conversation. 'You have no idea of what you have lumbered me with.'

'Go on with you,' Alinor laughed, 'you are absolutely loving every minute of it! I could tell as soon as I arrived that everything was going on swimmingly, so don't try telling me you can't cope.'

'That's your impression,' muttered Semira, and then smiled. 'Yes, all right, it isn't so bad. The staff are working so hard, and even the ministers have stopped arguing about precedent and procedure and are enthusiastically working on their own particular roles.'

'Got to be a first time for everything. Don't get your hopes too high, though, someone is bound to stir it up before much longer.'

'Don't say that. I don't want to think about it.'

'Right then, Mistress, what I need most now is a bath and some dinner. Tomorrow will be soon enough to catch up with what I've missed.'

It poured with rain that night, but Alinor slept deeply, untroubled by dreams or worries. She woke refreshed and eager to tackle any matters that were awaiting her attention. Mirantha assured her at breakfast time that she intended to have a chat with various people in the palace and town and do a bit of exploring. She would see Alinor again that evening.

Half of Alinor's morning was taken up with her ministers. From listening to their reports she was confident that matters of state were running smoothly and the new incumbents of various departments were making good progress. A number of trade delegates had been in touch and there were hopes of some new, lucrative deals being arranged before too much longer. A couple more months will see everything settling nicely into place, she thought; it needs to, as Sirad and I will have our own challenge to undertake.

With the last of her councillors gone, Alinor took herself down to the barracks to seek out Dhalen. She found the worthy veteran sat in a training room with a number of young men who had applied to join the queen's forces. She kept out of sight so as not to disturb his talk, interested to listen herself. He had obviously covered much of what he wanted to say and now wished to hear what the hopefuls had to say for themselves, but first he gave anyone who felt that they couldn't match up to the expectations that the Senior Commander had made very clear the opportunity to leave, without any sense of failure. It was not a life that would suit everyone; the training was long and arduous, and not all would succeed. Two of the group opted to go, and were not ashamed to be honest about their reasons, for which Dhalen commended them. Alinor turned away slightly as they left so they never realised how close they had come to their sovereign.

She listened with great interest to what these young people had to say. Her father had been justly proud of the men of his Elite Guard and some of those here today could eventually join those ranks after a year or two if their general service warranted. A few sounded quite promising; a couple more needed taking down a peg or two, but she felt that they would probably make good soldiers in time. Generally, she felt they all had potential. As Dhalen drew their session to a close she slipped in the door and he rose to his feet and saluted her. There was a great clattering as the youngsters jumped up, not knowing whether to salute or what.

Alinor surveyed them all and nodded.

'Remember what the Commander has said to you today,' she addressed them, 'and you will succeed and become good soldiers. You have chosen to serve your sovereign in a time-honoured way and I thank you and wish you all good luck in your training.'

There was a chorus of thanks, not too loud for fear of embarrassing themselves, and Dhalen dismissed them. As the last one disappeared to join his comrades outside eagerly discussing their first glimpse of the Lady of Ancor, Dhalen limped over and bowed to Alinor.

'Glad to see you safely home again, My Lady,' his voice was gruff, but the warmth was genuine.

'New recruits?'

'Yes. They're the third group I've had in recent weeks. Our numbers are growing well.'

'Anything I should know about?' she asked.

'Not particularly. There have been a few reports about lawlessness and banditry – coming up from the south like before. I don't expect it to get much worse during the winter, but that depends on the weather. I have heard that the situation in all the countryside down towards Mekad is still very bad, the military there still maintaining a stranglehold despite the continued absence of that magician. I am rather hoping that we will not just let it go?'

'No, we can't ignore it, Dhalen. But, and it is a big but, it is going to be a long campaign I fear, and not one that can be prepared for in a hurry. Too much is at stake and I for one will not send my men to their certain deaths, however strongly they want to right the wrongs. The situation is far more complex than you know, and at the moment I cannot explain it to you. I would just ask you to trust me.'

'I take it that Prince Sirad is of the same mind?'

'He is.'

'Then I trust you both. You are your father's daughter, and I would never have gainsaid him, so I don't intend to start with you.'

'You are a good man, Dhalen, and an excellent Commander. I trust you too.'

With that Alinor went back to the palace, grabbed something to eat and was ready when Semira came to take her over some details for the coming event. Her head was reeling by the time Semira said they should stop and get ready for dinner; the trouble was, Semira promised that the next week would be just the same. Fittings for her new gowns, plans for the various entertainments for all her guests and their entourages, musicians to be chosen, menus to discuss. The list was endless.

'I shall be exhausted before we get anywhere near the day,' sighed Alinor, 'so someone is going to have to hold me up if they want to put a crown on my head!'

'It will all be fine, and you will be fine. In fact you will be quite amazing, I just know it.'

Alinor gave her a look that said everything.

'I think you are a bully,' she said, 'but on the grounds that I gave you this job, I suppose I have to put up with it.'

'Quite right,' said Semira happily and waltzed out of the room.

The next few weeks simply disappeared in a coronation fervour. Alinor was able to get some time with Mirantha and was assured that the Healer was enjoying taking the opportunity to make a few trips away from Thorgiliad into the surrounding countryside while she had the chance. Relieved, Alinor submitted to the calls of duty. The first of the guests were due in a day or two, but, beyond all of Alinor's expectations, everything was in place. Later that night she walked the corridors of the palace, admired the newly restored hangings filling the halls with colour, wood gleaming softly in the lamplight, delicate crystal scattering sparkles on walls, ceilings and floors. Her people had done a wonderful job, she decided, and was determined that they would all have something to enjoy on this special occasion. It was quiet almost everywhere; there were occasional sounds of footsteps as the last of the servants made their way to their beds, but other than that she could have been completely alone. Without consciously thinking about it she found herself in the enormous great hall – the Throne Room – where in not too many days from now, she would take her place on the great seat of kings and be crowned Queen of Ancor. Slowly she walked its length, aware of the ghosts of generations past, sensing that they were somehow smiling on this most recent member of the House of Thormeyern to take on the burden of ruler. It was an oddly comforting feeling.

She stopped about twenty feet away from the steps leading to the dais upon which the throne stood. There were very few lamps left alight overnight but Alinor could see easily enough. There was a faint glow beside the throne which gradually started to grow brighter. In doing so she could see that it surrounded the figure of a man, a kingly being. This was no illusion from the catacombs of her trance. This was here, real. She had no doubts. It was her father.

She sank to the floor in a deep curtsey.

'Rise up now, my beloved child, for you are a queen and have no need to salute me.'

The figure approached her and reached out a hand to raise her.

Slowly Alinor too reached her fingers out and encountered real flesh, warm and strong.

'The powers that be have granted my greatest wish of seeing you once more, Alinor. I know how you have suffered but I can see that my little girl has become a beautiful woman, a great warrior and a wielder of power. What father could ever have wanted more for his child? I would have wished that you did not have to face the coming destiny, but you know that no-one can change what must now be.'

'Oh father,' Alinor managed to say, tears streaming down her face. 'I so wanted to see you again. That awful day has always haunted me - I never had the chance to say goodbye . . .' she broke off as the nightmare memories filled her mind.

The tall man gently took his daughter into his arms and she buried her face in the safety of his embrace.

'Let them go, those memories, for we cannot change what was, only what is. You carry your mother's legacy which, although it is a burden is not as bad as you believe it to be. I am not alone in the faith which I have in you and in this life you are not alone. Just as I found a love which made my life complete so you also have found yours. Nothing in the world can take away that love. Together you will restore much that has been lost, I am sure of that. Although you grieve that I cannot be with you, this could not have come about any other way.

Be at peace, my child, as I am now at peace. My wish has been granted and all I would ask of you is that you stay true to yourself.'

'I will not let you down,' Alinor raised her eyes to the loving face, 'you taught me what was most important in life and I will always honour you for what you have helped me become. I will never stop loving you.'

'Nor I you. But,' the gentle voice was heavy with sadness and he held her at arm's length. 'I cannot stay now. These precious minutes are all too short. Be strong, little Alinor, and brave. Be the queen you were always destined to be.'

She closed her eyes momentarily and felt his lips kiss her forehead one last time. She opened them again to empty space, although she was sure she could still feel the slight pressure of his hands on her arms.

'Goodbye, father,' she whispered into the shadows, 'and thank you.'

Alinor walked slowly to her rooms, her sadness now replaced by a feeling of great comfort. Her life had been changed forever the day her father was killed, but seeing him again, feeling his steadfastness and love flow into her being she finally felt that she was ready to face her future, whatever that may bring. She hugged that liberating emotion to herself as she drifted off to sleep.

The palace was full to overflowing; in fact it did overflow with retainers and escorts being accommodated throughout the city. The kitchens worked overtime to prepare vast amounts of food for all the guests that had descended on Thorgiliad to see the new queen crowned.

Semira was rushed off her feet as she darted here and there to make sure that everything was going smoothly, which it was to her surprise and delight. Musicians turned up when and where they were required, as did the various entertainers. Occasionally she would find courtiers lost in the maze of corridors and laughingly would direct them back to where their own people were housed.

Noise, colour, a tangible excitement in the air. The day had finally come for Alinor, daughter of Teleston of the House of Thormeyern, to be crowned the new Queen of Ancor.

Guests from all the countries of the Alliance crowded the halls of the palace, filling everywhere with their chatter. Soft perfumes wafted as people moved here and there, gradually making their way towards the centre of the day's ceremonies, the Throne Room. Fellow sovereigns and eminent leaders took their places guided by palace staff in their new uniforms, whilst those further down the hierarchy filled the remaining space, leaving a narrow pathway down to the throne itself. The loud talking gradually died down and stopped completely as two heralds sounded a fanfare to announce the commencement of the formalities. Heads turned towards the great entrance door to the Hall.

On previous coronations there had been a huge procession before the monarch even got to the Throne Room, but Alinor had over-ruled this and drastically reduced the number of those who preceded her. A dozen noble couples entered bearing gilded lamps and flowers followed by the most venerable of the palace ministers, Imberhan by name, with a page carrying Alinor's mother's crown on a velvet cushion.

They progressed up the length of the Hall; the couples dispersed to either side at the base of the steps, whilst the minister and his page ascended to stand beside the throne itself, the page setting the cushion upon a small table set apart from the display of other royal regalia ranged behind the throne.

To the strains of a beautiful melody played by several harpists, Alinor entered following two young women with jewelled rods. She was dressed in a fairly simple long gown with a short train, silvery in colour but seeming to flash with colours as she moved, her hair gathered at her neck with a fine golden jewel catching the light. Tall and elegant she walked confidently past the gathering who murmured appreciative comments as she went. She did not turn her head, but her eyes took in the faces of familiar friends and lesser known allies, all taking in the measure of the new sovereign.

She did not need to look to know where Sirad was next to his father Sothan, standing right at the front in deference to his seniority. His thoughts came clearly into her mind.

You are so beautiful, he was thinking, and I am so proud of you my love.

Alinor took the few steps up, turned and stood in front of the throne; the music ended.

Breaking with tradition again, she addressed the gathered dignitaries.

'I did not expect to be standing here today, to be taking the place of that great king Teleston. Some of you may perhaps have questioned that a young woman would be able to fill such a role. Let me assure those of you who do not yet know me well that my father raised me in his own image, and though none could ever replace him I have pledged to uphold everything he stood for – justice, compassion and integrity – and work to defend all good peoples from whatever evils may threaten us.'

A wave of commendation swelled from the crowd, her words carrying a conviction that they found compelling.

The formalities continued with the customary words from various celebrants invoking the blessing of the gods before finally Imberhan took up the crown and showed it to the congregation. He then showed it to Alinor who reached out to place her mother's gem Eletha into the space in the intricate golden structure. That done she took her seat on the throne.

Once more Imberhan raised the crown, turned and placed it on Alinor's head.

It seemed to all present that the crown blazed with light, surrounding the queen with a halo of gold. Gasps of astonishment filled the Hall before someone shouted out a salute, which was taken up by all, the air reverberating with the noise of their approbation.

Alinor stood. She opened her hands and there was brightness everywhere. The jewelled rods carried by the two young women sent sparks high up to the ceiling which was now filled with coruscating stars and musicians struck up a grand anthem. The Hall was simply awash with colour and light as she slowly descended the few steps and moved onto the main floor.

One by one her noble guests saluted her; with effortless dignity she accepted their congratulations as she made a very slow progress through the crowd. Eventually she managed to exit the Hall to where Semira was waiting, her eyes still damp with the joyful tears she had shed earlier.

Semira dropped into a low curtsey.

'Your Majesty,' she said.

Alinor took her hand and smiled.

'Thank you, dear Semira, for making this day such a success.'

'No, no, it was never down to just me. Others have done far more than I have.'

'Nonsense,' chided Alinor. 'But now, I have to go and change before the main reception begins and I need your help. Let's get away from all these people so I can get my breath back.'

Some time later the new queen made her way down to face the crowds again. Sirad had been waiting for the opportunity to catch her alone and she sent out a thought to him to come to her apartment when Semira had finally put the finishing touches to her dress and hair. With a knowing smile she rapidly disappeared as the prince entered, warning Alinor not to be too long.

For a moment Sirad just looked at her, his heart almost bursting with emotion. She threw her arms around him and they kissed as if they had been apart for months instead of a few hours.

'Well, your Majesty,' he said finally, 'that was an amazing demonstration.' He could have been referring to the ceremony, or was it the kiss?

'It was pretty wonderful, wasn't it? And no, it wasn't trickery, although I hope the guests will assume it was. When the crown was put on my head there was the most extraordinary feeling right through me.'

'I could see that. It all seemed to come from Eletha, as if your mother was showing you how proud she was today.'

'Oh Sirad, I could almost sense her presence. She . . .' Alinor blinked several times to prevent the tears from falling.

'Hush now, no need for tears,' said Sirad. 'This is a day to celebrate the start of a new reign.'

He kissed her again.

'Now, we'd best go before Semira comes to tell you off!'

'I'd rather stay here with you.'

With a chuckle, Sirad firmly led Alinor to the door, opened it and said, 'Your people await, your Majesty.'

'Said you were a bully,' muttered Alinor, and went out to face the celebrations.

The occasion of the coronation of the new queen in Ancor would provide an endless source of conversation for many months to come. Once the guests had finally left following what they described as a truly memorable and enjoyable stay in Thorgiliad it took some weeks to return the palace to normal again.

Sirad was the last to leave, having taken some time to spend quietly with Alinor. He was finding it increasingly hard to tear himself away from this woman he loved so much, and was not looking forward to having to spend the next few months back in Pelamir and unable to touch her, hold her, look into those misty blue eyes. He wanted so much more, and was painfully aware that she felt the same. To be able to share their thoughts was no consolation, and he held himself firmly in check to avoid letting her see how deeply he felt. They needed to be together, he was sure of it; how much longer would they have to wait?

He would catch up with his father's retinue well before the king reached home again. Fortunately for all concerned, the weather, although damp and miserable at times, had not proved a problem, although snow would blanket most of Ancor before too much longer.

'We have a couple of months before we can think about setting off again,' said Sirad, as they talked quietly the day before he was due to leave. 'There's no point in enduring bad weather if it is not absolutely necessary.'

'No, I suppose not.'

'I've been thinking about what Amiros said about tracking down the sword. It's difficult to be prepared for something when you have no idea what is required.'

'Just do what we can,' said Alinor. 'I'm sure the answers will come to us in due course, they usually do.'

She looked at her sword Shenbran, lying on the table in front of her.

'Nearly time to find your partner,' she said to it.

Was it a trick of the light, or did the blade really shimmer in response?

I hope you have enjoyed reading this second book as much as I have enjoyed letting my characters find their way in the saga. Writing can be hard work and any writer needs and appreciates feedback from their readers.

If you would be so kind as to take the time to place a review on Amazon, I would be very grateful. It will serve to encourage me to tackle the final episode in this series!

Website: harrietmjwood.uk
Email: harriet@harrietmjwood.uk

Printed in Great Britain
by Amazon